EARTH'S REQUIEM

DYSTOPIAN URBAN FANTASY

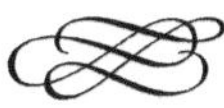

ANN GIMPEL

Edited by

ANGELA KELLY

Illustrated by

FIONA JAYDE

CONTENTS

EARTH'S REQUIEM

EARTH RECLAIMED, BOOK ONE

Dystopian Urban Fantasy
By
Ann Gimpel

COPYRIGHT PAGE

BOOK DESCRIPTION: EARTH'S REQUIEM

Resilient, kickass, and determined, Aislinn's walled herself off from anything that might make her feel again. Until a wolf picks her for a bondmate, and a Celtic god rises out of legend to claim her for his own.

Aislinn Lenear lost her anthropologist father high in the Bolivian Andes. Her mother, crazy with grief that muted her magic, was marched into a radioactive vortex by dark creatures and killed. Three years later, stripped of every illusion that ever comforted her, twenty-two-year-old Aislinn is one resilient, kickass woman with a *take no prisoners* attitude. In a world turned upside down, where virtually nothing familiar is left, she's conscripted to fight the dark gods responsible for her father's death. Battling evil on her own terms, Aislinn walls herself off from anything that might make her feel again in this compelling dystopian urban fantasy.

Fionn MacCumhaill, Celtic god of wisdom, protection, and divination has been laying low since the dark gods stormed Earth. He and his fellow Celts decided to wait them out. After all, three years is nothing compared to their long lives. On a clear winter day, Aislinn walks into his life and suddenly all bets are off. Awed by her courage, he stakes his claim to her and to an Earth he's willing to fight for.

Aislinn's not so easily convinced. Fionn's one gorgeous man, but she has a world to save. Emotional entanglements will only get in her way. Letting a wolf into her life was hard. Letting love in may well prove impossible.

ends. The characters are colorful, the friendships deep and the story grabs hold of you and does not let you go. Niki Driscoll

This story was amazing. Gimpel really knows her world building. We are thrust into this new world and you feel like you are there. It was very easy to get lost in this book. Offbeat Vagabond

The world of magic and mythology comes to life, the prophecies so fascinating it's easy to lose onself in Ann's stories and forget everything in the real world. Definitely a hit right out of the park. InD'-Tale Magazine

FIRST PROLOGUE

Salt Lake City, Utah

AISLINN TRIED TO STOP IT, but the vision that had dogged her for over a year played in her head. She squeezed her eyes shut tight. Mental images crowded behind her closed lids, as vivid as if they'd happened yesterday. She raked her hands through her hair and pulled hard, but the movie chronicling the beginning of her own personal hell didn't even slow down. She whimpered as the humid darkness of a South American night closed about her...

Her mother screamed in Gaelic, "Deifir, Deifir," and then shoved Aislinn again. She tried to hurry like her mother wanted, but it was all too much to take in. Stumbling down the steep Bolivian mountainside in the dark, she ignored tears and snot streaking her face. Her legs shook. Nausea clenched her gut. Her mother was crying too, in between cursing the gods and herself. Aislinn knew enough Gaelic to understand her mother had tried to talk her father out of going to the ancient Inca prayer site, but Jacob hadn't listened.

A vision of her father's twisted body lying dead a thousand feet above them tore at Aislinn. Just a few hours ago, her life had been normal. Now her mother had turned into a grief-crazed harridan. Her beloved father, a gentle giant of a man, was dead. Killed by those horrors that had crawled out of the ground. Perfect, golden-skinned men with long, silky hair and luminous eyes, apparently summoned through the ancient rite linked to the shrine. Thinking about it was like trying to shove her hand into a flame, her pain too unbearable to examine closely.

Aislinn was afraid to turn around. Tara had already slapped her once. Another spate of Gaelic galvanized her tired legs into motion. Her mother was clearly terrified the monsters would come after them, but Aislinn didn't think they'd bother. At least a hundred adoring half-naked worshipers remained at the shrine high on the mountain. Once Tara had herded her into the shadows, her last glimpse of the crowd revealed one of the lethal exotic creatures turning a woman so he could penetrate her. Even in Aislinn's near-paralyzed state, the sexual heat was so compelling, it took all her self-discipline not to race to his side and insist he take her instead. After all, she was younger, prettier. It didn't matter at all that he'd just killed her father.

…Aislinn shook her head so hard, it felt like her brains rattled from side to side in her skull. Despite the time that had passed since her father's murder, she still fell into these damned trance states, where the horror happened all over again. Tears leaked from her eyes. She slammed a fist down on a corner of her desk, glorying in the diversion pain created. Crying was pointless. It wouldn't change anything. Self-pity was an indulgence she couldn't afford.

Pull it together. The weak die.

Even though she wasn't sure why life felt so precious—after all, she'd lost nearly everything—Aislinn wanted to live. Would do anything to hang onto the vital thread that maintained her on Earth.

A bitter laugh bubbled up. What a transition: from Aislinn Lenear, college student, to Aislinn Lenear, fledgling magic wielder. A second race of alien beings, Lemurians, had stormed Earth on the heels of that hideous night in Bolivia, selecting certain humans because they had magical ability and sending everyone else to their deaths.

It was a process. It took time to kill people, but huge sections of Salt Lake City sat empty. Skyscraper towers downtown and rows of vacant buildings mocked a life that was no more. In her travels to nearby places before the gasoline ran out, Aislinn had found them about the same as Salt Lake.

Jacob's death had been a harbinger of impending chaos—the barest beginning. The world she'd known had imploded shockingly fast. It killed Aislinn to admit it—she kept hoping for a miracle to intercede—but her mother was certifiable. Tara may as well have died right along with her husband. She hadn't left the house once since they'd returned a year before. Her long, red hair was filthy and matted. She barely ate. When she wasn't curled into a fetal position, she drew odd runes on the kitchen floor and muttered in Gaelic about Celtic gods and dragons. It was only a matter of time before the Lemurians culled her. Tara had magic, but she was worthless in her current state.

The sound of the kitchen door rattling against its stops startled Aislinn. On her feet in a flash, she took the stairs two at a time and burst into the kitchen. A Lemurian had one of its preternaturally long-fingered hands curved around Tara's emaciated arm. He crooned to her in his language—an incomprehensible mix of clicks and clacks. Tara's wild, golden eyes glazed over. She stopped trying to pull away and got to her feet, leaning against the seven-foot tall creature with long, shiny blond hair, as if she couldn't stand on her own.

"No!" Aislinn hurled herself at the Lemurian. "Leave her alone."

"Stop!" His odd alien gaze met hers. "It is time," the Lemurian said in flawless English, "for both you and her. You must join the fighting and learn about your magic. Your mother is of no use to anyone."

"But she has magic." Aislinn hated the pleading in her voice. Hated it.

Be strong. I can't show him how scared I am.

Something flickered behind the Lemurian's expression. It might have been disgust—or pity. He turned away and led Tara Lenear out of the house.

Aislinn growled low in her throat and launched herself at the Lemurian's back. Gathering her clumsy magic into a primitive arc, she focused it on her enemy. Her tongue stuttered over an incantation. Before she could finish it, something smacked her in the chest so hard she flew through the air, hit the kitchen wall, and then slumped to the floor. Wind knocked out of her, spots dancing before her eyes, she struggled to her feet. By the time she stumbled to the kitchen door, both the Lemurian and her mother had vanished.

An unholy shriek split the air, followed by another. Aislinn clapped a hand over her mouth to seal the sound inside and clutched the doorsill. Pain clawed at her belly. Her vision became a red haze. The fucking Lemurian had taken her mother. The last human connection she had. And they expected her to fight for them? Ha! It would be a cold day in Hell. She let go of the doorframe and balled her hands into fists so hard her nails drew blood.

Standing still was killing her, so she walked into blindingly bright sunlight. She didn't care what happened next. It didn't matter anymore. A muted explosion rocked the ground. She staggered. When she turned, she wasn't surprised to see her house crack in multiple places and settle. Not totally destroyed, but close enough.

Guess they want to make sure I don't have anywhere to go back to.

Her heart shattered into jagged pieces that poked her from the inside. She bit her lip so hard it ached. When that didn't make a dent in her anguish, she pinched herself, dug her nails into her flesh until she bled from dozens of places. Fingers slick with her own blood, she forced herself into a ragged jog. Maybe if she put some distance between herself and the wreckage of her life, the pain sluicing through her would abate.

As she ran, a phrase filled her mind. The same sentence, over and over in time to her heartbeat. *I will never care for anyone ever again. I will never care for anyone ever again.* After a time, the words etched into her soul.

Ely, Nevada
Two Years Later

Rune paced from the kitchen to the living room and back again, hackles at half-mast and tail twitching behind him. Marta, his bondmate and the woman who'd rescued him from a trap when he was just a wolf pup, was resting. At least he hoped she was. Something between a whine and a growl slipped past his clenched jaws.

Damn her, anyway.

Didn't she understand she'd been targeted by the dark gods? Ever since she took to spying on the Lemurians in Taltos, their underground city, things turned to rat shit. Something hideous happened on her last trip. He wasn't certain quite what because he wasn't with her, and she refused to tell him. Many moonrises had passed, and she was only just now beginning to talk and think normally.

Rune paused to stare out a large window. The front yard was absolutely silent. So was the road fronting Marta's house, but then it would be since most of the humans were dead, and gasoline to make their cars run had long since run out.

He shook his fur out and came to a decision. Should he tell Marta now or wait until she woke?

She solved the problem for him. The sound of her footsteps made him spin to face the door into the living room. She was dressed to go out and had shoes on. Not a good sign.

"There you are." She favored him with a maternal smile, the one that made him want to bite her. She may have rescued him when he was too young to care for himself, but that was long ago.

"Here I am," he agreed and trained his amber eyes on the woman who meant everything to him.

"I'm leaving for a while—"

Rune's decision roared out of him. "Not without me, you're not. Never again. Look what happened last time."

"Be reasonable." She smiled again, and Rune felt magic prowl beneath her words.

He slapped up power of his own. "Reasonable has nothing to do with it. Last time they nearly killed you. I wasn't certain until yesterday you'd get enough of your memories back to be yourself."

"Neither was I." Her smile developed grim edges. She sank to the thick Oriental carpet and held out her arms.

Rune stayed where he was. "All the more reason to take me with you. You can merge your senses with mine. Together we're stronger. It's why we chose the Hunter bond."

"Aw, Rune." Sadness etched lines around her eyes and into her forehead. "You don't understand. None of us will get out of this alive, but we have to fight until we can't fight anymore. If we don't, it's like turning Earth over to those bastards, and I won't do that." She slapped the floor with the flat of her hand. "I won't."

"Neither will I." He gazed cooly at her. "Where are we going?"

"I can't take you with me. It's too dangerous."

"If you don't take me, you're not going, either." The wolf stood his ground, but it was shaky. She could order him, and he'd have to obey. It was how the Hunter bond worked.

Marta looked away, studying her hands. Her long coppery hair was in its usual tight braid, and she was dressed in loose-fitting black trousers and a black jacket, with stout lace-up boots. She was tall, almost as tall as the Lemurians, and she sat with her legs splayed in front of her.

Rune kept his gaze glued to her, willing her to capitulate. He was fully prepared to take her on in combat to keep her in the house, if she refused his company. "I'm not being stubborn," he said. "I need to be with you for me, not just for you. How do you think I'll feel if you don't return? How can I live with myself if you die in a place where I wasn't there to help you?"

"I could die anyway." She did look at him then, her clear green eyes filled with something he didn't have a name for.

"So could I, but if we're together at least we'll know we did everything we could for each other."

Marta nodded once. "All right. I don't have enough energy to argue with you. We're going to one of the mining camps to the west of us. Some humans are still alive, and they need my medical skill."

"How do you know anyone's alive?" he countered.

She shrugged. "Call it a hunch. I dream things sometimes, and this came to me not long ago. We'll do a travel jump. It's not far. If the place is deserted, I'll bring us right back." The same, sad smile returned. "With luck, we'll be home in time for supper."

"Ready when you are."

She got to her feet. "Are you going to come closer than that? I already said I'd take you, Rune. Bondmates don't lie to each other."

Shame filled him because she'd nailed his reticence. He didn't trust that she wouldn't trick him. He made his way to her side and felt her magic as she opened a portal for them to travel to the place she'd seen in her dream.

They rolled out into high, arid desert, and the remains of a mining camp sprawled about them, buildings falling into disrepair. Bullet holes riddled tin roofs and corrugated siding. Rune sent his senses spinning outward.

Nothing lived anywhere near here.

"Curious," Marta murmured. "I was so sure."

Rune's hackles hit full alert, standing on end the length of his back. "We must leave," he snarled. "It has to be a trap."

Before Marta could reply, another gateway opened a little way away. Bal'ta poured out. Marta flung magic at the disgusting creatures, minions of the dark, but she barely made a dent. They stood between five and six feet tall, with barrel chests, and their bodies were coated in greasy-looking brown hair. Thicker hair hung from their scalps and grew in clumps from armpits and groins. Ropy muscles bulged under their hairy skin. Orange eyes gleamed, and their foreheads sloped backward.

Rune had faced them before. At least they didn't have magic of their own beyond a shared intelligence. The flood had slowed, and he gathered himself for action. He and Marta could take them. They'd faced worse odds. Apparently she agreed, and he felt her merge her consciousness with his.

"I'll take this side," Rune growled and thrust himself into the thick of things, avoiding the cudgels and maces they used in battle. Rune knew to stay out of the line of Marta's magic. He sliced into one neck after another until he was coated in blood. The air was thick with the coppery stench of it. For some reason, Bal'ta avoided him. Something about his animal energy burned them, and he took full advantage of their hesitation.

He glanced at Marta from time to time, grateful beyond thought she was still on her feet. In addition to magic, she held a knife in one hand. A knife dripping blood. Dead bodies piled around both of them.

Rune danced to one side to avoid a cudgel aimed for him skull. He sent out a call for forest wolves, but none came to their aid. Maybe there weren't any living here—or maybe they didn't see the point in taking a stand in someone else's battle.

No matter. He and Marta were winning. Only a few Bal'ta remained. He'd begun to work his way back to his bondmate, when another gateway opened, this one black and edged with flames. A man sashayed through. Rune stopped cold, staring in disbelief. The remaining Bal'ta faded away from that gaping maw; in moments they'd summoned another portal and left.

Rune focused on the newcomer. It had to be one of the dark gods. No one else held that level of deadly beauty. Long dark hair streamed behind him, and he trained his shrewd dark eyes on Marta. She squared her shoulders and stared back.

"Kill him," Rune urged.

"I can't," she ground out. "Much as I'd love to."

The dark god tossed his shapely head back and laughed; the sound was disturbing, discordant. "Your bondmate is wise," he told the wolf. "She's clever not to get too close."

"Which one is he?" Rune demanded.

"You may as well ask me, since I'm right here." Dark eyes crinkled in chilly humor, and he mock bowed. "My name is Tokhots. I'm also known as the trickster." Dark robes fluttered around him, sashed in gray.

While Tokhots had been talking, Marta sidled farther from Rune and severed her connection with him. Worried, he tried to determine just what she was up to. If she planned an attack, he didn't want to be in the way and ruin things. Nor did he plan to leave her to the mercy of the dark god. Maybe if he kept Tokhots chatting…

"What do you mean by trickster? It's not a term I'm familiar with."

Tokhots did a funny little side step. "I play tricks. I'm funny. I'm a hell of a nice guy. If you got to know me, you'd—"

A ball of fire immolated one side of his robes. Tokhots' pleasant expression shattered, and he batted at the flames—and at jolts of power Marta hurled his way. Rune wanted to launch himself at the dark god, but Marta's power kept him rooted in place.

Finally giving up on extinguishing the flames, Tokhots shucked his robe, revealing golden-hued skin beneath. "Bitch!" he spat and raced to Marta so fast he beat Rune, who was also headed that way at breakneck speed.

"Don't bite him," Marta shrieked. "His blood is deadly poison."

Rune aborted a leap in midair and crashed to the rocky ground. He'd been about to close his jaws around Tokhots' neck.

The dark god held a writhing Marta in his grip. "You can't hurt me either," he taunted. "One drop of my blood and you'll be deader than the shades that roam the countryside."

"What do you want with me?" Marta gave a mighty heave.

Rune thought she might free herself, but Tokhots tightened his hold. "You've become an inconvenience. I sent the Bal'ta as a diversion until I could get here."

"What happens next?" Marta's voice was steady, but Rune sensed her fear, and it filled him with fury. He worked his way closer to the pair, not moving very fast.

"That's for me to know." Tokhots laughed again.

Caution departed. Rune judged the distance and leapt. So what if he died? At least Marta would go free. The air around him thickened, holding him suspended above the ground. Darkness dropped over him like a curtain until he couldn't see. He thrashed against the magic holding him and plummeted to earth, landing hard on jagged rocks. Ignoring pain, he vaulted toward where Marta had been, still running blind in unnatural darkness.

She wasn't there. Neither was the dark god.

He still couldn't see, but he could smell and hear. He employed both senses, ears pricked forward and nose snuffling so hard it began to bleed.

Nothing.

Marta's scent was strongest right where he stood.

Rune threw his head back and howled his desolation to the skies. He'd failed. The dark god had his bondmate, and he had no way to go after them.

By the time the darkness receded, his throat was raw with grief. He called for other animals, birds, even insects, to tell him what they'd seen. If they knew anything, but no one answered.

Despondent, guilt-stricken, Rune put one paw ahead of another.

No point in staying with the dead Bal'ta. Tokhots would never bring Marta back here.

The dark god had taken his bondmate on a oneway trip. Rune knew, as clearly as he knew anything, she'd never run by his side again. She was still alive, but her life force ebbed through their Hunter bond.

Soon she'd be no more, and it was his fault. If he'd been quicker, hadn't hesitated…

He shook his head hard and broke into a run.

CHAPTER 1

*A*islinn pulled her cap down more firmly on her head. Snow stung where it got into her eyes and froze the exposed parts of her face. Thin, cold air seared her lungs when she made the mistake of breathing too deeply. She'd taken refuge in a spindly stand of leafless aspens, but they didn't cut the wind at all. "Where's Travis?" she fumed, scanning the unending white of a high altitude plain that used to be part of Colorado. Or maybe this place had been in eastern Utah. It didn't really matter anymore.

Something unnatural flickered at the corner of her eye and she tensed. Standing still bought trouble with a capitol T. She swiveled her head to maximize her peripheral vision. *Damn! No, double damn.* Half-frozen muscles in her face ached when she tightened her jaw.

Bal'ta—a bunch of them—fanned out a couple hundred yards behind her, closing the distance eerily fast. One of many atrocities serving the dark gods that had crawled out of the ground that night in Bolivia, they appeared as shadowy spots against the fading day. Places where edges shimmered and merged into a menacing blackness. If she looked too hard at the center of those dark places, they drew her like a lodestone. Aislinn tore her gaze away.

Not that Bal'ta—bad as they were—were responsible for the

wholesale destruction of modern life. No, their masters—the ones who'd brought dark magic to Earth in the first place—held that dubious honor. Aislinn shook her head sharply, trying to decide what to do. She was supposed to meet Travis here. Those were her orders. He had something to give her. Typical of the way the Lemurians ran things, no one knew very much about anything. It was safer that way if you got captured.

She hadn't meant to cave and work for them, but in the end, she'd had little choice. It was sign on with the Lemurians—Old Ones—to cultivate her magic and fight the dark, or be marched into the same radioactive vortex that had killed her mother.

Her original plan had been to wait for Travis until an hour past full dark, but the Bal'ta changed all that. Waiting even one more minute was a gamble she wasn't willing to risk. Aislinn took a deep breath. Chanting softly in Gaelic, her mother's language, she called up the light spell that would wrap her in brilliance and allow her to escape—maybe. It was the best strategy she could deploy on short notice. Light was anathema to Bal'ta and their ilk. So many of the loathsome creatures were hot on her heels, she didn't have any other choice.

She squared her shoulders. All spells drained her. This was one of the worst—a purely Lemurian working translated into Gaelic because human tongues couldn't handle the Old Ones' language. She pulled her attention from her spell for the time it took to glance about, and her heart sped up. Even the few seconds it took to determine flight was essential had attracted at least ten more of the bastards. They surrounded her. Well, almost.

She shouted the word to kindle her spell. Even in Gaelic, with its preponderance of harsh consonants, the magic felt awkward on her tongue. Heart thudding double time against her ribs, she hoped she'd gotten the inflection right. Moments passed. Nothing happened. Aislinn tried again. Still nothing. Desperate, she readied her magic for a fight she was certain she'd lose and summoned the light spell one last time. Flickers formed. Stuttering into brilliance, they pushed against the Bal'tas' darkness.

Yesssss. Muting down triumph surging through her—no time for it—she gathered the threads of her working, draped luminescence about herself, and loped toward the west. Bal'ta scattered, closing behind her. She noted with satisfaction that they stayed well away from her light. She'd always assumed it burned them in some way.

Travis was on his own. She couldn't even warn him that he was walking into a trap. Maybe he already had. Which would explain why he hadn't shown up. Worry tugged at her. She ignored it. Anything less than absolute concentration, and she'd fall prey to his fate—

Vile hissing sounded behind her. Long-nailed hands reached for her, followed by shrieks when one of them came into contact with her magic. She snuck a peek over one shoulder to see how close they truly were. One problem with all that light was it illuminated the nasty things. Their backward sloping foreheads leant them a dimwitted look, but they were skilled warriors, worthy adversaries who'd wiped out more than one of her comrades. Their insect-like ability to work as a group using telepathic powers scared her more than anything. Though she threw her Mage senses wide open, she was damned if she could tap into their wavelength to disrupt it.

Chest aching, breath coming in short, raspy pants, she ran like she'd never run before. If she let go of anything—her light shield or her speed—they'd be on her, and it would be all over. Dead just past her twenty-second birthday. *That* thought pushed her legs to pump faster. She gulped air, willing everything to hold together long enough.

Minutes ticked by. Maybe as much as half an hour passed. She was tiring. It was hard to run and maintain magic. Could she risk teleportation? Sort of a *beam me up, Scotty,* trick. Nope, she wasn't close enough to her destination yet. Something cold as an ice cave closed around her upper arm. Her flesh stung before feeling left it. She snapped her head to that side and noted her light cloak had failed in that spot. Frantic to loosen the creature's grip, she pulled a dirk from her belt and stabbed at the thing holding her. Smoke rose when she dug her iron knife into it.

The stench of burning flesh stung her nostrils, and the disgusting ape-man drew back, hurling imprecations in its guttural language. She snaked her gaze through the gloom of the fading day, as she assessed how many of the enemy chased her. Aislinn swallowed hard around a painfully dry throat. There had to be a hundred. Why were they targeting her? Had they intercepted Travis and his orders? Damn the Lemurians anyway. She'd never wanted to fight for them.

I've got to get out of here.

Though it went against the grain—mostly because she was pretty certain it wouldn't work, and you weren't supposed to cast magic willy nilly—she pictured her home, mixed magic from earth and fire, and begged the Old Ones to see her delivered safely. Once she set the spell in motion, there'd be no going back. If she didn't end up where she planned, she'd be taken to task, maybe even stripped of her powers, depending on how pissed off the Lemurians were.

Aislinn didn't have any illusions left. Her world had crumbled three years ago. She'd wasted months railing against God, or the fates, or whoever was responsible for robbing her of her boyfriend and her parents and her life, goddammit, but nothing brought them back.

Then the Old Ones—Lemurians, she corrected herself—had slapped reason into her, forcing her to see the magic that kept her alive as a resource, not a curse. In the intervening time, she'd not only come to terms with that magic, but it had become a part of her. The only part she truly trusted. Without the magic that enhanced her senses, she'd be dead within hours.

Please... She struggled against clasping her hands together in an almost forgotten gesture of supplication. Juggling an image of her home while maintaining enough light to hold the Bal'ta at bay, she waited. Nothing happened. She was supposed to vanish, her molecules transported by proxy to where she wished to go. This was way more than the normal journey—or jump—spell, though. Because she needed to go much farther.

She poured more energy into the teleportation spell. The light around her flickered. Bal'ta dashed forward, jaws open, saliva dripping. She smelled the rotten crypt smell of them and cringed. If they got hold of her, they'd feed off her until she was nothing but an empty husk. Or worse, if one took a shine to her, she'd be raped in the bargain and forced to carry a mixed breed child. They'd kill her as soon as the thing was weaned. Maybe the brat, too, if its magic wasn't strong enough.

The most powerful of the enemy were actually blends of light and dark magic. When the abominations, six dark masters, had slithered out of holes between the worlds during a globally synchronized surge linked to the Harmonic Convergence, the first thing they'd done had been to capture human women and perform unspeakable experiments on progeny resulting from purloined eggs and alien sperm.

Aislinn sucked in a shaky breath. She did *not* want to be captured. Suicide was a far better alternative. She licked at the fake cap in the back of her mouth. It didn't budge. She shoved a filthy finger behind her front teeth and used an equally disgusting fingernail to pop the cap. She gripped the tiny capsule. Should she swallow it? Could she? Sweat beaded and trickled down her forehead, despite the chill afternoon air.

She'd just dropped the pill onto her tongue, trying to gin up enough saliva to make it go down, when the weightlessness associated with teleportation started in her feet like it always did. Gagging, she spat out the capsule and extended a hand to catch it, but it fell into the dirt. Aislinn knew better than to scrabble for the poison pill. If she survived, she could get another from the Old Ones. They didn't care how many humans died, despite pretending to befriend those with magic.

Her spell was shaky enough as it was. It needed more energy—lots more. Forgetting about the light spell, Aislinn put everything she had into escape. By the time she knew she was going to make it—apparently the Bal'ta didn't know they could take advantage of her vulnerability as she shimmered half in and half out of teleport mode—she was almost too tired to care.

She fell through star-spotted darkness for a long time. It could have been several lifetimes. Teleportation jaunts were different than her simple Point A to Point B jumps. When she'd traveled this way before, she'd asked how long it took, but the Old Ones never answered. Everyone she'd ever loved was dead—and the Old Ones lived forever—so she didn't have a reliable way to measure time. For all she knew, Travis might've lived through years of teleportation jumps. No one ever talked about anything personal. It was like an unwritten law. No going back. No one had a past. At least, not one they were willing to talk about.Voices eddied around her, speaking the Lemurian tongue with its clicks and clacks. She tried to talk with them, but they ignored her. On shorter, simpler journeys, her body stayed with her. She'd never known how her body caught up to her when she teletransported and was nothing but spirit. Astral energy suspended between time and space.

A disquieting thump rattled her bones. *Bones. I have bones again... That must mean...* Barely conscious of the walls of her home rising around her, Aislinn felt the fibers of her grandmother's Oriental rug against her face. She smelled cinnamon and lilac. Relief surged through her. Against hope and reason, the Old Ones had seen her home. Maybe they cared more than she thought—at least about her. Aislinn tried to pull herself across the carpet to the corner shrine so she could thank them properly, but her head spun. Darkness took her before she could do anything else.

∿

NOT QUITE SURE what woke her, Aislinn opened her eyes. Pale light filtered in through rough cutouts high in the walls. Daytime. She'd been lucky to find this abandoned silver mine with shafts that ran up to ground level. It would've drained her to keep a mage light burning.

Is it tomorrow? Or one of the days after that?

Aislinn's head pounded. Her mouth tasted like the backside of a sewer. It was the aftereffect of having thoroughly drained her magic, but she was alive, goddammit. Alive. Memory flooded her. She'd been within a hairsbreadth of taking her own life. Her stomach clenched, and she rolled onto her side, racked by dry heaves. Had she swallowed any of the poison by accident?

A bitter laugh made her cracked lips ache. Of course she hadn't. It didn't take much cyanide to kill you. Just biting into the capsule without swallowing would have done it. She struggled to a sitting position. Pain lanced through her head, but she forced herself to keep her eyes open.

The world stabilized. She lurched to her feet, filled a chipped mug with water that ran perpetually down one wall of her cave, doubling as faucet and shower, and warmed it with magic. Rummaging through small metal bins, she dropped mint and anise into the water. Then a dollop of honey, obtained at great personal risk from a nearby hive. When she looked at the mug, it was empty. Her eyes widened in a face so tired any movement was torture, and she wondered if she'd hallucinated making tea. Since she didn't remember drinking the mixture, she made another cup for good measure.

Liquid on board, she started feeling halfway human. Or whatever she was these days. As she moved around her cozy hobbit hole of a home, she glanced at beloved books, a few odds and ends of china, and her grandmother's rug—all that was left of her old life. By the time she'd developed enough magic to transport both herself and things short distances, most of the items from the ruins of her parents' home had been either pilfered by someone else or destroyed by the elements. She'd come by her few other possessions digging through the rubble of what was left of civilization.

Aislinn sucked in a deep breath and blew it back out. It made her chest hurt. Had the Bal'ta injured her before she'd made good on her escape? She shucked her clothes—tight brown leather pants, a plaid flannel shirt, and a torn black leather jacket—and took stock of her body. It looked pretty much the same. The long, white scar from under one breast catty corner to a hipbone was still there. *Yeah, right. What could have happened to it?* There might be a few new bruises, but all in all, her lean, tautly muscled form had survived intact. Before the world had imploded, she'd hated being a shred over six feet tall. Now she blessed her height. Long legs meant she could run fast.

She wrinkled her nose. A putrid stench had intensified as she removed her ratty leather garments. Realizing it was her, she strode to the waterfall in one corner of her cave and stood under its flow until her teeth chattered. Only then did she pull magic to warm herself. It seemed a waste to squander power on something she should be able to tolerate. Besides, despite sleeping, she hadn't totally recharged her reserves. That would only happen if she didn't use any more magic for a while. Aislinn thumbed a sliver of handmade soap and washed her hair, diverting suds falling down her body to clean the rest of her.

Something threw itself against the wards she kept above ground. She felt it as a vibration deep in her chest. It happened again. She leapt from the shower and flung her long, red hair over her shoulders so she could see. Soapy water streamed down her body, but she didn't want to sacrifice one iota of magic drying herself until she knew who—or what—was out there. Mage power would alert whatever was outside to her presence, so she snaked the tiniest tendril of Seeker magic out, winding it in a circuitous route so no one would figure out where it came from. Seekers could pinpoint others with magic. That gift was also useful for sorting out truth, but it wasn't her main talent, so it was weak.

Her magic found a target and she gasped. Travis? How could it possibly be him? He didn't know where she lived. Had her Lemurian magelord told him?

"Aislinn." She heard his voice in her mind. *"Let us in."*

Us no doubt meant his bond creature was with him. When Hunter magic was primary, humans had bond animals. His was a civet with the most beautiful rust, golden, and onyx coat she'd ever seen. *Should I?* Indecision rocked her. Her cave meant safety because no one knew about it. No one who would tell, anyway. She dragged a threadbare wool shift—once it had been green, but there were so many patches, it was mostly black now—over her head and shook water out of her hair.

A high-pitched screech reverberated in her head. Something must've pissed off the civet. Travis shouted her name again. He left the mind speech channel open after that. Locked it open so she couldn't close it off. Edgy, she wondered if he was setting some sort of trap. Aislinn thought she could trust him, but when it came right down to it, she didn't trust anyone. Especially not the Old Ones. The only thing that made working with them tolerable was she understood their motives. Or imagined she did. She still hadn't forgiven them for killing her mother. Poor, sick, muddled Tara.

"Aislinn." A different voice this time. Metae, her Lemurian magelord. The one who'd made it clear two years before that, magic or no, they'd kill her if she didn't come to terms with her power and fight for them. *"Save your comrade. I do not know if I will arrive in time."*

All righty, then.

The civet yowled, hissed, and then yowled again. Travis made heavy, slurping sounds, as if at least one lung had been punctured. Was saving anyone even possible? Dragging a leather vest over totally inadequate clothing, Aislinn slipped her feet into cracked, plastic Crocs and took off at a dead run along a passageway leading upward. The Crocs gave her feet some protections from rocks, but not from cold. She veered off, picking an exit point that would put her behind the fighting. When she came to one of the many illusory rocks that blocked every tunnel leading to her home, she peeked around it. No point in being a sacrifice if she could help it. Travis wasn't that close of an acquaintance. No one was.

She froze, disbelieving. Christ! It couldn't be. But it was. Though she'd only seen him once, that horrible night in Bolivia when her father died, the thing standing in broad daylight had to be Perrikus —one of six dark gods holding what was left of Earth captive. Bright auburn hair flowed to his waist and fluttered in the morning breeze. Eyes clear as fine emeralds one moment, shifting to another alluring shade the next, were set in a classically handsome face with sharp cheekbones and a chiseled jawline. His broad shoulders and chest tapered to narrow hips under a gossamer robe that left nothing to the imagination. The dark gods were sex incarnate, which was interesting, since the Old Ones were anything but. Promises of bottomless passion had been one of the ways the dark ones seduced Druids and witches and all those other New Age practitioners into weakening the gates between the worlds.

Heat flooded Aislinn's nether regions. She wished she'd paid better attention when humans who'd actually run up against the dark gods had told her about it. Something about requiring human warmth to feed themselves, or remain on Earth, or...shit, her usually sharp mind just wasn't there. She couldn't focus on anything except getting laid.

Her groin ached for release. One of her hands snuck under her clothing before she realized what she was doing. *No!* The silent shriek told her body to stand down, damn it. Now was *not* the time, and Perrikus definitely not the partner, but her body wasn't listening. Her nipples pebbled into hard points and pressed against the rough wool fabric of her hastily donned shift.

Wrenching her gaze to Travis—and her mind away from sex— she was unutterably grateful he was still on his feet. Wavering, but standing. The civet, every hair on end, stood next to him, a paw, with claws extended, raised menacingly.

"You know where the woman is," Perrikus said, his voice like liquid silver.

Aislinn heard compulsion behind the words. Hopefully, so did Travis.

"I followed you here," the dark mage went on. "I heard you call out to her. So where is she? Tell me, and I'll let you go."

The civet growled low. Travis spoke a command to silence it.

"I'm right here." Aislinn stepped into view, glad her voice hadn't trembled, because her guts sure were.

"Aislinn," Travis gasped. He lurched in a rough half circle to face her. "I'm so sorry—"

"Can it," she snapped.

The civet hissed at her, probably because she'd had the temerity to raise her voice to its bonded one.

She leveled her gaze at Perrikus. "You said he could go. Release him—and his animal, too."

That lyrical voice laughed. "Oh, did I say that? I'd forgotten."

"Let him go, and I'll, ah, give you what you want." *Should buy me a couple minutes here.* "Just turn off the damned sex fountain. I can't think."

His hypnotic eyes latched onto hers. "Why would I do that, human? You like how it feels. I smell the heat from between your legs."

"Bastard. I liked it a whole lot better when I thought you were just a comic book character." Aislinn wondered how much juice she had. This was one of the gods. Even if she was at her best, she didn't think she'd prevail in anything that looked like direct combat. "What do you want with me?" she asked, still seeking time to strategize. It wasn't easy with what felt like a second heart pounding between her legs. She wanted to lay herself at his feet and just get it over with.

"What do you think?" He smiled. Fine, white teeth gleamed in that perfect jaw. "Children. You have power, human. Real power. And you've only now come to our attention." He walked toward her, nice and slow. Sauntered. His hips swung with his stride. He was ready, huge and hard, under those sheer robes. Unfortunately, so was she, but she clamped down on her craving.

Aislinn ignored the moisture gushing down her thighs and reached for her magic. Travis limped over, joining hands with her. The civet wedged itself between them, warm against her lower leg. She felt the boost immediately, and her sexual hunger receded a tiny bit. Enough to clear her mind. *"On my count of three,"* she sent. *"One, two..."*

"No. Do just the opposite. He won't be expecting it. Pull from air and water. I'll blend fire. Aim for his dick. It's a pretty big target just now."

Power erupted from them. Even the civet seemed to be helping. Since she'd never worked with an animal before, she wasn't certain just how the Hunter magic worked. Aislinn concentrated hard to keep the spell's aim true. Travis was injured, so she took more of the burden.

Perrikus chanted almost lazily. Maybe he was drunk on his own ability, so egotistical he wouldn't guard himself. Her spirits soared as soon as she realized Travis's gambit had worked. Perrikus was using the counter spell for air and water. He hadn't counted on the tenacity fire would give their working. Moments later, a muffled shriek burst from him, and he grappled at his crotch.

"Bitch." No honey or compulsion in *that* epithet. He lunged for her.

Aislinn sidestepped him neatly, letting go of Travis. In a half crouch, she trained all her attention on their adversary. Hands raised, she began a weaving she hoped would unbalance him. Air shimmered at the edges of her vision.

"I am here, child. Take your comrade to safety. He carries an important message from me."

"Me—"

"Do not speak my name aloud. Go."

The shimmery place in the air sidled in front of Perrikus. Fiery motes lapped hungrily at his transparent robes. Not waiting to be told a third time, Aislinn shooed the civet into Travis's arms, draped an arm around him, and pulled invisibility about the three of them. The last thing she heard as she guided them toward the warren of passageways leading to her home was Metae baiting Perrikus.

"I was old before you were hatched. How dare you spread your filth?"

"Wh-Where are we?" Travis's voice gurgled. It had taken time to help him cover the half mile back to her cave. The civet made little mewling noises as they walked, sounding worried about its human partner.

"About two hundred feet below whatever's happening up there." Aislinn flung a hand upward. "Do you have Healing magic?" She pushed him through the thick tapestry that served as a door to her home and caught the civet's tail between fabric and rock. It hissed at her and then ran to Travis, light on its feet.

He nodded.

"Use it on yourself. It's not one of my strengths." Aislinn knew she sounded surly but couldn't help herself. She'd never wanted anyone anywhere near her home. Her body, ignited by Perrikus's execrable magic, screamed for release. Nothing she could do about that so long as she had company. Not much privacy in the one room she called home.

"Make a power circle around me."

Grateful for something to do, Aislinn strode around him three times, chanting. She felt Travis pull earth power from her as he patched the hurt places within himself. Satisfied he had what he needed, she retrieved her mug, got one for him, and made tea. In addition to goldenseal, she added marigolds to the decoction. Both held healing qualities. By the time she finished brewing tea, his color had shifted from gray to decidedly pink. His eyes were back to their normal brown. Moss green was his power color. She wondered if it was sheer coincidence that the civet's eyes were the same odd shade. She understood her Mage and Seeker gifts. The other three human magics—Healer, Hunter, and Seer—remained shrouded in mystery.

Aislinn looked hard at Travis when she handed him the tea. Dirty blond dreadlocks hung halfway down his back. He was well past six feet, but thin to the point of gauntness, his skin stretched over broad shoulders. A leather belt with additional holes punched in it held baggy denim pants in place. Battered leather boots, split along one side, and an equally worn leather vest over a threadbare green cotton shirt made him look about as ragtag as she always did. No one ever had new clothes. She patched what she had until the fabric fell apart. Then she looted amongst the dead, or possessions they'd left behind, for something else she could use.

"Thanks." He took the tea and shifted uncomfortably from foot to foot. "You have books." Surprise burned in his tone. "How did—?"

"You didn't see them," she broke in fiercely. That's what happened when you let people into your house. They saw things they weren't supposed to—like books banned by a Lemurian edict.

"Okay," he agreed. "I didn't see a thing." He hesitated. "Don't worry. I wouldn't get you in trouble. You just saved my life."

"Did you fix your body?" Aislinn grimaced. *That didn't sound very friendly. Pretty obvious I'm trying to change the subject.* "Sorry. I'm not used to entertaining."

He looked away. "Yeah, I'm better. I'm not used to being anyone's guest, either."

"How'd you find me?" she blurted. Not all that polite either, but she really did want to know.

"Metae and Regnol, my Lemurian magelord, told me to give you this yesterday." Scrabbling inside his vest, he drew out an alabaster plaque. About the size of a domino, it contained an encrypted message. "I tried to make our rendezvous on time, but everywhere I turned, something went wrong." He paused long enough to take a breath. "I won't bore you with the details, but it was past dark when I made it to the coordinates. You weren't there, but I knew you had been. Traces of your energy remained." He ground his teeth together. "I also sensed the Bal'ta. Because I feared the worst, I called the Old Ones—"

"What?" she broke in, incredulous. "We're never supposed to—"

"I know that." His voice rose over hers. "I was desperate. They told me not to bother reporting back if I didn't get the message to you. Anyway, they didn't even lecture me for insubordination. Metae told me where to find you. And a whole bunch of other stuff about how she'd wanted to tell you herself, but couldn't break away from something or other."

Aislinn gulped her tea. It was hot and made her mouth hurt, but at least the lust eating at her like acid ever since Perrikus turned those gorgeous eyes on her, receded a bit. Maybe it might, just might, leave her be. She'd even been wondering about a quickie with Travis—after he healed himself. Heat spread up her neck as she blushed.

"What?" He stared at her.

The civet had curled itself into a ball at his feet, but it kept its suspicious gaze trained on her.

"Nothing." She put her mug down and held out a hand for the plaque. "Let's find out what was so important."

Nodding silently, he handed it to her before sinking onto one of several big pillows scattered around the Oriental rug. The cat followed him. "Do you mind?" He pointed at a faded Navaho blanket folded in one corner of the room.

"Help yourself."

"Thanks." He unfolded it and draped it around his shoulders. "Takes a lot of magic to do Healings. I'm cold."

With only half her mind on him, Aislinn held the alabaster between her hands. It warmed immediately and began to glow. She opened herself to it, knowing it would reveal its message, but only to her. The plaques were like that. The Old Ones keyed them to a single recipient. Death came swiftly to anyone else who tampered with their magic. Metae's voice filled her mind.

"*Child. Your unique combination of Mage and Seeker blood has come to the attention of the other side. They will stop at nothing to capture and use you. The Council has conferred. You will ready yourself for a journey to Taltos so we may better prepare you for what lies ahead. Take nothing. Tell no one. Travel to the gateway. Do not tarry. Once you are there, we will find you. You must arrive within four days."*

"What?" Travis squirmed clearly uncomfortable. He knew he shouldn't ask, but couldn't help himself.

She shook her head. *Alone. Destined to be alone—always.* Sadness filled her. Images of her mother and father tumbled out of the place she kept them locked away. Memories of what it had felt like to be loved brought sudden tears to her eyes.

"Come here." Travis opened his arms. "You don't have to tell me a thing."

The civet growled low. Travis spoke sharply to it, and it stood, arched its back, and walked to a spot a few feet away, where it circled before lying down.

Mortified by how desperately she wanted the comfort of those arms, Aislinn dropped to the floor and crawled to him, taking care to give his bond animal a wide berth. The blanket must have helped, because when she fitted her body to his, it was more than warm. The sexual heat she thought she'd moved beyond flared painfully in her loins. When he cupped her buttocks with his hands and pulled her against him, she wound her arms around him and held on.

"There," he crooned, moving a hand to smooth her hair out of her face. "There, now. Let's take comfort where we can, eh? There's precious little to be had." He laughed, sounding a bit self-conscious, before adding, "Even I could feel Perrikus's spell. Got me going, too."

He closed his lips over hers. She kissed him back, too aroused to be ashamed of her need.

CHAPTER 2

he gateway to Taltos. How the hell was she supposed to find it all by herself? Travis was long gone, making a journey jump to wherever he lived. At least, that's where he said he was going. Aislinn blew out a breath, feeling guilty. She hadn't exactly asked him to go, but she'd hinted strongly that she needed time to herself. Travis was sweet—and a surprisingly adept lover. A reluctant smile tugged at her lips. She hadn't expected him to be so skilled. Or so attuned to what she needed, which had been rough and tumble sex without much in the way of seductive undertones.

The smile vanished abruptly. Ever since she lost her family, she'd made a point of staying away from anything that could turn into an emotional entanglement. It hurt too damned bad when you lost someone you loved. She could go the rest of her life without that kind of pain again, thank you very much.

Doesn't matter. It will be months before I see him again. If then.

Relegating her tryst with Travis to the infrequent dalliances she'd given in to when need outweighed reason, she gazed about her cave. It wasn't much, but it was all the home she had, and she was loathe to leave it. Aislinn shrugged off her ambivalence about the upcoming journey. Since her instructions were to take nothing and

29

tell no one, she wouldn't be wasting any time in preparations. Only problem was she needed to figure out where she was going. She closed her eyes and sifted through Lemurian memories that had been embedded within her at the time of her initiation. She kept two fingers centered in tattooed marks—black ink in the form of ankhs and stars—on her opposite arm as she concentrated.

Rather than a map of how to get to Taltos, what filled her mind was the first Harmonic Convergence of August, nineteen eighty-seven, and its globally synchronized surges. The Surge three years ago had been the last one as far as she knew, though there'd been many prior to it. Resentment filled her, and she ground her teeth together. Of course it had been the last one. The dark gods had used it to leapfrog their way to Earth. They didn't need to mastermind any more of them since they were already here.

Her parents had taken her to a remote location in the mountains of Bolivia during that last Surge. There'd been a surprising number of people, given it had taken several hours of strenuous climbing on slippery, muddy trails to get to a sundial supposedly placed by the Incas. Or maybe it had been the Aztecs. She couldn't remember. She'd been tired and not listening especially carefully to her father lecture about the history of the Convergence, as they made their way to the ancient shrine. He talked about it all the time. It had been his life's work, his and Doctor José Argüelles's. They'd spent over twenty years tracking every aspect of it at power points all over the world. This wasn't the first time he'd taken her and her mother to some remote location to view a Surge.

The trek began in thick jungle, but they'd climbed beyond the line where trees grew to an arid, high plain, pocked with huge craters and the ruins of primitive dwellings. Small scrubby plants dotted the landscape. Herds of llamas grazed nearby. Aislinn had been fascinated by their huge, liquid eyes and long, graceful necks. When she'd reached out to touch one, her father had called her back, telling her they weren't nearly as friendly as they looked. The journey had taken most of the day. Light was fading when they reached the sacred power point.

Her father told her about dozens of such spots scattered around the globe. "People are gathering there, too," he'd said with a knowing smile.

Her parents offered her cocaine leaves to chew. They'd given her a mild high. When the ground around the sundial began to undulate, she chalked it up to the drug. The rest of the crowd had rushed forward, though, chanting something in a guttural language. A vast hole formed in the earth, and two naked alien beings swarmed out of it. Several of the worshipers threw themselves at the feet of the things, chanting fervently.

The creatures had been so horribly inhuman, with eyes that radiated infinite power and colors shifting and changing under golden skin. Christ! An army of zombies wouldn't have looked any more terrifying—or shocked her more. Danger rolled from them in waves, setting her teeth on edge and making her stomach ache. Though she hadn't known it then, one was Perrikus, the other D'Chel.

That had been the beginning of the freaky part. Her world unraveled right along with it.

With a despairing look on her face, her mother had whispered in Gaelic so garbled it was tough to follow, telling her and her father to fade into the shadows behind nearby ruins. They'd begun a surreptitious retreat, when one of the things materialized right in front of her father. One minute, he'd been behind them; the next, he stood in front of Jacob Lenear, blocking his way. Jacob stood six feet four, but the glowing figure was at least half a foot taller. Up close like that, his multi-hued eyes glowed menacingly. Shiny black hair hung past his waist. The colors flowing into one another under his skin held a hypnotic quality.

"Where do you think you are going, *human?*" The last word sounded like a curse.

"It's late," her father began, spreading his hands in a placating gesture. "And—" Those were his last words.

The thing wrapped a long-fingered hand around Jacob's neck and snapped it. The whole event happened so fast, the only part Aislinn remembered clearly was her mother screaming. The humans who'd welcomed the abominations began to chant something like, "Kill the unbelievers. Bring on the New Age. New Age. New Age. New Age…"

A woman had stepped forward then and tugged at the other alien being's arm. Dark hair blew in her eyes. She was half naked, her small, conical breasts painted with runic symbols. "I am Amaya, queen witch of this coven. Where are the others? I was told six of you would emerge."

The thing smirked at her and shoved reddish-gold hair over broad shoulders. "If you ever speak directly to me again, it will mean your death. Depending how closely your kin followed orders, our brothers and sister are already here. This is not the only power point in this world."

Looking mildly shaken, Amaya lowered her hazel gaze and slunk backward. She joined hands with several others. They raised their voices in a song that only partially muffled Aislinn's mother's wailing. Draped over her husband's body, red hair dragging in the dirt, Tara Lenear's Irish heritage rampaged to the fore as she shrieked a wake for her beloved. Aislinn tried to join her, to hug her father one last time, but in what was one of her last sentient moments, her mother stopped screaming and hustled them off the mountain.

It was only later, after the madness took root, that Aislinn realized it would've been far more merciful if Tara had joined Jacob that day. Her mother hadn't been the only one to lose her mind in the face of the invasion—the six dark gods hadn't lost much time creating gateways for their hell-spawned minions to scare the crap out of people—but Aislinn had *needed* her mother, goddammit. It hadn't taken long for the truth to sink in: she'd lost both her parents on that South American mountain.

Not long after, the Lemurians had shown up with their own brand of alien power. While they'd dealt fairly with her, Aislinn knew it was because she was gifted. The chilly indifference with which they dispatched humans who were either crazy or without magical ability still felt like an affront. She'd been raised to believe all life held intrinsic value. The first time she'd floated that idea to a Lemurian, he'd laughed for a good thirty minutes. She hadn't brought it up again.

Aislinn twisted her face into a bitter grimace. Even three years later, the memories horrified her. She shut her eyes, squeezing them so tightly colors flashed behind her lids. Her father and mother were dead. They couldn't help her anymore. There was no percentage in thinking about either of them. All it did was make her sad.

Pressing harder on the tattoos, she asked the Old Ones how to find Taltos. When the answer came, she understood she'd known all along. It was part of the embedded memories, but she'd been so upset by Perrikus—and thinking about her parents—she'd been at cross-purposes with herself.

Confident the gateway would show itself to her, assuming she survived the journey, Aislinn wondered about her invitation. Insofar as she knew, other than the brief indoctrination she'd gotten once she accepted her magic and agreed to help the Lemurians, no additional training had been offered to other humans. Had any of them ever been invited into the Old Ones' domain before? Was she the first? The thought excited and frightened her at the same time.

"Let's see." She ticked off on her fingers. "Mage, Seeker, Seer, Healer, Hunter." The spectrum of human powers. She had both Mage and Seeker talents. Her Mage gift gave her facility with spells. Most humans had only one skill. It was unusual, but not unheard of, to have two. Travis, for example, was a Hunter, but he had Healing talent also. Why would the Old Ones suddenly take such an interest in her? So what if one of the dark ones planned to rape her? It wasn't any different than they'd done with countless human women. A harsh laugh escaped. Actually, the Old Ones and the enemy had one thing in common: a blatant disregard for human life. Aislinn figured the Old Ones were simply using her and others like her as pawns in their million-year-old battle against Perrikus and his cronies.

Feeling confused and vulnerable—and angry that her compliance with Metae's orders was a foregone conclusion—Aislinn mapped out her journey. She needed to get to a sacred mountain in northern California. It was about a thousand miles from her current location, so it would take several jumps and at least two days. Maybe even three because her magic would need time to recover.

Take nothing—that's ridiculous. I have to take food.

No, she argued with herself, *I can hunt. Probably better to follow Metae's instructions exactly.*

A familiar voice broke into her reverie. *"Aislinn."*

"Travis? Didn't you go home?" She winced. He'd been kind to her. He deserved better. *"Uh, sorry. Didn't mean to be rude."*

He chuckled. *"Yeah. I went home. Just wanted to tell you I hope I see you again."*

Sudden tears sprang to her eyes. She brushed them away. *"Damn it, Travis,"* she hissed, her mind voice almost a growl. *"Do not start caring about me. I don't think I could stand it."*

"We've all lost a lot, Aislinn. Don't let it blind you to the rest of your life."

She began to answer, but he severed the link. She sent magic spinning out to resurrect it, but pulled it back almost immediately. Travis was a complication she did *not* need right now. What she needed to do was get moving. On her feet before the thought was done percolating, Aislinn stripped off her shift, then dressed carefully in layers, snugging into long underwear and wool pants that used to be black, but had faded to gray. A red flannel shirt—it clashed with her hair, but so what?—topped by a leather vest and her torn black leather jacket completed her usual *mercenary for hire* outfit. She glanced down at herself and laughed. There'd been a time when she'd actually cared what she looked like. Now the only thing she cared about was if her clothing was warm and functional.

Eying her boots, she shook her head. She needed to be on the lookout for a replacement pair. She tossed a battered rucksack over her shoulders to hold some of her clothes in case it was warmer than she thought it would be, made sure she had a water bottle and her cook pot, and held a westerly location in her mind as she entered a journey jump.

Aislinn arrived at her planned destination easily. Under the watchful eye of a weak sun trying hard to put out a little warmth, she patted the walls of a deserted tin mining shack a couple hundred miles from her home. Compared with her last journey, the first leg of this one had been easy. The next few should be, too, at least until she traveled into terra incognita. When she couldn't picture her location, she wasn't sure quite what she'd do. Coming out in unknown terrain was always risky.

She'd been to the tin shack before. Once when her mother was still alive, and later, when she was teaching herself how to use magic to travel. The miner who'd built the humble structure had left a diary about losing his wife to cancer. His pain, splashed across the grime-streaked pages of a journal, pierced her heart. She thought about going inside to see if the journal was still there, but resisted. She didn't really have time to spare. Aislinn reached out cautiously with her magic to see if any threats were near. And froze.

She wasn't certain what she sensed, but it had wrongness stamped all over it. She hadn't expected to run into trouble so soon, and it rattled her. Silent in her cracked leather boots, she faded into the hut through a door hanging half off its hinges. The diary was right where she'd left it, tucked into a clear plastic bin so rodents wouldn't chew it to bits. Drawing power, she looked through the walls of her shelter.

Ghost army.

Had they seen her arrive? Shades of human dead, robbed of life far too soon, roved the countryside in packs. They holed up in what was left of the cities, too. Not unlike feral dogs, they refused to leave. Enough of them could suck the life out of you, which was how they swelled their ranks. Aislinn ground her teeth together. While easier to fool than instruments of the dark, she couldn't afford to take chances. Dead was dead, and shades would kill her just as eagerly as Bal'ta. Her corporeality was an affront to them.

Because they weren't magical, they shouldn't be able to sense her. If she sat tight, she could wait till they moved on, but that might make her late. The alabaster had given her four days' time. It seemed like enough, if everything went smoothly. She peered at the ghost army again with magic-enhanced senses. As she watched, one of them pointed a bony finger her way. She sat up straighter. Shit. They must have seen her flicker into being after she'd first arrived.

She girded herself for moving on, pulling magic, visualizing a location, when the shades closed in. They slithered through the walls and surrounded her. When she reached for her magic, a barrier stood between her will and the reservoir that held her power.

What the hell? They're not supposed to be able to do that. The reek of long-decayed flesh pricked her nose. She stifled a gag. Skeletal fingers with strips of flesh hanging off them reached for her. A high-pitched, wavering howl filled the air, and chills ran down her back. The shades sounded hungry. Aislinn forced herself to look at the remnants of humanity surrounding her. "Did this shack belong to one of you?" she asked, as she scanned the group.

"Aye. What's it to you?" One of the men stepped forward. Even dead, with flesh peeling off him in strips and a caved-in place where it looked like someone had buried an axe in his skull, it was obvious he'd been a big, powerfully built man.

Aislinn met his dead, brown gaze. "I read your journal. I'm sorry about your wife." She hesitated. "I know what it is to lose someone you love."

"Do you now?" he snarled. Half-eaten away lips drew back from teeth with exposed roots.

"Yes," she said simply. "Both my parents were killed. All my friends, too."

The man stepped closer. Raising a hand, he ran it down her arm. Then, more familiarly, cupped a breast. "Warm," he breathed, showering her with rancid breath. "So warm." He tightened his hand, pulling her close.

Swallowing revulsion, Aislinn laid a hand over his. "Don't you want to see your wife again?"

He tossed his shaggy head. Long, gray-flecked dark hair crawling with maggots swatted against her body. "Stupid girl," he brayed. "If you're going to give me some prattle about heaven, don't waste your breath. Stopped believin' when Betty died."

"Doesn't matter what you believe." Aislinn met his gaze. "Spirits of the dead live on, but you have to pass the light to know that."

He was kneading her breast now, rubbing the exposed bone of his fingertips over her nipple. "And how would you know, missy?"

She wasn't certain, but Aislinn thought she saw hope flicker behind his dead eyes. "Because I have to believe I'll see my parents again one day. Either I'll be killed in battle, or after I'm through fighting for the Lemurians."

He dropped her breast as if it burned him. A hissing sibilance passed his lips, spraying her with spittle. "You're one of them. Turned by the other side."

Outraged shrieks battered her ears, and the dead closed in on her.

"Grab her," one of them shouted.

"We need her."

"She's warm."

"Lemurian magic might bring us back."

"Oh no, it won't," Aislinn countered, swallowing pity and fear. "They're the ones who killed most of you. Remember?" She hurried on. "If you keep killing the few of us that are left, who will avenge your deaths?"

The remains of a plump woman sidled close. She stroked

Aislinn's hair, sending ice chips into her guts. "Warm," she mumbled. "I remember what it was to be warm."

The miner shoved his body between them. "Go," he hissed at Aislinn. "You do devil's work. We will let you leave, but you must make me a promise."

"What?" Aislinn wondered if she'd have to lie.

"Fight those who killed us. I want revenge."

We all do.

Sucking in a deep breath and letting it out, she took a chance, hoping the Lemurians weren't in her head to listen. "Once the dark are defeated, if that's even possible, I give you my word I will do what I can to see that the Old Ones return to Taltos and remain there."

The man turned to the rest of the ghost army. Aislinn hadn't been paying attention, but most of them were crowded into the miner's shack. Bodies merged into bodies in one stinking, gelatinous mass. "What do you think?" he demanded.

"She spoke true," one ventured.

"Aye, I thought she'd lie to save her sorry hide," another spat.

Her jaws were clamped together so hard they ached, and Aislinn forced her mouth open to ease the pressure. Some of the dead were determined to keep her, while others argued one more life couldn't possibly help them. She reached for her magic again, inhaling sharply when she didn't sense the barrier anymore.

May as well be ready, she reasoned and started the spell to take her away from this place.

The miner grasped her wrist. "We did not release you."

A wry smile split her face. "You let me access my magic. It's pretty much the same thing." She held her breath.

He smiled back at her, ghoulish with non-existent lips and snagly teeth. "Maybe it is. Go, human. Never forget what you are." He made shooing motions toward the door.

Aislinn didn't wait to be asked again. Swallowing down bile, she raced outside, hungry for air not tainted with the reek of dead meat.

What the hell? She stopped in her tracks as soon as she'd cleared the lintel. Sitting on its haunches, staring at her with amber eyes, was the most intelligent-looking wolf she'd ever seen. It cocked its head to one side. Gray fur, streaked with silver and black, gleamed in the sun.

I'm not a Hunter. Why would it come to me? Those with Hunter gifts had animal sidekicks, like Travis's civet. Following instincts, fueled by her magic, she reached toward the wolf and asked in mind speech, *"You want something of me. What is it?"*

Feeling foolish—after all, her hunches were sometimes wrong—Aislinn glanced sidelong at the wolf, and she readied herself to leave. It wouldn't do to tarry in case the shades changed their minds.

"I'm coming with you."

"I am not a Hunter. You've made a mistake."

The wolf rose lazily to its feet, lush tail swishing. *"I never make mistakes. Include me in your spell. If you do not, the Hunter Covenant gives me the right to kill you."*

The wolf stalked to her, and she saw it was male. Aislinn culled through her memory banks for what she knew about Hunters and their animals. Humans with Hunter skills were the most adept at finding the enemy—and killing them. Somehow, the blend of animal magic boosted whatever the human brought to the table. She couldn't remember what happened to humans who refused an animal bond. Who knew? Maybe rejection did give the wolf the right to kill her.

Covenant or not, it didn't pay to get off on the wrong foot. She'd never tolerated being bullied and wasn't about to start now. *"Now see here."* She hunkered so their gazes met directly. *"No threats."*

He just looked at her, tongue lolling.

"Great," she muttered and expanded her casting to bring wolfie-boy along. "Ghost army, talking wolf. What the hell else will I find between here and Taltos?"

CHAPTER 3

*A*islinn brought them down in the ruins of Salt Lake City—an asphalt nightmare. She'd been aiming for her old neighborhood and the bomb shelter her father and some of his friends had hogged out under their home in the nineteen eighties. She was tired and knew she needed food and sleep before she could travel again. So far, wolfie hadn't been any trouble, but it took almost double the magic to move both of them. She'd felt power from the civet. If wolfie had any, he was doing a fine job hiding it. She did some quick calculations. The four days that had seemed generous now seemed as if they might not be quite enough.

The wolf morphed into being next to her and made a whuffy noise, midway between a whine and a snarl. *"Where have you brought us? Nothing to hunt here but corpses."* He wrinkled his nose in lupine disgust.

Ignoring his question, she asked, *"Do you have a name?"*

He gazed at her with interest. *"Why?"*

"So I have something to call you besides wolfie?"

"Rune will do."

She rolled the name around in her mind. It chimed sourly. Raising her eyebrows, she looked at him. *"That's not your name."*

"Names have power. Even you should know that, human."

Biting off a sarcastic retort, she said, *"Just make sure no one follows us."*

Feeling thoroughly chastised, and by a wolf no less, she trotted in the direction of the house she used to live in, leading them across a rubble-filled alleyway, through a culvert, and finally underground, down badly decomposed steps. Many were missing, and she stumbled, catching herself on what was left of the handrail. The doorway was still in place, right along with the punch code lock. She keyed in seven-seven-four-three, and the door swung inward.

Aislinn stepped inside with Rune at her heels. As soon as his tail cleared the door, she pushed it shut and sank into a dusty chair. It was dark as pitch with the door closed, but she didn't need to see. The smell in the small enclosure reminded her of her father, and tears rose, threatening to spill over.

"Your pack lived here."

Wondering how he could possibly know that, but too weary to puzzle it out, her eyes fluttered shut.

When she opened them, she knew she'd slept, but not very long. She was hungry and thirsty, but rested enough. Rune had curled his body around her chair. She felt his fur, soft against her ankles, and the heat rising off his body. For some inexplicable reason, his nearness brought a smile to her face. Now that her eyes had adapted to the dark, she could see threads of light filtering around the door where it no longer fit tightly in its frame.

"Time to hunt?" he asked, stretching out one paw at a time once he'd gotten to his feet.

She nodded, rising. *"There used to be food here. Let me look."* She called light—a glowing rose orb—into being. It followed after her like an obedient puppy.

Since the combination lock served as a decent deterrent, quite an array of canned goods remained. Most likely all of them. Beckoning her light closer, she peered at a can of Hormel corned beef hash. Then she laughed. "Use by September nineteen ninety-nine, huh?" She poked at the can. It seemed intact. The lids on either end weren't pooched out like they'd have been once botulism set in. Returning to the cans, she got peaches, green beans, Vienna sausage, and the can of hash. The can opener still hung by its hook on the side of the cabinet. She grabbed it, too.

Rune waited by her chair, his ears pricked forward. She waggled the can of hash at him. *"Interested?"*

"I don't think so." He wrinkled his nose. *"Whatever's in there died a long time ago."*

"Well, try some. It will save time." Using the opener, she removed the lid and upended the can on the packed dirt floor. The wolf nosed it, shrugged his furry shoulders, and began to eat. Hesitant at first, once he'd taken a couple bites, he snarfed down the rest.

She went to work on the beans and sausage, eating with her fingers. Everything tasted okay. She saved the peaches with their sticky syrup for last. "Go capitalism," she muttered, popping the last peach into her mouth. The canned good manufacturers probably underestimated the shelf life of their products on purpose to make people buy more. She looked around the twelve by twelve subterranean space. It had been underneath their kitchen. In addition to the faded, corduroy easy chair, there was a card table with four chairs, shelves built into every wall, and hooks for a kerosene lantern. Her father hadn't been sure there'd be enough ventilation to use it for very long, but two five-gallon tins of kerosene sat in one corner, along with their battered Coleman lantern and a supply of mantles she was certain had long since turned to dust.

Her family. This was the last of what was left of them and their home. Not very fucking much. Resisting an urge to sift through the rubble above to see if she could find anything else, she set the peach can on the floor. The bomb shelter had been built before she was born. She remembered playing down here on hot summer days when the temperature climbed into the nineties in Salt Lake.

Rune's voice broke into her memories. *"I thought we were in a hurry, human."*

"Yes." She shot out of the chair as if the wolf had bitten her, disgusted with herself for her unauthorized trip into yesterday-land. *"We are."*

"Where are we going?"

She pulled the door open, withdrew the magic supporting her light, and cocked her head to one side. *"Can you help when we travel?"*

"Certainly. You did not ask."

Certainly, her inner voice mimicked. *As if I knew I had to.*

"Well," she ventured, aiming for a neutral tone, *"I'd really appreciate it. We have a long way to go."*

"I need to know our destination."

"I can't tell you."

Rune, who'd started up the stairs, whipped his body around. Golden wolf eyes glared down at her, glinting amber in the low light. *"I am your bond animal. There are no secrets between us."*

"I shouldn't have a bond animal," she argued, pushing past him up the steps. *"I already told you. I'm not a Hunter."*

"Yes," he insisted, *"you are."*

They were still quarreling when they emerged into daylight. Realizing too late that she should've been more cautious, she scattered magic in a full circle, seeking threats.

"I already checked," Rune informed her haughtily. *"If there had been danger, I would not have allowed you above ground."*

Aislinn rolled her eyes. Not only did she have a talking wolf who was convinced he was bonded to her, now the wolf had decided he was her guardian angel. Ignoring him, she began setting up her magic so they could leave. Spell mostly in place, she whistled for Rune. He was facing away from her, sniffing something fifty feet away. He didn't turn around. *"Rune,"* she hissed, struggling to contain the spell. It tugged at her, ready to launch itself. *"We're ready."*

He swiveled his head to look back at her over one shoulder. *"Oh,"* he inquired caustically, *"are we?"*

"Fine." She threw up her hands, and her spell lost its punch.

Christ, but she hated to waste magic. *"Did you decide you're not coming?"*

"I don't know." He turned to face her.

She opened her mouth to answer, and then it fell open. "You just answered me," she sputtered. "And not in mind speech."

"All bond animals can talk," Rune informed her. "But only to our bonded one or others with the Hunter gift." His voice was deep and rumbly, like a friendly grizzly bear might sound.

Aislinn sank to a convenient piece of concrete. "Look." She held out her hands. "I have no training in Hunter magic. Zero. Zip. Zilch. I'm a Mage with weak Seeker ability. At least, that's what I thought I was. Also, I'm used to working alone. I like it that way. That doesn't make me very good partner material."

Rune walked a bit closer. He hung his head. "You probably should know my last human was killed in a Bal'ta raid led by Tokhots. I tried to protect her, but she did not listen to me. I killed all those godless whelps, except Tokhots, that murdered my bonded one, but Tokhots vanished as soon as the first few Bal'ta died." The wolf's lower jaw quivered. He threw back his head and one long, low, anguished howl burst from him. "You were the first Hunter I've come across since her death. I listened outside that cabin while you bargained with the dead. I liked what I heard." The wolf hesitated for a long time before his next words. "If you truly do not want me, I will seek another. I do not want a forced bond. Even though the laws say I could kill you for refusing me, I would not do that."

Oh, God. What do I do now?

The wolf's distress was so palpable, it seared her, but he was proud, too. She could see it in the determined set of his shoulders. She'd never wanted to hurt anyone. In that moment, she understood on a visceral level that she'd chased away the possibility of support —and love—to shield herself. Aislinn felt ashamed. What had Travis said? *We've all lost a lot...*Something like that. She'd used her losses as an excuse to check out of life. Drifting from assignment to assignment, she'd never let herself think too deeply about anything.

Guess I assumed I'd be killed sooner or later.

Scooting over, she hunkered next to Rune and held out a hand to him. "If you go into this knowing you'll have to help me because I don't know shit about being half of a bond pair, well, I'm willing to give it a whirl."

"You don't have to," he said stiffly, still not looking at her. "I didn't tell you about losing Marta so you would pity me. I told you so you would understand."

She stifled a bitter laugh. "I don't pity you," she said. "I pity me. I lied to you just now. It's not that I prefer working alone. I've chosen to so I don't have to feel responsible for anyone else's death. If you still want me for your bondmate, I'd be honored."

Rune looked at her then. Really looked at her and sifted through her soul, taking her measure. At length, he shut his eyes and whuffled softly. "You still have not told me where we are going. I must know if I am to help boost your magic."

Aislinn let out a breath she didn't know she'd been holding. This was the first time she'd offered anything touching the core of herself since her parents died. Granted, it was only a wolf—*No, a stern inner voice kicked in. He is far more than a wolf, and you know it. He is love and risk. And vulnerability.*

"*I am going to Taltos,*" she sent in shielded mind speech. "*I do not know if they will let you in.*"

What he said next shocked her. "*They may not exactly welcome me, but I've already been there.*"

She was a little show on the uptake, because she was well into pulling their traveling spell together when it dawned that if Rune had been there, he must know how to find it.

"Of course," he said, obviously having read her mind.

"You know my thoughts?" For a second time that afternoon, her spell frittered away on the winds.

The wolf nodded. "You should know mine, now I've dropped my shielding. It is part of the bond gift."

She smiled at him, liking this new development, even though it felt scary. It'd be like having a twin, where each knew the other's innermost feelings. She'd always wanted a brother or sister—

Alien energy bombarded her. She snapped her head hard right and heard Rune's voice in her head. *"Down the stairs, human. Get that door open. Do it now."*

The old Aislinn would've hesitated, wanting to see exactly what they faced. Today's Aislinn dove for the stairwell, trusting Rune's hyper-tuned senses. She was only twenty feet from the break in the earth leading downward. Because she knew where the damaged steps were, she made the bottom in seconds and entered the code from feel without drawing magic for her light. Rune nosed her forward as soon as the door opened.

She pulled it shut and stood in the dark, the harsh sound of the wolf's panting loud in her ears. "What was out there?" she whispered, loathe to use any magic in case something with Seeker or Hunter ability lurked above.

"Dark magic."

"Can you still sense it?" She hesitated. "More importantly, can they sense you?"

"Yes and no."

"How are you invisible to them?" She was curious. Maybe she could borrow from his skills. That would be a handy one.

"I do not need magic to smell and hear things."

Aislinn felt stupid. Of course he didn't. Lupine senses were far more sensitive than her own. Feeling for the chair, she sank into it. And waited. At least half an hour ticked by. "I think we should face whatever's out there," she said softly.

"No."

"Well, we can't stay here."

"Why not? There's food and plastic bottles with water."

"Because I have to be at the gateway in three more days."

"Or?"

"Or they may not let me in."

In the faint light filtering in from around the door, she saw Rune shift from an alert sit to his feet, tail pluming behind him. "I will go." He nosed at the door. "Open it for me."

"Now just a damned minute." She rocketed to her feet and buried a hand in the thick ruff of his neck. "We can be partners, but I won't have you fight my battles."

He turned and met her gaze, eyes gleaming in the dim light. "I will not lose another bondmate."

Shit, he's more like me than I realized...

She squatted and wrapped her arms around his neck, breathing in the clean animal scent of him. He smelled like the forest and wild things. It was a good smell. Pure and bracing. "None of us can predict the future. I will do my damnedest to stay alive, and so will you. We can help each other, but no matter how hard we try, one of us might die." She blinked back sudden tears. "It's not the life I was born to, and I don't like it very much, but it's the way things are. I say we go out there together."

His body stiffened beneath her touch. She stroked his coat from shoulders to haunches again and again. Finally, he said, "It would not be my first choice, but we can leave."

"Do you know what kind of creature we face?"

When he didn't answer, she sent out the finest spindle of Seeker magic. It came back almost immediately, and she blew out a breath. "Only wargs. Not that many of them. We should be able to mow our way through them and be gone."

"They are my blood. I would prefer not to kill them if there is another way."

His answer stopped her dead. She thought about wargs—wolves turned by the dark and infused with their insidious magic. Like all creatures of the dark, they'd surrendered their will. "You feel sorry for them?" She was incredulous. It had never occurred to her to feel anything but anger for men stupid enough to sell their souls to the dark gods.

"No, I still hold hope they will come to their senses."

"Oh."

Rune's compassion for his kin filled her with embarrassment. Ever since that night in Bolivia, all she'd wanted to do was inflict pain on the ones who'd been irresponsible enough to invite disaster to Earth. The power of their chanting at multiple weak spots between the worlds had opened gateways for the dark. Stupid idiots.

"Well," she said, "we can try to leave from here. It's always harder traveling from underground, but if you help…"

He shook his head, still cradled between her arms. "No, you are right, human. This is a battle to the death. For each of their foot soldiers we vanquish, they have fewer to launch against us. Come. Let us do what we must and be gone from this place."

"There are ten," she told him, "feeding on the dead. There must've been fighting here recently. We have the element of surprise. I'll pull fire from the earth. Don't get between me and my targets."

"I will start with the ones on the right." He growled. Hackles rose along his spine.

"Fine. I'll start left. We'll meet in the middle. I want to test out this Hunter magic you think I have."

Using two hands, she opened the locking mechanism silently. Rune went first. When he gathered his rear legs under him and sprang out of the hole in the earth, she was on his heels, power blazing from her hands. Whatever she targeted fell before her. Aislinn blinked in amazement. Could it be that Hunter magic meant she never missed? *Christ! Wish I knew more about this.* It wasn't that she couldn't be overpowered, but her aim was always true. Once she sent magic after something, it couldn't escape the death that flew from her hands.

Son of a bitch, maybe I'm a Hunter after all.

Amidst yelps and howls, three impossibly large, gray wolves fell before her. Then two more. She didn't have time to look Rune's way. Snarling and snapping suggested he was well engaged. She pulled power to send it spiraling after another wolf when her target, apparently sensing his imminent doom, turned tail and ran. She could still kill it, but it didn't feel fair to nail an enemy in full retreat.

Now who's the bloody bleeding heart?

She looked for Rune. Two wolves lay dead, and he battled with a third, his powerful jaws closed around its neck. The last wolf turned and ran after the one she'd let go, tail tucked between its legs.

Once she jockeyed with her perception, she could hear Rune's thoughts. He and the wolf beneath him were talking. Rune agreed to withhold the deathblow if the wolf would leave. He stepped back, gaze trained on his adversary. For a moment, it seemed the other wolf—coal black with shiny green eyes—would keep his end of the bargain. He half turned in the direction the other two deserters had taken.

Out of nowhere, with a tremendous spring, he twisted his body in the air and landed atop Rune, burying his teeth in Rune's neck. Aislinn loosed a battle cry and sent a killing blow straight to his head. The other wolf toppled into the dirt.

She ran to Rune and flung her arms around his neck. Harsh panting filled her ears. Warm liquid gushed under her hands. Goddammit! The lying, cheating, sack-of-shit wolf who'd welched on the kindness Rune offered had punctured a major vessel. Ignoring an inner voice that reminded her she wasn't a Healer, she closed both hands over the wound. A chant she'd never heard before rose from her throat. She imagined the damaged tissues beneath her hands and what would need to knit itself together so Rune didn't lose any more blood.

"Help me," she urged, not knowing who she asked. Tears ran down her face. She would not lose him. Not now. They'd just found each other. So what if she wasn't a Hunter or a Healer. The wolf would be her friend.

If she could keep him alive.

CHAPTER 4

It was so long since she'd had a friend, the word was more concept than emotion, but she'd do just about anything to keep Rune alive. For him to die because he'd been protecting her would open the scabs coating her heart all over again. She'd tended those scabs ever since her parents' deaths, adding magic to make them impervious to stray emotion. In spite of all that, Aislinn knew the truth. She was scared shitless to peer beneath them. The tough girl veneer she'd cultivated these past three years was only the thinnest of coatings.

Her heart thudded against her ribs as she worked on the wolf that was soaking the ground in front of her with crimson streaks. *Please,* she sent up a prayer, hoping someone was listening. *Don't let him die.*

She berated herself, muttering, "Shouldn't waste my breath. Rune needs all my attention."

Blood welled, hot and sticky on her fingers. The coppery smell was thick in her nostrils. She willed the blood to stay within, sent cells from her own body through her fingertips with instructions to patch the punctured blood vessel. When the flow didn't stop, panic filled her, but she shoved it aside.

I have to believe I can do this. She lectured herself. *That's how magic works.*

Aislinn wasn't sure how long she knelt there, weaving water, fire, and her own flesh into the blood vessels in Rune's neck. Finally, when hope had nearly died, the blood slowed, then stopped.

Rune, who'd somehow stayed upright through her ministrations, sank to his haunches, panting. He leaned against her. "Bondmate," he breathed. "Thank you."

She sent her Mage senses into him. He was well enough to travel. Mage magic *knew* things. It also helped with what she'd always thought of as *parlor tricks*. Things like seeing through walls and finding water. Seer magic, which she didn't have, foretold the future—at least, parts of it—and could alter the flow of time.

"We need to leave," she told Rune.

"Not a Hunter. Not a Healer. Yet, it would appear you are both." His voice was thick, but he was talking, goddammit. And thinking, too.

"Never mind that. We need to get out of here before those two who left come back with reinforcements. I was afraid they'd show up while I was working on you." Her face twisted as if she'd bitten into something sour. "I don't know what I would've done if that happened."

"It didn't. No point borrowing trouble, human." Gathering his feet under him, Rune stood and shook himself.

She thought about asking for his help, but decided not to. He needed all his energy to finish healing. Running the geography of what had been the western United States through her mind, she settled on a jump that would bring them to the eastern reaches of Nevada. Not too far. It should be within the scope of what magic she had left.

She gazed back at the bomb shelter. It would be convenient to bring some of the food along, but she couldn't transport aluminum cans. The one time she'd tried, the cans burst, made a God-awful mess in her rucksack, and peppered her back with sharp bits of metal. Generally, anything traveling had to be either flesh and blood, or something inert strapped to her body—like clothing or a backpack. Her dirk and cook pot didn't pose a problem, but they weren't sensitive to pressure changes like canned food. She blew out a tired breath. All the more reason not to go too far. She'd have to hunt once they got there. If she brought them out in one of the many mountain ranges in that region, there'd at least be cover.

"Ready?" She stroked Rune's head.

He moved to her side, panting and wobbly, but determined. Holding an image in her head of where she wanted to go, she drew her traveling spell again. Weightlessness began in the soles of her feet. She tightened her arm around Rune and willed them out of there.

The wolf did something while they were en route. It felt as if he pushed inside her body, merging with her. It made things easier, so she didn't fight the sensation, but it was so unusual it took her breath away. She looked through two sets of eyes and heard through two sets of ears, her common world overlaid by the wolf's enhanced senses. She'd expected the journey to be dull, but it filled with unexpected wonders. Scents bombarded her. She smelled growing things and wild horses and bees at work. The scent of honey was so thick, it almost coated her tongue. An eagle's hunting cry came out of nowhere, followed by a pack of wolves howling.

When they tumbled out on a rocky hillside, she blinked several times, trying for a return of her normal perspective.

Rune stood next to her, tail twitching and head turning from side to side as his nostrils flared. "I am going hunting," he announced and took off at a lope.

Aislinn was hungry, too. Reaching out with magic—or trying to —she understood she was far too depleted to do much of anything. "Unless a mouse happens to run over my foot and I'm lucky enough to catch it, guess I'm out of luck," she groused.

"Stop feeling sorry for yourself. Find water for us," drifted back to her.

Good advice. Opening her senses, she sought the tang that meant water. It would've been easier with magic, but it wasn't impossible without. Nevada wasn't as dry as it looked. Once her mother had checked out, Aislinn spent several weeks wandering from one miner's shack to another, hunting for a place to shelve her grief. There'd still been cars and gasoline then, so it was relatively easy to leave Salt Lake—and return.

Tara hadn't seemed to understand Jacob was dead. She talked to him all the time, and she'd reverted to Gaelic, stopped bathing, and almost stopped eating. It was as if Aislinn hadn't even existed anymore. Once when she'd returned after a month of knocking around Nevada, Colorado, and Utah, her mother just looked blankly at her, apparently not having noticed she'd been gone.

Water.

She wrenched herself back to the present. A spring was just over the next ridge. Either that, or an artesian well. Trusting the wolf could find her, she started for it, stumbling over rocks littering a talus field. Maybe she might have enough magic to help her pick a path... No go. She stubbed a toe, cursed, gave it up, and used her eyes.

The spring was exactly where she'd sensed it. It wasn't much, a trickle oozing out of moss-coated ground. She'd just eased herself down next to the slick, algae-coated rocks when she spied Rune walking toward her. His mouth bulged with two fat rabbits.

She dug a small circle around the water to encourage it to pool and lurched back to her feet. "Nice!" she exclaimed. "Dinner." Gathering sage, she piled it between rocks. When she had a respectable heap, she lit it with a thought. Fire was the first magic and by far the easiest. Aislinn waited for the blaze to die down so she could cook over it.

She picked up a rabbit and looked quizzically at the wolf. "One of these is yours."

"I can get more."

"No," she insisted. "Eat one of these. If we're both still hungry, you can hunt for more."

The wolf snatched up the smaller of the two rabbits and hauled it a few feet away. She heard the crunch of bones breaking. Gutting her rabbit with the dirk that hung from her waist, she tossed the entrails Rune's way. Once she'd skinned the carcass, she threaded the meat onto thick pieces of scrub oak and warmed them over her fire. Not caring the meat wasn't fully cooked, she ate as soon as blood stopped dripping from it, delighting in succulent flesh bursting on her tongue. Sometimes, she thought she could taste the desert grasses the rabbits fed on.

Who knows? Maybe I can.

Rune edged closer, snout painted with gore. He stuck his nose in the sandy declination she'd hogged out and drank, slurping loudly. Then he walked to her small stack of rabbit bones and crunched them down. *"Do you want more?"*

"No, I'm good. We need to sleep. I don't have enough magic right now to move a raccoon out of here, let alone the two of us."

He nudged her with his nose. "Sleep, human. I will take first watch."

She stuffed the last of the rabbit into her mouth, chewing. "Okay," she said, her words garbled by the meat, "but wake me so you can rest, too."

He didn't, though. When she opened her eyes, the sky was thick with stars. It was cold, like it always was in high desert places in the dead of night. Rune lay next to her, warm against her side. Even though she'd only known him for a few hours, it felt as if they'd been together forever. A part of her wondered how that could possibly be. Another part accepted—and welcomed—that she was no longer alone.

"You were supposed to wake me."

"I would have. The night is not yet over." His voice rumbled against her.

She draped an arm around his warmth and fitted her body

against his back, almost like she would've done with a lover. "Sleep, Rune. We'll leave when it's closer to dawn."

She felt his body relax against her, heard his breathing slow, and smiled to herself. Yes, it was a lot like having a lover, though simpler in many regards. She thought about their next jump. It would be the first one beyond where she'd been before. She didn't have an image to hold in her mind.

Maybe Rune will know. He's been to Taltos.

In the cold stillness of the darkest part of the night, when dawn was still at least an hour away, he rolled over, and she knew it was time to go. Darkness would help them, giving cover when they came out at the next place.

"Rune," she said softly, "send me an image of places between here and the gateway." She was hesitant to give voice to the word *Taltos* aloud.

A jumble of views filled her mind. She shook her head. "Send me the next place," she clarified. "So I know where to tell the spell to take us." Once she'd gotten it, she murmured, "It looks just like here."

"Trust me, human. It may look the same, but it is farther west."

THE MORNING WAS MOSTLY GONE when they came out two jumps from where they'd spent the night. Aislinn took in their surroundings. A thick pine forest stretched in all directions. Small animals rustled in the undergrowth. "Where are we?"

"I do not have the answer you seek. You want a place name. I do not know such things. We are closer to Taltos. That is all I can tell you."

She did some internal calculations. The first jump in the cold pre-dawn had taken them to more desert. She'd assumed they were still somewhere in Nevada, since the entire state was desert, but this looked different. Could possibly be in California already? Maybe somewhere around the Sierra Nevada Mountains that bisected the state?

The wolf seemed fully recovered. She'd asked him how he was so many times that he'd bared his teeth and growled. She didn't see how all that damage could've mended so quickly—after all, she wasn't a Healer—yet he appeared whole and strong, and she was grateful. *Yeah, I'll take all the miracles I can get here.* "How many more jumps?"

The wolf looked at her. His mouth opened in a grin. "I will tell you when we get there."

She laughed—and then started, realizing how long it'd been since she'd heard the sound of her own laughter. Real laughter, not the bitter chortlings she'd taken to indulging in. "Fair enough." Her gaze lingered on the trees around them, and she sent Seeker magic zinging out, searching for threats. "We need more to eat. It feels safe enough to hunt."

Rune lifted his muzzle and scented the air. He cocked his head to one side, a quizzical expression on his face. "There is something here, but I do not recognize it. Look again, Seeker."

When she did, the fine hairs on the back of her neck stood on end. Evil was faint, but there. It was possible she sensed residue from one who'd been there minutes, months, or years before. Rune, who'd snapped up a couple of unidentifiable rodents while she was scanning, threw her a knowing look. She ran the six dark gods through her mind: Perrikus, Majestron Zalia, Adva, D'Chel, Tokhots, and Slototh. She'd only come face to face with three: Perrikus, his mother Majestron, and D'Chel. So she had no idea what the others felt like. She wondered if the wolf might.

"Rune," she whispered into his mind, *"what do you know of the dark ones?"*

He sidled to her and dropped a still-twitching vole at her feet. Aislinn picked it up and brushed the dirt off. She was famished. Hungry enough to eat it raw. She wouldn't have enough magic to get them out of there if she didn't eat, and she didn't dare risk a fire. Not until they could pin down whatever it was both of them felt.

"You look as if it were poison," he said, sidestepping her last question.

"Really?"

"Your face is all drawn up into the same expression I'd have if someone served me shit."

Suppressing a giggle, she split the rodent down its belly line. The gut sack dropped into her hand, and she held it out for Rune. With a couple decisive cuts, she loosened the skin. "You didn't answer my question," she pressed while she chewed still-warm flesh. It wasn't as bitter as she'd thought it would be.

"No, I didn't."

Two rodents later—one more for her and his third, or maybe his fourth, she hadn't been paying terribly close attention—the faint miasma hadn't gotten any worse. She relaxed fractionally. Surely, if something was there, it would've shown itself by now. Their enemy wasn't known for restraint.

"Take us here." The wolf shoved an image into her mind.

His voice in her head startled her, since she'd been lost in thought. *"How far is it?"*

"Not very. I know you are tired."

Aislinn reached for her rucksack, and then realized she hadn't taken it off. Somehow, Rune knew things—like how close to exhaustion she was. She buried a hand in his ruff, and they were gone.

They crashed down almost as soon as they'd left. "You weren't kidding that this wasn't very far. We could've walked."

"No. We couldn't. Look around you."

Purple sky stretched from horizon to horizon. Dual suns were on their way down. *We jumped through a veil.* Her eyes widened, and she swallowed hard. "Okay. Where are we?"

"One world over. You wanted to have a conversation about the dark. It is not safe anywhere on Earth. The bad ones have ears everywhere. I showed you a place we could talk. And now we are here."

She mulled that over, shifting from foot to foot. Part of her training in mage craft had included the existence of parallel worlds that shared a boundary with hers, but she'd never been to one. "Is there food here?"

"No. Here is talk and rest."

The rolling grasslands beneath her feet looked soft and inviting. She sank down, resting her back against a boulder. It reminded her of her rucksack, so she unclipped it and arranged the small backpack behind her to make her seat more comfortable.

"Do we need to use mind speech?"

"I don't think so," Rune replied, his ears pricked forward. "I believe us to be alone."

Sending her magic outward, she blew out a relieved sigh when it pinged back clean of taint. "All right." She was so tired, her words slurred. *Too much magic. Not enough rest and food.* "What do you know of the six dark gods?"

"Beyond their names?"

She nodded.

"I am sorry, human, but little enough. I was hoping you could tell me about them. It is why I brought us here."

"But your last bondmate—"

"—tried to protect me," he interrupted. "We spent years together. I was little more than a pup when she found me, long before the dark ones broke through. Our relationship changed afterward. It was then we became bondmates."

"Oh." Aislinn looked away. She could see why Marta would've tried to shield her wolf, especially since she'd raised him. Silence hung between them. She felt Rune next to her, alert, waiting. His energy had a vigilance that rubbed off on her.

"First of the six is Perrikus. He rules power and energy. His mother, Majestron Zalia, is their leader. Other than that, I'm not sure quite what she does. I came upon her once, and she frightened me so badly I soiled myself. She takes hold of your mind, and you can't think anymore."

Aislinn sucked in a breath. She looked about and then sent magic in a tight circle to make sure they were still alone. The twin suns clung to the sky, low on the horizon, and the day was pleasant, but she felt chilled to her core.

"The other four?" he pressed, leaning close.

"I've never, ah, discussed them before. With anyone."

"How did you learn of them?"

"Read scrolls from the Old Ones." She bit her lower lip, remembering. "Metae hung onto them the whole time I was reading and whisked them into her robes the second I finished." Aislinn's mouth burned. Human tongues weren't designed to shape the names of evil. She licked her lips, but her saliva made them hurt.

I can finish this.

"Adva rules portals and knowledge. D'Chel is the god of illusion. Tokhots is a trickster and master rhymer. Slototh is filth and all that is discarded."

Her mouth felt swollen. So did her tongue. For a moment, she thought her airway would close. She pulled a water bottle from her rucksack and drank deeply. It helped a little.

"It is better for me to know." Rune's voice seemed as if it came from a long way away.

Her head spun. It was impossible to focus her gaze, so she closed her eyes. She gulped air like a landed fish. Something warm and wet laved her face over and over. It took a ridiculously long time for her to realize the wolf was licking her. Even longer for her to hear the wordless song he sent into her mind.

CHAPTER 5

*P*art of her was surprised to wake up. Before darkness claimed her, she'd wondered if speaking those six names aloud, within the same few minutes, would be her undoing. The inside of her mouth ached. Exploration with her tongue and fingers found blisters extending outward in large pustules that nearly covered her lips.

Something sharp grazed her arm. She forced her eyes to focus and realized Rune had just bitten her—but gently. "Time for us to leave this place."

"We just got here," she protested. It was hard to make her sore mouth form words.

"The border worlds do not tolerate us for long."

"How do you know that?" In spite of her discomfort, she was curious.

"Marta was a messenger."

So they must have done a lot of world-jumping... "That's why you know where Taltos is."

He just looked at her. Sorrow rimmed his eyes. Aislinn guessed it hadn't been all that long since Marta's death. Being a messenger was exceedingly dangerous. It was the way information flowed to those fighting the dark. The Old Ones had their own ways of communicating with one another. If they were close enough, they used telepathy with humans, too. At least those with Mage and Seer abilities. For humans who were too far away—or who lacked those particular skills—the Old Ones used alabaster plaques and runners to deliver them. Messengers were nearly always in the thick of things. Travis doubled as a messenger. She was pretty sure Hunting was his main function, but those weren't the kinds of things people talked about. Survival depended on secrecy. It was better if no one knew your talents. Travis had used telepathy to tell her he wanted to see her again. So he must have Mage or Seer skills, too, at least to some extent. If her supposition was true, he'd taken quite a risk reaching out to her.

There's a whole lot I don't know about human gifts. Maybe Travis is using something entirely different. Something I've never even considered. She made a mental note to ask Rune more about Marta and which skills she'd had.

A deep rumble beneath her drove Aislinn to her feet. The world seemed to be trying to expel them. Furling her eyebrows at Rune, she asked, "So do they send little green men with a hook out next?"

"I am not sure I understand   "

"Never mind. It was a joke. And not a very good one." She walked over to him. "I need the next place."

"How strong are you?"

Turning her Mage sense inward, Aislinn took stock. "Medium," she said after a pause. "I think we could go a ways." *At least, I hope we can.*

"Your mouth."

"Yeah, it hurts, but it probably looks worse than it feels. I'll work on Healing it later."

Another pine forest filled her mind. This one bordered a large lake. Holding the vision close, she buried a hand in Rune's neck and called up a spell. Winds—so strong they ripped the breath from her lungs—buffeted her as soon as she and Rune left the border world.

Grit blew in her face. The blisters on her lips ruptured, and fluid dripped down her chin. *What the hell?* Wary and confused, Aislinn wondered if it was always this hard to leave the borderlands. She tightened her hold on the wolf, determined to ride it out. What choice did she have? Once committed to a destination, it was suicide to switch locations mid-jump.

Struggling to infuse enough magic to keep her spell going got progressively harder. *It's like trying to drive into a headwind. Takes more fuel.* A harsh laugh escaped her. *That* world, the one with cars and gasoline, was gone. She still thought about it, because she'd understood it—and because she missed its relative predictability. In that world, soldiers got furloughed—R&R they'd called it. In this one, you fought until you died. The Lemurians had never heard of battle fatigue.

The wind left as quickly as it had come. She drifted in a familiar black void, trying to get her breath, the thud of her heart loud against her ears. She ran an experimental tongue over her lips. They actually felt better now that the blisters had broken open. Like he'd done the other day, Rune inserted part of himself inside her. It boosted her flagging energy and reminded her of the fine edge between survival and failure. When the wolf had first shown up, she'd been afraid he'd slow her down. Now it seemed he might make the difference between her actually finding the gateway. Or not.

They clunked out of the void. She didn't have enough power for an elegant transition. One minute, they were weightless. The next, Rune shoved her behind him, hackles on full alert as he scanned the seemingly deserted forest. In spite of being tired and scared, she heard her stomach growl. It didn't care about anything beyond its empty state.

Knowing they had to hunt, Aislinn tried to summon enough magic to see if they'd come out somewhere safe. Rune sank into an alert sit, and she knew she could save herself for something more important. Like finding game. Or greens. The wolf would never sit if he'd sensed danger.

She looked around them. A lake glistened through pine boughs in rays from a setting sun. Judging by how she felt, today ought to be long since over. Or maybe it was already tomorrow. She'd heard that time flowed differently in the borderlands. *If I got really lucky, it's still yesterday.* She took off at as brisk a pace as she could manage toward the water.

Catching her up quickly, Rune nipped at her calf. "Where are you going?"

"To see if anything edible's growing in the shallow part of the lake." She happened to be looking at him, so she saw something like a grimace cross his furred features and grinned. "Not meat, but I like it."

AGAINST RUNE'S PROTESTS, she made a small, sheltered fire between two large boulders and Healed her mouth while she waited for her meal to cook. The hunt had been good. She'd found both watercress and wild onions in abundance. The wolf contributed three fat rabbits. She made a stew of sorts in the battered cook pot she always carried. Rune ate his share of the meat raw. Belly really full for the first time since before she'd lain in wait for Travis, she carted water from the lake to douse the coals.

Rune eyed the rising smoke. Every aspect of his body, from his tautly held tail to the set of his shoulders, told her he thought her fire posed a huge risk.

"Stand down, silly." She made an expansive gesture with both hands, sure she'd sleep well since she'd had such a sumptuous meal.

He threw an injured look her way. "I will take first watch."

Too tired to argue, she pulled all her clothes on to ward against the chill of the night, laid her head on her pack, and closed her eyes. Sleep came, but it was almost worse than none. Aislinn stood outside herself, suspended above her body, which tossed and turned on the hard ground. Metae morphed into being, shrieking just like she had when Aislinn was about to throw her magic down the vortex. Except this time, the Lemurian dunned her for being late.

"I told you four days."

"I still have two," Aislinn protested.

"Not by my count."

Guess I wasn't so lucky in that border world.

Chastised, Aislinn understood she was awake and in astral form. Somewhat stiffly, she bowed her head. *"What would you have me do?"*

"How came you by Marta's wolf?" As she often did, Metae switched topics.

"He picked me." Aislinn glanced at Rune. He sat still as a carved statue, staring straight ahead, frozen in time. Apparently, Metae didn't want him to overhear their conversation.

The mage eyed her, scrutinized her soul and memories through a tightly woven web. The inside of her head burned. Tears leaked from her eyes. When she brushed them away and looked at her fingertips, they were red.

Christ. She made my eyes bleed.

"Sorry. I forgot how fragile you humans are." Metae didn't sound the least bit sorry. *"A Hunter picked you, and you Healed him when he was hurt?"*

"Why ask? You already know those things." Aislinn heard a peevish undercurrent in her tone, but her temper was on the uptick, and she didn't bother to modulate her anger. *"I'm not asleep. May I rejoin my body?"*

Disorientation blurred her vision as astral and physical bodies collided. She'd never cared for the sensation. It made her nauseous. Taking little, panting breaths to make sure her dinner stayed in her stomach where it belonged, she raised her gaze to Metae. The mage was in a female phase. The Old Ones were hermaphroditic, sometimes appearing as one sex, sometimes the other. Aislinn tried to ask one time about how they managed to have children.

All her blushing and stammering bought her was a bunch of doublespeak.

The Lemurian was over seven feet tall. Male or female, that part never changed. Blond hair shrouded her. It was so long and thick that the white robes beneath were all but obscured. Gold jewelry shone like a queen's ransom. A thick torc sat round her neck. Another circled her brow. Rings set with enormous gemstones sparked from nearly every finger. An iridescence to her skin made it hard to look directly at her. Her eyes were the worst, though. Deep, dark pools, they swirled hypnotically. Aislinn learned early on to avoid gazing at any Old One's eyes. Once ensnared, she couldn't turn away until they released her. The first time it happened, the Old One—not Metae—had laughed at her, but didn't let her go, for an endless time. The lesson sank in, and she hadn't made that mistake again.

"Thank you." Aislinn bowed slightly, feeling rigid and awkward like she always did around the Old Ones. "I'm sorry I'm late. What would you have me do?"

The Lemurian moved around her in a circle. Aislinn became stillness itself, waiting. They remained like that, Metae moving and Aislinn immobile, until dawn lightened the eastern horizon. Sometimes, Metae moved so quickly Aislinn could only feel her, and sometimes so slowly the only hint she moved at all was her position shifted subtly as time flowed past.

"I think," Metae said after Aislinn had given up on the Old One telling her anything, "I shall leave you in your world—"

An odd mixture of disappointment and relief swept through her. She'd wanted to see the mysterious Taltos, but was apprehensive about what she'd find. Her humanity felt like it was shrinking. One of the fears she'd kept to herself was that the Old Ones would complete the transformation, and she'd become something alien. Like them.

Laughter like pealing bells filled the dawn. "Oh, you are far from off the hook, child. You are developing into something…interesting.

Amazingly, with little intervention from us. I find that fascinating. I am simply giving you more time on your own to, shall we say, discover your talents. Then we shall welcome you to Taltos."

So I can entertain all of you? I don't think so. She clamped down on her thoughts. The Old Ones could read them easily if they were paying attention. Though Metae narrowed her eyes, she didn't say anything.

If Aislinn hadn't been so shocked by the turn of events, she'd have been ready. She knew how Lemurians came and went: in a puff of light so bright, it blinded you, leaving spots dancing in front of your eyes for hours. The blast rocked her. She slammed her lids down, but was a fraction of a second too late. Light seared her corneas, burning into her brain.

Rune yelped. She remembered he'd been frozen in place, his eyes wide open. Finding him by feel, she pulled him to her. "It's all right. She's gone." Laying hands over the wolf's eyes, she sent her magic—fairly fully recovered to her relief—edging forward. When she found healthy tissue instead of sizzled cells, she blew out a breath and smoothed his fur back along the sides of his muzzle. "Your eyes will be fine, Rune."

"What do you mean *she's gone?*" he demanded.

"One of the Old Ones was here."

"Why couldn't I sense her?" Rune wriggled out of her grasp, blinking furiously.

"She immobilized you."

The wolf growled. "I will have a word with her when we get to Taltos. Or him, if she's shifted."

Aislinn cocked her head to one side. "That's just it," she muttered. "Now we aren't going."

Rune squeezed his eyes shut, grimacing. "I'm going to the lake to douse my head. My eyes are burning. When I come back, you need to tell me everything."

The sun was well up in the sky by the time they'd finished another meal. While they ate, Rune peppered her with questions as she relayed Metae's visit, asking for clarification on several points. He growled, rose to his feet, and shook himself from ears to tail, before head-butting her with his snout. "Because you have become an interesting specimen for them to watch, they are not going to give you any assistance. At least not now."

"That's about the size of it." Aislinn sucked the last shreds of rabbit flesh off a bone, following it with a thick wad of watercress. Her fire had bothered the wolf so much the night before that she'd opted for raw this morning.

"We treat pack puppies with more respect."

Aislinn shot him a look. "I'm scarcely a puppy."

"In terms of your knowledge of magic, that is exactly what you are."

Ouch. "Touché."

"And that means?"

"Even though it pains me, I agree with you."

Rune whuffed low in the back of his throat. She could have sworn he was laughing.

"So, human, where do we go next?"

She stuffed a wild onion into her mouth, delighting in the bitter sweetness of it as she chewed. Waving the stalk in his direction, she said, "I've been thinking about that."

He waited, watching her closely.

"I believe we should go home. To my home, that is," she clarified.

"Why?"

Good question. "Because all my things—well, the few I have —are there."

"Would you like to see where Marta and I lived?"

A sudden flash of insight slammed her between the eyes. Rune wanted things from what had been his home. "I'd love to." Her reward was a quick flip of his tail as he bounded to her side, his eyes bright and filled with what looked like anticipation. She met his golden gaze full on. "We can get whatever you want while we're there."

"Maybe you'll want—" Head rearing up, his voice broke off.

Senses on red alert, she leapt to her feet. It took a few seconds before she heard it, but wing beats filled the still morning air. *"Just birds,"* she sent, reverting to mind speech.

"No. Ready yourself. We need to fight."

Trusting Rune's instincts, she melted into the shadows of a tree that would shield her from something airborne. The wolf didn't bother. He didn't have to. His natural form was an effective disguise. For a ridiculous moment, she wondered if she could learn to shapeshift along with Healing and Hunting, and then she laughed silently to herself. Taking different forms was a Lemurian skill. No human had mastered it. At least, she didn't think any had.

She trained her senses on the skies, eyes narrowed in concentration. As surreptitiously as possible, she pulled power from the Earth, keeping her magic out of the air. The wing beats got louder. Clearly, whatever was coming wasn't interested in stealth—which meant they hadn't zeroed in on her. Or else they were so strong, they didn't fear anything. Not a comfortable thought.

Aislinn caught sight of a leathery wingtip and cringed. Bats, but probably not normal ones. It was rare to find animals nowadays that hadn't been turned by one side or the other. Hunters used bond animals like Rune to expand their ability to seek out and destroy the enemy. If Rune thought the bats were a threat, they probably were.

"Draw one breath and fire," the wolf said.

"What will—?"

"I will help you when they get close enough to pull out of the skies."

The minute she loosed her magic, the bats would be on them. So far, they hadn't been discovered. If she stilled her power, and Rune acted more like a forest wolf and less like a bond animal, the bats might pass on by. They had to be headed for their cave. Nocturnal creatures, the daylight must be uncomfortable for them.

"We may not have to fight. Pretend you are hunting. I will mute myself."

He didn't answer, but she knew he'd heard. He sauntered away from her, sprang, and pulled a mouse from scrub grass and pine needles. The next rodent he pounced on looked larger, more like a marmot. Rune dragged it into the shadow of a boulder and proceeded to rip its guts open.

Aislinn became one with the tree next to her, borrowing its energy to cover hers. Barely breathing, she willed the winged mammals on their way. They filled the skies above her now. Their sharp, high-pitched squeals loud in her ears. They sounded angry about something. The bulk of them flew on. She was close to congratulating herself on calling this one right, when half a dozen wheeled back, heading right for Rune.

What the fuck? Bats don't attack things fifty times larger than themselves.

"Rune. Swim to the middle of the lake. Stay there."

The wolf exploded from his place. Long before the bats reached where he'd been, she heard a splash and knew he was following her directions. She'd been afraid he'd argue. Chittering like little mad things, the bats picked up the remains of the marmot and suspended it between four of them. Burdened by the dead animal, they flew low, but at least they left. She waited before she risked sending magic skyward to make certain they were gone.

Inhaling a steadying breath, letting it out, and pulling in another, Aislinn thanked the tree for shielding her, shouldered her rucksack, and loped to the lake. Her wolf paddled in slow circles, wearing an annoyed expression.

"Come on. Let's get moving while we can." She smiled at him. He looked like a large drowned rat.

Rune made the shore far faster than she expected. The second he hauled his body out of the water, he stalked over to her and shook himself, spraying her with droplets. "You will never order me away from you again when there is danger."

"I'm glad you listened," she retorted. "Don't you see? This was better than having to fight. Neither one of us are hurt—"

"We must be equal partners." He growled low in the back of his throat, hackles at half-mast. "The bond means I obey you, whether or not it's what I want. I loved Marta, but she forced her will on me. In the end, it meant her death."

She looked at Rune and extended compassion through their bond, hoping it would soothe his obvious pain. "I didn't know. Truly. Remember, I'm not trained as a Hunter." She sank a tentative hand into his wet ruff. "When there is little time to discuss strategy, what would you have us do?"

"I had a plan—" he began and then snapped off the next words so hard, his teeth clacked together.

"It may well have worked." She stroked his head and shoulders. Water squeaked beneath her fingers. "Rune, we are newly met. It'll take time for me to discover your strengths, and for you to appreciate mine."

"I am sorry." He really did look contrite. "Wanting you to do my bidding was not any different than you ordering me about." He nuzzled her side.

Except you're bound to obey me. Wish I'd known that...

The tang of magic zinged through the air. Rune's tail swished. Aislinn sent power in a protective arc over them both.

"Sister Hunter!" a decidedly masculine voice boomed from behind them. With barely a rustle, a tall blond man stepped out of a thick pine grove. The biggest raven she'd ever seen rode on his shoulder, its curved beak open in greeting.

CHAPTER 6

$\mathcal{A}$islinn took him in as he strode toward them. He moved with an understated grace that hinted at barely suppressed power. A tattered corduroy jacket hung off impossibly broad shoulders. It was open, showing a well-muscled chest covered with golden hair that glistened in the sun. The day wasn't really all that warm. She wondered why he wasn't wearing more. A flat, hard stomach disappeared into faded dungarees that hugged narrow hips. His hair had been hacked off to shoulder length. She supposed it helped keep the bird's claws from tangling in it. Bright blue eyes gleamed at her. He was smiling, and it made the corners of his eyes crinkle into happy little creases. A scraggly beard covered cheeks and chin. He had very straight, white teeth nested in a square jaw.

What a gorgeous man.

"I'm Fionn." He extended a hand. "This is Nevermore." He glanced at the raven.

"That is not my name, and you know it." The raven sounded pissed. She trained beady, avian eyes at Aislinn. "My true name is Bella."

Realizing she'd been gawking, Aislinn took Fionn's hand, gave it a firm shake, and pulled hers back. She felt color stain her cheeks and hoped it wasn't too noticeable. "I am Aislinn, and this is Rune."

Wolf and raven stared at one another. Something passed between them, but she wasn't quite sure what. With a little hop, the bird fluttered from Fionn's shoulder to land atop Rune. More of the silent energy flowed.

Aislinn furled her eyebrows. "Are they talking?"

Fionn drew back a pace and stared hard at her. Feeling him gather power, she held up both hands, palms facing outward. "Until a couple days ago, I thought I was Mage and Seeker," she explained. "I was, ah, on my way somewhere at the Old Ones' behest when the wolf chose me. I tried to tell him I was no Hunter, but he insisted." She shrugged. "I know it sounds odd, but my talents are still developing."

"You speak true, though it makes little sense." Fionn's words sounded grudging. He kept a respectable distance between them and eyed her, as if she were a powder keg about to blow.

A corner of her mouth quirked upward. "How do you suppose it makes me feel? Part of me still misses being a teenager with parents in our house in Salt Lake. It took a while to get used to the magic I was supposed to have. To find out I have more—" she rolled her eyes "—is deucedly unnerving."

"You look older than that."

"Lost my dewy-eyed youth, huh?" She snorted. "It's because I am older now. Twenty-two."

"Youngster. I'm thirty."

"So you had some sort of established life before—"

"Stop." He raised a hand and trained his gaze on her. It spoke a warning, as clearly as if words had passed his lips.

She understood. One of the unwritten rules was never talking about the past. "Sorry." She shifted gears. "You didn't answer my question. About Rune and Bella."

"Bond animals have their own network. If they don't know one another, they will know others who know someone in the other's circle. They're comparing notes. And complaining about their bondmates. Though I've never gotten Bella to actually admit that." He laughed, and she felt the tension bleed out of him.

"Do you Hunt alone? Or are there others like, ah, us nearby?" When she stumbled over the *us*, Aislinn realized she still didn't see herself as a Hunter.

An awkward silence hovered before he answered. "For now, I Hunt alone." Moving alongside her, he draped an arm over her shoulders. "Come sit with me. We can share conversation, food—and perhaps other things as well over time."

She slipped out from under his arm. Her flush from earlier had to be back in full force on her suddenly overheated face. "Now wait a minute," she sputtered. "You're being pretty presumptuous—"

He shook his head and laughed. "*No mas.* I thought you might like to learn about your Hunter skills. That's all." He resettled his arm companionably around her shoulders.

The heat from his body felt comforting. His fingertips caressed her, light as butterfly wings. She felt need in him with a sharp, desperate edge to it, sexual, yet more than that, too. Questions bubbled, but she didn't ask any of them. All the humans who were left lived with loneliness. She thought about Travis and what he'd said about taking comfort when it was offered. *Good advice,* she realized, walking next to Fionn. Against her better judgment, she let herself enjoy the feel of his body where it brushed against hers.

They passed Rune and Bella. The animals were so deep in conversation that neither acknowledged their human. Fionn made a chirping noise, but the raven cawed so disapprovingly he looked cowed.

"What was that all about?" Aislinn asked, curious.

"I asked her to come with me, and she told me to piss off."

"Hmph. Are all bond animals temperamental?"

They reached a sheltered cove a hundred yards down the lakeshore. He gestured for her to sit. "Only strong-minded animals seek the Hunter bond. So the answer to your question is probably *yes*. Bella's been my only bondmate. She's certainly volatile, and the reason—" He broke off, looking uncomfortable.

Reason for what? Aislinn thought about Travis's civet. The cat had seemed somewhat retiring, maybe because she'd never been included in conversations with it. *Lots to learn here.*

Aspens grew thickly next to the shoreline, their leafless branches twining together. Sand and marsh grasses formed a rough beach. The two of them sat with their backs leaning against a sun-warmed rock. After his earlier familiarity, Fionn kept his hands to himself. She'd liked it when he touched her, but didn't know how to ask him to do it again without him taking it wrong.

He pulled some dried meat out of a pocket and handed it to her, along with a few withered blackberries. He hadn't said anything after his last words, but his sharp-boned face had reddened. Perhaps he wasn't used to taking comfort either. She smiled wryly at the thought. Everyone was lonely. And afraid. The person you started to care about might die soon. It was easier to keep that door shut and not care at all.

"You look about fifteen when you do that."

"Do what?" She met his gaze. His eyes were the most incredible shade of blue, with long, dark lashes.

"Smile."

I'd do just about anything to be fifteen again, before all this started. "Thanks."

"Do you want to know about the Hunter magic?"

She nodded eagerly. "Yes, everything, but do you think we're safe here? Right before you showed up, we diverted a flock of bats that had obviously been turned by the dark."

He quirked an eyebrow. "Really? I thought they were on our side."

Aislinn considered that and then realized she'd moved beyond expecting any species was immune to corruption. "Better not to have assumptions. False confidence means dead."

He'd been leaning toward her and drew away, an odd look on his face. "You could freeze the tits off a boar, lady. If you think I'm wrong, there are kinder ways to tell me."

Like a flash flood rising out of nowhere, anger ripped through her. She leapt to her feet and paced in an attempt to contain her rage. How could he be so naïve? Apparently, the last three years had been a hell of a lot better for him than they'd been for her, if he still expected *kind*. She recognized jealousy, and it made her feel ill. Aislinn tried to keep her mouth shut, but failed miserably.

She rounded on him and placed her hands on her hips. "Kind? Who the fuck is kind anymore? Or gentle. Or considerate." She pounded a fist into her other hand for emphasis. "What world do you live in? There are no friends. No place is safe. And just in case you hadn't noticed, no one is *kind* anymore."

Because she couldn't stand there, looking at the incredulity—and something else, was it hurt?—in his eyes, she took off at a dead run back toward Rune and Bella. *What's wrong with me? Have I been by myself for so long that I can't even have a conversation with someone else if they don't see the world just like I do?*

Yeah, it's a whole lot easier to screw 'em and move on.

Arms closed around her. She'd been so lost in herself that she hadn't heard him come up behind her. He held her against him. She felt his heart thud against her shoulders. Heard him breathing into her tangled hair. "Aislinn, Aislinn. Don't run from me. Please. You carry so much pain, you remind me of a cactus. All spines. What happened to the human parts?"

"They died a long time ago." To her horror, she wanted to cry. Wanted the relief of tears. Her eyes stung, but tears refused to come.

"Ssssh." He held her easily with one arm. The other hand smoothed her hair. "Ssssh."

She leaned into the hand cupping her head. *If the only way I can feel anymore is sex, I know how to do that.* Twisting in his arms, she pressed herself against him and turned her face up for a kiss. His lips covered hers, and he tightened his arms around her. Their kiss deepened until it was the only thing in the world. He drank her in, and she smelled the musk of his arousal. Her nipples hardened into peaks where they pressed against him, and a low, frantic moan escaped her.

She insinuated a hand between them to grasp him, but he pulled back. His breath came fast, and color was high on his face. "No." He shook his head. "Not yet. We'd just be using each other. Besides—"

All she could think about was wanting him inside her. She'd felt him straining against her, hard and ready. Glancing at the bulge tenting the front of his jeans, she saw that he still was. Squirming, she pressed her thighs together and ran her tongue over lips swollen from their kiss. It wouldn't take much to bring her over the edge. She locked her gaze on his, too proud to beg, but willing him to want her.

With a sound midway between a moan and a sigh, he pulled her back against him and shoved a leg between hers. He closed his arms tight around her body and held her, raining kisses down her face and neck. She came almost the minute she touched him, shuddering with release.

Wanting to return the favor, she reached for him again, but he caught her hand. "I can wait," he murmured. "I want to get to know you." A crooked smile lit his face. "Besides, we have to figure out how to get along out of bed first."

Is that how it's done?

She'd been so young when the world turned to shit, her only experiences with sex had been furtive groping in the back seat with her boyfriend. Sex since then had been quick and impersonal. Needs filled without any emotional baggage attached. She found herself smiling back. "If we're going to do that, we need to find some way to talk about who we are."

He looked sheepish and reached a hand to rearrange himself. "So we do."

Feeling unaccountably shy—after all, he'd just brought her to orgasm—Aislinn bit her lip and said, "Maybe for starters, neutral ground would be teaching me about being a Hunter."

He laughed. Joy lit his features with a warm glow. She liked the way he laughed. It made tiny crease lines around his eyes, and the merry sound made it seem the world was still normal. His blue eyes glowed in the morning light. "That is how we started."

"And look how we finished." She giggled and then realized with a shock that she sounded like a girl again. "Do you think it's safe for us to stay here?"

"Oh, right. The fucking bats. They're what got you into such a temper."

"Well?" She met his gaze and raised a questioning brow.

"We'd probably be safer at my place. It's warded."

"Or mine," she countered and then thought about the logistics of getting there and decided his was probably a better idea.

"Mine's much closer."

"It would almost have to be," she said.

He shot her a thousand-watt grin and took her hand. "Let's round up the animals. It's only about a ten-minute walk."

HE TOOK her to a cunningly constructed dugout that looked just like the neighboring hillside. She had to close her eyes and let him lead with his magic to get inside. His home was surprisingly spacious. It consisted of a cooking space, a living area, and an alcove where he'd piled pine boughs and blankets. Books sat on rough shelves, away from the dirt floor. Though a mage light obligingly followed him once they were inside, lanterns hung from hooks, too.

"Recapping, because the Old Ones knew humans would take time to become adept at flushing out the dark, they gave us animal companions. Their sharper senses, coupled with our intelligence, made for a good team. Together, we hunt the enemy, flush them out, and work with the other gifted to kill them."

"You are not smarter than I am." Bella squawked, flapping over to where they sat.

"It's not polite to eavesdrop." He smiled fondly and ruffled her feathered head.

"What's eavesdrop? It sounds dirty."

"It means listening to conversations you're not a part of," he informed her.

"We are part of all conversations that include our human." Rune jumped into the fray and padded over to stand next to Aislinn.

"See." Bella pointed a wing at Fionn. "I'm not the only one who thinks that way. If you weren't such a loner—"

Fionn jumped to his feet, knocking a book off the table they'd been seated at. "Silence," he thundered and thudded his fist down on the table.

"She was not right for you," Bella said sweetly. "I merely encouraged her to move on. And her bond animal was simply impossible."

Aislinn's ears pricked. So there had been a lover, or maybe a wife, but the bird hadn't liked her. "Do bond animals have a say in such things?" she asked, glancing from Fionn to the bird.

"Of course we do," Rune answered. "We see these things more clearly sometimes."

"I didn't ask you," she told the wolf. Aislinn shifted her attention to Fionn. "Maybe you could tell me what happened."

"Later," he snapped, jaw tight. A small muscle twitched beneath one eye.

Aislinn understood he was still angry. Angry enough to throttle his bird. *Glad I'm not the only one who gets out of control.*

"So, uh, how long have you lived here?" she asked, trying for a neutral topic.

"Since the beginning."

"Before that?"

He blew out a tense-sounding breath, sucked down air, and exhaled again.

Sensing he was too tightly wound to sit back down, she got to her feet. "How about if we go hunting? It's about time for supper, and I'm hungry." *And it's okay by me if we put off the "I'll show you mine if you'll show me yours" conversation. Makes me just as uncomfortable as it makes you.*

"Good idea." He slammed a hand over her eyes and ushered them out of his house. She felt his magic at work. Once they were outside, he chanted, resetting the wards to render his dwelling invisible. The familiar tasks seemed to relax him.

Looks like the animals aren't the only temperamental ones. She chuckled inwardly. What a pack of oddballs they were. "How about rabbits and greens?" she suggested a shade too brightly.

"Ever eaten marmot?"

"Yeah, I like them, too."

"We'll get the meat," Rune volunteered.

"Excellent." Bella's wings pumped air. "Two each," she called back. Apparently feeling challenged, Rune took off at a lope and disappeared into thick timber.

"I'm surprised she left us alone," Fionn commented dryly.

Seems like a good lead-in. Maybe if I keep quiet, he'll tell me more. She followed him back toward the lake, plucking edible greens she recognized along the way. By the time they reached the water's edge, her hands were already full.

"Can't carry any more."

He turned toward her, taking in the mixture of growing things draped over both arms. "I've always just gotten watercress or onions. What are all those things?"

She pointed with her nose. "These are Fairy Bells. This one is False Mermaid. Here's Burdock. And these are Mariposa Lilies." She plucked a small plant from underneath the others. "Mint."

"Even I know that one, but not the others. How'd you learn about them?"

"My father. He was interested in things like that and took me into the backcountry with him—a lot." Fionn seemed relaxed, so she took a chance, infusing a smidgeon of calming magic into her next words. "What did you mean about being surprised your bird left us to ourselves?"

He shifted from foot to foot, but held her gaze. "Oh, that. Ah, I've had a couple female partners. Bella didn't like either of them."

"What'd she do?"

He bent and pulled a bunch of wild onions out of the ground. "Why do you want to know?"

"So I can be ready if she tries the same thing with me."

"She likes you."

"How can you tell?"

"She wouldn't have left us otherwise. And she likes your wolf." He spoke matter-of-factly. "The other problem was she hated the wolverine and the owl."

"How could anyone hate an owl?" Aislinn was mystified. "They're so beautiful."

He shrugged. "If you ask Bella, I'm sure she'll tell you her reasons. I think we have enough. Let's head back."

Curiosity burned a hole in her guts. He still hadn't told her very much. What the hell could a bird do that would run a human woman off?

"She has a sharp beak. And a sharper tongue," Fionn muttered.

"You can read my thoughts?" Aislinn stopped walking, thunderstruck.

He nodded. "Uh-huh. It's my second gift. A variant of the Healer magic. It's why I knew how, uh…never mind."

She understood. It was why he'd known how desperate her body was earlier. "It's okay." Walking close, she stood on tiptoe and kissed his stubble-covered cheek. "When Rune told me he knew my mind, it was a shock. Like my privacy had been violated. Guess I've had a chance to get used to the idea." Stepping back, she turned and headed the way they'd come. He fell in next to her.

"Both my Hunter partners really tried to make peace with Bella, but that bird is intransigent. Once she makes up her mind, there's no reasoning with her. And…" He paused for a beat. "I suppose they weren't all that important to me. Bella knows me better than I know myself sometimes."

"Well, thank God she's taken a shine to me." The fine hairs on the back of her neck prickled. Aislinn froze, pulling invisibility about herself. *"Don't say anything, but we're not alone."*

"I know. Trust yourself to me. I won't hurt you."

He closed his arms around her. She felt the shift and knew he was moving them. In seconds, the walls of his home shimmered into being. "What was out there?" She dumped her armload of plants on a rough counter. His impromptu embrace when he'd transported her had crushed the greens. The front of her shirt was sticky with aromatic plant juices.

"Not sure." His brows knit together. Then his frown deepened. She felt him pull earth magic, lots of it. "Stay here," he barked. "Bella's under attack. She needs me."

"Not a chance." Aislinn locked her hands around his arms. "Either I'm coming with you, or neither of us goes. Rune is out there, too."

CHAPTER 7

The stink of dark magic thickened the air. What had been a mere hint a few moments before turned into a positive stench.

"What's your strongest suit?" she hissed as soon as they were back in the forest.

"Earth. Then water."

"Okay. You draw earth. I'll mix in fire and stoke it with air if we need more." Using a dollop of magic to partially mask her presence, Aislinn started off at a fast trot.

Fionn made a grab for her arm. *"Not so fast. You could be running right into a trap. Mind speech only from here on."*

She stopped, spun to face him, and jabbed an impatient finger into his chest. *"If you have a better idea, let's hear it."*

"I don't recognize what this feels like. Do you?"

Reaching out with tendrils of her Seeker sense, she realized with a shock that she didn't either. *"No."*

"Since neither of us knows what we're facing, we go really slow. And I go first."

She fumed, but didn't want to jeopardize them by arguing, so she followed him, her senses hyper alert. What the hell was out there that felt so putrid? And why couldn't she sense Rune?

She heard the bird squawking long before they found her. Either Rune wasn't with her, or he was already dead. A cold edge of fear knifed into her gut. She fanned magic around herself, less concerned about invisibility than having power at hand if she needed it.

"Good that you're ready," Fionn said approvingly.

A bat dive-bombed them. She swatted it away and then stopped dead. Bats. Were they the same ones she'd seen earlier? Half running, she caught up to Fionn. *"I think it's the bats I was worried about."*

"I don't. Hurry. Bella's dying."

The bird's life force was weakening. Aislinn felt it flicker, flare up, and pulse and knew the bird was waiting for Fionn. Trepidation chilled her. She'd seen it happen often enough in battles. People waited for those special to them, only to die in their arms. She wondered what it would do to Fionn to lose his bondmate. It would tear his heart out, but would it sap his will to go on?

Aislinn swallowed hard. She knew. She'd struggled against just packing it in—and more than once. It would've been easy enough to toss herself in front of the enemy dozens of times. But something inside—maybe a misplaced preservation instinct—kept her fighting to stay alive. Damned if she was going to simply hand her world over to the invaders.

Lost in her thoughts, she wasn't paying attention and ran right into Fionn. She heard his sharp intake of breath and peered around him.

Fuck. Aislinn lunged forward, but Fionn snagged one of her arms and held on tight. Something that morphed from form to form held Bella suspended by her wings. One moment, it appeared as a man, then a large, growling cat that looked like a cheetah, then an impossibly tall bird. Realization slammed into Aislinn: it had to be D'Chel, the dark god who controlled illusion. Blood dripped from the raven.

Was she truly mortally wounded, or was her appearance another of D'Chel's trickeries?

At least I know why the evil didn't feel familiar. D'Chel must've twisted it somehow.

A tortured sound burst from Fionn. Letting go of Aislinn, he raced into the clearing. "Loose my bird," he snarled. "If you want to fight someone, fight me."

Maniacal laughter with an ice-cold edge filled the air. "It would scarcely be a fair contest, Celt."

Aislinn groaned. They were supposed to be in this together. Fionn had stormed into the fray as if he'd forgotten she existed. Rustling sounded behind her. Worried it might be D'Chel's minions, she pivoted in the direction of the noise.

Rune charged past at the head of a pack of at least a dozen forest wolves. Quick as a thought, they launched themselves at D'Chel in a blur of gray and black—and were tossed through the air like a gaggle of rag dolls. Rune screamed his disapproval. She heard him encourage the others with a mix of snaps and snarls. Regrouping, they charged again. *"Lend your magic,"* sounded in her mind.

Using her Mage skill, Aislinn cast a protective net over the pack, begging the Old Ones for strength.

D'Chel dropped Bella and twisted to give the wolves his full attention. Still laughing, he matched their form, making himself into a wolf, but one three times as large as any of them, with glittering copper eyes. Aislinn moved closer so she had a clear view of the impromptu battlefield and upped the ante on her spell. She still didn't understand why she hadn't been able to sense Rune until he flashed past her.

I'll have to ask Fionn about that later.

The bird lay as if dead. Fionn scooped her up, held her close for one heartbreaking moment, and then cried to Aislinn to come take her. Grief etched in the hard line of his jaw, and his blue gaze flashed fury.

She couldn't protect the injured animal and help fight. Rune needed her. So did Fionn and Bella. Aislinn edged forward, holding out her hands for the bird while trying to maintain the spell helping Rune and the wolves. Blood ran warm down her fingers.

The raven croaked weakly, "Put me somewhere safe. Help my bondmate."

She truly is dying. Hoping it would stem what felt like the inevitable, Aislinn sent as much energy into Bella as she thought she could without shorting out something important. She cursed her lack of Healing knowledge. When she'd worked on Rune, it had been guesswork. She'd had an opportunity to experiment then, but time was in short supply right now.

Fionn charged into the battle. His magic collided with D'Chel's, creating a series of sparks so bright spots swam before her eyes. She laid Bella in the shadows between two large fir trees. The bird folded her wings around herself. "Don't you dare give up," Aislinn hissed.

Back in the clearing, a quick assessment told her things were deteriorating. One of Fionn's arms seemed broken. When had *that* happened? Somehow, he was still calling magic, lobbing jolts one-handed at the dark god. Two wolves lay dead. Rune danced just beyond D'Chel's reach, but she sensed his energy fading. The other wolves were nowhere to be seen. She didn't blame them. No point in getting killed in someone else's war. She made a mental note to tell Metae they had to involve all the animals, not just Hunter bond-mates, in this fight. After all, it really was everyone's battle. If they lost Earth, no one would have a place to live.

I need to make this work.

Gritting her teeth, she strode forward and placed herself dead center in front of D'Chel. He'd shucked the wolf form and looked like a man again. He turned slowly to face her. The same lambent sexuality she'd felt from Perrikus oozed from him. Strange she hadn't felt it before. Maybe when he was working illusion, it muted his charismatic qualities. Long hair so black that it had a bluish cast was braided close against a finely-boned head. Clear coppery eyes shone out of a perfect face with chiseled features. He wore hunting leathers that encased his muscled shoulders and slim hips like a glove, leaving little to the imagination. She let her gaze roam appreciatively over him, hoping to draw his attention away from Fionn and Rune.

"Hey, pretty man," she cooed, hoping against hope he was as susceptible to lust as Perrikus. He sure had the same effect on her. She planted her feet shoulder width apart so her thighs wouldn't rub together and ignored the heat in her loins.

His gaze shifted. He looked at her appraisingly just before his eyes turned a delectable shade of pale blue. "Do you know who I am?"

Should I tell him?

She inhaled sharply to buy herself a moment to think. Because she couldn't come up with a better strategy, Aislinn turned a brilliant smile his way and purred, "Of course I do."

Eyes hooded, he said, "Tell me."

"D'Chel, god of illusion."

"You do not have to do this," Rune's voice sounded in her head. *"We can find a way that does not involve you sacrificing yourself."*

Fionn limped to her side. He tried to take her arm, but Aislinn shook him off. "Let me do this my way."

"No," Fionn muttered. "It will be his way or no way. He'll fuck you and turn you to their side. Christ, didn't they teach you anything?"

"Believe in me," she sent, focusing her mind voice only for Fionn. *"Please don't make this harder."*

A cunning smile graced D'Chel's face. "Your bond animal?" He gestured toward Rune. "And your mate?"

"Well, you got one right."

The god's eyes flickered dangerously. Apparently, he wasn't used to making errors—or having them pointed out.

"Let them leave," Aislinn continued, holding his gaze. In a sudden flash of insight, she deployed a risky gambit and added, "I was visiting with Perrikus the other day, but one of the Old Ones showed up. Ruined our fun."

Surprise fluttered across his far-from-human features. *Good. Let him try to figure out which side I'm on.* Lots of humans, starting with the ones who'd helped open the gateway during the globally synchronized surge, fueled the dark ones' powers by their adoration —and lots of sex.

Fionn clamped a hand around her wrist in a viselike grip and tugged. "Come on," he snarled. "We're leaving. Now."

"I'll find you later," she murmured. "Bella needs you. Take Rune." She held her breath. Would D'Chel let them go if she stayed? She hoped he'd find her interesting enough to release the others. After all, most humans who followed the dark didn't have much power. Perrikus had wanted children with her.

"I am staying with you," Rune growled.

Aislinn clamped her teeth together so hard, she was surprised they didn't shatter. It went against the grain to force Rune, but she had to see him out of harm's way. "You will go with Fionn and Bella."

Anger, disappointment, and betrayal flashed from the wolf's eyes.

Fionn's gaze moved from her to D'Chel. Giving her a terse nod, he moved toward where she'd left the bird. Rune followed him, refusing to meet her gaze.

"Nicely done, human." A lascivious smile lit D'Chel's face as he drank her in. His hand snaked out, stroked her face, and then moved familiarly down her body. "Your loved ones are out of harm's way—for the moment. What will you barter for their continued safety?"

"I am under the Old Ones' protection."

He drew his full lips back in a sneer. "So what? Besides, I don't see them racing to your defense."

His unnerving gaze shaded back to coppery-green and bored into her. A jolt of lust so hot it made her come where she stood turned her knees to jelly. At least the sexual tension ratcheted down a notch or two, but not for long.

His gaze never left her face. He smiled knowingly. "We could have a lot of fun, you and me. You're a ripe one."

He pulled her to him. Close up like that, she saw flecks of silver in his ever-changing eyes. She also saw how alien they were. Despite his humanoid form, he was anything but. His perfect body felt cool against hers when he slashed his mouth atop hers. He drew heat from her until she started to shiver and pulled away from his mouth and his roaming hands. Away from the length of him pressed against her crotch.

"Would you take me against my will?" Her teeth chattered. All the heat leached out of the world. *Holy shit! He's going to drain the life right out of me.*

"I am a god. I take what I want."

He reached for her again. A feral gleam shone from the depths of his eyes, desperation for something to warm him. She wondered how many thousands of years old he was.

I have to do something before I freeze to death. She hadn't understood before that if he entered her, he'd steal everything warm and living. What would be left? *Not very fucking much.*

Sudden terror energized her. Because it burned inside her all the time, Aislinn drew fire. She made the surface of her body hot, so hot D'Chel yanked his hands away. She stumbled and nearly fell.

"What are you doing?" he demanded. "Stop that at once."

"You're cold. I'm hot." She panted with the effort of holding her magic. So long as she kept it within and didn't turn it to energy for spells or fighting, it would heat her. Apparently, he couldn't touch her when she was like this.

He tried again, laying a cold hand against her breast, but he snatched it away at once. Barely contained rage built. She saw it in the set of his jaw and his narrowed eyes.

"Let's just agree we made a mistake," she suggested smoothly.

"I could blast you out of this world with a thought."

"I don't think so," she replied evenly. *If he could, I'd be dead now.*

His man-form wavered. A cobra stood before her, weaving its dance of death. Before it could strike, Aislinn mobilized the magic simmering inside her. First, she called invisibility, and then she jumped, ameliorating all traces of her destination.

The journey buffeted her and was far harder than she thought it should've been for such a short jump. Something subverted her magic—from both sides. Fear clotted in her throat, and sweat ran down her sides. When she finally came out in Fionn's grotto, she was unbelievably relieved to find all three of them there. Fionn cradled Bella against him. Rune turned his back on her.

"This place is a whole lot deeper than I thought," she said, eying Fionn. "I had a hell of a time getting here." She sucked in a shuddery breath. Jump spells weren't reversible. Either you came out the other end at the planned destination—or you didn't. "For a while there, I was afraid I'd be trapped in my own working."

He drew his brows together. "Sorry. I had to release my warding to let you in. It took me a while once I sensed you outside. I hope you covered your tracks." He stumbled to his feet, Bella still in his arms, and glanced about, as if expecting D'Chel any moment.

"I did. I also understand why you used magic to ferry me in and out of here." Tension whooshed out of her, and she shot him an impressed smile. "Nicely done. No one could ever blunder into this place by accident."

He looked surprised. "Thanks. I don't get many compliments."

Aislinn strode to her wolf and crouched next to him. "I apologize for forcing you. I wanted you safe. You need to know I'd do the same again if it meant your life." Rune's fur rippled beneath her touch, but he ignored her.

Coming to her feet, she made her way to Fionn and Bella. "How is she?"

Fionn shook his head and sat back down. "Weak. She's lost a lot of blood. I was just getting ready to see what I could do for her when I had to stop to dismantle my wards for you." He looked at Aislinn. "We only beat you here by a few minutes."

"I healed Rune. Would you like me to try to help?"

Nodding, he moved over to make room for her. Aislinn held out her arms for the bird. "I did what I could in the forest. Like with Hunter magic, I didn't think I had Healing abilities either, but it appears I do."

She linked to the bird and tried to figure out what D'Chel had injured. Fionn was right. His bird had lost blood, but nothing critical seemed damaged. One of her wing bones had snapped. That would be an easy fix. Taking her time, Aislinn infused Healing energy into the large raven. She felt Fionn in her mind, working alongside her. When she was certain the bird could tolerate it, she mended its broken wing.

Looking up, she met Fionn's gaze, grateful he hadn't tried to talk to her while they'd been navigating through unfamiliar avian physiology. "She'll be fine. A good rest, and she'll be good as new."

"I think the same. Thank you." His heart was in his eyes. He lifted the bird off her lap and placed her on a cushion off to one side. Turning back to Aislinn, he said, "Do you feel like telling us what happened?"

Sidestepping his question, she quirked an eyebrow. "How's your arm? And you were limping earlier."

"Hmph. Ankle was just a sprain. Not so sure about my arm. I'd planned to see to it once I was done with Bella. Didn't expect you back quite so soon." He paused for a beat and skewered her with his gaze. "Truth was, I didn't expect you back at all."

She snorted. "Oh ye of little faith. Would you like me to look at your arm?"

Wordlessly, he held it out. Her Healer magic was still close to the surface. She laid a hand on either side of his arm and called her power front and center again. "Something took a hell of a chip out of the bone right here." She pressed gently, trying to get a sense of what she needed to fix.

"Whooph." He winced, apparently biting back the rest of what would've been a yelp.

"Sorry." She chanted softly and wove strands to bring new bone cells to patch the weak spot. His body heated under her touch. She smiled as she felt the damage recede, replaced by healthy tissue.

"Thank you a second time." He dipped his head her way. "I didn't want to disturb you while you were working, but what in the name of the gods happened out there?"

"If Rune will forgive me for forcing him to go with you, I'd like to tell all of you." The wolf still faced away from her and didn't budge. Not so much as an ear twitched, even though he had to be listening.

A corner of Fionn's mouth turned downward. "I want to know, even if he doesn't. We have all those greens we gathered earlier. I could cook them while you catch us up."

Aislinn realized she was famished. "That would be great."

"Would you like dried meat along with them?"

"Even better." Pushing heavily to her feet, she made her way to Rune. The wolf drew away, and she knew how badly she'd hurt him. Settling next to him, she stroked his fur. After a time, he turned reproachful eyes on her.

"I do not care if it means my death," he said with dignity. "I do not want you to ever order me away from your side again."

"You left me earlier," she pointed out. "While we're on that topic, why couldn't I sense you?"

He dropped his amber gaze. "Because I know how to shield myself."

Aislinn glanced at Fionn, who was using magic to cook their meal. "Is that a common bond animal trait?" He shook his head. She refocused on Rune. "Yet you can do this."

"Yes."

"Why didn't you want me to know where you were?"

"So you wouldn't stop me. I was trying to help Bella."

Confusion rocked her. "Why would I have interfered?"

"Because his first loyalty must be to you," Fionn answered, handing her a cracked earthenware plate.

"Thanks." She sat on the floor next to Rune and shoveled food into her mouth. Now that it was in front of her, it was all she could think about. When she came up for air, she gazed at Rune, who'd laid his head next to her thigh, and at Fionn, who sat across from her. "I need a tutorial on Hunter bondmates. There's a whole lot I don't know about them. While we're at it, there are things about myself I guess I don't know, either. I got away from D'Chel by concentrating my magic. But I kept it inside, so it made the surface of my skin uber hot. Turns out, he couldn't tolerate touching me when I did that. He shape-shifted, and I took the opportunity to jump."

"Did he fuck you?" Fionn's stark question startled her.

She shook her head. "No. The closer he got, the more I understood it would kill me—or turn me into some sort of mindless zombie—if he got his dick inside me. That's when I came up with my idea to use fire. I was so damned cold from his touch, I had to do something."

Deep worry lines etched into Fionn's forehead relaxed. "Thank God," he breathed. "I tried to tell you back there. Mortals who fuck the gods end up, well, not exactly human anymore. They turn you so they can pilfer your power. I don't know about the zombie-thing, but sex with them makes you useless to our side."

"Yes," Rune seconded. "Do not ever do that again. You thought you could control a god. Ha! You got lucky."

"I am lucky—" she grinned at them "—because I have both of you to care about me." As soon as she said the words, she knew how true they were. After three years of being alone, she had a family again. Joy, a feeling so unfamiliar she barely recognized it, warmed her heart.

"We need to leave as soon as Bella's strong enough to travel," Fionn said.

"Agreed." Aislinn nodded. A daring thought took root. "Even

though Metae called me off, I think we should head for the gateway."

Fionn shot her an appraising glance. "Bold move. Especially without an invitation."

"Well, she didn't tell me I wasn't welcome. Just that she wanted me to have a few more experiences in the real world, first."

He chuckled. "You're certainly racking those up."

"So I am." Her eyes felt suddenly heavy.

"Sleep. You've earned it. Plus, you're exhausted." Fionn reached across the space between them and laid a hand on her arm.

Aislinn sensed his spell, but didn't fight it. Leaning against her wolf, she fell asleep before she could say another word.

CHAPTER 8

The murmur of Bella's and Fionn's voices woke Aislinn. It was impossible to tell what time it was, since, unlike her cave, no daylight filtered into Fionn's home. She pulled air into her chest and took stock of how she felt as she blew it back out. *Hmph. Not too damned bad.*

Rune padded over to her and licked her face. "Bella is much better today," he told her.

Good. One less thing to worry about. Since she didn't know all that much about the dark gods, she hadn't been sure how sophisticated, or interested, D'Chel might be in terms of his ability to track them. Fionn kept wards about his place—they'd nearly been the death of her—and she'd taken care to cover her tracks, but she doubted if either strategy could stymie a god. "How late is it?" she asked Rune.

"The morning is close to gone."

"You're awake." Fionn walked over to her, a broad smile on his face. "Bella is—"

"I already know," she interrupted. "Rune told me. I'm so glad. That means we can get going."

"I need to check outside to make sure it's safe." The air around Fionn took on a shimmery hue as he pulled magic.

"Why can't we leave from in here?"

He spun and looked hard at her. Enough illumination shone from his mage light for her to see an odd look on his face. "It's almost impossible to travel from underground."

"It is harder." She stood and rose on her tiptoes to stretch. When she tried to run her fingers through her hair, they tangled in hopeless mats. "With two of us, I think we can manage it. I really pissed D'Chel off yesterday. Unless something more pressing came up, I'd bet my last dollar—if I still had one—he's out there, hanging around and waiting for the first wisp of magic to surface."

"You'll have to show me how to help you." Fionn was still eying her strangely.

"Why are you looking at me like that?"

He bit his lower lip and looked away. "Because you seem to have more magic than any other human I've come across since this whole travesty began."

Her muscles tensed, and the sense of peace she'd wakened with dissipated, leaving her edgy. What he'd said made her just as uncomfortable as it obviously made him. "Okay. Makes meeting up with the Old Ones that much more critical. They know things."

He snorted. "They certainly do. And it's a sure bet they've told us as little as possible to secure our cooperation. Have you ever wondered why we never heard of them before the dark gods stormed the gates?"

She frowned. "Now that you mention it, we'd heard of them. I Googled 'Lemurians' for a high school project."

"Yes, and everything you came up with said they weren't real."

She shrugged. "We didn't know as much then as we do now."

"Or maybe they're linked to the dark in some way we don't know about."

She sucked in a breath. "Mmph. I suppose they could be. Both sides are into killing us off. It's just the Old Ones seem so much more honest about it."

"Oh, you *liked* the culling?" he inquired archly, his voice liberally laced with sarcasm.

"Of course I didn't like it." She huffed. "How could anyone like seeing their friends and family drop into some vortex that was a one-way trip to hell?"

"The thing that blew me away was why no one organized against them."

"Did you?" It was her turn to gaze appraisingly at him. She'd been so inexperienced and naive when everything happened, it never occurred to her to do anything other than follow orders.

He nodded, jaw set in a defiant line and chin tipped upward. "Yeah. I tried, but no one seemed interested. It was weird. Like there'd been some sort of mass hypnosis."

"It didn't affect you?" She crossed her arms over her chest, still looking at him.

"Guess not."

She shifted her gaze to Rune. "How did you become a Hunter's bondmate? Was there something special you had to do?"

"I cannot tell you that."

Both she and Fionn stared at the wolf. "Why not?" she demanded.

"It is a condition of the magic."

She exchanged glances with Fionn. "Looks like a conspiracy to keep us in the dark."

"No shit." He bit off the words and looked cowed. "I'm actually embarrassed I never thought to ask Bella the same question. I simply accepted that she was mine, and we were bound."

"Maybe they did...something so you wouldn't be curious." She hurried on. "See, I didn't start as a Hunter—or a Healer. Until Rune approached me, I assumed I didn't have that type of magic." Aislinn pressed her tongue against her teeth. "I've asked lots of questions these past few days. Mostly in my head, mind you."

"We should trade all the information we have," Fionn said slowly. "Together, maybe we'll be able to figure things out."

She wasn't so sure about that. It seemed like far more puzzle pieces were missing than the two of them could provide, but at least it would be a start. More than they had now.

She walked to where Bella sat on her perch. "May I touch you?"

The raven squawked sarcastically, clearly back to her irascible self. "You don't have to ask. You saved my life. You and my bond-mate together."

Aislinn thought about explaining she'd only been trying to be polite and considerate by giving Bella a choice before touching her, but decided against it. Laying a hand on either side of the feathered body, she ran the Healer equivalent of a scan. Surprise sent her brows crawling up her forehead. Just to be sure, she scanned Bella again, but the information was the same. Even the broken wing bone was completely healed. "My," she gasped, "you're better than good."

"Exactly." Fionn joined her next to the raven. "Even more reason we should tell each other...everything."

"I disagree. We should leave." Rune paced nervously.

Trusting the wolf's senses, Aislinn exchanged glances with Fionn and said, "We can talk once we've put some distance between us and D'Chel." She held out an arm. Bella hopped onto it.

"Uh-uh. This will work better if Bella's with me." Fionn gathered the bird into his arms.

"Send me an image of the next jump," Aislinn told the wolf, already drawing the mix of energy that would get them out of there.

"I need it, too," Fionn said.

"Ready?" Aislinn asked. Fionn moved next to her. Rune closed in, too.

"Okay, everybody." Familiar power built within her. The previous night's meal and a decent rest had worked wonders. She felt as if she could move them all, even if no one else did a thing. Fionn put his arms around her, sandwiching Bella between them. Taking care to hold everyone's life force separately so no one would get lost in the transition, she loosed her spell. Aislinn felt magic flow around them and waited for the weightless sensation, but it didn't come.

"What the hell?" she sputtered. Magic was thick in the small space. They should be gone. She couldn't gin up any more power. Had D'Chel trapped them in some way? Fear surfaced. Her heart hammered against her chest.

"Here." Fionn added to her working. "Let's try it this way. As you guessed last night, we're deeper underground than you might think, and there're my wards to get through. I should've disabled them before you began."

Pathetically grateful to have a reason her magic had failed, she pushed her power outward again and was rewarded with the buoyancy that told her it was working. "Thank God," she muttered. Then Rune was in her mind, and she saw through his senses. Fionn hadn't been kidding about being far beneath the earth. They were at least five hundred feet down, with ward bands every fifty or so. She developed a new respect for his magic as she passed through each of them.

They came out on a long stretch of deserted asphalt. It was so open it gave her the creeps. Aislinn fanned magic in all directions, but didn't feel anything out of the ordinary. "We need cover," she said.

Fionn looked around. "Pretty barren."

Rune padded in a large circle, looking in all directions and scenting the air. "This is not the image I sent." He flooded her mind with another.

Aislinn wondered what had happened. Now that the wolf mentioned it, this stretch of roadway certainly wasn't the image she'd held in her mind. Why hadn't she realized that? *Christ, am I losing my mind?*

"I'll take us from here," Fionn said. "Ready?"

Grateful no one commented on her lack of stewardship for the current jump, Aislinn just nodded. The next jump brought them back into forested terrain. She sank into a shaded spot under an oak tree. *Oaks. That means we're fairly low.*

"Feel like hunting?" Bella asked Rune.

"Stay close," Fionn cautioned.

"We will." Bella flew off, with Rune tracking her from the ground.

Fionn sat next to her and asked, "What happened?" Concern cut deep into his features, making little crinkles spill around his eyes.

She shook her head. "I've been asking myself the same thing. It's like something—or someone—got into my head and swapped the first destination for the second. Makes me nervous. Once I set the traveling spell loose, there's no way I can control it en route."

"I know." He closed his jaw in a tense line. A muscle twitched beneath one eye, which probably meant he wanted to say a bunch of other things, but was holding his peace.

"Tell me about yourself."

He looked at her, half a sour smile on his face. "Not much to tell. I was an archaeologist. I'd just finished my doctorate and begun teaching at Oregon State. I had a wife and two kids." The muscle twitch got worse. "They were culled. I was spared, though at the time, I wished they'd sent me through the gateway, too. Sometimes I still do." His blue gaze bored into her, testing how much truth she could stand.

He lost his entire family. She didn't know what to say. "I'm sorry" seemed inadequate. She laid a hand over his, trying to infuse compassion through her touch, but he shook her off.

"Don't," he snapped. "Makes it worse."

Yes, it does.

She thought about her own closet full of skeletons locked away in a corner of her mind where they couldn't hurt her anymore—or at least, not as much. Dragging out a couple, she told him about Bolivia and the Surge. About her father being murdered and her mother going mad. "The madness turned out to be a good thing," she said, grateful to be close to the end of her tale. It had hurt more than she'd thought it would to dredge up the memories. "Being checked out shielded Mom from what the world had turned into. I don't think she even knew what was happening when they herded her to her death."

Aislinn looked hard at Fionn. "Do you know why they thought they had to kill everyone without magic? I've wondered about that."

"No, but it's why I think there has to be some connection between the dark gods, those who serve them, and the Old Ones."

"Maybe they use our magic—you know, siphon off little bits of it —to somehow help themselves," she ventured. "The rest of humankind would only have been a drain on resources—"

"—and if they'd left enough of us alive, there could've been some sort of unpleasant uprising that might've sent the whole lot of them back across the veil," he finished for her.

She smiled bitterly, her mouth puckering as if she'd bitten into something unspeakably sour. "Well, now that we've solved the puzzle, what do we do about it?"

"Nothing. We do nothing, or they'll ship us through the vortex. I've spent the past three years shielding my thoughts."

"Oh." She felt woefully unequipped to deal with the squatters who'd taken up residence on Earth. "Have you ever talked about any of this with anyone else?"

He laughed, but it held a chilly edge. "Of course."

"And?" She thought she knew the answer, but needed to hear it out loud.

"Everyone told me I was nuts. Like I said, it's as if there was some sort of mass hypnosis that passed me by." He paused. "And apparently you as well."

Rune loped back to her, a marmot hanging out of his mouth. *"Bella has one, too—a small one,"* he informed them.

"Do you think we could risk a fire?" she asked, looking from Fionn to the wolf.

Rune bristled. She knew his opinion about fires.

"Better if we cook with magic," Fionn concurred, apparently having read the wolf's stiffened posture.

The raven's wing beats filled the air. She dropped her kill into Fionn's outstretched hands.

Aislinn grinned. It was obvious they'd done this before. "I hear running water," she said. "There has to be a creek not far from here. Let's go. It will give us fresh water for the cook pot—and maybe some greens, too."

"Grand idea." Rune's tail swished. "Bella and I will get more meat."

Aislinn watched his retreating form, glad he'd forgiven her for forcing him to her will.

It all worked out. We're still alive. Now if we can just stay that way.

After they'd eaten, Fionn pulled some badly stained topographic maps and a compass out of his rucksack.

She drew close, fascinated. "Do you know where we are?"

"Not precisely. Give me a minute."

"I always wanted maps to help me figure things out—"

"It's like with the books. The Old Ones either took them all or destroyed them," he cut in.

"But you still have these." She tapped the map with an outstretched finger.

"Only because I didn't give them up, and they don't know I have them."

"You have books, too." *And so do I.* She wasn't sure why she was reluctant to let him know about their shared civil disobedience. She opened her mouth, but shut it before her secret could spill out. *He's not telling me everything, either,* her inner voice noted, as if the quid pro quo made it all right to keep things hidden.

Fortunately, he wasn't looking at her, or he might have read guilt on her face. He was doing something with the compass; it lay against one of the sides of the map. "We're here." He stabbed the map with a begrimed finger.

She bent over his arm, looking. "So that roadway we ended up on earlier was Interstate Five." Her nostrils flared and her eyes widened. "We're practically walking distance to Mount Shasta."

"Uh-huh." He nodded. "Best I can tell, we're near Castle Crags, only about twenty miles from the gateway to Taltos."

"Where'd we come from?"

He pointed to an area north of Susanville, scribing a circle with his finger. "I've moved around a bit, but I've stayed in this same basic area for the last couple years. It was safe enough—until you showed up."

She ignored his comment. "Do you suppose the Lemurians know we're here?" He shot her a look that said he thought she was smarter than that. She tried again. "Have you ever been there before?"

"No. Told you I've kept my distance."

If you've done that, why come with me now? It didn't make a whole lot of sense. Aislinn turned her attention to Rune. "Why'd you go to the gateway?"

"Because I wanted justice—for Marta." Aislinn was just about to ask him another question when he added, "They sent me away."

She considered digging deeper, but it upset Rune to talk about his last bondmate. She saw it in the squared-off way he stood. Instead, she got to her feet. "I'm going for a walk. I need to think. If we're going to be there tomorrow, I have to figure some things out, so maybe the Old Ones will answer my questions."

She felt Fionn fall into step next to her before she'd gotten a hundred yards from the flat rocks near the rushing creek where they'd eaten. He circled her waist with an arm. "You don't have to do this," he said.

She snorted. "Yeah. I've been thinking the same thing. I can turn tail and run back to my little hovel, fight when they call me, and spend the rest of my time hoping this will all go away."

"Except it won't."

Aislinn stopped walking. She turned to him and laid her head in the nook between his shoulder and neck. After the briefest of hesitations, he pulled her close. His breath was warm in her hair. She wanted to kiss him. To lose herself in sensation so she wouldn't have to think about all the rest. But that was the easy way.

Moving back so she could meet his gaze, she said, "How about this? I'll go there by myself tomorrow. You can take the animals and return to your home. I'm sure I can find it again. It's easy to find places I've been before."

"What will you do after you get to the gateway?"

She shrugged, trying to lighten the anxiety nagging her. "Play dumb. Like I didn't understand what Metae meant. Ask a few questions about my magic and how to deal with things like D'Chel. I've met up with two of the dark gods in the last few days. Makes sense I'd be rattled about it. Maybe the Old Ones have an anti-sex charm or something."

When he didn't say anything, she hurried on. "That way, there'd only be one of us hiding secrets from them." *Rune would be safe, and I wouldn't have to worry about them hurting you,* she added silently, surprised by the strength of her feelings for him. She hadn't known Fionn all that long. She didn't understand why it felt so important to protect him.

He pulled her to him again. This time, she laid her head against his chest. The beat of his heart sounded loud in her ear. He knotted his fingers in her hair and kissed her forehead gently. *He's just as scared as I am,* she realized. *Scared to love. Scared to lose anything else to the scourge that's taken over our planet.*

Twining her arms around his neck, she slipped her fingers under his hair, and then turned her face upward. With a soft moan filled with need, he covered her lips with his and kissed her. His tongue plumbed her mouth; she sparred with it, licking and sucking. His breath was sweet. He tasted of summer meadows and something spicy and exotic she couldn't name. Her body heated under his touch as he ran his hands down her back and cupped her ass, drawing her firmly against him. The swell of his erection pressed against her lower belly.

This time when she reached between them to touch him, he pressed himself into her curved fingers. She sensed something untamed in him that ran close to the surface. He kept the energy tightly reined in, but need simmered, barely contained. She felt the shift when he released whatever brakes he'd imposed on his sexuality. Aislinn opened her eyes. His had darkened to midnight. Hunger blazed from their depths, and he pushed her down onto the ground. Shoving her clothing aside, he latched onto one of her nipples, suckling and nibbling, and then switched to the other.

She arched her back and wound her arms around him, trying to draw him closer. Electric sensation sparked from his mouth on her breasts, setting her nerve endings on fire. She buried her hands in his hair and rained kisses down the side of his face. Ever so slowly, he moved his mouth upward to her throat and mouth.

She let go of him long enough to fumble with the fastenings of her pants, undo one boot, and free one leg. When she reached for his pants, she saw he'd beaten her to it. Aislinn pushed Fionn onto his back. Wrapping a hand around his shaft, she straddled him and then guided him inside her. The shock of his body within hers rocked her. She'd had plenty of sex, but the intensity of his flesh buried inside hers stunned her with its immediacy. Orgasms crowded against one another until she wasn't sure when one ended and the next began.

His hands gripped her hips. She heard breath rattle in his throat, and color splotched his face and chest. He cried her name, voice hoarse with wanting her, before his own release took him. Fionn shuddered inside her for a very long time.

Aislinn collapsed over his body. He stroked her back and her hair, murmuring wordless endearments. "Look at me," he said at last.

She pushed away, feeling cold where his body no longer lay

against hers, and rolled into a sit, legs tucked beneath her. "I'm looking. What I see is beautiful."

He colored. A tender smile tugged at the edges of his mouth. "That's not why—" he began. Fionn shook his head, levered himself up, and sat across from her. He laid his hands on her knees. "I'm of two minds about your plan to go to Taltos alone, but I do think it's better than letting them see us together. Especially after what we just shared."

Realization raced through her. Like books and maps, relationships were also on the *best not do it* list. No one had any problems with humans having sex. They just weren't supposed to develop feelings for one another. *One more way to keep us isolated. And them in control.*

He must have divined her thoughts, because he laughed wryly. "Oh, it wouldn't have mattered whether or not we actually fucked. They'd sense that we lusted after each other. It would make them...uncomfortable."

Intuition chimed a sharp note. "That's not all you want to tell me."

He nodded. Smiles and laughter gone, he looked serious as death. "You will not do anything to jeopardize yourself. You will come home to me." He moved one of his hands from her knee and closed it about her wrist like a vise. "I will not lose anything more to *them.*" Because he'd stopped shrouding them, heat from his emotions seared her.

She swallowed. This was what she'd feared—and wanted. He cared about her. *And I care about him. Christ, I hope this wasn't a mistake.*

If Fionn was one type of problem, Rune had been another. To say the wolf was not pleased by her plan was an understatement. He'd run off into the woods and shielded himself so she couldn't find him.

"I'm afraid he'll track me on foot," she said to Fionn, returning after a fruitless hour hunting for the wolf. "After all, he knows where the place is."

"We have some time yet." Fionn's deep voice sounded reassuring.

"I suppose we do. There's nothing magical about me showing up at the gateway tomorrow. We can wait him out, but it makes me nervous setting up a camp so close to Taltos."

"Hmph. They'll probably think we're spying on them," he concurred, scratching at his beard. "Actually, taking your bondmate with you isn't such a bad idea—"

She whirled to face him. "What if something happens to him?"

Fionn tipped her chin upward with a finger, forcing her to look at him. "Something could happen to any of us. It's why we've avoided entanglements."

So I'm not the only ambivalent one here. "Guess I haven't gotten used to having an animal companion." She prevaricated, finding it easier to focus on her feelings about Rune than the jumbled mess inside her whenever she thought about Fionn.

"They're pretty good at taking care of themselves." He smiled. It was a toned-down version of his ten thousand-watt grin, but it still made her guts go all mushy.

"Rune," she tried again, using mind speech this time. "Come to me."

"Mistress." His voice dripped censure.

"I am not your mistress. But I'd like to be your friend."

"Then stop trying to foist me off on others. We are bondmates for a reason."

"Can we talk about this?"

"We are talking. If you're trying to get me close enough to trap me, forget about it."

She looked at Fionn. "Did you hear that?"

"Every word."

"What do you think?"

"Rune definitely has a mind of his own. I say we ask him what he thinks of your plan and take his counsel into consideration."

The wolf sauntered out of a grove of blue firs. "At last, a human with sense." He growled, keeping his distance from her. His hackles were at half-mast, his amber eyes chilly.

"Okay." Aislinn placed her hands on her hips. "What do you think we should do?"

A surprised look spread over the wolf's face. "You have to take me with you. Metae already knows we are bondmates. She would think it odd if you showed up alone."

Aislinn hated to admit it, but Rune had a point. "I was just trying to keep you safe," she snapped.

"We are safer together," the wolf replied in a patronizing tone. "You have much to learn, *bondmate*." His sarcasm escalated with the last words.

"It's true," Fionn concurred. "Part of the magic cementing the bond is a synergistic energy that's more together than its individual parts."

Aislinn squatted next to Rune. "Just don't disappear on me again," she muttered. "I'll have my hands full, and I don't know if I can pull this off if I'm worried about you."

"Then don't send me away."

From a nearby branch, Bella squawked an unintelligible opinion. Aislinn assumed the bird agreed with the wolf.

"Okay." She stood and spread her hands in surrender. "I know when I'm outnumbered. Let's strategize. What are the most important things we need to know from the Old Ones?"

MORNING CAME ALL TOO SOON. She'd slept wrapped in Fionn's arms with Rune against her other side. It felt right somehow. Like she belonged between the two of them. She was tempted to retreat. It was unlikely her gambit would pay off, and she would've put herself and her wolf in harm's way for nothing.

"They know we're here," Rune told her. "You have to go. The Old Ones would think something was very wrong if you came all this way, only to turn around."

She eyed the wolf. "I'd forgotten you could read my mind."

"Good thing." He met her gaze, tongue lolling. "Someone has to keep you on the straight and narrow." Surprised he'd know about human idiomatic expressions, she asked how he'd come by it. Pain flickered behind his eyes. "Marta used to say that."

"Wolf has a point." Fionn crouched by a nearby creek, making them breakfast out of crushed pine nuts and some berries he'd located the night before. "Your plan depends on the Old Ones thinking you still trust them."

"So I have to act like I do." She squared her shoulders. This was going to be hard. She'd never been a very good liar. "Is the food ready?" She didn't feel much like eating, but she'd need energy.

"Bring your cup over here."

~

SHE WAS JUST CLEANING the dregs of pine nut flour paste out of her eating mug when Fionn reached into one of his many pockets. He handed her what looked like a piece of river-washed quartz, clear with green flecks in it. "You want me to take that?" She raised a quizzical eyebrow, and he nodded. "Why?"

"It's linked to my magic. If you get into trouble, lay your lips against it and breathe my name into the stone."

"Just Fionn? Or will I need a last name, too?"

Leaning close, he whispered to her.

She drew back, her mouth rounded into an "o." Breath caught in the back of her throat. "B-But you aren't really," she stammered. "It's not possible. I mean, that just happened to be your father's last name. Right?"

He looked at her. Flickers of green danced around his sea blue irises. "Time for you to get going." He paused a beat, added, "lass," and winked.

This gets stranger and stranger. I feel like Alice without the white rabbit. She lurched to her feet, located her rucksack, and started stuffing things into it. She felt the heat of him behind her before he touched her. It sat like a living thing between them.

He circled his arms around her. "Turn about," he said.

Maybe because she was listening for it now, she heard the faintest of Irish lilts in his voice. It reminded her of her mother. If she hadn't grown up fed on Celtic myths, she wouldn't have recognized his last name. Pivoting in his arms, she looked up at him.

"I took a bit of a risk, telling you what I did," he said.

She stammered, "Ah, not to worry. I won't—"

"Sshh." He closed his mouth over hers.

The kiss was sweet, not demanding a thing from her, but it still made her knees weak. When she opened her mouth for more, he drew back.

"Uh-uh." The tiny creases around his eyes deepened as he smiled.

"No more today. There are other things for you to focus on. Don't be thinking about me or Bella. Get what you can from those bastards who see themselves as rulers here. Maybe we can find a way—"

"Maybe we can," she echoed. It wasn't easy to pull back from his embrace. She wanted to take up residence in those arms and never leave. Instead, she shouldered her pack, clucked to Rune, and pulled the magic she'd need to jump.

Tears were dangerously close to the surface as her spell made the air around her shimmer. *What the fuck am I doing?* she asked herself roughly. *I got along fine without him until now. I don't need anything that will make me hurt again. Nothing.*

"Think about the Old Ones and our task." Rune was in her mind, his voice stern.

Good advice. She spat out the words that would take them to Taltos, still feeling ridiculously conflicted.

Because she'd aimed for Mount Shasta City, thinking it held the gateway, Aislinn was surprised to find a collection of dilapidated buildings and nothing more. Usually cities retained more in the way of debris. It looked as if no one had lived here for fifty years. Rune broke from her side and dropped a paw onto a mouse that had the bad luck to scurry by at just that moment. Its small bones made little crunching sounds between his powerful jaws.

"So where is it?" she asked, eying him.

"Follow me. We can walk from here."

At first, she was annoyed he hadn't sent her the right image, but as she stretched her legs into a long-strided lope, she was grateful for time to organize her thoughts. They climbed a hill that led due east out of town. The bulk of Mount Shasta towered above them. Snow spilled down its flanks nearly to the remains of the town. Rune disappeared into a hillside. Even though she couldn't see the opening, she figured there had to be one and followed him.

A cave so large that she couldn't see its other end stretched before them. Rune sat on his haunches, a dark shadow barely visible in the cavern's dusky gloom. She dribbled magic to her mage light. Breath whistled through her teeth. Lava formations made whimsical archways. Multi-hued crystals glittered in the depths of some of them. The effect was dizzyingly beautiful. Water ran down one wall. She grinned in spite of herself. *Gee, that part's a lot like my house.*

"What now?" she asked the wolf.

"We wait. They know we're here. They likely knew last night."

"Your animal has wisdom." Metae's unmistakable voice, something like temple bells with a buzz saw behind them, preceded her form as it oozed through one of the walls. "I wonder about you, though." The tinkling bells cooled perceptibly. "Did I not tell you I would let you know when to come here?"

"Oh?" Aislinn did her very best to look surprised. "I knew you were angry because I didn't get here in the four-day time limit, but I thought you meant for me to get here as soon as I could. See," she prattled on, working to infuse truth into her voice, "we ran into more troubles. D'Chel—"

"What about that charlatan?" Metae demanded.

Well, that seems to have gotten her attention. "I met a fellow traveler. Also a Hunter, bonded to a raven. D'Chel attacked the raven—"

"And me, too, but I got away," Rune cut in. "I marshaled the forest wolves to help fight." He leveled his amber gaze at the Old One. "But we were not strong enough. Two were killed."

Metae's gaze shifted from Aislinn to Rune. Something unspeakably alien and undeniably ancient shone from her iridescent eyes. Aislinn shook her head to clear her thoughts. *Wonder why I never noticed how strange her eyes were before?*

"Because I titrate which parts of me humans can see," Metae sent. The temple bells pealed again. "Never forget I can read your mind, child. Now, what happened to the raven bondmate?"

Aislinn sucked in a breath. "I, uh, offered myself in exchange for D'Chel letting the raven, her human, and Rune go."

That inhuman gaze drilled into her. "Apparently you got away. How?"

Opening her mouth to try to talk felt strange. Suddenly, she knew anything shy of unvarnished truth wouldn't pass her lips. "He stopped shape shifting and took on human form. He touched me and kissed me, but he was so cold." Aislinn shuddered at the memory. "I'd planned to just have sex with him and figure out a way to escape after, but he was leaching everything warm out of me. I, uh, knew if he fucked me, I'd lose myself."

"Good you figured that out." Dry amusement ran beneath Metae's voice. "You still have not told me how you escaped."

"I told you how cold I was. Well, I drew fire. Since I didn't have a spell in mind, I held it within me." Aislinn squared her shoulders and clasped her hands behind her back. "The heat made me feel a whole lot better, especially when I figured out my skin was so hot that he couldn't touch me. He tried a couple times and then turned into a cobra." Aislinn shrugged. "Since I already had power to spare, I diverted it into a jump and was gone."

"And he did not try to follow you?" Metae sounded incredulous. "You had better be telling me the truth, Daughter."

"You know I am. You're in my mind." Aislinn tried to keep defensiveness out of her voice. "He may have followed me, but he didn't find me. I took refuge underground. My next jump left from there.

"Anyway," she hurried on before Metae could question her more closely about exactly where underground she'd been, "that's why I'm here. I need an anti-sex charm or something to protect myself. Christ, I've had run-ins with two of them in as many days. Perrikus would have had me if you hadn't shown up. I don't know if he's another refrigerator man like D'Chel, but…" Aislinn let her voice trail off, hoping she'd done a decent job convincing Metae of her continuing trust in the Old Ones.

No one said anything for what seemed like hours. Rune moved close to Aislinn and leaned against her side. Her legs grew tired, but she knew better than to sit in an Old One's presence.

"I must confer with some of the others," Metae said at last. "You and your bond animal will remain just outside the entrance to this cave. Hunting is plentiful. It is safe to have fires, and the water flowing down yon wall emerges as a spring not far from here."

"How long do you—?" Aislinn caught herself and bit off the rest of her sentence. She knew better than to question Metae.

"Maybe you have more in the way of wisdom than I thought," Metae muttered just before she vanished in a blast of light so bright that spots danced in front of Aislinn's eyes.

Rune padded toward the cave's entrance.

Cunning! It's illusion. That's why I couldn't see it from outside. Either her magic had sensitized itself to it, or Metae had done something to make it visible.

"Do you think it's safe to talk?" she asked the wolf.

"No." He headed through a stand of Jeffrey pines.

"Where are you going?" she called after him.

"Hunting. Want to come?"

Aislinn realized she did want to come. The thought of parking her butt outside the entrance to Taltos for an indeterminate time chilled her. She understood what a dangerous game she played and how few tools she had in her arsenal—especially compared with ancient creatures who'd been alive for thousands of years.

My biggest asset is they think I'm stupid, she realized. *I'll have to capitalize on that.*

"Coming?"

"Huh?" With a start, she glanced at the wolf. "Sure. Lead out."

Loping after him, she wondered just how long it would be before Metae returned—and how many Old Ones would come with her. Aislinn had seen enough to know they operated in small groups. It was rare to find one alone, as Metae had been the other day in the square outside her cave, or just now at the gateway to Taltos.

The chirrups of an outraged group of marmots pulled her out of her musings. *Good. Must mean Rune got one.* The thought of meat cooked over a fire until it was actually done made her mouth water.

CHAPTER 10

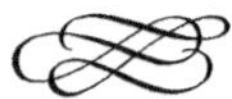

*A*islinn gutted the marmot and was ready to head back, but Rune ran downhill, toward the remains of the town, saying, "We need at least two more." She wondered about that. The animal hanging from her hands weighed a good five pounds. They still had a couple hours of daylight, though, so she followed him. Walking was always better than waiting. The wolf's tail disappeared into a thickly wooded grove. Willows grew so close together, they scratched her skin and tugged at her clothing. She came to a spot where she couldn't go any farther and wondered if she'd missed a turn in the undergrowth. "Rune?"

"Look down."

Sure enough, the willows formed a rough archway that began on the ground and ended at knee level. Dropping to all fours, she slithered through, cursing the wolf for making her follow him. She could've waited outside until he chased down his prey. Wet ground soaked her wool pants and flannel shirt. The rich smells of loam filled her nostrils. She looked around, surprised to discern a passageway. Someone had cut away branches to make a rough opening in the thicket.

"Ouch!" She pulled her hand back from something sharp and summoned her mage light. Its gentle glow bounced off a veritable jungle of crystals in all shapes, sizes, and colors. The cleverly hidden passageway led into a six by ten foot cave. Its gently rounded roof was high enough for her to stand upright, if she crawled a foot or so toward its center. Swiveling around, she pushed her feet forward and stood as soon as she could. The thick soles of her boots cushioned her from the sharp crystals. "This is amazing. How'd you find it?"

Rune shifted from paw to paw. "I think it is safe to talk here. The crystals should mask our conversation."

"Yes, but how did you find it?"

"Marta knew about it. She cut the path."

Marta was at Taltos? "How about if you start at the beginning?" Aislinn suggested. "You told me you came here for justice for Marta. There's more to it than that."

Rune's amber gaze skittered sideways. "I believe the Old Ones killed Marta. Set her up."

"Why would they have done that?"

"Because she was getting too close to the truth about what they are."

"Do you know what she found out?"

The wolf looked her way, and his eyes glittered dangerously. "No. She would not tell me. Said it was too risky. She figured out a way to keep me out of parts of her mind, so I could not find out that way, either."

"So when you came here after her death—?"

"I pretended to be crippled with grief. It was not difficult, since it was hardly an act. I was hoping that if they saw me as a bereft bondmate, I could learn something."

"Did you?"

"No, they made me leave."

Aislinn walked carefully across the uneven floor. When she got to Rune, she squatted next to him and put both arms around his neck. "I'm sorry you lost her." She buried her hands in his thick coat and breathed in the musky wild animal scent of him.

A low growl vibrated in his chest, but he didn't shake her off. "If they take you down into Taltos, tell them you want me with you. I can merge with you."

"Like you do when we jump?"

"Yes. I can lend you my senses. It will help protect you."

"Do they know you can do that?"

"I do not think so. I have spoken with many other bond animals. Except for Bella, none admit to merging minds with their mates."

"I wonder why they'd take me to their city?" she mused, still hugging the wolf.

"To turn you into one of them."

"But they're reptiles under some sort of coating that only looks like skin. They lay eggs. They're not even male or female all the time." Her skin crawled. The last thing she wanted was to be transformed into what they were. She craved Fionn, the warmth of his arms and the heat of his body pressed against her, rigid with need.

No, don't go there. I need my wits front and present. Not in my crotch. Besides, I haven't even tried to wrap my mind around his last name and what it might mean.

She stopped petting Rune. "You never told me your true name."

"And I am not going to."

"Why?"

"It is safer for both of us if things go wrong. The Old Ones can hurt me, but they cannot control me if they do not have my name to hand."

Something nagged at her, the same something that had been bothering her ever since she'd asked Fionn for his last name. She knew about Celtic mythology from her mother. Aislinn doubted Fionn would've told her his full name, no matter how much he wanted to see her again, if she hadn't asked. Power and knowledge had to be earned. They weren't bandied about freely.

"Is there anything more you need to tell me?" She straightened, but couldn't unkink her back entirely. A hank of hair had caught on a down-sweeping crystal. She untangled it and crab-walked to a place she could stand upright.

"Yes. Unless they plan to kill you, which is unlikely, they cannot hold you in Taltos against your will. It disturbs the magic they need to maintain their home to have negative energy present. Besides taking me, your other condition for going with them is that your visit will be short."

"Do you think a day is enough?"

"More than enough. Half a day is better. If you stay too long, you will lose your will. Once that happens, they will suck the energy out of you and remake you into one of them."

She stared hard at Rune. "How do you know these things?"

He woofed softly. The sound echoed in the small space, amplifying itself again and again. Silvery highlights glinted in his coat, reflected by the glow from her mage light. "It took Marta a while before she figured out just how dangerous the Old Ones were. You see, she visited them, too."

Aislinn's mouth went dry. "How long did she stay?"

"Two days once. She was a shell when she escaped. After that, she closed her mind to me and told me if she ever talked about returning to Taltos, I should do anything in my power to stop her—including killing her."

"How long after that did she die?"

His upper lip drew back into a snarl. "Only one turn of the moon. It probably would have been sooner, but she stayed inside our warded home where no one could get to her, trying to get her mind back. She had me recount our years together because the Old Ones stole her memories." Rune's tail swished angrily. "Marta finally thought she was strong enough to face whatever they could throw at her. She said she couldn't hide forever."

"What happened?"

Another snarl, this one louder. "A pack of Bal'ta, led by Tokhots, lured her to her death. She used the last of her magic to protect me."

Aislinn swallowed hard. "Anything else?" *Do I really want to know?* She shivered, wanting the warmth of a cook fire.

"No. We can leave."

～

STRONG MAGIC ZINGING through the air brought Aislinn bolt upright out of an uneasy sleep. The night was well on its way toward dawn. Three of the Old Ones glimmered in the darkness. They all looked like Metae, with long, thick blond hair, iridescent, golden skin, and whirling pools for eyes. Where Metae favored gold ornaments, her two companions wore heavy silver bracelets and rings. Metae had traded her white robes for pale green. The other two wore black, sashed with peacock blue silk. No matter how many times Aislinn saw them, their height was still unnerving. She wondered what the bodies under those robes looked like. Were reptilian claws and scaled skin hiding beneath the long, dagged sleeves?

"We have come to a decision," Metae announced.

"Yes," an unfamiliar voice seconded. It was deeper, but the multi-faceted voice tones were genderless.

Aislinn scrambled to her feet and hastily stuffed her few things into her rucksack as she waited to hear the results of their discussion.

"We offer you a choice," the third Old One said.

"Uh, look," she said a shade too brightly, to mask her pounding heart. Did they knew how nervous she was? "All I really wanted was an anti-sex charm, so I can hold the dark gods at bay. Once I have that, I'll be on my way." She was chickening out, but she wanted to put as much distance as she could between herself and the Old Ones. Her conversation with Rune had been unnerving. She wished they'd had it *before* she'd dragged them to Taltos.

118

"What you want is of little consequence," an Old One informed her.

"We have decided you need help developing your...potential," Metae added.

"Yes, we will be taking you into Taltos," the third one said. "It is a great honor."

"Please don't take this wrong"—Aislinn spread her hands in front of her in a self-deprecating gesture—"but what if I don't want to go?" She had no idea where her sudden burst of courage came from, but she welcomed it. "I have a home. I don't need yours."

"We think you do."

An Old One took hold of her arm, his fingers ice cold. It was the first time one had actually touched her, and she was appalled. Their touch was just as frosty as the dark gods' had been. Pulling fire, she yanked her arm away and stepped out of easy reach, the sound of her own breathing loud in her ears.

"Now, now," Metae said, a placating spell woven into her words. "She must come willingly as our guest. We agreed on that point. You've frightened her."

"Yes, he did," Aislinn agreed quickly. Had it been a *he*? She wasn't sure, but it didn't really matter. "I've been scared enough lately." She tried to infuse just the right hesitation before her next words. "If I can bring my wolf, I'd be willing to come for a short visit. Maybe half a day, but I must be free to leave if I'm uncomfortable." Suspicion gnawed at her insides. Her stomach burned. "What choice were you talking about earlier?"

Between when she'd wrenched her arm away from the Old One and now, Rune had positioned himself between her and it. The clicks, clacks, and buzzing that comprised their language filled the air. Aislinn had never been able to interpret it. Untangling their speech was as impossible as trying to make sense out of a buzzing beehive.

"That would be...acceptable," the Old One who hadn't grabbed her said.

The one who'd touched her bowed stiffly from the waist. He looked like a marionette, bobbing on unseen puppet strings. "I am most sorry if I made you uncomfortable. Metae has told us much of you. I was simply…eager for your visit." Something feral shone from his swirling, multi-colored eyes.

"The choice," Metae made a chopping motion in his direction, "was which of us you wanted to apprentice yourself to. We all possess slightly different skills. Would you like me to tell you about them?"

Aislinn shook her head, trying to figure out a diplomatic way to get out from under the Old Ones' gun sights. The last thing she wanted was to antagonize them. "I'm sure you're offering me quite an honor." She picked her words with care. "Maybe, someday, I might be interested, but not just now. I'm still rattled from Perrikus and D'Chel. And from finding I have Hunter and Healing talents. I need time to assimilate them before I add any more magic."

Metae inclined her head. "I understand. Perhaps, once you have seen Taltos, you will change your mind."

"If the half day begins now"—Aislinn wanted to get things moving before she completely lost her nerve—"that means Rune and I will be back outside in this clearing by noon."

"Child," Metae purred, "whatever has happened to you?" Compulsion ran beneath her words. "You used to trust me."

"It's been a rough few days," Aislinn answered honestly. "I'll fight all the Bal'ta, wargs, bats, and human shades I run across, but those dark gods are downright creepy. I particularly didn't like it when Perrikus told me he wanted to use me as a brood mare."

More clicks and clacks. She thought there might be an outraged undercurrent, but she wasn't sure.

"Let us care for you. If only for a few hours." Metae's voice was honey. "Mayhap you will decide to stay longer—"

"Not this time. Promise you won't force me." The fear in Aislinn's voice was real. *Don't be a fool,* she chided herself. *Their promises don't mean shit. I sound like a ten-year-old.*

"No, no. Of course not. Are you ready?" Metae held out a hand. Despite the Old One's neutral tone, Aislinn picked up a note of impatience.

With Rune sticking to her like a shadow, Aislinn shouldered her pack and walked toward Metae, avoiding her touch. Whatever the Old Ones were did not include warm-blooded. Somewhere beyond the bulk of Mount Shasta, dawn was probably lightening the eastern sky. Aislinn stole a final glance at the world she knew, hunting for evidence that the sun was truly rising. She'd always craved its warmth. Something about retreating into the bowels of the earth—God only knew how deep—curdled her stomach. This was different than her cave, or Fionn's. She was free to come and go there. What if they tried to trap her once she was in Taltos? Aislinn clamped down on her thoughts.

"So tentative," Metae murmured.

A pronounced alien cadence in Metae's voice knotted Aislinn's muscles. Maybe it had always been there, and she'd just never noticed before. Rune leaned closer to her, warm and reassuring. The air began to shimmer, then to burn. Fire licked at her. She fought the urge to pull magic of her own and run. The fire would burn her long before it had any effect on the Old Ones, with their forty-degree body temperature. As quickly as they'd ignited, the flames died. The earth beneath her and Rune dropped away. For one gut-wrenching moment, they were suspended in midair, just before they fell into a void.

She traveled through blackness for a long time, an arm around Rune's thick neck. Finally, the inky curtain around her shaded to a pallid gray. Lights took shape beneath her, like she was in an airplane looking down on a big metropolitan area. They glided to a stop in front of a gilt plaza with a fountain shooting blue-green water at least a hundred feet into the air. Gemstones glittered under the water. Aislinn looked around, trying to get her bearings. Twin suns sat halfway up the sky. *Is this another world?* Old Ones passed in groups of twos, threes, and fours, chattering away.

"Welcome to Taltos," one of her guides announced.

"This is the central square. The city is arranged in spokes spiraling outward from this point," Metae noted.

Feeling like a tourist, all Aislinn could do was gawk. Tall, glittering buildings in pastel colors stretched as far as she could see. The roads were crowded with Old Ones walking purposively. Everybody seemed to have a destination in mind. She looked for cars and then laughed at herself for her stupidity. Of course there wouldn't be any. The Old Ones used magic to go places.

Something jostled her mind. Her perspective shifted, and she realized she was looking through Rune's eyes. She sucked in a surprised breath, turning it into a cough to cover her shock. The grand buildings were illusion, since the wolf didn't see them. The fountain and gemstones were real enough, but the fountain was closer to twenty feet than a hundred. Rather than being paved with something golden, the streets were dirt. Aislinn adopted a neutral expression and tried not to stare. She shielded her thoughts, so nothing would give her away. Her heart beat wildly in her chest, but she couldn't do much about that, other than keep breathing.

"This way." One of the Old Ones trotted down a street.

Aislinn wanted to ask where they were going, but didn't trust herself to talk. She was afraid her voice would tremble and betray how anxious she was.

It wasn't just buildings and streets that Rune perceived far differently than her. He saw the Old Ones for what they truly were. She bit her lower lip hard. While still tall with whirling eyes, the creatures striding along with such purpose had lizard-like faces, scaled skin, and clawed appendages. They wore neither clothing nor jewelry and looked more like tailless dragons walking on two legs than anything else. If she hadn't been so nonplussed, that last thought might've made her smile. She'd had no idea illusion could stretch so far. D'Chel was a piker by comparison. That thought did bring a grin to her face.

"That's better," Metae said, mistakenly interpreting Aislinn's facial expression to mean she was relaxing.

"Why yes, it is, isn't it?" Aislinn turned her smile on Metae. It was getting easier now that the shock of seeing what she—no, it—really was had worn off a little. "Where are you taking me?"

"Why, to the alchemists, of course. You wanted a charm, or a spell. It must be matched to your energy. By the time that is accomplished, the time you said you were willing to spend with us will be all but gone."

A door in one of the illusory buildings opened. They walked down many stone steps into an underground grotto. Lanterns masquerading as cut crystal lights hung from hooks. Shelves crowded with scrolls lined the walls. A raised pallet sat in the middle of the room. Under the illusion, it was really an earthen platform splotched with red and green stains. A coppery scent tickled her nostrils. Aislinn wondered what color their blood was.

"Lie down, child." Metae's voice was gentle.

"I'd rather not." Aislinn backed stiffly toward the stairs.

"How else can we match a charm to your energy?" The voice exuded reason, promised shelter.

With every fiber of her being in full rebellion, Aislinn propelled herself toward the platform. When she lay down, the wolf positioned his body next to hers. Forcing herself to relax, she reached for her magic. It was muted, as if some sort of shielding stood between her and it, but she thought she could punch through it if she had to. *They think I'm weak.*

An Old One positioned itself at her head. The wolf's withdrawal from her mind was immediate. He obviously did not want the Old Ones to know what he could do. A chilly foreleg—that looked like a hand and arm again now that Rune was no longer in her mind—dropped onto her forehead. Energy shot through her brain, probing. She wondered what the thing was hunting for, when her head began to spin. Before she could marshal her resources to fight against it, consciousness ebbed.

From a long way away, she heard herself scream, "Noooooooo —" Aislinn arched her back and kicked her heels to stay awake, but something dark and insistent leached the will out of her. The last thing she felt before slipping into oblivion was Rune, warm and solid against her side.

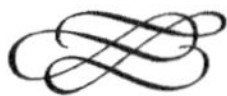

islinn ran. Something was behind her. She heard the scrape of claws on stone, felt hot breath against her back. The whoosh of what sounded like huge wings filled the air, but the passageway was so narrow, the thing probably couldn't spread them. Her lungs burned. She didn't know what was back there and couldn't afford the time to look. If she did, her slender margin would vanish, and the thing would snap her up. It wanted to kill her. Hatred raked her back each time it breathed.

Rock walls glimmering with tiny lichen flashed past. The floor had slimy spots. She slipped more than once. *Where the fuck am I?* Leg muscles aching and a stitch cramping her side, she blundered on. *Am I dreaming? Can you die in dreams?* Aislinn careened around a corner. Her booted heel landed on a slick spot, and she sprawled on her ass, the breath knocked out of her.

Terror pounded. She couldn't run much farther. Struggling to make her lungs work, she leapt to her feet, spun, and faced the thing closing fast behind her. Aislinn yanked her dirk from her belt and grappled to find her magic. It was there—sort of—but fire, always her first preference, was missing. She dragged air and earth into the beginning of a protection spell. Fire was for fighting. If she couldn't have that, maybe she could at least slow down whatever was after her by warding herself.

The monster was enormous. It filled the cave-like passage nearly to its ceiling. The creature looked the way she'd always imagined dragons would, with burnished reddish scales covering a reptile's body. A long tail curved over its head. Small forelegs and sturdy hind legs were tipped with wicked-looking red talons that had to be six inches long. It had the same eyes as the Old Ones: spinning pools of night.

Aislinn stood tall, squaring her shoulders. If this was truly where things ended, she'd go out strong, not cowering. "What do you want with me?" She infused compulsion into her question, then wondered why she'd bothered. Surely her puny magic was no match for the thing of legend standing before her.

A gout of fire spewed from its mouth, landing a foot shy of her boots. It stared at her. She looked anywhere but at its eyes. They were too much like the Old Ones' for comfort. If she met its gaze, she'd be lost. It came closer, hot breath oddly comforting in the chilly air of the cave. The dragon—what else could it be?—smelled of sulfur and blood. A rough, taloned foreleg skittered down her body, first one side, then the other. Aislinn relaxed fractionally. If it wanted to kill her, she'd be dead. She tried again, "What do you want with me?"

Did the Old Ones have gods? Was that what this was? Something even older than them?

Without warning, the talons casing her body moved to her head. As they traveled down her cheeks, she felt searing heat on one side, followed by intense cold. Then nothing. The dragon pulled its foreleg back. Blood dripped from its talons. Her blood. Aislinn raised a hand to her face. A large gash traveled from eyebrow to chin, and her skin was icy to the touch. Once the flesh thawed, it would hurt like hell. The dragon lifted its foreleg to its mouth and licked the blood off its talons.

Great wings lifted in the still air. It could only deploy them halfway before they met the sides of the passage. On the third wing beat, the dragon twirled. Moving amazingly fast for something so large, it strode down the tunnel away from her, its feet slapping the muddy floor. Now that she wasn't running from it, Aislinn noticed the earth shook each time one of its feet landed. Darkness settled about her like a winding sheet, and she realized the light in the tunnel had come from the creature.

Can I make light without fire?

Knees trembling, she wondered what would happen next as she coaxed a very feeble light into being. "No point in hanging around to find out," she muttered and ran as fast as she could manage in the opposite direction. A half-formed mage light—the best she could do —clung to her. After a few steps, it felt like she was plowing through Jell-O. The cave walls moved toward her, closer and closer, until she was certain they were going to crush her, grinding her into nothingness. Her head spun. Nausea gripped her.

Just when she was certain she was going to die in this nameless, dark place, she rose through the ceiling and flowed through stone as if it wasn't there. She looked at her body thrashing about on the raised, earthen dais in the Old Ones' alchemy lab and understood what had happened. *It was my astral self down there. Not me. Did they send me there, or did I do it on my own?* So relieved she almost couldn't breathe, Aislinn hurtled toward her physical self. No wonder she hadn't been able to draw fire. She needed her *body* to do that.

But she needed her body to bleed, too. When she gazed at herself lying on the table, she was shocked to see a wicked-looking gash running the length of one side of her face. The collision of astral and physical bodies jarred her before she could figure out how the dragon had managed to carve her up when her body hadn't actually been there. She'd already been nauseated. Dry heaves racked her as she forced herself to a sitting position.

Aislinn wiped bile from her mouth with the back of one hand and gazed at Rune. Gratitude to find him unharmed nearly undid her, and she blinked back tears. When she'd returned to her body, he'd jumped off the platform and stood in front of her. Concern shone from his amber eyes. Craning her neck around, she identified Metae and the other two Lemurians. "I need water," she demanded, her voice raspy.

Someone shoved a flask into her hand. It occurred to her that it might be poison. She swished some around in her mouth. It tasted okay, so she took a long drink. "Where was I?"

"The place where we learn things," Metae said carefully.

"Who was the dragon? One of your gods?"

Surprise registered on all three alien faces. "You saw him?" one of them asked.

"I just asked you about him, didn't I?" Aislinn sounded bitchy, but she didn't care.

"He is wise beyond reckoning," Metae said. "It is a great honor that he has shown himself to you."

"Yes," another Old One concurred, practically bowing to her. "You cannot leave us now. We need to—"

"Oh yes, I can." Aislinn leapt to her feet and headed for the stairs, with Rune hard on her heels. "Whatever it was scared the shit out of me. I wouldn't go back to that subterranean tunnel system again for anything."

"Her face," one muttered.

Aislinn felt blood dripping down her cheek and neck. "Yeah," she called over a shoulder from halfway up the stairs, "the damned thing took a swipe out of me. Except my body wasn't there. It was up here. How the hell—?" Since it was impossible to put what she was feeling into words, she snapped, "Never mind."

"It tasted you." The Old Ones crowded behind her, so she couldn't see which one had spoken. "We noticed when the cut formed, but had no idea what happened."

"You must tell us," Metae chimed in with her musical voice, "everything."

Aislinn nodded agreement Lent before realizing maybe it wasn't such a good idea to confirm that the thing had swallowed her blood.

Outside again, she looked up and down the street. "Where's the best place to leave from? And where is the anti-sex charm you were supposed to make for me?"

All three spoke at once, trying to persuade her to stay. Not for long, just for a little while. They needed more time to match her energies to a charm. They needed to tend to her wound. She was hungry, tired… Compulsion in the words had her half believing them before Rune slid into her mind.

"I will help you." He sent her an image of the area outside the cave where they'd spent most of the previous night.

She shook her head, hard. Christ, they'd almost seduced her. They definitely had her number. She *was* weak—and stupid. Latching onto Rune's sending like a dying man who sees all his possibilities vanishing into a fine mist, she reached for her magic. *Fire. Where was fire? Thank God.* Tapping into a rich vein, she pulled as much as she could, not bothering to be elegant. Fingers buried in the wolf's ruff, she felt her spell take hold.

"We cannot let her leave." Though it was clicks and clacks, Aislinn realized with a start that she understood them. What had the dragon thing done to her?

Fingers seized her. She fought to hang onto her spell.

"We cannot hold her against her will. She would contaminate our magic in no time." Metae's voice was stern.

"Orione has the taste of her blood. It will be simple enough to get her back."

"Yes, we can retrieve her whenever we want."

The fingers clutching her arm hard enough to draw blood loosened. Aislinn considered kicking the Old One in the crotch, but didn't want to spare the energy. Besides, it wasn't like he had balls, and she figured it would take everything she had to get out of Taltos. She poured power into her working until the false golden city wavered; blackness took hold.

Aislinn didn't know if she could have done it without Rune. The wolf's presence in her mind steadied her. Kept her on course when she was so weary she let go of their destination. It was dark when they tumbled out onto the packed earth in front of the cave. Aislinn fell on her face in the dirt, so tired she couldn't keep her eyes open.

Something sharp closed on her upper arm. "No." Rune's voice was harsh. "Not here."

Knowing he was right, that this place wasn't safe, Aislinn staggered down the mountainside after him. She sprawled on her ass because she couldn't see and then tried to raise her mage light, but it wouldn't come. Not so much as a flicker. *Tapped out. Got to eat and sleep.* Every time she fell, thinking she didn't have enough starch to lurch back to her feet, the wolf was there. Sometimes licking, sometimes biting, he urged her along. Finally, she recognized the willows and understood he'd herded her into the crystal cave. Her last thought before blackness took her was how wretchedly uncomfortable the cave floor was pressed against her butt and legs.

PAIN FROM HUNDREDS of sharp spines poking into her chivied her awake. Light spilled into the cave's entrance. Rune wasn't there. Groaning, she flipped over, pulled herself along on her belly and crawled out onto the dirt. She scuttled along until the willows eased enough for her to stand upright.

Her wolf sat next to freshly killed rabbits. He must've stood guard over her while she was passed out. Now he'd gotten her food. A wave of appreciation so profound it brought tears washed through her. "Thank you."

"You would have done the same for me," he said gruffly. "Eat. The quicker we are away from here, the better." Shucking her pack, she pulled a water bottle out and drank deeply. Her hands shook as she gutted and skinned the rabbits, hungrily sucking raw meat off the tiny bones.

She was midway through the second rabbit when she looked up guiltily. "Was one of these supposed to be yours?"

"I ate while you slept."

She wanted to talk with Rune, but knew how dangerous that could be. And she didn't want to waste time retreating to the crystal cave to have a conversation. Once she'd eaten, she reached for her magic to see if she had enough to jump them out of there. If possible, she wanted to be much farther away than Castle Crags. Maybe, if she planned well, she could get close enough to Fionn for him to come meet them.

Pushing to her feet, she put her things in her pack. "Ready?"

Rune moved to her side. Aislinn waited until she felt the magic build inside her. Her reserves were still dangerously low. It would take more than half a single night's sleep and one meal to bring her back to full strength. Weightlessness took her. Rune claimed what was starting to feel like *his* place in her mind. For once, this jump was easy. They came out on the banks of a fast-running creek. A deserted building nearby sported a faded sign announcing, *Welcome to the McCloud Fishing Lodge.*

Aislinn felt dirty from her time in Taltos. She glanced at the winter sun. It was high in the sky, so her clothes might have time to dry if she washed them. Hastily stripping, she walked into the creek, enjoying the feel of the sand against her bare feet. A deeper pool gave her what she needed. She sank into the icy waters and let them close over her head. Aislinn surfaced, gasping from the cold, and grabbed handfuls of sand from the bottom to scrub her hair and herself. The gash on her face ached, but at least it was clean. She wondered if she could Heal herself, then discarded the idea. She'd need a mirror to do a good job. More importantly, she didn't want to spare the magic. In another life, she would've gone to an Emergency Room for stitches. "Ha." She snorted. "Another life indeed."

"What?" Rune, who'd been sunning himself on the bank, raised his head off his paws.

"Nothing." *I was just feeling sorry for myself.* She gathered the clothes she'd scattered around the bank and dragged them into the water, scrubbing at them. She couldn't get them really clean without soap, but at least they wouldn't smell quite so bad. When she was done, she wrung them out and draped her long johns, wool pants, and flannel shirt over bushes. She hefted the pants, grimaced at how heavy they still were, and tried to wring more water out. Gathering wood, she started a fire, moved her clothes closer to it, and set about cooking more rabbits Rune had caught while she'd been bathing and doing laundry.

The wolf lay on the riverbank in scrub grass. He waited until she was done eating before asking, "What happened?"

Well, what did happen? She sorted through her thoughts. "I think we came within an angstrom of being trapped there. If you hadn't gone into my mind when we were all standing outside that travesty they called a lab, we never would've gotten away. Before that, though, my astral self separated from the rest of me." Rune opened his mouth to ask a question, but she shook her head. "Wait till I'm done. I don't know how the separation happened. If I did it, or they forced it. Anyway, I was in some sort of long, curving tunnel, and this dragon thing was chasing me. It's what bloodied my face, so it could taste my blood. I thought I was dreaming, but I wasn't. Ugh." She shivered. The paltry warmth of the day wasn't enough to keep a chill from slithering down her spine.

Needing to do something to force her mind away from the tunnel and the dragon, she checked how dry her clothing was. Satisfied that at least her long underwear would be dry soon, she turned them over and stoked the fire.

"It was them," the wolf offered. "The one with his claws in your hair forced your astral self out of your body. I felt it."

That solves one riddle. "So they must've wanted me to go somewhere, but they looked surprised as hell when I told them what I'd seen." A thought surfaced, and she stared at Rune. "Would you have had a way out of there if I'd been trapped?"

"No."

Wish I'd known that. She opened her mouth to berate him, but then bit her tongue. Yes, he'd pushed his way onto this journey, but the truth of things was he'd saved them both. If not for him, she'd still be locked in Taltos, at the mercy of the Old Ones.

"The Old Ones were arguing right before we finally left." Rune sounded thoughtful. "I wonder what they said and why they decided to let us go."

"I know why."

"You can understand them? When did that happen? When I was in your mind earlier, you couldn't."

She nodded. "That's right. Something happened when I was in that tunnel."

"Are you going to tell me?" He came to his feet and padded to where she stood.

"I suspect the dragon had something to do with why I can understand the Old Ones now." A corner of her mouth quirked into a grin. "I'm not complaining. I'll take my gifts where they fall. In terms of what they said to one another, apparently they can't hold us against our will. It's like what you told me in the crystal cave. It creates some problem with their magic to have a bunch of reluctant recruits gumming up the works. Must be why they kill everyone."

"That's not all." Keen intelligence shone from the depths of Rune's lupine eyes. "I'm waiting."

"The thing I met up with is named Orione. The Old Ones said he could *retrieve me* for them anytime they want me. I didn't like the sound of that."

Rune growled. "Neither do I."

"Not much I can do about it." She shrugged pragmatically. "I'm sure not going to hide behind wards for the rest of my life."

"That's eerily similar to what Marta said." Rune blew out a whuffly growl. "Are your things dry?"

She felt them again. "Not really. They can dry the rest of the way on my body. Why?"

"Let's walk a bit."

Aislinn shimmied into her damp long johns and dragged the wool pants over them. She tugged her faded flannel shirt over her head and slipped into her vest and jacket. She'd given up on panties and bras long ago. She blessed her woolen clothing. It was still wet, but it warmed almost immediately next to her skin. She sat in the scrub grass and pulled on wool socks, followed by her battered boots.

The sun disappeared behind a bank of clouds, almost as if it sensed she didn't need it anymore. A stiff breeze blew her still-wet hair into her face. With a sigh, she gathered it together, fished in her rucksack for a length of leather, and tied it out of the way. "Ready." She got to her feet and shouldered her pack. "But I want to look through that old fishing lodge first."

"Why?"

"Maybe there's food or something." Because she had to scrounge for everything, she always searched abandoned buildings, particularly those in the middle of nowhere like this one. The door hung half off its hinges; it made a creaking sound in the wind. She took a tentative step inside, realized the flooring was rotten, and determined where the support beams were. She didn't find food, but on the second floor, consisting of four large bedrooms, she found clothes. Pants and shirts and a Gore-Tex jacket that looked as if it hadn't ever been worn. It still had a plastic bag around it. Shoving a dusty coverlet off one of the beds, she tried things on. Nearly everything fit, even the silk panties and lacy bras.

"They're ridiculous," she muttered, but the feel of the smooth material, soft against her skin, made her reconsider. Once upon a time, she'd loved nice things. She settled on a finely woven, long-sleeved wool shirt, sturdy pants with lots of pockets, and the Gore-Tex jacket to wear. Then she filled her pack with three more shirts, another pair of pants, socks that miraculously didn't have holes in them from resident moths, bras and panties, and a wool-lined vest. Unfortunately, whoever had owned the clothes had feet that were smaller than hers. She looked longingly at a pair of leather boots, but they'd make her feet hurt every time she wore them. She did tie a pair of Teva sandals to the outside of her rucksack, though. They were a big step up from the cracked, plastic Crocs she had at home.

She thought about folding her old clothes and placing them in dresser drawers, but they were still quite damp. She draped her threadbare garments over the furniture. "For the next person," she told the silence of the room. "There's still wear left in them."

"What are you doing?" Rune called.

"Shopping." Something that sounded a lot like a giggle escaped before she started down the broken staircase.

"You found food?" the wolf asked, nose twitching. "Must be in cans. I can't smell it."

"No, silly, I found clothes. I don't have an all-weather fur coat like you."

"We're losing the light," he observed. "Maybe that walk wasn't such a good idea—unless we end up staying here for the night. Then we'll need to scout a protected campsite. Do you have enough magic for another jump?"

"Sure." She was astonished by how good she felt. Between food, lolling in the sun—even though it hadn't been all that warm—waiting for her clothes to dry, and finding new ones, her energy was back online. She thought just maybe she could conquer the world. Or what was left of it, anyway. "Let's surprise Fionn and Bella."

CHAPTER 12

Surprise was a mild term for what Aislinn encountered. Fionn grabbed her shoulders the minute her spell dispersed and shook her. "I've been expecting you since this morning. Tell me everything. Everything, lass. Leave nothing out. Christ! What happened to your face?" He let go of one shoulder to trace the gash down her cheek.

"Welll, nice to see you again, too." She drew back and stared at him. His jaw was set in a hard line. His brows were drawn together. Blue eyes snapped dangerously. He looked furious—and worried.

"You were supposed to call for me if you got into trouble." He balled his hands into fists at his sides.

So I was. "You're yelling at me. Stop it. And I'm not sure you would've been much help." *Ah, whoops, that didn't come out quite right.* "Er, I mean, if you'd been there, of course—"

He turned away, sucking air like a bellows, clearly trying to get himself under control. When he turned back, the tense planes of his face had relaxed a little. "You're right, of course. It's just that I was so damned worried about you. And I felt fucking helpless. Told myself if you weren't back by midnight, I was going after you."

"We didn't agree on a time when you necessarily expected me

back." Aislinn trod cautiously, aware of how tired she was. The euphoria she'd felt leaving the fishing lodge had gotten sucked up and spit out by the magic she'd summoned to ferry Rune and her to Fionn's grotto. Apparently, she wasn't as fully recovered as she'd thought. The last thing she wanted was an argument. "What if Rune and I had spent the night next to the McCloud River? We talked about it. Then you'd have been gone tomorrow morning when we finally got back here, and I wouldn't have known where you were. Plus, I'd never have been able to get in if you weren't here to open your wards."

He stared at her. No, it felt as if he was staring *through* her. "What would you have done?"

She threw her hands up. "I don't know. Waited for a while, I suppose."

That twitchy place under his eye was back. "Just a while?"

She stalked over to a pile of cushions, unbuckled her rucksack, and flopped down. "Christ, Fionn. I'm tired. I've had a hell of a couple of days. Can you just tell me you're happy to see me and leave it at that?"

"No."

She thought about asking *why not* and then decided she didn't really want to know. Next, she thought about asking if he wanted her and Rune to leave. She glanced about for the wolf. He and Bella chatted companionably in a corner. It appeared the raven had offered a far warmer—and less complicated—greeting for her fellow bond animal than Fionn managed for her. *Nah, even if he told me to leave, I couldn't go anywhere without sleep.* "How about if we both get some rest?"

"Not until you tell me what happened."

She blew out an exasperated breath. "Won't it keep till morning?"

Fionn shook his head so hard, unbound hair fell into his face. He pushed it back with an impatient gesture.

"Okay, I give up," she said. "It shouldn't take all that long. We could spend more time arguing about it than it will take to tell…" Fifteen minutes later, she was just finishing her description of Orione and her discovery that she could understand the Old Ones' language, when he held up a hand.

"I know you're tired. And I'm sorry I pounced on you, but could you describe the dragonesque thing again. Close your eyes, take your time. I need every detail you can remember."

"Can you get me something to drink?"

"Sure." He got up and went into an alcove. In a few minutes, he handed her a cracked cup of something decidedly alcoholic.

She took an experimental sip that exploded on her tongue. It tasted of flowers and summer. She met his gaze for the first time since he'd raised his voice. "What is it?"

"Mead." In answer to the question in her mind, he added, "I made it from honey." He gestured with two fingers for her to concentrate. "The dragon?"

She did the best she could describing Orione. It seemed to satisfy Fionn, because he didn't ask any more questions. Somehow, her cup was empty. The warmth of the liquor relaxed her tense muscles. Her eyelids drifted toward half-mast.

He laid a hand on her knee. "Let me hold you, lass. Morning will be here before we know it."

A feeble protest rose to her lips that she really was too tired to do anything other than sleep, but he shushed her. He helped her to her feet, and leaning on him, she let him lead her to the bed. He pulled off her boots and then lifted her legs onto the low platform fragrant with pine boughs. She curled into a ball on her side and felt him fit his body behind her. His breath was warm and soothing on her neck. It felt good to be held and cherished. But it felt awful to have to answer to anyone else. Her brain tried to find words to express the dilemma, but drowsiness befuddled her tongue. All she could do was murmur his name. She didn't know why, maybe because she was so tired, but she called him by his whole name, the one she'd been supposed to breathe into the green-flecked quartz crystal: Fionn MacCumhaill.

"Aye, lass," he murmured against her ear. "Ye are bound to me, just like ye are to yon wolf. And like him, I will protect you forever."

She fell asleep trying to tell him she belonged to no one but herself.

～

WHEN SHE WOKE in the depths of the night, his body was still curved around hers. She turned to face him and called her mage light. It played over the bones in his face and reflected the blue of his eyes when he opened them.

"You're awake," he said softly, Irish lilt all but gone from his voice. Maybe she'd imagined it just before she fell asleep. "I would've thought you'd sleep till morning." Reaching out with tenderness at odds from his earlier ire, he smoothed hair away from her face.

She smiled sleepily. "Nice to wake in your arms."

The arms in question tightened about her. He found the hollow in her neck with his mouth and trailed kisses downward until he ran into the opening of her shirt.

"I can take it off," she murmured. Heat ran like molten silver through her veins. She'd never met anyone who got her going so quickly, except the dark gods, and they didn't count.

"Let me help you." His voice roughened with need.

As soon as she pushed the wool top over her breasts, he moved her bra aside and closed his mouth over a nipple. His teeth grazed sensitive flesh. She pressed her body against him. He sucked harder, bringing her nipple to a hard, aching point of sensation. Fionn switched to the other breast. Knowing fingers twirled and tugged, replacing his mouth. She felt a climax build and embraced the exquisitely sensitive nerve endings driving her toward it. She started to shove a hand between her legs and then knew she wouldn't have to. The combination of his mouth and fingers was plenty. She came, grinding her crotch against him, hands and teeth digging into his shoulders.

Fionn raised himself over her and brought his lips down on hers. His tongue slipped inside her mouth. She sucked on it hard, drawing him in so deep, she lost track of where she stopped and he began. He tasted of nearly forgotten summers, of abandon and freedom.

The length of him pressed against her thigh, hot and hard. With a shock, she realized the bottom half of his body was naked. Shoving frantically at the waistband of her pants, she finally remembered these were different pants and they had both buttons and a zipper. Somehow, she managed to get them down enough to pull one leg out. He rolled her onto her back, probing for entrance almost immediately. Drawing her knees back, she gripped his hips and pulled recklessly. She wanted him inside. Deep. Now. Gasping and panting, she arched her back, trying to get as close as she could. His breath mingled with hers. He took her lower lip between his teeth and bit down. She bit back, all fire and claws, taking his gambit and giving him one better.

Fionn groaned as he sank into her and began the same long, slow strokes that had driven her crazy last time.

Aislinn lost track of how many times she came before she felt the spasms of his release. She tightened her grip on his shoulders and drew him against her. They fell back asleep like that before he shifted his weight off her and drew her into the circle of his arms, crooning softly. It was only when she woke again that she realized he'd been singing to her in Gaelic. It felt like she was a child again and her mother was holding her. She even thought she remembered that particular song. If it was the same one, he'd been telling her he'd care for her always and keep her safe.

Feeling more awake, she snorted to herself. *Nice try, but nowhere is safe anymore. No point in deluding myself.* He stirred next to her, but the cadence of his breathing told her he was still asleep. *Wonder if Rune and I should leave?*

Are you kidding? the other side of her brain demanded. *He's the best fuck I've ever had. Why would I want to walk away from that?*

It comes with strings. Remember last night?

She rubbed her eyes, not wanting to wake him before she'd had time to sort out her thoughts. Yes, Fionn did come with strings. Was she already tangled up in them? She'd barely had a chance to get used to sharing her life with the wolf. Maybe she and Fionn could take a short break from each other. See how they really felt before they got in much deeper.

Nope, not a good idea. The way things were today, with no reliable way to communicate over distances, either they stayed together—until one of them decided they were done—or they parted right now. She didn't see any other choices. Besides, survival was scarcely a foregone conclusion. If they went their separate ways, one of them could be killed, and the other would never know. She thought about how it would be to have him dead, and a part deep inside her ached, the pain so intense it felt like a knife in her guts.

How could I be so attached? I barely know him. She tried to slip quietly out of their bed, but the movement woke him. He closed a hand about her wrist and pulled her back, said something in Gaelic, and then switched to English. "Sorry. Sometimes when I'm half asleep, I forget."

She gaped at him. "That's an old form of Gaelic."

"And how would ye be knowing that?" He aped an Irish accent so perfectly, it made her laugh.

"Because my mother was Irish, and she used to talk to me—in Gaelic and in Irish. I recognize the difference. Gaelic has a different cadence."

"So it does. Come back here. There's nothing so pressing we can't have a good morning hug." The accent was very nearly gone. The words such perfect English, she might not have noticed the slight twang beneath them if she weren't paying attention.

His body was warm against hers. And quite naked. Just the touch of his full length against her was enough to start her blood humming. She squirmed, trying to get away. "We'll never get anything else done," she protested.

"And what could be more important than this?" he demanded, his perfect teeth very white against his scraggly beard as he smiled at her. Gently taking one of her hands, he pushed it downward until her fingers curled around his shaft. Ridged flesh jumped in her hand, once and then again, obviously ready for more of what they'd shared the night before.

Good question. She tried to gin up an answer, but couldn't come up with anything. Rune and Bella could take care of themselves. She had no job to go to. No school. Only this man and her and the magic their bodies made together.

"Just remember"—she cupped the side of his face with her free hand—"you asked for this."

Aislinn let go of him and yanked the covers out of the way so she could look at him. Really look at him. She kindled her mage light, since his wasn't bright enough for her purposes, and the sight of his body made breath catch in her throat. Lean muscled arms and shoulders funneled to a flat stomach and slender hips. A light dusting of golden hair sparkled against bronzed skin. She ran a fingertip from shoulder to groin and then traced his leg all the way to his feet. He flexed his toes and made a feral, possessive noise deep in his throat.

"And do ye like what ye see?" Blue eyes sparkled.

Her throat was thick with desire, but she managed to croak, "Oh my God, how can you even ask? You're the most beautiful, the most perfect—"

"Nay, lass, that would be yourself ye're describing. Your hair is like liquid fire, and your eyes are golden. I've never seen eyes like that afore. And your breasts... If ye'd lived hundreds of years ago, poets would have written odes to them." He opened his arms. "Come here. I canna stand the distance between us."

She understood, because neither could she.

When they finally got up hours later, her nether regions were sore as she shifted around to pull on her clothes. "Ouch."

"Och aye, and I have just the cure for that." He winked.

"Och aye isn't Irish. It's Scottish."

Fionn rolled his eyes. "The era I came from, that expression was in common usage throughout the northern British Isles. What about my cure?" He waggled his eyebrows suggestively.

She swatted him. "Nope. I need a break. And a bath. I can smell myself."

"We can go to the river. I'll even make the water warm for you."

"You can do that?"

"Uh-huh. So can you. I'll show you how." Fionn stood and collected his clothes strewn on the floor. He stretched his arms above his head and pivoted his torso from side to side before getting dressed.

She finished dressing, got to her feet, and made a mock bow in his direction. "Lead on."

He took her hand and opened a path through his wards for all of them. Rune and Bella were more than ready to hunt, dashing off the minute they were above ground. As she followed him to the river, Aislinn wondered if she'd ever had so much sex before in such a short time frame. It didn't take long to realize she hadn't. For one thing, no one ever stuck around very long once their most immediate needs had been sated.

Fionn was talking to her, but she hadn't heard him. "Tell me again," she said. "I was thinking."

He eyed her. "About what?"

She shook her head.

The look he gave her sharpened, but he went on. "I was giving you a tutorial on how to warm water in a circle about yourself. Mix water and fire in equal proportions—"

"Water will extinguish fire," she protested.

"Watch." He gave her that ten thousand-watt grin again, shucked his clothes, and stepped into a deep pool in the river.

She couldn't help it. She smiled back and got out of her own clothes. Splashing over to him, she was pleasantly surprised to find that he stood in the middle of truly warm water. "Wow! I'm impressed. Water and fire, eh?"

He inclined his head. To his credit, he didn't say, *I told you so*.

Warm water really did go much farther than cold. It soothed her inflamed tissues, too. He showed her a root that soaped when you crushed it between rocks.

"What is that?" she asked delightedly as she squished slimy goo all over her body in bath temperature water.

"Indian soap root. An older name is Bear Onion."

She memorized what it looked like so she could find it again. It even did a pretty good job with her hair. Of course, it wasn't all that dirty, since she'd just washed it the day before. She had a feeling soap root would manage the oils better than sand, though. Aislinn fingered the gash down the side of her face. It still hurt, and it would leave a hell of a scar.

Thoroughly clean, they lay naked on rocks warmed by a combination of magic and the sun. It was temperate for so late in the year, and she luxuriated in not being swathed in layers of clothing. Fionn used his shirt for a gathering basket and brought them wild blackberries that had dried on their vines. She popped one after another of the tiny black globes into her mouth, enjoying the combination of sweet and tart. Rune padded over and flopped down beside her, part of a mangled rodent hanging from his mouth. Bella overflew them and then flapped her way to a nearby tree limb. She cawed raucously. Aislinn wondered if it was the avian equivalent of laughter.

"This is the first time I haven't been scared in..." She hesitated. "Maybe in years." She bit her lower lip. "I'm not sure it's good. I need to be scared so I'm alert." She glanced around them, half expecting some dark creature—or maybe a human shade—to jump out of the foliage.

"There's safety in numbers," Fionn said. "With four of us, it's not likely something nefarious could slip past."

Aislinn wasn't so sure about that, but she held her peace. She didn't want to ruin what felt like the most perfect day since before her father had been killed. Swiveling so she could look at Fionn, she asked, "Tell me why you can speak Gaelic. Are you from the United Kingdom?"

His face darkened, and she wondered what she'd said wrong. There'd been a time when she could speak German. If anyone had asked her, she'd have told them she learned it in school.

When the silence started to feel uncomfortable, he said, "Let's just say I was born in the Old Country." He met her gaze, but his eyes were hooded, as if he didn't want her to probe. "I've been in the States for a very long time, though. My home is here."

That's an odd answer. And not quite what I asked about. "If things are going to work between us," she said, keeping her voice very quiet, "there has to be absolute truth. I can't stand by your side in battle, wondering what you're not telling me." She took a breath and went on, finally recognizing what was bothering her. "Because that's it, Fionn. It's not that what you said wasn't true. It's that you left a whole bunch of things out."

"Did I now?"

Her neck stiffened at the mocking challenge in his voice. "Och aye, and ye did," she muttered. "Two can play that game. Now talk."

"I will. But not outside the wards. Are you ready to go in?"

She started pulling on her clothes. "Yes," she managed through gritted teeth. What was it with this man? He could make her so hot her body was awash in lust so intense it obliterated everything, and so angry she wanted to choke him. He was the only man she hadn't been able to walk away from.

Maybe I can. I haven't tried.

Who am I kidding?

Well, I haven't tried—not really. Let's see what he has to say for himself. Then I'll decide.

CHAPTER 13

Fionn tried to make small talk once they were back underground, but Aislinn wasn't having any of it. The animals retreated to a far corner after she raised her voice the first time. "Talk," she shouted, pounding a fist into her other hand for emphasis. "Tell me who you are and where you came from." She made an effort to gentle her voice. Christ, she sounded like a fishwife. "If I'm going to link my life to yours, I have a right to know."

That must've gotten through, because he said, "Yes, you do. I'm sorry. I've been hiding who and what I am from everyone for so long, it's not easy to stop dissembling."

Her Seeker senses, attuned to truth, corroborated his statement. At least it was a start. Aislinn pursed her lips. "Did your wife know?"

He shook his head and gave her a lopsided smile. "At least, not the most current one, nor the several who came before her."

She took a step away from him. "You're not really Fionn MacCumhaill. You couldn't be." Breath clogged in her throat as she waited for his answer. Her heart thudded against her ribcage.

"Yes, I did give you my name." He spoke as if to himself. "Maybe I made a mistake, but I was wild with fear for what would happen once you delivered yourself to the Old Ones like a trounced pig."

146

"You gave me a name," she clarified, still keeping her distance. "But there's no way you could possibly be *the* Fionn MacCumhaill."

"And why not?"

"Because you'd have to be hundreds of years old. Maybe as much as a thousand," she sputtered. "He was a Celtic god."

"Do you remember which one?"

Irritation stung her. "What is this? Twenty Questions?"

"Well, do you?" His voice, the American one, was so soft that she had to strain to hear.

"Of course I do. He ruled, ah, wisdom. And overcoming enemies." She racked her brain, culling her mother's fairy stories from wherever they lived when she wasn't thinking about them. "Creation, protection, knowledge, divination." She put her hands on her hips, feeling pleased with herself. "That about covers it."

"Aye, lass, that it does." The Irish lilt was back. He smiled at her. Or he showed her his teeth. It didn't feel much like a smile. Now that she was looking at him, really looking, something ancient and brimming with knowledge lurked behind his blue eyes.

I'm imagining things. It isn't possible.

"Of course it is."

"Damn it." She was so frustrated, she punched him. He didn't make so much as a *whuff*, but her knuckles stung. "Stay out of my head."

"As you wish." He inclined his head.

She brought her fisted hand to her mouth, sucking at the sore parts. "No, it's not. You can't be hundreds—maybe thousands—of years old."

"The others, they told me I'd die if I left the Old Country. They thought the magic wouldn't stretch so far. But it did—and I didn't."

"What others?"

"The other gods, of course." He chuckled. "The Celts had many gods. Well over a hundred at the apex of our strength. Once I knew everyone's name, but not anymore." He looked sad, his eyes pinched at their corners. "Many have faded out of time and memory."

What the fuck have I gotten myself into?

Aislinn slowly crossed the room and sat on one of the cushions piled against a wall. She propped her head on an upraised hand and tried to use her Seeker sense to see into him. Something stopped her, though.

"What are you doing?"

"Trying to figure out if you've told me the truth."

He nodded, looking serious. "Try again. I've dropped my wards."

Aislinn slid effortlessly into his mind. She started sifting through his memories. The first one had men—lots of them—on horseback, riding across a heavily forested plain. When she saw their banners, she did a double take. *The Crusades. He has memories of the Crusades. It can't be. Must be another war.* Fascinated, she figured out which one he was. He didn't look all that different. Not really. His hair was longer, down to his waist, and he rode a huge, black horse with some sort of armor trappings. It looked like he was a king, or at least a commander, since he rode at the head of a large company.

In the next memory, Fionn was in a squalid cell. Rats ran up and down the walls. Water dripped incessantly. He sat on a raised platform against one wall. When she looked more closely, she realized he was chained. Dirt streaked his bruised face. His head had been shaved.

Shivering, she hunted for a better memory. And found one. This time, he was in a lavishly hung bedchamber. A woman with long red hair done up in intricate braids, and very little else on, rode atop him. Her back was bowed in pleasure. His hands cupped her breasts. Feeling like a voyeur, Aislinn watched their lovemaking until the woman shuddered on top of him. His hands came round to her hips then, shifting her so she faced away from him. Seemingly understanding what he wanted, she ended up on her knees with him behind her. When she raised her face, Aislinn gasped. The woman looked so much like her that she could've been a twin.

She dropped that memory fast, sifting for another. Time passed. Maybe hours. She heard his voice, but thought it was in the memory she held before her now. He was in a vast library, hunched over a leather-bound volume that had to be a foot thick. Monks glided up and down the aisles between bookshelves, chanting. It sounded Gregorian. *Must be the Middle Ages sometime.*

"Aislinn." A brisk shake pulled her back into herself. "I said it is enough. You have been in my mind for hours."

She felt woozy, as if she'd had too much to drink. She tried to remember all the things she'd seen. One stood out. "Who was the woman who looked like me?"

At first, he looked shocked, then he began to laugh. "Moira. You must mean Moira. I'd nearly forgotten about her." He cocked his head to one side. "Now that you mention it, the two of you do look a great deal alike."

She sucked in a breath to steady herself. And then another. Somehow, she thought it was more than that. Maybe some sort of reincarnative thing, but she didn't have the energy to pursue her line of thought.

"Do you believe me now?" he asked, settling next to her.

She nodded. It wasn't possible that he could hold all those memories if he hadn't lived through them. "The Crusades?" she managed. "Did you fight in the Crusades?"

A confused look screwed his features into a question mark. He shook his head. "Those were on the Continent. They started in France and Italy. No, I've been in plenty of battles, but I never rode in the Crusades." He laughed. "I'm a Celt and a god. Why would I want to lay myself on another god's altar?"

Why indeed? Now that she thought about it, she understood he'd have had little interest in a Christian war. She described his horse and the banners the men had been carrying.

"Oh aye, I remember now. 'Twas one of the times the Vikings had landed. Pesky souls. Mostly, they simply marched across Ireland. Or sailed around it. But not always. I was truly young then." He smiled reassuringly.

"When was that, and how old were you?" Her heart beat too fast. Both her trip through his mind and this conversation unhinged her.

He rolled his eyes. "I believe that battle was around 1250, maybe 1300. Let's see. That would've made me about a hundred and fifty, give or take a few years."

"Wh-What year were you actually born?"

His eyes on her said, *give it a break, woman,* but he finally answered, "Near as I can tell, 1048."

Aislinn kept breathing. She was afraid if she didn't stay on top of things, though, carefully instructing her lungs to inflate, they might not. One thing stuck out in the confusion her mind had become. If he'd really been around all that time, maybe he could help figure out how to send the dark ones back to their worlds. And keep the Lemurians in Taltos.

"I've been working on how to do that."

She rounded on him. "Do. Not. Do. That. Just because you can read my mind, don't. Unless I give you permission." She thought about it for a moment and added, "Or if things are truly desperate."

"Ready to eat something?"

His rapid shift of topics was dizzying, and it pissed her off that he didn't acknowledge her request for the privacy of her thoughts. When she focused on her midsection, though, it felt hollow. She shot him a wry grin. "More than ready."

He got up, went to a sideboard, and carried two plates filled with berries and biscuits over to where she sat. Strips of dried meat were laid over the bread.

"When did you do all this?" She broke a biscuit in half and stuffed it into her mouth. "Mmmmm, pine nut flour. I hated it at first, but it grows on you."

He shrugged. "When you were in my head. It's not easy, letting someone sort through my thoughts, nor is it anything I've allowed before. I never thought you'd stay so long. I needed a diversion, so I made us a meal. Would you like mead to wash everything down?"

Her mouth was full, so she nodded and looked around for Rune and Bella. Before she could ask where they were, he said, "They wanted to hunt, so I opened a passageway for them to leave."

"Do you suppose they're all right?"

Resettling himself next to her, he nodded. "Yes, Bella would let me know if she ran into trouble."

"What about all the stuff you told me before?" she asked.

"What *stuff?*" He cocked an eyebrow, mimicking her tone.

"You know. Stuff that made it sound like you had a normal life with a university teaching job and a wife and two children—" Her eyes widened. "Your children must've had magic. How'd they end up in the vortex?"

"It was all true," he said carefully. "The children weren't mine. She had them before we married. And I'm used to making it sound as if I'm *normal.* It's how I've gotten by all these years."

"What about other children?" Aislinn persisted. "Surely..." Her voice ran down.

"I've been careful about that."

"Good. Maybe it means I'm not pregnant."

A corner of his mouth turned down. "You're not. Conception is a simple enough thing to control."

She ate in silence, questions rioting—no, make that stampeding—through her head. "What were you doing here all those lifetimes before the dark ones broke through? Uh, no, how about starting with when you came over from Europe."

"It's the United Kingdom, not Europe. And that would have been in the late seventeen hundreds. Although I did travel back and forth, once I determined I hadn't lost my magic by migrating to the New World."

"Did you just sort of fade from life to life? Didn't people notice when you, ah, didn't die?"

He shot her a look. It said he'd indulge her this once, but there'd be a finite number of stupid questions he'd answer. "Let's just say I planned well. And I have been many things. It gave me a certain latitude to blend in."

"Have you ever told anyone else who you are?"

He shook his head. "Not since I arrived here. In the Old Country, everyone knew who I was—at least up until the sixteen hundreds or so. After that, people stopped believing in magic."

"Why'd you tell me?" She wasn't certain she wanted to hear the answer.

"Because you're…different."

She waited, but he didn't elaborate. "What's that supposed to mean?"

"I'm not sure. There's something…ethereal about you." He drew in a breath and then blew it out sharply. "I believe you are only at the barest beginnings of discovering who you are. It's something I'd like to help you with."

She bristled. "That's easy. I'm Jacob and Tara Lenear's only child."

"And are ye now, lass?"

"Either talk one way or the other," she snapped peevishly. "Stop going back and forth."

"You're frightened," he said in American English.

"No, I'm not."

"Aye, ye are." He looked at her, and she saw the truth of his words reflected in the depths of his eyes. He laid a hand over hers. "It's a lot to take in all at once. Why don't we switch to a more neutral topic?"

"Such as?"

"Orione. Aren't you curious about the dragon?"

Something clicked deep in her mind. "You're old. So's it. Does that mean you know what it is?"

He smiled. This time, it reached his eyes and was way more than simply teeth. "Yes, I know what it is. At least, I think I do from your description."

"Are you going to tell me?"

The smile morphed into a grin. "I was just waiting for you to ask." His expression took on a somber hue. "Some knowledge must be requested. I believe Orione is actually Dewi—"

"The Celtic dragon god," she gasped.

"You know about her?"

Aislinn nodded. "Yes. Mother used to tell me she'd protect me."

"Turns out your mother was prophetic." His eyes narrowed. "Did she ever say why the dragon would protect you?"

Aislinn drained the rest of her mead and held the cup out for more. He pulled a flask from a shirt pocket and poured. She tried to remember what her mother had told her, but nothing came. Finally, she shook her head. "No. I mean, yes, she told me some things, but I'm damned if I can remember a one of them."

"Want to spend some time outside?"

She looked at him. "It's night, isn't it?"

"Aye, lass, and there's a killer moon out there."

"Maybe we can hunt with the animals." She got to her feet and rifled through her pack, pulling on warmer clothes. In her hurry, the things she'd pilfered from the fishing lodge spilled onto the floor.

He came up behind her, scooped up a flimsy pair of blue thong panties, and looked at them. "Never would've figured you for the type. You're more practical than this."

She quirked a brow. "If you're very, very nice to me, I may just model them for you."

He made a grab for her ass. "Something to look forward to." His dark blue gaze drew her like a magnet. Somehow, she found her way into his arms. He settled his mouth over hers, and desire flamed bright as she kissed him back.

Before things got out of hand, she put her hands against his chest and pushed. "Outside," she panted. "Let's hunt. We can fuck later."

"Tired of me already?"

She laughed. "No. That's the problem. I don't think I'll ever get tired of you." She clapped a hand over her mouth, thinking she'd said too much.

He grinned. "I would hope not. We're just getting to know one another. There are lots of things I haven't done to you—or you to me. For example—"

Because she was afraid he'd start listing them and she'd be lost, she yanked on his arm. "If you don't set the magic to get us out of here, I will."

"You're a hard woman."

She snorted. "No, the problem is, you're hard all the time. Come on, let's get out of here."

Fionn had been right. The moon was nearly full. It shone so brightly, she didn't need her mage light. What a beautiful night. Cold and crisp, with a million stars lighting the sky. She wondered what it would be like to be hundreds of years old like him. To have seen the stars hundreds of thousands of times.

Rune found her within minutes of her arrival. He licked her hands, nuzzling them. "The hunting is good tonight. Little animals all love the full moon."

"Have you fed well?" She ruffled the soft fur behind his ears, and he leaned into her.

Bella landed on her shoulder. The bird's wings made a fluttery sound as she folded them against her body.

"You must really like her." Fionn smirked. "My shoulders are broader." He patted one.

"Hers are softer." Bella smirked right back, staying put.

"Does Bella know?" Aislinn reached for Fionn's hand.

"Does Bella know what?" the bird asked, her claws tightening on Aislinn's shoulder.

"Of course." Fionn ignored the raven. "Bond animals are mind-linked."

"What?" the bird cawed. Her claws dug in so deep Aislinn was sure there'd be bruises, if not actual cuts.

"Hey," she protested. "That hurts." The raven's talons relaxed a little. "I was curious what you knew about your bondmate."

Bella loosed another raucous cry and preened her feathers. "That's easy, human. I know everything."

Intuition that had nothing to do with magic burned in Aislinn's midsection. "She's been with you for a lot of your life?"

Though she'd asked Fionn, the bird answered. "Of course, missy. He and I have been together forever."

Rune nipped her. *What's this all about?*

We'll talk later. She turned to Fionn. "Let's hunt. I need to stretch my legs. I'll take this area." She pointed off to her right. "You choose another. That way, we won't nick one another by mistake with our magic."

"See you in a bit, lass. Good hunting." He melted into the forest.

She tried hard not to think. When she did, her brain drove in crazy circles, coming back to the same impossibilities every time, but without any answers. If she wasn't careful, she found herself reexamining the things she'd found in Fionn's mind. When she realized she wanted to spend more hours in what was a walking, breathing history lesson, she reined herself in.

The Old Ones have been around forever, so why not him? And Dewi...

Dewi was a fairy story.

Apparently not.

She wondered why the Old Ones had another name for the dragon thing, thought maybe Fionn might know, and turned toward home. Despite her musings, she'd managed to snag a marmot and a ridiculously fat raccoon. They had a strong gamey taste, but made excellent soups and stews.

The dragon has two names. Fionn has a name right out of legend. I don't even know Rune's other name. Shit, am I the only one around here with a simple, normal name?

"Come on." She clucked for the wolf. "Let's go home."

"I knew if I waited long enough, you would show yourself," something chuckled from the shadows.

She twirled and dropped her game so she'd have her hands free to fight. "D'Chel?"

"Who else?" The god stepped from a grove of lodge pole pine, wearing his human form. "Nice you were expecting me."

CHAPTER 14

*R*une growled. Hackles rose the length of his back. His body vibrated with outrage where he touched her leg.

"Easy," she cautioned him. *"No heroics."*

D'Chel threw his head back and laughed. "By all means, keep your bond animal under control, so I don't have to kill him."

She ground her teeth together. "Leave us alone."

"Here I thought you wanted me." Luminous eyes, copper this time, glittered against the moonlit night. Shiny, dark hair fluttered around him, moved by a gentle breeze.

"What did I ever do to make you think that?" Though she tried to infuse venom into the question, her voice came out high and squeaky.

"Last time, you sent your mate and animals away so we could be alone." He smiled, perfect teeth nested in a strong jaw. A jab of sexual heat seared her.

"I sent them away so they'd be safe."

"Oh, I see." The lascivious grin widened. "You're into sacrifice. I know some wonderful little games we could play. Besides, I like my women subservient."

She drew her lips into a snarl, baring her teeth. "Never. I'll die first."

"Is that your choice?" He raised a hand lazily. "It's all the same to me, human. There are many more where you came from. I simply thought your spirit might make things more...interesting for a change."

"You can't touch me if I don't want you to. I proved that last time."

"True. But I can kill you from where I stand." Another jolt of lust stabbed her. Fluid gushed down her thighs, reminding her how sore her labia were. "We really could enjoy one another. Look how hot I make you from ten paces. Think what I could do if I were actually touching you."

Memories of bone-chilling cold oozing from his hands rioted through her mind. Maybe he could kill her, but she was damned if she'd let him touch her again.

"Look." He pulled his richly embroidered black robe open and stroked himself. She tried to look away, but couldn't. His cock was mesmerizing. Perfectly formed, perfectly hard, perfectly beautiful...

Stop that! Just stop it. The fucking thing is cold and dead, just like the rest of him. It doesn't matter what it looks like.

"Mmmm," he purred, stroking faster. "If that's the problem, I can make it warm just for you. Come touch me. See for yourself." His hand worked harder.

Something in the air shifted. It felt as if he were stroking her as well. Aislinn fought against it with everything she had, but she came anyway, shaking all over. *Fuck! Another "look, Ma, no hands" orgasm.* Breath jangled in her throat.

He took a step closer, still working himself. A drop of semen glistened on the end of his cock. She yanked her gaze upward until she met his eyes: copper slits, glinting dangerously. Compulsion poured off him. If she didn't do something right then to break his hold on her, she'd close the distance between them and give herself to him.

Aislinn commanded her body to move right that second, goddammit, but she was rooted to the spot, staring into those mystical, alien eyes. Rune growled. Pain rocked her ankle. She glanced down and saw the wolf's jaws circling her lower leg.

"Thank you. Do it again."

Pain tore through her as the wolf tightened his hold—and broke D'Chel's. Aislinn pulled fire as fast as she could and heated her body so D'Chel couldn't actually touch her. Footsteps pounded through the thick undergrowth. She stiffened. Was it another dark god?

"Aislinn!" Fionn shouted. He and Bella crashed into the clearing.

"I was just leaving," she panted, still so hot that all she could think about was getting a cock—anyone's would do—inside her.

"No." His voice was stern. "Let's try to get rid of this bastard." Raising his hands, he released power. It flew straight toward D'Chel. At least the god of illusion had let go of his dick. It bounced outside his robes in an obscene parody of desire as he ducked and wove to avoid Fionn's volley.

She grasped the power filling her and loosed it in jolts, sending it toward D'Chel, but the space where he'd been was suddenly empty. The dark god apparently hadn't liked the odds.

Why am I not surprised?

Aislinn tensed, waiting to see what he'd morph into. After ten breaths, she began to hope he was gone. After twenty, she was sure he was, at least for the moment. Her hands dropped to her sides.

"I think we can go home." She bent and picked up the marmot and the raccoon.

"Why didn't you call me when you knew you were in trouble?" The same unsettling edge that had been there when she'd returned from Taltos ran beneath his voice.

"I thought I could handle it." She drew herself up tall and looked at him. "And I was handling things."

Fionn made a rude sound somewhere between a grunt and a snort. "Och aye, and ye were *handling things* just fine. I smell sex in the air. He had his cock to hand, and ye were standing like a vestal virgin sacrifice, staring at him with cow eyes."

Heat flooded her face, fury mixed with shame. "I didn't go to him," she hissed. "I'll admit I wanted to, but I didn't. When you showed up, I was drawing magic to get myself away from him. Away, not toward." Spinning on her heel, she stalked back through the forest.

His footsteps pounded behind her. Hands settled on her shoulders. She stopped dead because he held her in place. She thought he'd come round in front of her, but instead, he dropped his mouth close to her ear. "You're a proud one, lassie. Your pride will be your undoing."

"Where I come from, we call that spirit," she snapped. "It's what's kept me alive."

"What was your mother's last name?"

"Huh?" Confusion rocked her. Where had that question come from?

"It's a simple enough question. What clan did your mother came from?"

"McLaughlin. Her last name before she married Daddy was McLaughlin."

The hands on her shoulders tightened. "And her family came from Inishowen?"

"That's right. Hey!" She wriggled her shoulders. "You're hurting me."

"Sorry." His fingers, which had felt a lot like Bella's claws, loosened. Something electric radiated from them.

"Did you know," his voice was very quiet, "that you are descended from kings?"

It was so preposterous she threw her head back and laughed. "Don't be ridiculous. There's nothing special about the name McLaughlin. It's as common as rain. If you look in any phone book, there are dozens of them."

"The original spelling was MacLochlainn." He spelled it out for her. "They were the first kings of Ireland." When she heard him again, it was deep in her mind. *"I know, lass. I was there."*

~

SHE STOOD over a pot of water warmed by magic. The raccoon, its meat cut into strips, simmered along with greens and wild mushrooms. Fionn had tried to talk with her after they returned to his home, but she'd asked to be left alone—at least for a while. Still rattled from her confrontation with D'Chel, she didn't want to let slip that Rune was the only thing that stood between her and disaster. The slick place between her thighs reminded her how weak she'd been.

I never should've talked to him. That was my mistake. The minute I saw him, I should have pulled magic and gotten myself away.

"What about calling for me?" Fionn's voice was quiet. "You never did tell me why you didn't."

She twirled so quickly, hot liquid from the pot splattered from her spoon and dripped across the floor. "You're in my head again."

He sat in a rickety chair, watching her, arms crossed over an old fisherman's sweater he'd shrugged into when they returned. A corner of his mouth quirked upward. "Well, you won't talk to me..."

"That doesn't give you the right—" she began and then bit off the rest of her words. She blew out a breath, hoping the simple action would cool the fury raging through her. Giving the stew another stir, she stalked over and sat across from him in the room's only other chair. "I don't understand why I get so angry at you." He opened his mouth, but she shook her head. "No, let me do this my own way. Before I talk about the hard stuff, what would you like me to call you if other people are around? Do you have a more Americanized name?"

His blue eyes twinkled merrily. "I've tried that. Didn't work, because none of them ever got my attention. Call me Fionn." He

161

lapsed into his Gaelic accent. "Just doona be including the rest of my name."

She rolled her eyes. "Stop that. What if I slip up?"

"You'll figure something out. Look, lass, I can't stuff the cat back into the bag."

She pinched the bridge of her nose. "Okay. Next question. Why do the Old Ones have another name for Dewi?"

"They had a dragon god before Mu sank. They must believe Dewi is that god."

"They called it Orione, not Dewi," Aislinn pointed out. Fionn just looked at her, so she went on. "Why are you so sure who I met is your dragon god and not theirs?"

"That's a good question. I suppose at the root of things, I'm not. I'd have to lay eyes on the thing myself to be certain, but Dewi would never have harmed a MacLochlainn. Your mother was right when she told you Dewi protects your clan."

Aislinn turned the information over in her head. The Old Ones had seemed truly shocked Orione hadn't hurt her. "What about the blood part? Is that something Dewi would have done?"

"I could tell you a carefully crafted lie to make you feel better, but I truly don't know. Any magical creature might use blood to determine what sort of being it faced. As it stands, we know two things." He counted on his fingers. "One, it tasted your blood. Two, it let you go. I believe it discovered who you were through your blood."

"Which is why it left," she finished for him and got up to give the stew another stir. "Earlier, you said the Old Ones came from Mu. So that's a true story? About the continent sinking and all."

"Of course. Never could figure out why it dropped out of the histories. Unless the Lemurians wanted to cover their tracks. It was their own damned fault they lost their land—"

She held up both hands. "Uh-uh. Maybe sometime I'd like to hear about it, but my head's too full right now."

A corner of his mouth turned down. "I'm guessing now would

not be the time to tell you the history of Ireland and the MacLochlainn clan, either?"

"Prescient of you." She smiled as she sat back down. Her earlier anger scattered like so much dust. She reached a hand across the small table that lay between them, and he took it. Her next words came hard. "I'm sorry I didn't call you. I just kept thinking it wasn't all that bad. After all, it was just D'Chel. It wasn't as if he had an army at his back—"

"Not that you knew about," Fionn growled.

She waved him to silence. "Hush. I'm trying to apologize. It isn't easy. Anyway, I promise I'll try to do better. It's hard to see myself as part of something. It's been just me for three years."

He lifted her hand to his lips and kissed it. It was such a courtly, old world gesture that it warmed her. "I think our meal's nearly ready," he said. "Not sure what time it is, but it might qualify as a romantic midnight supper."

"Sounds good to me." Her smile widened into a grin. "I'm hungry." Aislinn rose, intent on filling bowls with stew.

Rune had been asleep since feasting on raccoon scraps. He got to his feet and rubbed against her as she crossed the room. Something nagged in the back of her mind. "Oh." She laid a hand on the wolf's head. "Sorry, Rune, I'd forgotten." She turned to face Fionn. "Rune wanted to go back to where he and Marta lived. There are things he thinks I should look at."

Fionn glanced at the wolf.

Rune's tail swished from side to side. His amber gaze shifted from one to the other of them as he spoke. "Marta kept notes about the Old Ones. They may help you. And I would like to visit my home one last time."

"How long since she died?" Fionn asked. "And where exactly did you and Marta live?"

"In a town named Ely. I'm not exactly certain how much time has passed since I lost my last bondmate." Rune shook himself from head to tail tip.

"About a month, maybe a bit more," Aislinn cut in. "Animals measure time differently than we do."

"We should leave tomorrow, then. We don't want anyone to get there ahead of us, and it seems much time has already passed." Fionn got to his feet. Looking at Rune, he asked, "Did Marta ward her home?"

"Of course."

Fionn exhaled sharply. "Then we may not be too late." He placed his hands on Aislinn's shoulders. "Sit. I'll get our food."

She returned to her chair, thinking about looters. Christ, she'd looted the McCloud Fishing Lodge just yesterday. Or had it been the day before? Bottom line was everyone took whatever they could, wherever they could find it. Unless Marta's house had been very well hidden, wards or no wards, they may well find it stripped of everything. No one else would care about her notes. They'd see paper as something to start a fire with.

"Thanks." She beamed at Fionn, who'd just set a steaming bowl, fragrant with herbs and spices, in front of her.

"Eat. You could use a bit more meat on your bones." He looked down his nose at her. "Don't crinkle up those golden eyes. Do you know they're almost exactly the same shade as Rune's?"

"Mother's eyes," she mumbled. "I have my mother's eyes."

"They're a MacLochlainn trait," he informed her with a hint of a supercilious grin.

They ate in silence. Once she started on the thick stew, she realized she was half-starved. It was easy to follow one spoonful with another, washed down by several cups of mead, and not think at all.

"Maybe," she ventured after her bowl was empty, "as long as we're heading to where Rune and Marta lived, we could take whatever we find there to my place. It will be much closer than this. We're still in California. Where I first met Rune was only a couple hundred miles from home."

"Where's that?"

She held up her hands, palms outward. "Near the Utah-Colorado border, about halfway down Utah."

Fionn crinkled his brow in thought. "I can't tell for certain without dredging out my maps, but if Rune means Ely, Nevada, he and Marta lived just about dead center between our two homes." He nodded. "Sure, we can go to your house if you'd like."

Remembering Travis's interest in her library, she felt uncomfortable. "There's something I should tell you."

His gaze zeroed in on hers, suddenly wary. He crooked two fingers as if to say, *out with it.*

"I, ah, I have books, too."

A long, uneasy silence bounced back and forth between them. "That's it?" he demanded. "You made a point of telling me you have books? So what?" He flung an expansive arm skyward. "I have books. Without them the knowledge of the world will truly die out."

"I-I felt the same way," she murmured, "which is why I kept all I could from Mom and Dad, even though it was forbidden."

"Are you done?" He glanced at her empty bowl. When she nodded, he put it on the floor for Rune. Getting to his feet, he came to her, pulled her upright, and led her to some cushions. "Sit with me.

"People have been trying to outlaw books on-again, off-again, ever since the fourteen hundreds, when Gutenberg invented the printing press. The thing I fail to understand is how the combination of the dark gods and the Lemurians managed to break the will of billions of people on this planet."

"I wonder if there's even a single billion left," she muttered.

"Oh, I think there is."

"How would you know?"

He draped an arm around her shoulders and pulled her against him. "I know because I'm not the only Celtic god left. We have ways of communicating with one another. And,"—his eyes glinted darkly —"we number far more than the dark gods. I'm not so sure about the Lemurians. No one has ever been certain of their numbers."

She thought about the hundreds she'd seen. "There were a lot of them in Taltos. It was odd, though. They all seemed to be hurrying somewhere. I wondered at the time what they were up to."

"It could've been illusion. Maybe they wanted you to think there were lots of them. It's possible that only the three you actually spoke to were real."

Aislinn considered it and wished she'd paid closer attention. "I just don't know. I suppose I might've been able to use my Mage senses to figure that out. Sorry. I was so nervous, it never occurred to me." She thought of something and cocked her head to one side. "They must've been real, because they were still there when Rune merged his senses with mine."

"Hmph. Not the answer I'd hoped for, but it's good to know all the same. Come closer." He tightened his grip around her shoulders.

He was murmuring wordless endearments, breath warm against her neck, and caressing her shoulder with calloused fingers, when something occurred to her. Drawing away slightly, she tilted her head and gazed at him. "If there are more of you than them, why haven't you gotten together with your buddies and blown the dark gods back to the hell they came from? I'm pretty sure the Bal'ta and other abominations would go away if that happened. Then we'd just have the Old Ones to contend with."

"It seems like a long time to you since the dark gods came."

He posed it as a statement, so she continued to study his face. Of course it was a long time. What was he, brain damaged?

He must have been inside her head, because the corners of his mouth twitched. "Lass, three years is nothing in real time. It's the blink of a cosmic eye. We were waiting to see if the human inhabitants of this planet could rescue themselves. Generally, we don't like to interfere."

"Were you going to wait until we were all dead?" She bristled and pulled away from his embrace. "Shot to shit in that damned movable vortex? If you had some means to alter what was happening and didn't use it—"

Fury ripped through her. She'd been fighting with everything she had, even though she knew it wouldn't be enough. Earth, her Earth, was worth it. What had he been doing all that time? Nothing! Fucking nothing, that's what. "Damn you." She drew back a hand to slap him, but he caught it midair.

"It's my turn to apologize." He laid her hand gently in her lap. "We kept thinking humans would mobilize. We didn't count on the Lemurians slaughtering so many. By the time we got worried, millions had walked into that damned vortex like sheep—"

"What exactly is it?" she interrupted, still furious. "Do you know?"

"It's a gateway. They can open it wherever they want."

"Yes, but where does it go?"

He shrugged. "To Hell." At the look in her eyes, he held up both hands. "Near as we can tell, it emits a highly specific radioactivity that scrambles human brains. It kills instantly. The cells just explode."

"It sounds…unnatural." She went cold inside.

"It is. Why do you think there are so many shades? The vortex interrupts their journey across the veil. Makes them forget what their spirits need to do once their bodies are no longer living." Pain floated behind his eyes.

"Do you think it's too late?" The anger drained out of her, replaced by fear.

"I hope not." He set his jaw resolutely. "The silver lining in this cloud is all those humans who discovered they carried magic within them. Were it not for the Harmonic Convergence and all those synchronized Surges, the majority of humans would've remained magic-less."

"I'm not sure I understand."

"The Convergence, and the Surges that followed it, distorted the energies binding this world with others parallel to it. Those energies created the possibility of magic here on Earth, not just for the gods, but for everyone."

"So everyone who threw their lives away had magic?" she asked, aghast.

"Not all, but many. Just not enough magic to satisfy the Lemurians. They're up to something. I'll be damned if I know what it is, though."

"Mother," she murmured. "If anyone was magical, it was Mother." She thought about Tara Lenear's wild hair and dead eyes once the madness took hold. Sorrow tore through her like a riptide, tears so close to the surface it took all her will to keep from collapsing into helpless sobs.

His mage light fluttered close. He studied her face. "You, *mo croi*, my heart, would have found your magic even without the Surges." She opened her mouth, aching to talk about her mother—to tell Fionn about her—but he shook his head. "Not tonight. We need sleep. I want to be out of here as close to dawn as we can."

CHAPTER 15

They initiated the jump from underground, even though it meant they couldn't go as far. Fionn insisted, saying, "If that dark hellion waylays us the second our heads pop out, we'll burn a lot of energy that could be spent traveling."

"Where are we?" She looked at terrain a little more arid than what they'd left, but nothing like the innards of Nevada.

"Does it matter?" He gave her a crooked grin. "You take the next jump."

It felt good to be away from the forest around Fionn's. Though it was ridiculous, she'd nearly talked herself into D'Chel living nearby. *There are lots of reasons I saw him twice that don't include him living there,* she lectured herself. *For all I know, he has his own private hell on one of the border worlds.*

"Doona be making that mistake." The Irish lilt was back in force. "The dark gods can go anywhere. Quickly, too. It was coincidence he found us. Once found, though, he saw us as easy pickings and decided to stay." Fionn winked at her. "Delectable morsel that ye are, lass. What man could resist?"

"Bah!" She tapped into magic as she talked. "And ye'll be turning this lassie's puir head with all that balderdash."

He made a sour face.

"If you don't like having Irish tossed back at you," she said, "then don't use it in the first place. There. Ready when you are."

Rune came to her side. Bella lit on her shoulder. Fionn put an arm around her. "Lead out."

She pictured one of the many places she knew in northern Nevada, gratified when her magic worked and they came out within spitting distance of her planned location. Squinting, she looked at the sun. "This may do it for today." She checked around them for traces of dark magic and blew out a relieved breath when she didn't find any. "Let's figure out a place to camp."

"I can take us farther. Remember, there are two of us now." Fionn walked to where Rune and Bella had begun hunting rodents in a sagebrush thicket. He clucked, and the wolf loped to his side. Fionn shut his eyes. "Send me an image of where you lived with Marta. Thanks! Good hunting. I'll tell you and Bella when we're ready to leave."

He returned to where Aislinn sprawled in the dirt, drinking from her water bottle. She turned her gaze upward. "Fine by me if we can get all the way to Rune and Marta's today." She smiled to herself. It was actually much more than fine. It was incredible that they could cover so much distance in such a short time. Made things easier. She recalled the time it had taken her to get from her home to Mount Shasta. Of course, it was farther, and she'd stopped off in that other world, but still... Maybe pairing up with someone could work to her advantage.

Yeah, I've spent so much time avoiding entanglements, it never occurred to me that having someone else around could actually be helpful.

"You're only just now coming to appreciate that?" Fionn was on his knees, facing away from her bent over his maps.

"Awk. Damn it! What? Do you live inside my head?" She crawled over to him and studied the map he'd laid out.

"No, lass. I merely visit there occasionally. It's fair interesting, though. Maybe I should spend more time—"

She slugged him in the thigh, but he just laughed. "Ye canna hurt me, lassie."

"Stop that, too."

"Why does it bother you?" He looked at her. Curiosity shone from the depths of his eyes.

She swallowed hard. *May as well tell him. If I do, maybe he'll quit.* "Because it reminds me so much of Mother, it hurts."

"Och aye." He pulled her into his arms. "Speaking in a brogue is more comfortable for me, but I'll try to honor your wishes."

Wanting to change the subject, she wriggled free and jabbed a finger at the map. "Show me where we are."

"Here." He pointed. "According to Rune, we are going there." Fionn tapped at a spot not far from the Utah-Nevada line.

She gauged the distance. "Shouldn't take long."

"No, not long. What do you think we'll find?"

She turned her palms upward. "Don't know. Depending on how voluminous Marta's notes are, though—assuming they're still there —we might spend a couple days sifting through them."

"I thought the same." He rolled back onto his heels and then proceeded to fold the maps and stuff them into the pocket of an old khaki field jacket. Patched pants made of the same fabric, battered leather boots, and a faded sweatshirt blazoned with *Go Bears* hung off his tall, well-muscled frame. Fionn extended a hand and helped her to her feet.

"I should've shopped for you while I was at that fishing lodge. This"—she fingered a hole in his jacket—"isn't long for this world."

He shouldered a North Face backpack. It looked newer than his clothes. "Get your things," he suggested and then whistled. Rune came at a run. Bella dive-bombed Fionn, spreading her wings at the last possible moment.

Aislinn laughed. "What's that? Her version of chicken?"

Bella cawed at her, sounding annoyed.

Fionn eyed his bird. "Looks like she has your number, sweetheart."

Another displeased avian sound burst from the raven. "I am not a chicken."

"Oh, so that's it!" Aislinn dissolved in laughter.

Fionn joined her.

~

AISLINN HAD BEEN correct that the jump wouldn't take long. Between Fionn's magic, which was stronger than hers, and the relatively short distance, they stood in front of a dilapidated yellow and blue Victorian before Rune even had a chance to merge with her.

"Great!" Aislinn bounded forward, hit something invisible that tossed her backward through the air, and landed on her ass.

"Hmph. Answers one question," Fionn muttered. "Wards are still intact."

"No shit." Taking his proffered hand, Aislinn pulled herself upright and dusted dirt off her pants. She looked reproachfully at Rune. "Why didn't you stop me?"

"You moved so quickly, I did not have a chance."

"Can you disable them?" she asked the wolf.

"No, but they'll let me in." As if to demonstrate, he sashayed up to the front door and placed a paw to the right of it. The heavy, ornate oak slab swung inward. Rune disappeared inside.

"Good for him. Less good for us." Aislinn took off her pack, dropped it in the dirt, and sat on it. She sent her Mage senses spinning outward to try to figure out how to dismantle the warding. When she sensed the complexity of Marta's work, she groaned. "This will take days," she muttered.

"Maybe not." Fionn returned from walking around the house. "The back is far less complicated. I say we attack it from there." He pulled her to her feet for a second time. "What is it about you and sitting in the dirt. Do you like it down there? Get your pack."

They worked together. He illuminated the working so it was visible, while she clipped a large enough hole in the weave to let them through. "Well," she said as the last piece fell, making a hissing noise, "that wasn't so bad."

"I wouldn't be too cocky, lass. Marta may have other surprises for us. I know I would." He eyed Bella. The raven was perched in a large cottonwood tree, preening her glossy black feathers. "You stay there. I'm not sure we have a safe path yet. Or that we need you inside at all."

"Yes, I do not care for inside." With a squawk, the raven went back to grooming herself, apparently still annoyed about Aislinn's chicken analogy.

They crept forward. Spooked by Fionn's pronouncement, Aislinn kept her Mage senses alert and fanned about her. They'd no sooner cleared the warding surrounding the house, when a muted buzzing that grew louder by the moment broke the late afternoon's silence.

"Bees," Fionn hissed.

"No," Aislinn corrected, seeing them, "wasps." She slapped a ward around herself. For a time, all she could see was wasp bodies trying to get to her, stingers embedded in her ward. Suddenly, they fell away en masse. "What the hell?" she muttered and cautiously withdrew her protective spell. She tried to avoid stepping on the wasps, but there were so many it was impossible. Small bodies squished under her boots.

"I killed them." Fionn's voice was harsh. Angry welts covered his face and neck. "Let's tackle the house."

"How many stung you?"

Glancing at her, he shook his head, looking annoyed. "Oh, not more than a couple dozen. You were damned quick with your warding. Nice work." Grudging admiration rang beneath his words.

"Once we get to the bottom of Marta's protections, I can Heal those."

"Thanks. I may take you up on that." He hesitated fractionally and then favored her with a wanton grin. "I am perfectly capable of healing myself, lass, but I far prefer the feel of your magic against my skin than my own."

"You're thinking about sex?" she demanded. "Now? We have to figure out a way in—" Realizing what she'd just said, she laughed.

"Yes," he chuckled. "I am all about finding ways into things. Especially you. Careful now." They made their way to the front of the house and up the steps, stopping a short distance from the door. "Rune," Fionn called to the wolf, "open the door for us."

"Smart," Aislinn murmured. "He'll have a way both in and out that won't hurt him."

"Maybe."

The door swung inward soundlessly, as if someone had just oiled the hinges. Fionn held up a hand. "Let me go first."

She pushed outward with her Mage senses.

"Stop that!" Fionn's voice was sharp. "The wolf may have a way through the wards, but you could blow it to smithereens with magic."

"Sorry. Hadn't thought about a self-destruct aspect." She hastily pulled every shred of her power back inside herself and then tried to make herself close to invisible, even quieted her breathing.

Fionn crept forward. At the last moment, he dropped to his knees and leaned back. The swoosh of metal grated, harsh against her ears. Blades sprang from the upper doorsill, crisscrossing in the middle. They would've sliced Fionn in half if he'd stepped over the lintel.

"How did you know?" she cried.

"Sensed it. Marta left the lower portion open. Maybe she thought someone might force Rune to bring them here."

A low whine sounded from just inside the house. "I did not know. I am grateful you were not injured," Rune said. "Sorry—"

"Hush." Fionn ducked under the crossed blades. "Your bondmate loved you very much. No need to apologize for that. Aislinn, come on."

She looked at the half doorway, took off her pack, kicked it through, and followed Fionn inside. Straightening, she looked around. In contrast to the rundown appearance of the outside, the interior was spotless. Not so much as a speck of dust lay on anything. Furnished with antiques to match the age of the home, it looked as if she'd stumbled into a nineteenth century museum. The low hum of magic reached her ears. *Must be why the house is still clean.* "What did Marta do for a living?" she asked Rune.

"She was a doctor. And she kept on doctoring until close to the end. People still got sick after the dark ones came." Rune's voice resonated with pride.

Aislinn ruffled his fur. "Wonderful news," she murmured. Then she thought about her Healer magic. Perhaps she didn't really need anything as prosaic as penicillin anymore, but she'd look through whatever Marta had just the same. "Do you suppose there are medicines left here?"

"We don't require them, but it seems likely," Fionn said. "No one else would've been able to storm the fortress. By Brigid's tits, we barely got in."

Aislinn giggled. "Goddess, eh? Is she a friend of yours? And does she have nice tits?"

"Yes to all three."

"On a more serious note, do you think we've hit the last of Marta's little surprises to trap the unwary?"

He cocked his head to one side. Strands of blond hair swung across his eyes. "Not sure. We won't know until we're through searching the rooms."

"I can show you where her study was," Rune offered, "and where she saw patients."

"Let's save the study for last," Fionn said. "If there are more wards, that's where I would've placed them."

They started with the kitchen. Aislinn pulled cupboards and drawers open. "Oh my God," she exclaimed excitedly. "There's food here. Real food. Flour and sugar. Where the fuck would she have gotten those? And rice and noodles." A broad smile split her face.

"We might stay here until it's gone. I don't have anything nearly this sumptuous at my house." She looked at Fionn. "Neither do you."

"We could take some of it with us," Fionn suggested.

"You don't understand." She stopped in the center of the kitchen and turned to face him, hands on her hips. "I've been hungry for most of the last three years. Besides, I've never had much luck transporting food. Though it might work if it wasn't in cans."

"Och aye, and I do understand." He met her gaze. "But you're not alone anymore."

So that means I don't get to make my own decisions.

"Yes." His voice was even. "It means that and other things as well."

She pounded a fist on the stone counter. "Damn it." Her voice rose to a shriek. She tried to modulate it, but it was too late. "Stay out of my head." She barreled out of the kitchen and right into something that felt like a thousand watt fence. The last thing she remembered before losing consciousness was feeling like all her cells had fried.

~

THE HIGH CEILINGED room swam into focus. Fionn chanted something in Gaelic, breaking off to shout, "Yes!" as soon as her eyes fluttered open. Aislinn felt magic leave her body as he withdrew his spell. She lay on her back on the hardwood floor in the kitchen, her head cradled on his lap. Rune was licking her face and saying her name over and over in her mind.

She struggled to sit, but Fionn held her in place. "Not yet, *mo croi.* I nearly lost you. Go easy. Here."

He tipped a flask against her lips. She sputtered as he poured mead down her throat, but felt better once its heat spread through her. Apparently satisfied that between him and the mead, she'd been reclaimed from death's door, he helped her sit.

"Have some more." He handed her the flask. "Just so you're not surprised, I fixed your face while I was about things. Oh, and I got rid of the Old Ones' marks on you, too."

Memory of what she'd done flooded her. "Sorry," she mumbled and took another hefty swig of mead. Reaching curious fingers to where the dragon's gash had been, she found smooth skin. Aislinn tried to smile. "Uh, thanks. Why'd you remove the tattoos?"

"That's how they track you." Not only was he not smiling, his brows were drawn together, darkening his perfect features.

Her body tensed. "Why those dirty, fucking bastards. They told me it was so I'd have access to some of their memories."

"At least that part is true. I take it you didn't know the rest?"

She shook her head. "That was pretty stupid of me not to realize." She winced. "And incredibly stupid to go flying through that doorway."

"Glad you said it so I don't have to." He shot her a look. "It shortens the lecture, but doesn't excuse you entirely. Never, never, never run off half-cocked in a strange place where you don't know what booby traps someone might have set."

I deserved that.

"Yes, and likely a good deal more, but I'll stop there. Can you get up?"

"I think so." Her insides wobbled, but she felt mostly like herself.

Rune rubbed against her leg. "I am grateful to Fionn. When you hit the floor, I was certain you were dead."

"She was," Fionn said, his voice thick with emotion. "But we managed, you and me, didn't we?" He stroked Rune from head to tail. "Fortunately"—he looked pointedly at Aislinn—"your wolf follows directions."

"Not always," she shot back. "I presume I stumbled into the study." She gestured to a door on the far side of the kitchen, opposite to the one that led to the main hallway and front door.

Fionn nodded. "It's the only part of the house, other than the attic and basement, we haven't looked at. How about if you stay in the kitchen while I figure out how to get past her wards? It shouldn't be all that difficult since we untangled the ones around the house."

"I could go through her medicines while you do that."

Fionn frowned. "Show me where Marta kept them," he told the wolf. "You stay here," he called over one shoulder. "Don't even think about moving."

Her temper simmered at being ordered about, but she called it to heel. It had nearly gotten her killed with her headlong dash into the equivalent of an electrified fence.

I need to think more. React less.

To divert herself, she started with the kitchen cupboards, moving dry goods to the spacious stone countertops. It was obvious after the first cupboard that Marta had stocked far more food than they could ever carry away from her house. "I have it," she murmured. "We'll just reset those wards. That way, we can come back here to restock." She wondered how easy it would be to retract the swords guarding the front door, but assumed there had to be some way to accomplish it. They'd left the front door open, rather than taking time to figure out how to get it closed again.

She'd started putting food back into the cupboards when Fionn called her. She stopped what she was doing, stepped into the main hallway, and followed the sound of his voice. Polished interior doors graced both sides of the hall. Aislinn's booted feet sank into a lovely, patterned Oriental rug runner. Just before the passage ended, she turned into a room lined with glass-fronted cabinets.

"Marta's medical office seems safe enough," Fionn said, giving her a quick kiss. "I'm off to solve the study problem."

"Wait," she called after him. "What about the Lemurians' knowledge? What did I lose along with those tattoos?"

"Nothing," he grunted, glancing back at her. "I know everything they did and more." He disappeared down the hall before she could ask anything further.

"I will stay with you." Rune licked her hand. The wolf seemed pathetically grateful she hadn't died. When Aislinn thought about it, she could see why. Rune had loved Marta. It would've been hard for him if her magic caused the death of his new bondmate.

"Wonderful!" she exclaimed. "I like your company."

Low whines, mingled with small whuffy sounds, filled the air. If Rune had been a cat, he would've been purring, but she decided not to tell him that. Aislinn squatted next to him and hugged him hard. He licked her face, and she realized she was crying. *What's happened to me? I'm an emotional mess. Got to pull myself together.* Snuffling, she stood and began checking the contents of Marta's medical office.

"Holy shit," she told Rune after a few minutes. "There's nothing she didn't have here. Wonder how the hell she restocked her medicines and medical supplies after the places she bought them closed down?"

"Probably the same way she came by all that food. She used her Hunter magic to find far more than the dark." Fionn stood in the doorway. She hadn't heard him approach, possibly because the thick carpet muffled his footsteps. "I cleared the electrical field."

"Wow! You did that really fast."

"Magic wielders use similar patterns for all their spells. It was akin to the outside wards, so I was able to figure it out easily enough."

Aislinn turned to gaze at him. Lines creased his face that she didn't remember seeing before. She could only guess the strain of watching her die and being afraid his magic wouldn't be up to the task of bringing her back. "Thanks," she said softly, "for saving my life."

He closed the distance between them in two long strides. "Don't you get it yet?" he said against her hair as his arms closed tight about her. "I'm not sure how it happened, but you and I are fated to be together. The blood of the earliest Irish kings dances in your veins. For years, I sought you, settling for others when it seemed an impossible task. In truth, I despaired ever finding you. I tried everything. Nothing ever worked. You asked me before about children. That was why I never had any. I couldn't find their proper mother."

He drew in a ragged breath and pulled her even closer. "I don't understand how it is I've found you now, with the Earth standing at the edge of a precipice, yet here you are. And I am grateful."

"I was foretold somehow?" Her voice was muffled against his chest. What he said didn't seem possible. In spite of the warmth of his arms, it gave her the creeps.

"Och aye, lassie. My lassie. Heart of my heart, breath of my breath. I shall be holding you still when light leaches out of the world." The Gaelic words swirled, soft against her ears.

"My mother used to sing me that."

"Of course she did. Because you are royalty from the ancient line. Your mother was an Irish queen."

CHAPTER 16

"How could you possibly know that?" Aislinn pushed back far enough to look at him.

"I've been inside you. Held your blood in my hands. In my soul. You've done enough Healing. You understand how it's done—"

"Not what I meant. How could you know Mother was some sort of queen?"

"I recognize your blood—and hers. We thought Tara was the last of her line," he said without missing a beat. "She disappeared from Ireland about thirty years ago. Some of my...associates have been hunting her ever since. Since she was the last living MacLochlainn, it was her duty to return to Ireland, produce children with a proper father—"

She waved him to silence, trying to think. "Mom and Dad met at Cambridge." She counted back on her fingers, realizing with a shock that it had, indeed, been thirty years ago.

"Did you never visit any of your mother's people?" His voice was soft, but insistent, as if he already knew the answer, but wanted to be sure she paid close attention to it.

"No. She told me she didn't get on with them. That they didn't approve of Daddy..." Her voice ran down. Could Fionn's story possibly be true?

"Och aye, and 'tis more than true. Naught but males were born to the MacLochlainn line for centuries. They even married well outside the clans, hoping against hope to produce a female. Tara was the first since, well in a verra long time. I thought 'twas she my future was linked to. I waited for her to grow a bit, but by the time I showed up to claim her, she was gone." He shrugged helplessly. "See, and I was wed to another. I needed to extricate myself."

"You knew Mother?"

"Aye, that I did."

Aislinn's head spun. Prophecies, matches that had been preordained, or some such thing, for centuries... It was too much to get her mind around. He was still talking, but she'd stopped listening. The last thing she heard was "...and so, 'twas not her, but you—"

She shook her head. "Stop. I need to eat. All I've had since we left your house this morning is mead."

"Of course." He sounded contrite. Hands on her shoulders, he maneuvered her toward the door.

She shook him off. "I can walk." She heard the sharp undercurrent in her voice and felt like an ingrate. He'd just saved her life. She took a deep breath. "Can we talk about something else, please? I know I started it by asking about Mother, but I need time to make sense of all this." *And I don't want you to be with me because of something written down hundreds of years ago...* She glanced over her shoulder, wondering if he'd read *those* thoughts, but he didn't give any indication. An iron bar of tension settled just between her shoulder blades. Her teeth were set so tightly her jaw ached.

"I'll make us a meal," he said, his voice tone carefully neutral.

"Great. Thanks." *I'm so scattered, if I cooked, God only knows what would end up in the mix.* "I can start on Marta's journals—or notes, or whatever she has." Aislinn strode through the kitchen to the study. She felt him behind her, but made a conscious effort to not look back. Her heart was such a muddle she needed some alone time.

Marta had bound journals. Years' worth of them. She'd apparently begun setting her thoughts to paper during medical school and had never stopped. It took Aislinn a while to determine just which of the leather-bound volumes covered the years since the Surge. Finally, she found one for each year. Thinking that felt manageable, she settled at a cozy antique mahogany desk with glass-fronted cubbies, called up her mage light since the afternoon was long gone, and began to read.

~

"HERE YOU GO." Fionn plopped a good-sized bowl in front of her. It smelled wonderful.

She smiled. It had been good to have a break from thinking about her family and his insistence she was his long-lost soul mate. "Looks good. What's in it?"

"Rice. Dried meat. Dried vegetables, herbs. I'll fetch mine. Do you want mead or water?"

"Both."

While they ate, she told him what she'd discovered in the first third of the first journal. Marta had still been spending most of her time with her patients. But she'd seen the writing on the wall and was already stocking up on food, medicines, and medical supplies. Much of her journaling had chronicled fears that shortages would plague her little town in eastern Nevada, though perhaps not quite as quickly as they hit the larger urban areas.

Aislinn was surprised to find that Marta had been married. She'd asked Rune, who was sticking to her like flypaper, what happened. The wolf had snarled one word: vortex.

"Anyway..." Aislinn set her empty bowl down. "That's about as far as I got. I need sleep before I can do much more."

"There's still running water in the house," Fionn informed her. "It's some sort of gravity-fed mechanism from a spring up the hill out back. Should work so long as the temperature stays above freezing. If you'd like a bath, I can warm the water." He smiled. "Or you can."

"Aren't you tired?"

He shook his head. "I will be, but not yet. I'll pick up reading where you left off."

She selected the bathroom off the hall, rather than the one in the master bedroom. The bathtub was an old-fashioned claw foot affair. It felt positively decadent when she sank into water warmed by the spell he'd taught her. She used real soap and shampoo, thinking how much she'd taken for granted in her old life. When she was drying off, she let her thoughts drift to Fionn. Though it was subtle, a formality that hadn't been there before their conversation in Marta's medical office marred his features when he looked at her. Replaying what they'd said, she cringed. He'd been so excited to have verified she was his specially selected life's mate. Something about the way he'd merged with her while he saved her life must have confirmed the information.

Specially selected by whom? I need to ask him about that.

Yes, he'd been thrilled, but she was horrified to find that she was little more than a pawn on a giant chessboard. She knew she'd hurt his feelings. Did she want to deal with that now?

Maybe it will be easier once we've both rested...

With a towel wrapped around herself—a real towel, deep blue terrycloth—she padded down the hallway. A light shone from the master bedroom, across from Marta's medical office. Aislinn stopped in the doorway. Fionn lay propped on pillows on one side of an enormous bed. It had carved head and footboards made of some rich-looking dark wood. Maybe mahogany, like the desk. The light she'd seen was his mage light hovering next to him. He patted the other side of the bed. "Best place in the house to sleep. I checked all the rooms. There's another full bathroom just through that door." He flicked fingers to his left.

"I know. I found it earlier." *Maybe he's not mad at me after all.*

"I was never mad. Just disappointed."

For some reason, his incursion into her head didn't bother her this time. Maybe she was getting used to it. Maybe she was just tired. Fionn smiled. There was hope in that smile. And determination. His blond hair looked damp.

"Did you get a bath?" she asked.

"A shower."

"Were you able to warm the water?"

He shook his head.

She grinned, her gaze wandering over him. Aislinn sucked in a breath. No one should have such a perfect body. "Well, you could've joined me."

"I thought about it. Wasn't certain you'd welcome me." Blue eyes augured into her.

She dropped her gaze. "Thanks for giving me some space. I needed it." She paused. "But you could have shared my bath. Tub's big enough for an army."

He laughed, and the tension between them evaporated.

Rune was in a corner. Somehow, she knew that had been his place. He lay there, looking incredibly relaxed, head atop his paws, tail curved around his hindquarters. She stopped next to him, hunkered down, and stroked his fur. It was matted in places.

"You're home."

"I am. It feels…different without her, but I slept here for many years. Sometimes, Marta was away. I have been pretending this is one of those times. That way I can enjoy my memories of her without grieving."

Aislinn wrapped an arm around the wolf's neck. "Sleep well, bondmate." Bending forward, she kissed him.

Fionn had Marta's journal propped open on his stomach. She looked at where he was and realized he was nearly done with the first volume. *Good.* The sooner they found out if Marta knew anything, the quicker they could put her information to use.

Draping her towel over an upholstered chair, Aislinn crawled onto the bed and sank into mattress springs. A real bed. "This is the first time I've slept in a bed since my house got trashed." The sheets felt silky against her skin.

"Have you missed it?" He laid the journal aside and turned to face her.

"Mostly, I don't let myself think about things like that. Why long for something I can never have again?"

"You didn't answer my question."

She looked hard at him. "It's the only answer you're going to get. No point in playing *Let's Remember*. It tears my heart out."

He looked as if he wanted to gather her close. Instead, he said, "Are you awake enough to hear what I found?" Something lay beneath his words. Was it excitement?

She turned onto her side and propped her head on her hand. "Sure."

"Seems we were on to something when we thought there might be a link between the dark gods and the Lemurians. At least, according to Marta…"

SHE WOKE to sunlight streaming through leaded glass panes. The bedroom faced east, so its windows caught the morning sun. Fionn's body was snugged up next to her back, his arm woven around her waist. He had a musky, exotic scent. She breathed it in hungrily. It reminded her of the mead he gave her. Sometime during the night, he'd pressed inside her, tentative at first until he was certain she wanted him there.

She snorted inwardly. She was damned near as helpless with him as she was with the dark gods. Once he got his hands on her, touching her, stroking her, all she could think about was fucking him. Apparently sensing she was awake, he nuzzled her neck and then trailed his tongue lazily down to the hollow in her collarbone. He shifted a hand and captured one of her breasts. She giggled.

"Again?"

"And why not?" he demanded, voice half-lost against her body.

She felt him harden against her ass, pressing against its curves. She pushed back, and he made a sound low in the back of his throat. She loved that sound. It was the same one he made when he came. Like a jungle cat purring. Aislinn turned in his arms so she could look at him. His eyes gleamed blue like the sea, with amber flecks around the irises. His hair splayed across the pillows in a golden cascade. She traced the lines of his face with a finger. Her breath caught in her throat. "You're so beautiful. It's not fair for a man to be so exquisite."

He caught her hand in one of his. Bringing it to his lips, he kissed it. "I'll take any advantage I can with you, lass. 'Tis a prickly one, you are. You could be a poster girl for Irish temper."

"At least I come by it honestly."

"Och aye, goes along with that bright mop of yours." He grabbed a lock of her hair and brushed the tips of her nipples with it.

"Stop." She batted playfully at him.

He took her hand again and sucked on her fingers, making the most incredible sensations shoot right to her crotch. What was happening between her thighs intensified as he worked his way down to her little finger. How was it possible? He wasn't even touching her, for God's sake. Suddenly, she couldn't wait another second. Straddling him, she opened herself and groaned when he thrust upward with his hips and plunged himself into her. He watched her, his gaze never leaving hers, as she rode him. She arched her back in delight as he probed deeper, discovering places no one else had come close to.

He gripped her hips, setting a rhythm. "Look at me, lass."

She did and lost herself in the hum of passion sparking from his eyes, which were alight with lust. Something shifted, and she was him, feeling the heat of her body around his cock, sharing the tension that shattered as he came hard deep within her. Her body dissolved around him in rhythmic release, but she was so caught up in the wonder of his orgasm, she barely noticed her own.

When he started moving inside her again, she realized she was back in her own body. "Mmmm… That was incredible, but this is a good place to stop." She clambered off him and dropped her legs over the side of the bed. "If it was up to you, we'd spend all our time fucking." She walked to his side of the bed and trailed a finger down his still-erect cock, glistening with fluids from their bodies. "Doesn't it ever go away?"

He laughed. "You sound as if you wish it would."

Aislinn's face heated, and she knew she was blushing. "No, not exactly. It's just…" She wasn't sure what she wanted to say. That other men weren't so interested after they came. That she wasn't, either. Christ, she'd come so many times since she met Fionn, she didn't understand why she was within a hairsbreadth of saying to hell with it and jumping on top of him again.

He snaked out a hand and grasped her wrist. "It hasna been like this for me afore either, lass. Where no matter how many times I fuck you, I'm left wanting more." She heard truth in his words, even without her Seeker senses. "We're fated for one another. 'Tis the reason I hunted you for centuries."

"Fated by whom?"

"The MacCumhaills were not always gods. 'Twas the link betwixt us and the MacLochlainns that made us so. Our lines have mated for better than a thousand years." He looked away. "Ye doona have a corner on the stubborn market, lass. I railed against that fate, told the others I should be able to pick whatever woman I chose. By the time I understood I was incomplete, that I needed a MacLochlainn by my side, I couldna find one." He looked at her again, a sheepish light in his eyes.

"This is getting way too woo-woo for me." She extricated her wrist. "I know I asked, but let's find something to eat. Then I want to look for Marta's personal gateway to Taltos—the one you told me about last night."

"We can look for it, lass." He was on his feet so quickly she wondered how he'd managed it. "But we're not going to try to open it." He caught her wrist again. "Agreed?"

"All right." Aislinn looked around for her clothes and then remembered they were sitting in a heap on the bathroom floor. "Do you suppose Marta has any coffee?"

"I'll look." Fionn slid worn khaki pants over his hips and pushed his cock out of the way to button them. He dragged the *Go Bears* sweatshirt over his head.

She drew her gaze away from his body. It wasn't easy. She'd never seen anything quite so perfect. Not even the dark gods were as beautiful as Fionn, with his well-formed muscles bunching over broad shoulders, hard, flat stomach, and golden-hued skin. "Wonder if Marta's husband has clothes here that might fit you."

"Feels like a pretty low priority." He grinned. "If it makes you feel better to dress me like a Ken doll, you can look."

"Where's Rune?" She glanced around, grateful the sexual tension inside her had lessened enough for her to think again. And for Fionn's return to normal English. Whenever he morphed into his Irish dialect, it felt like she was sinking into something ancient she didn't understand.

"I heard him leave during the night. Maybe he needed out."

"Yes, but why wouldn't he have come back?"

Fionn winked at her. "Think he wanted to give us some privacy. It was during our middle of the night tryst that he left."

After a breakfast of oatmeal, dried fruit, and powdered milk with real coffee to wash it all down, Aislinn tackled the front door problem while Fionn read. He was faster than she at sorting the important parts in Marta's journals from the parts he could skip over. Rune was back by her side. Both of them went outside to check on Bella and found the raven asleep with her head tucked under one wing. Sensing them, she squawked sleepily.

Aislinn made her way back to the front door and stared at the crossed blades, probing with her magic to see if there'd be an easy way to send them to their recessed homes in the wooden frame of the house. An hour later, she wasn't any closer to a solution. She reached out a tentative hand, wiggled the bottom blade, and jumped a foot when it slid back into the wall. "Not magic at all," she gasped. "At least, not in this direction." It was all about angle. When each blade hit a certain position, it retracted. Once she got the hang of it, it only took a few minutes to finish the job.

Feeling pleased with herself, she pulled the door shut and headed for the back of the house, intent on pilfering clothes—if she could find some that might fit Fionn. Rune's claws clicking on the entryway brought her up short. She turned to the wolf. "Uh, would you mind if I looked through Marta's husband's clothes and maybe took some?"

Rune cocked his head to one side and eyed her. "They are not doing anyone any good sitting in drawers."

Half an hour later, with work pants, sweaters, and jackets heaped over an arm and a pair of boots laid atop everything, she went hunting for Fionn. He'd pushed a carved wooden chair under a bay window with stained glass panels. He looked up from a journal. "What's all this?"

"Let's see if any of them fit." God or not, a long-suffering expression crossed his face. It was a combination of amusement and resignation that she remembered from her father, who'd looked the same way every time her mother brought something home that required trying on. To his credit, he set the journal aside, came to his feet, and stripped off his clothes.

"Just a ruse to see me naked."

"Hardly." She tried to ignore heat flaring in her loins as she passed garments to him. The pants were a bit short and wide in the waist, but a belt held them up. Everything else seemed all right. "Do you think this might fit?" She held up a boot.

"So now I'm Cinderella?" He snatched the boot and jockeyed a foot into it. "Yes, it's fine."

"It's a boot, not a slipper. And it's not glass." She plunked the other one in front of him. "I'd kill to find a new pair of boots for myself. I'll get you a couple new pairs of socks, too."

He scooped the faded *Go Bears* sweatshirt off the floor. "I'm keeping this, but I'm willing to swap out the rest."

Aislinn glanced out the window. Somehow, they'd lost most of the day. "How close are you to finishing those journals? Did you find anything?"

He grinned at her, eyes glittering with challenge. "Feel like hunting for the gateway? No wonder Marta knew so much about the Old Ones. She spent years spying on them. It's a miracle they didn't catch her before they did."

"Tell me." Aislinn plopped down on the edge of the mahogany desk.

"We can talk while we find Marta's entry point. I have a feeling it's hidden by magic, just like everything else important here."

Rune walked up to Fionn and nosed him. "Are you saying Marta had a direct way into Taltos from this house?"

Fionn furled his brows at the wolf. "I'm guessing you didn't know that."

Rune growled. "No. I do not like it that she kept things from me. Important things. All those nights she was not here, I thought she was with someone sick who needed her." Fionn squatted so he was eye level with the wolf. "Well, she may have been some of the time, but she spent many nights in Taltos."

Rune shifted his amber gaze from Fionn to Aislinn. "The two of you will not lie to me—ever." The words were nearly lost in a snarl. It was obvious he was upset, tail swishing back and forth, hackles at half-mast.

Aislinn felt the wolf's outrage in her gut. The Hunter bond depended on honesty. "Bondmate," Aislinn said, infusing formality into her tone, "you may not like what we have to say, but Fionn and I will always tell you the truth."

CHAPTER 17

"This has to be it," Fionn insisted, running his hands over the rough stone walls of the basement. "It feels different."

Aislinn circled the basement one more time, her mage light following after her. The small windows set high on the walls, just under the ceiling, didn't provide enough illumination to see by, even if the day hadn't been fading. The basement was one large, half-finished room, with a dirt floor and rock walls halfway up. The upper part of the walls was rock in some places and wooden planking in others. A washer and dryer sat off to one side, along with a freezer, its door hanging open. A washtub stood next to the ladder leading down from the trap door they'd found cleverly concealed under a removable hardwood panel in a corner of the kitchen.

"You have the incantation from the journals." Aislinn walked over to Fionn and touched the wall, trying to sense the change in the rock that had alerted him. Rune followed. He hadn't left her side, insisting on being helped down the ladder. The wolf had spent a lot of time muttering to himself about how Marta must've drugged him so he wouldn't follow her, since he hadn't known about the kitchen trapdoor.

Fionn looked at her. "Once I set the spell in motion, I have to enter."

She squared her shoulders. "I'm ready." Then what he'd just said sank in. "Oh, no," she sputtered. "You're not going alone."

"It's best if I do. Our likelihood of discovery doubles if we both go."

"No." Even though what he said made sense, she wasn't budging. "Either both of us go, or neither."

"What about me?" Rune demanded, pushing between them.

"You can't go," Aislinn said. "It's too dangerous."

Fionn jabbed her in the side. "There's an echo in here. Seems like that's what I just said to you—"

"That is the same thing Marta said." The wolf bristled, cutting off Fionn's next words. "I am far from a pup. And I sense things more keenly than either of you." Rearing up, he placed his paws on Aislinn's shoulders. She staggered under his weight. "I saved you the last time we were there. You have to take me."

"Okay. Okay. Could you get down before you drive me into the dirt?"

Fionn blew out an exasperated-sounding breath. "Let's have another meal," he suggested. "It's been hours since breakfast. We're all getting testy. If we're all going—and that is far from a foregone conclusion at this point—I suppose it includes Bella." He shook his shaggy head. "We need a better strategy. I was just going to dip my senses in there to see if the gateway even worked."

"Hmph." Aislinn turned and headed for the ladder, afraid if she opened her mouth, they'd get into an argument. Now that he mentioned it, food did sound like a good idea. She mounted the rungs and diverted her ill mood by thinking about what to make. After canvassing bins and canisters in the cupboard, she tossed barley, nuts, dried apricots, and strips of some sort of dried meat into a large pot and deployed magic to cook them.

"Start at the beginning. Tell me again what Marta was trying to accomplish." She poured half a bag of dried peas to her mélange.

"She was convinced she could find a way to seal Taltos off from Earth."

"Why focus on the Lemurians? Seems to me we'd be better off if we could send the six dark gods packing."

Breath hissed through Fionn's teeth. "If you'd stop asking questions, I might be able to come up with something that didn't sound quite so disjointed. I had trouble following Marta's reasoning, too." Bella, who'd been perched on Fionn's shoulder, flapped over to the cook pot and hooked her talons over the edge.

"What are you doing?" Aislinn made shooing motions.

"Seeing what's for dinner." The raven mock-pecked at her before settling on the back of a chair.

Fionn put out his arm for the bird. She hopped onto his shoulder. Turning a chair around, he crossed his arms over its backrest. "Marta had magic long before the Surge. I peeked in some of her earlier journals. It was why she went to medical school. She already knew when people were going to die, so she figured maybe she should study something that might help her do something about it.

"She stumbled on the gateway out of this house when she was still a teenager." In response to something in Aislinn's face, he added, "Yes, this is where she grew up. Of course, in the beginning, she didn't understand where she went when she called magic to take her through the basement walls. She'd go to her *special place* to think and get away from things."

"That's what she called it in her journals?"

He nodded.

"Must've been hard being her," Aislinn murmured. "No teen likes to be different, and she sure couldn't tell anyone about herself."

Fionn quirked a brow.

Reading his meaning easily, Aislinn nodded. "Okay, I'll shut up. Go on." She tasted her stew and added sage and basil.

"She met Dewi on one of her earliest trips, and they struck up an odd sort of friendship. The Lemurians were always there, but in those days, they came and went. Often as not, when Marta went to Taltos, she was the only living thing there. No Dewi, no Old Ones. During those trips, she spent time in a massive library. Most of the books were written in something similar to Greek, so she started to study the language on her own."

"Enterprising soul, wasn't she?"

"Now that you mention it," Fionn said with a grin, "she certainly was. How's dinner?"

"Barley's not soft yet. Maybe another twenty minutes. Keep talking."

"Obviously, she barely made a dent in the library, but she did find ancient tomes that detailed the fall of Mu. They also prophesied many future events, including what would happen during the last Surge." He stopped and raked a hand through his hair. "I guess when that came true, it rattled Marta. Magic or no, she saw herself as a scientist, and she became desperate to know what else was in the library. She tried to bring books back here, but they'd only go as far as the gateway. The first time she tried, when she realized she was back in her basement sans book, she hustled back to put the book away before anyone noticed it sitting out by itself."

Fionn pursed his lips. "She got caught sneaking the book back into the library. The Lemurians weren't terribly organized then. She played the *gee, I was experimenting with magic I don't understand* card, and they let her go with exhortations never to return."

"But she didn't listen," Aislinn interrupted. Since her concoction didn't need anything but time, she settled next to Fionn and Bella.

"She did for a while," Fionn said, a serious note in his voice. "After the Old Ones started herding masses into the vortex and after losing her husband, she felt compelled to find answers. I understand better why people ran into that damned thing like lemmings, though. They were hypnotized. Marta was careful to sedate her husband, Ryan, if she had to leave for very long. She was frightened of what might happen if he left the house without her."

"I remember that day." Rune, who'd been pacing as he listened to Fionn, spoke up. "I tried to tell Father not to leave. It was like his body was here, but his mind had left. When I took hold of his pant leg with my teeth, he hit me. He'd never hit me before. I was so shocked, I let him go." The wolf whined. "I wish I would have thrown my body over his. If I had known, I would have."

"Not your fault." Aislinn bent and stroked him.

"It wouldn't have mattered what you did," Fionn said. "Once the Old Ones put out the call, it was impossible to ignore. Anything shy of rendering him unconscious wouldn't have worked. Somehow, they did nose counts of who they called versus who threw themselves into the vortex. They would've known he was missing and upped the ante."

"I knew they had some way of figuring out who had magic and who didn't. Was their system so precise they could tack it down to every individual on Earth?" Aislinn felt flabbergasted. It was hard to breathe.

"According to Marta, yes." Fionn looked more discomfited than she'd seen him before.

So he's feeling it, too, she thought and tugged at the neck of her shirt. The kitchen suddenly felt far too warm.

"Och aye, lass, how could I not?" He inhaled sharply. "Anyway, once Marta lost her husband, she became far less cautious. Guess she felt she didn't have much left to lose."

"Me." Rune sounded hurt.

Fionn nodded. "Sorry." He beckoned with an open hand, and Rune came to him. "I don't really know how she felt, I was just conjecturing. Desperation probably played a role. Her notes suggest she felt time was running out. She found something in one of the books that made her believe the Lemurians and dark gods were linked. That one couldn't exist without the other. Sort of like the dark and light halves of the human psyche. Dewi told her something that may have clinched that, but she didn't put what it was in her journal."

"Damned inconvenient," Aislinn muttered.

He waved her to silence. "If you think about it," he continued, "it makes sense. The Lemurians have been here since Mu sank, and they never caused any problems. Enter the dark gods, and suddenly, they found the power to throw their weight around. They were always arrogant asses. I'm certain they sat around wishing they could rid Earth of everyone without magic for millennia. They've been trying to recreate Mu ever since they lost it. Everyone there had magic—to varying degrees, of course."

It was hard to sit still. Aislinn got up to check their food. What Fionn said made sense. And it was good news—sort of. Getting rid of the dark gods was still an impossible task, but for some reason, it felt slightly less impossible than before. She dished up the thick broth, filled a couple water glasses from the sink, and ferried everything to the table.

"So what was Marta trying to do?" Aislinn asked around a mouthful of food. She'd waited for Fionn to start talking again, but he'd been silent.

He laid down his spoon. "She didn't see how she could tackle the dark gods—"

Aislinn snorted and nearly choked. "No shit. At least if you're a woman, you can't get anywhere close to them without forgetting about everything but opening your legs. Wonder if Perrikus's mother has the same effect on men."

"She does. For the love of God, woman, stop interrupting after you've asked a question."

Aislinn shot him a look that she hoped was all injured innocence. "I get why Marta targeted the Old Ones. What I wanted to know was how she planned to get rid of them. There." She clapped her mouth shut. "I won't say another word."

"You just did." But he was smiling. "Apparently, there's an energy balance the Lemurians need to maintain Taltos. She was trying to subvert it enough that they'd have to leave."

Aislinn opened her mouth to ask how, but bit her tongue.

"Excellent." His smile grew broader. "You may not be learning, but at least you're trying."

"Good to get credit for something," she muttered *sotto voce*.

"Anyway, there's a harmonic running through Taltos. Its source is an underground tunnel—probably the place you met Dewi. Marta planned to disrupt it for long enough to change its oscillation and pitch permanently. I think Dewi was essential to her plan, but I'm not positive about that."

"That's all it would take?" Aislinn was incredulous. "Another harmonic would make them leave?"

"Marta seemed to think so," Fionn said thoughtfully. "I'm not so certain. The Lemurians are the Third Race. I believe them more resilient and resourceful than that, but I may be wrong." He scraped the bottom of his bowl. "If a different harmonic only severed their connection with the dark, it wouldn't really matter if they left."

"If they're the Third Race, what am I?"

"Fifth."

"Who was in between?"

"Didn't they teach you anything in school?" He looked genuinely surprised. "That would be those who sank along with Atlantis."

Biting off a snarky comment about it being hard to get an education after the world imploded, she asked, "Would you like more?" He nodded, so she took his bowl and ladled more dinner into it.

"What I really should do," he said, "is confer with some of the others. Now that we've sat and talked things through, it would be foolhardy for any of us to test the gateway without knowing more than we do."

"The other who?"

"Celtic gods."

Oh, sorry I asked... "How are you going to travel to Ireland?"

He gave her another odd look. "The same way you met Dewi: astrally."

Aislinn thought about it. She wanted to do something other than wait around while a bunch of ancient gods chewed the fat, but the stakes in this game were particularly high. If they went in hell for leather and screwed up, no one else would even know where they'd gone. And if they died, all of Marta's painstakingly gathered knowledge would be for naught. She raised her gaze to his. "How long would you be gone?"

Something like relief lit his face, and she knew he'd been afraid she was going to put up an argument. "Not more than a day or so. Depends who I can raise on short notice."

"When do you plan to leave?"

"Are ye so anxious to be rid of me, then, lass?" He narrowed his eyes. "Doona be getting any ideas in that flame-red head of yours. Ye will wait here with the bond animals till my spirit returns to my body."

"Stop with the Irish already." She blew out a breath, then sucked in another to buy herself time to get her temper under control. She didn't understand how something as simple as an Irish dialect could make her feel things so acutely.

"Okay." His gaze hadn't left her face. "You didn't answer me."

"No, I don't want to get rid of you—at least, not most of the time. And I will be here when you get back. Unless you take years or something. Then I might not be." Getting up, she carted their dishes over to the sink and walked back to the table.

He drained his water glass, pulled a flask out of a pocket, tipped it to his mouth, and swallowed. He held it out to her, but she shook her head. "Come hug me, lass." He opened his arms invitingly. "I would prefer to feel you against me through the night, but I will leave now. I fear there's not much time to waste."

"Something else in the journals?"

She sat on his lap and wove her arms around him. He pulled her close, and the fear that had surged at his last words subsided a little. Laying a hand against her head, he turned her face so he could kiss her.

"*Mo croi,*" he murmured, pulling away. "Keep everyone safe." He set her on her feet, got to his, and walked purposefully from the kitchen. "You'll have time while I'm gone," he called over his shoulder. "You can read her journals for yourself."

"Wh-Where will your body be?"

"In our bed, lass." He did turn then and gave her a broad wink. "Take good care of it."

SHE CURLED herself around his body through the night. The next day, she settled in with Marta's journals. What she found was so unsettling it was hard to keep reading. Once she'd lost Ryan, there'd been a part of the woman that went mad—or became highly irrational, to put a kinder spin on things. Aislinn wondered how Marta had managed to hide her craziness from the Old Ones.

Other than occasional trips outside, Rune never left her side. Bella flew into the bedroom and stood watch over Fionn. Aislinn tried to interest her in water and food, but the bird ignored her.

On a hunch, Aislinn riffled through drawers in the study and found photographs she assumed were Marta. She considered double-checking her assumption with Rune, but the wolf was edgy. He seemed to be asleep for the moment, and she didn't want to bother him.

The pictures were vaguely disturbing. Marta had been a tall, muscular woman, with long, coppery hair and clear, green eyes. She was built more like a man than a woman, with broad shoulders and a square jaw. In the pictures that included her husband, she towered over him by a good six inches. Aislinn squeezed her eyes shut to clear the afterimage from one particular photograph and then looked at it again. She shook her head. No matter which angle she chose, Marta didn't look entirely human. Something about her eyes and her posture were almost more Lemurian than human.

After searching further, Aislinn found family photographs with an older couple. Who were they? Marta's parents? She didn't look much like either of them, but perhaps she'd been adopted. Aislinn rubbed her eyes. The older couple had a distinctly alien cast as well. She shoved the pictures back in their drawer, feeling uneasy.

"Yeah," Aislinn mumbled, "if those were Marta's parents, what happened to them?" They couldn't have been more than about sixty or so. Had they been forced into the vortex, too? Returning her attention to the lines of careful script in Marta's journals, Aislinn hunted for something, anything, about the woman's parents. Coming up dry, she started on some of the earlier years. When she surfaced, light was fading from the sky. Pushing heavily out of the upholstered leather chair she'd sat in for hours, she stretched and walked into the kitchen, where she flipped on the tap and splashed cold water on her face to clear her head.

She'd found references—lots of them—to Marta's parents in those earlier journals. Apparently, they'd also been doctors—a pediatrician and a surgeon. But the references ceased abruptly the year Marta finished medical school and began her residency in Internal Medicine. *Why? What the fuck happened to them? The damned Surge wouldn't happen for another ten years.* The elder couple's disappearance would also have predated Rune, who likely wouldn't know anything, even if she asked. Marta hadn't had children, and she'd done a hell of a job playing overprotective mother with her wolf.

Marta's parents weren't the only element missing from the last thirteen years of journal posts. Other than a brief notation about her marriage and another about her husband's death, Marta hadn't written anything of substance about Ryan, either. Why? What was it about him that Marta didn't want to risk putting on paper? Speaking of which, why was she still using paper and not doing her journaling electronically? Unless they were hidden extremely well, Aislinn hadn't found a computer anywhere in the house. Not that it would've mattered, since the electricity to power them was long gone, but the lack of such a common device was another unexplained oddity.

Nibbling on leftovers from the night before, she tried to make sense of what she'd read. Fionn was right about one thing. The urgency in Marta's postings had escalated dramatically right before her death. It was hard to say whether something real lurked behind her frantic scribblings, or whether her insanity was spiraling out of control.

Because she couldn't do anything but wait, Aislinn culled through the study and selected an old underground novel, *Islandia,* by Austin Tappan Wright. By the time she realized it was a fictionalized account of a place like Mu—or maybe Atlantis—the story had sucked her in. She read herself to sleep, lying next to Fionn. When morning came and he hadn't returned, she began to worry. She'd had a restless night, waking with her heart in her throat twice, sure Fionn was dead. She'd even called up her mage light to look at his body to make sure he was still breathing. After the second time that happened, she gave up on sleep and went outside into the dawn with Rune. She tried to get Bella to come along, but it was like the raven had turned into a statue. Who knew? Maybe she'd sent her astral self after Fionn.

Gazing at pink edges on the eastern horizon, Aislinn longed to forget the last three years, just for a moment. The sunrise was normal, damn it. Why couldn't everything else be? She tried talking with Rune, but the wolf was uncharacteristically silent. When she finally understood that he wanted to be left alone, she worked her way back through the wards and into the house, using the back door, since it wasn't booby trapped like the front and she didn't have to spend half an hour re-sheathing blades.

To kill time, she read *Islandia* and made a pan of something like biscuits with real flour. She didn't realize how sick she'd gotten of pine nut flour until she concentrated heat in the oven with magic to bake them. They smelled incredible and melted in her mouth when she broke off a corner to taste, not able to wait for them to cool. She found unopened jars of homemade preserves and spread a strawberry-esque one lavishly on a hot biscuit. It tasted amazing.

Aislinn moved her feast into the study and read some more. When she looked out a window, she was shocked to find that it was growing dark. Fionn had been gone two days. Was he coming back? What if he'd run into some sort of trouble? She bit her lower lip, not liking that thought at all.

She considered the gateway beneath her. She knew how to activate it. Or she thought she did. That information had been in the journals, mostly because it was a trial-and-error process and Marta had memorialized her attempts.

By the next morning, Aislinn had made up her mind. She hadn't slept well again and felt incredibly out of sorts. It was stupid for her to spin her wheels waiting for Fionn. She could go into Taltos, look around, and come back, probably before he returned, the way things seemed to be going. At least then she'd have something to contribute to their combined knowledge.

If there was anything to combine with.

She had a bad feeling about Fionn's protracted absence. Aislinn pressed her tongue against her teeth. She didn't know Fionn very well, but assumed his caring for her was genuine. Surely he wouldn't stay away unless he was stuck somewhere. Or dead.

That clinched it. *I'm going. No point in waiting to be rescued. I gave up on that when I left Daddy lying dead in the Bolivian mountains. Or maybe it was when Mother marched into the vortex.* She thought about the wolf. He'd scarcely said a word to her in the last twenty-four hours. Should she take him? *I'll let him decide.*

"Rune."

The wolf trotted into the bedroom. When he looked at her, his eyes were sad.

"I am going into Taltos. Would you like to come?"

He sprang onto the bed in a single leap and licked her face effusively. *"I thought you'd never ask. Waiting has been eating into my guts like the frothy sickness."*

Surprised, she hugged him and then maneuvered around so she could get dressed. The clothing she'd found at the McCloud Fishing Lodge was coming in handy. She donned black multi-pocketed pants, a black knitted top, and tossed the black Gore-Tex jacket over everything. It had been cold the last time she was in Taltos. She shoved her feet into her worn-out boots and rifled through Marta's drawers until she found a black watch cap she could tuck her bright hair under. She hesitated over a pair of black wool gloves from the same drawer and then slid her hands into them. They were too big, but at least they'd cover her skin. If she'd had greasepaint, she would've blacked her face. As it was, she pulled the turtleneck top up to cover her chin and called it even.

CHAPTER 18

Getting Rune down the ladder by herself wasn't easy. He outweighed her. She tried to talk him into going down backward like she did, but he insisted on tackling the rungs nose first. It was a good twenty-foot drop to the packed earthen floor of the basement. After several false starts, she told him to back up into the kitchen, where she joined him and used magic to jump them down.

She ran her hands over the place in the wall that had drawn Fionn, but it didn't feel quite right. Moving back a pace, she shut her eyes, opened her Mage senses, and sent them outward. When she felt something connect, she walked toward the feeling, letting her magic guide her.

Fionn had been partially right. The glowing portal she unearthed was close to where he'd laid his hands. *Maybe the gateway shows itself differently to different sorts of magic wielders.* Before she lost her nerve, Aislinn began the incantation that would open a path into Taltos. Her heart beat so hard against her ribs, she feared it would come right out of her chest. Her mouth was dry, and she licked nervously at her lips. For a few moments, nothing happened, and then the rock wall moved inward, making a groaning sound as stones grated against one another.

Without waiting for her, Rune bounded through the opening, his tail pluming. Aislinn hurried after him. She waited for the portal to swing shut, understanding from Marta's directions that she'd need to mark the spot so she could find it from this side. In the muted glow from her mage light, she piled rocks in a pattern that looked different from all the other rocks littering the tunnel floor and then imbued them with a jot of magic that would light when she called to it. Glancing around, she wished she knew if this tunnel was the same one she'd wandered through during her first visit. Things felt different to her astral self, so she couldn't tell.

She looked for Rune and found him silhouetted against the pervasive gloom a few paces away. Catching him up, she said, *"Little talk, mind or no."*

He nudged her with his nose to show he understood. She shivered slightly. It was cold and damp in the tunnel. She was glad she'd layered on warm clothes.

Which way should I go? Cautious not to use too much magic, she sought the most expedient route to the surface. Mostly, she saw this as a reconnaissance, so she could figure out where things were. If the harmonic ran through the tunnel, there might not be a reason to ever leave it, but she needed some above-ground landmarks. According to Marta, the harmonic started under the library. It was most vulnerable there, and that was where she'd planned to sabotage it. *Let's see what I find.* Aislinn had never been one to trust someone else's magic. The few times she'd done that, she'd been sorry, and it had been a good object lesson.

Ever so gently, Aislinn tried to sense if any Old Ones lurked nearby. She used a form of radar, where she sent magic outward. It pinged back at her differently if it encountered life forms between her and the direction she'd chosen. When her power returned to her, sweet and clean, she let out a tense breath. It whistled loudly, and she clapped a hand over her mouth. *Whoops. Need to be more careful.* Other than her mage light, which she dimmed to nearly nothing, she shuttered her power within herself and started walking.

The tunnel widened after a few hundred yards. Light filtered in from somewhere, so she doused her mage light completely. The tunnel floor was definitely moving upward. She hugged one wall and proceeded slowly. In another hundred feet, it became obvious she was heading for an opening.

She made a clucking sound low in her throat. Rune, who was ahead of her, stopped and waited. She sank a hand into his fur. *"Stay close. Merge with me."*

Wolf senses exploded into her brain. She smelled Old Ones, heard them. They were close. Why hadn't her own magic picked up on them? Aislinn shoved that worry to a back burner, intent on determining where the Old Ones were. Understanding slammed into her. *They're walking right over my head.* As the tunnel closed on the surface, she was probably directly under their buildings. And right under their noses. Making herself still as the rocks, she listened, blessing Dewi for the ability to understand their language.

"I tell you, we need to bring the girl back here. She holds the key, since we lost the other."

"She does not want to come."

"I can sweeten that pie. She's besotted by one of those Celtic pests. If we lure him here, she'll follow."

"Really? Which one?"

They sound like a bunch of gossipy old women. In spite of her fear, Aislinn suppressed a grin. Wait, what had they just said? She strained to pay attention to the guttural clicking sounds.

"...living where our special one was."

"Yes, unfortunate she never saw herself in that light. She hated us."

"We should have intervened after she trapped her parents and diverted their magic—"

"Yesssss," someone interrupted with a hissing sibilance. "I told you at the time she had to be reprogrammed, but did any of you listen to me?"

"We can all see clearly behind us," another said in a placating tone. Was it Metae? Aislinn thought she recognized the intonation.

One of the Old Ones made a gagging sound, which cut off the other's words.

A new voice chimed in. "The parents were loyal, but their daughter fought us at every turn, clinging to her human side. Bah! We barely had enough power to keep Taltos intact. Dealing with her would have drained us."

"Surely we could have managed one lone human…"

"You have the memory of a sand fly. It is not that we did not try. She was uncontrollable, especially after she corralled her parents and tapped into their magic."

"Sssssht. That is not to be spoken aloud."

"At least it maintains the gateways so we don't have to—"

The sound of a sharp slap and a scuffle ensued. Though Aislinn listened for several minutes, hoping to find out more, conversation halted abruptly.

A flurry of movement up ahead sent her racing back down the tunnel. Aislinn didn't know if the Old Ones had somehow sensed her presence, but she wasn't waiting around to find out. She tried for silence, but rocks crunched under her boot heels. She ran by feel, using Rune's hyper-tuned senses for guidance.

"Back again, little one?" trumpeted in her mind.

She screeched to a halt and scanned the darkness. Rune vibrated against her. He'd be growling if she hadn't told him to maintain silence. Aislinn flattened herself against the tunnel wall. Pulling Rune next to her, she disengaged from his mind to keep him safe.

"Dewi?" Her mind voice was tentative. She didn't want to antagonize the creature in case Fionn was wrong about who it was.

"You know my name." The dragon sounded pleased. *"And I know yours. MacLochlainn. I recognized your blood. Flee, child. I will keep the*

Mu-spawn at bay. They revere me, but only because they have mistaken me for another."

Herding Rune, she sprinted for her rock pile. She'd hoped to find out more, but maybe this was good enough for a first trip. It seemed the dragon would be an unexpected partner. *Don't get too excited,* she told herself, recalling it had been Marta's ally, too. Maybe Dewi wasn't all that picky, since it looked as if Marta had murdered her parents.

Risking a small tendril of magic, Aislinn hunted for her marker, gratified to see it flare twenty feet ahead. She started her spell before they got there and slipped through the space in the rocks as soon as it was big enough to accommodate her and Rune.

As the door scraped shut, making so much noise that she was certain it would give them away, she heard Dewi assuring the Old Ones there'd been no one but them in the tunnels all day. Heart pounding in her throat, Aislinn collapsed onto the dirt floor. She hadn't realized how frightened she was. *Because I didn't let myself think about it.*

Rune sidled next to her and lay down, putting his head in her lap. "I was useful."

"You certainly were."

"That means I can go next time."

Until Rune said it, Aislinn hadn't realized she planned to go into Taltos again. Once she heard it spoken, though, she knew she'd return over and over. Either she'd destroy Taltos or die trying. For a moment, she wondered if Dewi could help Fionn. He wasn't back yet. If he were, he would've been waiting in the basement to chastise her. Or worse, he would've come through the gateway after her.

Calling up her mage light, she got to her feet. The first thing she needed to do was locate Marta's parents. The Old Ones seemed to think she'd done something to them, which probably meant bones were located somewhere around this house.

"Rune, did you know Marta's parents?"

"No. She never talked about them."

Aislinn trod carefully. She didn't want to upset Rune, who'd idolized Marta, despite the fact she'd treated him like a child. "The conversation you helped me overhear when you merged with me… Well, it suggested Marta's parents may be somewhere in or around this house. Could you either look for them, or lend me your senses?"

"We can do both, starting with the basement, since we are already here. What am I looking for?"

Well, what are we looking for? "I'm not sure. Corpses or people in some sort of stasis. Not dead, but not exactly alive, either."

Rune made a whuffy sound, his attempt at humor. "Anything unusual, then." He bent his nose to the wall nearest them and walked a circuit. Merging her senses with his, Aislinn stayed put. No need for her to follow along.

When they didn't find anything, she jumped them to the kitchen, where they kept looking. By the time they stood at the top of a spiral staircase leading to the attic, she wondered if the Old Ones might've been mistaken. They'd searched everywhere else, including the yard and a falling-down garage out back with two cars in it: a Subaru wagon and a Toyota sedan. Since they sat well outside Marta's wards, both had been looted for parts.

The attic door was locked. She blasted it with magic, but it didn't budge. Fanning power around her, she discovered more warding. Fortunately, Marta hadn't been particularly creative. She'd found one type of warding that worked and used it over and over.

It still took Aislinn close to half an hour to hack her way through. When she stepped into the large room running the length and breadth of the house, the air had a stillness to it that reminded her of a mausoleum. A few pieces of antique furniture were scattered about—mostly tables and chairs. Old chests with black metal banding and hasps sat in a row against one wall. There were no windows, and unlike the rest of the house, dust was thick.

"They are here." Rune's voice sounded from behind her.

Aislinn's Mage senses agreed. But where were they? She scanned the empty room, returning to a place in one corner that felt odd. "It's illusion," she muttered and strode across the attic toward the strange-feeling place. She stopped before she got there, having learned that Marta's wards packed quite a punch.

She sent her magic forward, but it zapped right back at her. Aislinn tried again from a slightly different angle. Two hours later, she'd tried every spell and counter spell she'd ever learned, to no avail. Absolutely convinced if she could only neutralize the binding, she'd find Marta's parents in some sort of suspended animation, Aislinn hissed in frustration.

"She protected them well," Rune observed.

Aislinn started to say something, but bit back the words and shielded her mind. No point in telling the wolf that Marta's parents had scarcely been willing victims. For one thing, she didn't know for sure. For another, if she couldn't figure out how to get to them, it was a moot point anyway.

Curious about the chests, she lifted their lids. Two of the four were empty. The others held clothing and bedding. Some of the clothes were lovely, fine silks in bright colors and soft woolens, but Aislinn wasn't in the mood. She turned toward the stairs. "I can't do any more tonight."

Once she wound down the staircase and made her way back to the kitchen, she was shocked to find it was night again. There hadn't been any way to judge the passage of time in the windowless attic. Where had the day gone? How long had she and Rune been in Taltos? It hadn't seemed like even an hour had passed, but it must've been much more than that.

Stuffing one of the previous day's biscuits into her mouth, she chewed automatically. Still no Fionn. What did that mean? She wondered if he'd be able to unearth Marta's parents. "Doesn't matter," she muttered around a mouthful of biscuit. "He's not here."

"Where do you suppose he is?" Rune asked. "Bella is still checked out. I think she went with him."

"Yeah," she agreed. "I think the same. And I have no fucking idea where Fionn is. He was supposed to be back two days ago."

"When are we going back to Taltos?"

Aislinn thought about it. *Since I'm on my own again, I can make my own schedule. I suppose that's one advantage.* "How about as soon as I'm done eating?"

∼

BACK IN THE TUNNEL, she rebuilt her cairn and checked to make sure her magic-imbued marker was still intact. This time, she led them in the other direction. Were these tunnels here before the Old Ones built Taltos, or did they excavate them for some reason? Borrowing Rune's senses, she listened for the harmonic. Even with his sensitive ears, she could barely hear it—and that was only because she knew it had to be there. It was a subtle hum, well below the range of human ears.

They headed deeper into the mountain. She'd just rounded a corner when something made her stop. It wasn't anything she could put her finger on, but the fine hairs at the back of her neck tingled. *Magic. And not mine.* Balancing on the balls of her feet, she debated whether to go back. She hadn't learned a damned thing this trip, though. What was the point in risking discovery if it didn't bring her closer to a solution?

Small rocks beneath her feet slid downhill. It became a struggle not to simply ride them down. What was happening? Was it an earthquake? One that had happened without perceptible shocks or sound? It felt as if she was on a conveyor belt. She seized a large rock outcropping and held on. Rune swept by, all four paws grappling for purchase. She made a grab for him and missed.

Shit! Because she couldn't let him face whatever was happening alone, she let go and slid down a slope that got steeper and steeper. Rocks bounced off other rocks. She dug her boots into the slide, hoping to stay on her feet. She didn't know what would happen if she fell, but figured it wouldn't be pretty. Just as soon as she found Rune, Old Ones be damned, she was going to jump them out of there. So what if they ended up near Mount Shasta. She knew the way back to Ely from there. It was better than being crushed to death by tons of rocks.

It felt like hours before the rock pile slowed and finally stopped, but it probably hadn't been more than ten minutes. Deploying her mage light, she peered hundreds of feet—maybe even a thousand— back up the slope. No way in hell they'd be able to climb back up it. The rocks would just keep sliding if either of them put any pressure on them. *"Rune."*

A faint whimper sounded. She got to him as fast as she could and brightened her light to see how badly he was injured. Her breath caught in her throat. She tried to hug him, but drew back when it was obvious he'd broken some ribs in the fall. And a leg. He panted, obviously in pain.

Should I jump us now, or heal him first? Healing magic might draw attention, but if one of those ribs punctured a lung, he might die when she tried to get them out of there. Gritting her teeth in frustration, she knew she had to patch him up before she could do anything else.

"Ssssh. It will be all right. I'm going to help you." She infused magic into the broken places in Rune's body. Because she'd been there before, it was easier this time. And quicker. She was just finishing, congratulating herself for having escaped a speeding bullet one more time, when she felt something coming. Rune got to his feet and shook himself. He must've sensed it, too, because hackles went up along his spine.

Aislinn hoped it was Dewi. She'd been so intent on the wolf, she hadn't noticed the stink of alien magic drawing near. Whatever it was was close. Too close for her to risk a jump. They'd nail her with her molecules half in and half out of the tunnel. She might never come out at her destination.

Knowing they'd been discovered, she let her light blaze so she could at least see what was after them. *Damn! Lemurians.* Aislinn readied her Hunter and Mage magic for a fight. She wondered if she could actually kill an Old One. No one had ever tried, that she knew.

"There you are, sweetling. Back for a visit so soon?" The honeyed tones belonged to Metae. Aislinn would've recognized her voice anywhere. "And you brought your wolf. Marvelous! That must mean you are planning to stay."

Three Old Ones came closer. They shed plenty of luminosity, so Aislinn redirected all her magic into fight mode and let her mage light wink out. She waited. They needed to be closer still before she struck.

"You are coming with us, child. Aren't you?" Metae was only about fifteen feet away. "Your place is here. I am so glad you realized that."

That's how she's always gotten to me, by pretending to be kind. Aislinn urged herself not to fall for it. The Lemurian was infusing compulsion into her words. Aislinn could practically see the spell. Still, being wanted was seductive. No one had wanted her since her parents died—except Fionn, and he was gone.

Bullshit. That's what she wants me to think. She walled her mind against Metae, even though a place inside her felt broken and bereft. Like losing her last friend.

Aislinn ginned up what she hoped looked like a convincing smile just before she lobbed a killing blow right for the Old One's throat. Metae yelped and jumped aside. Aislinn's magic barely grazed her. In the confusion, Rune launched himself at one of the others and sank his teeth into the side of its neck. Iridescent red and green blood geysered, spraying thickly through the air. The coppery smell was cloyingly sweet. It smelled like the promise of victory.

Thinking they just might win this one, if the Old Ones didn't call for reinforcements, Aislinn sent another bolt of magic toward Metae and the other Lemurian. She ducked and wove, avoiding their magic as she chucked power their way. It didn't seem like they were trying to kill her, only capture her, which made things easier.

Aislinn panted from fear and exertion. Her breath plumed white and frosty in the chilly subterranean air. Rune had killed one of them. The others danced out of his reach and erected magic barriers he couldn't jump through. She opened a hole in one of them just for him. Leaping through it, Rune latched onto another's throat, decimating it. Bones snapped. The wolf was coated in gore, but his eyes were alight with joy. This was what he'd been born for, and he knew it.

"Well," she gasped, trying to get near Metae. "That leaves the two of us. How do you want to die?"

"Why are you doing this, child?" The Old One sounded aggrieved. "Have we not been kind to you?"

Aislinn snarled. "Earth does not belong to you. You were barely noticeable down here before you teamed up with the dark. Either send them back where they came from, or leave."

"But we taught you about your magic—"

"And killed everyone else."

Metae's body moved under her robes in the Lemurian version of a shrug. Because the Old One seemed more intent on conversation than killing, Aislinn blasted her with magic. Metae twirled to get away from it, and Aislinn jumped her. With her legs twined around Metae's waist, she shoved her dirk home in the Old One's neck. The sharp iron blade slid easily between scales, burying itself deep.

"Y-You do not understand. We have never been your enemy," Metae gasped before enough blood gushed out of her wound to silence her forever.

Aislinn slipped to the ground along with the Lemurian's inert body. She yanked hard to get her blade back. Metae's reptilian scales had closed about it like a vise. "Let's get out of here," she said to Rune. Christ! She'd killed an Old One. In fact, they'd killed three. What would the rest of them do once they found out?

She answered her own question, suddenly iced to her bones.

Hunt me down to the end of my days, that's what. No longer worried about magic giving her away, she curved an arm around Rune's neck. She'd had time to rethink her exit strategy. It wouldn't take much magic to jump them back to the top of the rock fall near the place in the tunnel that led into Marta's house.

Half expecting a rush of Lemurians to mob them, Aislinn cast a jump spell. The rockslide fell away beneath them. She raced through the upper tunnel with Rune by her side and loosed the spell to open the gateway when they were still fifty feet away. As soon as it opened, she and Rune skittered through.

She was about to pat herself on the back herself for a mission at least partially accomplished, when hands grabbed her shoulders and shook her hard. Grabbing her dirk, she writhed against her assailant and prepared to fight. Rune raced to her side, whining. Why hadn't he launched himself at whoever held her?

Understanding slammed home. Fionn! The basement was dark, but she could smell him. Anger lent an exotic edge to his normally musky scent.

"Ye were supposed to wait for me. What the fuck, Aislinn? Where have ye been?" He shook her again so hard her teeth rattled. "Never mind that. I know where ye were. What the bluidy fucking hell were ye doing going there without me?"

CHAPTER 19

She tried to twist away, but his hands were like a vise. "You're hurting me," she said. "Let go."

Rune's whines shifted to low, warning growls.

Fionn's mage light flared. She heard his sharp intake of breath when he saw them. "Ach! Christ! Ye're covered in Lemurian blood. Talk." His hands loosened fractionally. At least he didn't shake her again.

"Not until you let go of me. And maybe not until after I've had a bath." She tried for dignity, but it was hard with his body leaned against hers. What she really wanted to do was turn around, throw herself into his arms, and never let go.

"Och aye." Breath whistled between his teeth, and she knew he'd been inside her mind. He spun her to face him, closed his arms around her, and crushed his mouth over hers. His hands moved down her back, gripped her ass, and pulled her violently against him. She felt the length of his cock press against her stomach, where it throbbed hot and hard. All the moisture in her body fled south, flooding her crotch with need.

She tore her mouth away. "So do you want to just do it right here in the dirt?"

She drank him in with her eyes. God, but he was beautiful. So perfect she almost couldn't breathe. If he said *yes*, it was fine by her. She couldn't wait to get him inside her. He didn't answer, just reached to unbutton her pants. His hands were rough, pushing the fabric down her legs.

"Wait." She was so hot, she could barely find words. Bending, she unlaced a boot, wriggled out of it, and got one leg free.

Grappling to get her hands on him, she realized his pants were already unzipped. "Convenient," she gasped as she crawled up his body, twined her legs round his hips and her arms about his shoulders.

He shoved into her, burying himself. She felt a shudder go through him. It made her come, shivering against him. He spoke to her in Gaelic, his voice raspy and urgent.

"You've got to be kidding," she managed. "I can barely understand English right now."

He gripped her ass, as if it was the only thing standing between him and drowning. Rocking against her, he rammed himself to the hilt again and again. Aislinn felt another climax build in her belly. She clawed his back and screamed that she needed him faster, harder, deeper. Release shot through her in multihued ecstasy, and her body arched against his, vibrating with lust. His cock swelled even more. He had to be close. A feral shriek split the air when he came. She heard desperation in that cry and knew he'd been frightened to the depths of his being that he'd lost her.

"Are the two of you going to stop fucking long enough to let us talk with the lass?" Understated humor ran beneath an unfamiliar male voice coming from the vicinity of the kitchen.

Rune barked.

Aislinn tightened her legs around Fionn. "Who the hell was that?"

He laughed. "'Tis why I was gone a wee bit longer than I'd expected. I brought reinforcements along, and they traveled with their bodies. Wouldna have been verra useful to have just their astral selves here." He cupped his hands around his mouth and called to whoever had spoken, "Stay topside till we're decent."

Raucous laughter rang from above.

Embarrassment engulfed Aislinn as she disentangled herself. How many strange men had listened to her shrieking to Fionn to fuck her harder, goddammit? "You should have told me," she muttered.

"And when would there have been the time for that?" The glow from his mage light had developed a decidedly randy hue, like an old west bordello. He quirked an eyebrow. "Never forget, lass. Death and sex are linked. Ye came from a battlefield, so ye got the death part. When I found you, ye were ripe for the plucking."

"Like a Christmas goose." Aislinn snorted and slid her exposed leg back into her pants. She fired her own mage light, hunted down her boot, and stuffed her foot into it. "Here, help me get the wolf upstairs."

"How'd ye get him down here without me?"

"Magic."

"Why dinna I think of that? And here I was deluding myself that 'twas one more reason ye wouldna try the gateway."

She ignored the sarcastic undercurrent in his words. Something he'd said earlier seemed impossible. "You can pull jump magic so potent it transports you across an ocean?"

"Aye, lass. It takes twice as long as astral travel, but 'tis certainly possible."

She opened her mouth to tell him about Taltos, but he stopped her with a kiss. "Wait until ye can tell us all."

Three men waited for them in the kitchen, along with Bella. The bird shot Fionn what looked like a reproachful glance. Aislinn wondered if he'd made the raven stay in the kitchen. Though the men tried to wipe knowing leers off their bearded faces, it was a losing battle.

Aislinn's cheeks flamed, but she squared her shoulders and said.

"I'm going to have a quick wash. Back in a flash." Rune trailed after her as she headed down the hallway.

She settled for cold water, not wanting to take time to run a bath. Aislinn did what she could to sponge blood off herself and the wolf. He didn't seem to appreciate the impromptu bath and skulked away as soon as she let go of him. "Where are you going?" she called.

"Hunting. I'm hungry."

She thought about telling him to be careful, but decided not to. Rune had been a hero tonight. You didn't tell heroes to be careful. You afforded them the respect of acknowledging they could take care of themselves.

Grateful for clothes that didn't stink of blood, she folded up the bottoms of a pair of Marta's pants and threw a faded blue flannel shirt on over the top of them. Christ, the woman had been a giant. Aislinn was tall at nearly six feet, so pants were generally too short. She'd never had to cut a pair down before. Feet bare, she padded toward the kitchen. The smell of food filled her nose the minute she hit the hallway, and her mouth flooded with saliva. She had no idea what time it was. Had she spent what was left of the previous night in Taltos?

She peered through the kitchen windows. Dawn lightened the sky to a muddy gray. "Hmph. Answers one question," she muttered and turned her attention to the men.

Seeming larger than life, they sprawled in chairs around the kitchen table. They were all about Fionn's size—around six feet four or so—their bodies thick with muscle. Two of the strangers were blond, the other dark. Everyone's hair was braided and tied out of the way with strips of leather. Four sets of eyes zeroed in on her, so full of questions it made her head spin.

Aislinn grabbed one of the biscuits she'd made, dropped it onto a plate, and spooned something fragrant from a large pot over it. "Who are all of you?" she asked, talking with her mouth full because she was too hungry to wait. Besides, manners had gone out with the demise of civilization.

"I am Arawn," the dark-haired man said, half bowing to her. His eyes were as dark as his hair. A beard flowed down his chest. When he smiled, his teeth were very white against it. He wore leather pants, boots that laced halfway up his shins, and a leather vest that left his chest bare. A gold medallion, heavy with runes, hung from his neck.

She inclined her head to him. "God of the dead. Also revenge, terror, and war." Aislinn glanced at Fionn. "I'm impressed. Where'd you find him?"

"That's only because ye havena yet heard who I am." One of the blond giants leapt to his feet and bowed from the waist. "This is how 'tis done," he told Arawn, humor sparking from his eyes. "Ye rise in the presence of the fair sex." Dark blue robes fluttered. He tightened a black sash so vigorously that leather pouches swung from it. Aislinn wondered what was in them. A carved wooden staff, glowing with an inner light, was propped against the table next to him. His reddish beard was close cropped, following the lines of his jaw. Like her, his feet were bare.

"You are?" Still on her feet, Aislinn took another mouthful of her meal.

"Gwydion." He looked hard at her out of eyes as blue as Fionn's. "Ye seem to know your mythology. Can ye tell me who I am?"

A smile tugged at the corners of her mouth. "You're a warrior magician. Greatest of the enchanters." She cocked her head to one side, thinking. "You also control illusion." Setting down her plate, she snapped her fingers. "Hey, you could take on D'Chel."

He threw back his head and laughed. "Aye." He looked at the others and winked. "The lass has faith in me."

"There's another problem you might be able to help me solve," she said before shifting her gaze to the third man. "First, though, tell me who you are." She met coppery eyes set in a tanned face. His beard was scraggly like Fionn's, and he was dressed in leathers like Arawn, except rather than a vest, he wore a full leather shirt.

"I am Bran." His gaze never left hers.

"Prophecy, war, sun, music, arts." She held his frank stare.

"'Tis a pleasure to be recognized. Nice to meet you, lass." Bran smiled.

Aislinn blew out a breath and sank into a chair with her food. "My, what an august group. Guess I can retire to the back bedroom while you save the world."

Fionn handed her a glass filled with mead. "What did ye mean about there being something Gwydion could help you with?" It sounded as if he was jealous, and his next words clinched it. "I can do anything he can."

"The hell ye can," Gwydion snarled.

Better start at the beginning. Aislinn leveled her gaze on Fionn. "You're going to be angry with me, but stuff it, okay? When you caught me downstairs a little bit ago, Rune and I were coming back from our second trip—"

"What?" He was on his feet and by her side in an instant. Fionn locked his hands on either side of her face and stared at her in disbelief. His eyes shaded to midnight, and she understood how pissed he was.

"Stand down, man." Arawn rolled his eyes. "Ye doona own her."

"Aye, leave the lass to tell her tale," Gwydion said. Coming to his feet, he took one of Fionn's arms and yanked hard. Grumbling, Fionn let go, but didn't return to his seat. She heard him behind her, pacing.

Aislinn shook herself. "Thanks." She smiled at Gwydion. "You can rescue me anytime."

"I don't fucking think so," Fionn snapped.

"I was teasing," she protested. "Trying to lighten things up a touch."

"Don't encourage them. They'd lure you to bed in a heartbeat if I turned my back."

She couldn't believe how out of sorts he sounded. *Guess it'll take more than that roll in the basement hay to calm him down.* "You don't trust me—" she began.

"Nay, it's that I've known them for hundreds of years." His tone softened ever so slightly. "Aislinn, we need to know what ye did in Taltos."

She closed her eyes for a moment, trying to organize her thoughts. "The first trip, I mostly wanted to see if I could get through. I eavesdropped on the Old Ones, and Dewi talked to me." Turning, she spoke to Fionn. "I was careful. I noted the place I came into Taltos, even marked it with magic so I could find it again."

"What'd ye overhear?" Fionn still didn't sound very friendly.

Aislinn looked around for Rune, but he wasn't back yet. *Good.* "I'd rather Rune didn't know this, but according to the Old Ones, Marta did...something to her parents. They're upstairs in the attic, slathered in layers of illusion and spells. I don't know if part of them is still alive, but Marta may have used their energy to boost her own magic."

Bella cawed and flapped over, landing on Aislinn's shoulder.

She turned to the bird. "You will not tell Rune, either. Understand?"

The raven pecked gently at her hand. Aislinn took that for a *yes.*

Fionn looked interested in spite of himself. "Did you try to break the spell?"

Good, he's back to American English. Means he's at least trying to get along with me. "Did I ever. Spent hours. Nothing worked." She ate some more. "Rune sensed them there, too. We searched the entire rest of the house, and the yard, before we found them."

"What about Dewi?" Bran asked. "We sent her to, ah, blend in with the Old Ones eons ago. Since then, she's ignored my requests to return."

"Aye, and 'tis precious little in the way of spying she's done for us," Arawn added, sounding irked.

"I don't know," Aislinn replied, glad the dragon seemed impervious to being bullied about. "The Old Ones call her Orione. She, ah, recognized me as a MacLochlainn and covered my butt so I could hustle Rune and myself out of there."

Even though she wasn't looking at him, she felt Fionn glare at her. "Ye had such a close call, then, and went back for more. What are ye, lass, stupid? Are ye so intent on throwing your life away—?"

"Leave her be." Bran snorted. "Ye are so deep in rut for your long-lost soul mate, ye canna see straight. Lass." His coppery gaze found hers. "If ye ever tire of him and his overbearing ways, I wouldna boot you from my bed."

That brought a laugh from the others. Aislinn held her breath and blew it out once Fionn joined in, saying, "There just might be a wee bit o' truth in that, though ye can forget the bedding part." He clapped Bran on the back and returned to his chair.

Aislinn drained off half her mead, relished its heat traveling to her belly, and then launched into the second installment of her story. *I could have my own television show. Aislinn's Adventures in Taltos. Bet it would sell as well as Alice in Wonderland.*

She noticed Gwydion looking oddly at her long before she stopped talking, but ignored him so she could finish what she had to say. His blue gaze grew unnerving, so she faced him and asked, "What?"

He shook his head. "I suppose I was marveling that ye managed to kill a Lemurian. Had ye stuck with magic, ye would have failed. Why ever did ye choose hand-to-hand combat against an adversary so much more powerful than yourself?"

She shrugged. "Rune had already killed two of them. I figured if he could do it, so could I."

Gaelic flowed around the table. She followed some of it. Mostly, the men were speculating why Metae hadn't fought back harder.

Aislinn broke into the conversation. "For some reason, Metae wanted me alive. She must have thought she had a special enough bond with me that we could leverage to work through the bad feelings." Aislinn spread her hands in front of her. "She used compulsion like always. For some reason, I was impervious to it this time."

"Dewi," Fionn muttered. "She's got to be behind this. She's the one who opened your mind to the Old Ones' language."

More Gaelic. They'd been hunting Dewi for centuries, but she'd hidden herself, ostensibly deserting them after they'd sent her to spy on the Lemurians. They argued about what Dewi had up her sleeve, masquerading as Orione. Aislinn heard *MacLochlainn* over and over, but couldn't decipher the parts before or after.

Once she finished her meal, she asked, "What are you saying about me?"

"I thought you understood Gaelic," Fionn said in perfect English.

"I do—sort of. But not when it's so fast."

"It doesna matter," Arawn said. "According to Fionn, ye are not interested in Irish history. Besides, it would take far too long to give you a crash course in your ancestry. The short version is that your family and Dewi have primordial links dating back to the fifth century. She would protect you. 'Tis part of an ancient bond."

Aislinn narrowed her eyes in thought. "It's not so much that I'm not interested, but it feels a bit overwhelming."

She'd begun formulating questions, when Gwydion flowed from his chair to an upright position in one supple movement. Like Fionn, he was incredibly light on his feet for such a large man. "I would look on that spell in the attic that defeated you, lass."

Rune padded into the kitchen, a rabbit clutched between his jaws. Aislinn hoped everyone would remember not to implicate Marta in whatever had happened to her parents. "We're going back to the attic," she told the wolf. "You can stay here and eat. Bella will keep you company." She glanced meaningfully at the raven.

Aislinn led the way to the back staircase. Fionn trooped after Gwydion. She smiled to herself. *He doesn't want to leave me alone with one of his buddies. Is he really afraid I'll take a shine to one of them?* Aislinn couldn't help herself. She laughed at the absurdity of it. Fionn was almost more than she could handle. The last thing she needed was two of him.

"What's so funny?" Fionn asked, but she just shook her head, grateful he hadn't chosen that particular moment to read her thoughts.

Once in the attic, Gwydion stalked to the corner Aislinn indicated. He raised his staff, spoke words in a language she didn't recognize, and the length of polished wood in his hand came alive with light. The minute it did, she saw a spell hovering around two crypts.

Fionn pulled her toward the stairs. "Guard your eyes, lass. His spells can get extremely bright."

She waited, peering through spread fingers, but nothing happened.

"What manner of being made this?" Gwydion asked, sounding curious.

"Why, I suppose she was human." Aislinn dropped her hands to her sides.

"Nay. Not possible." Gwydion turned to face them. "Magic spreads from the two lying here to the rest of the house and beyond —far beyond. I doona think the house is illusion, yet I wonder what will happen to it—and whatever is linked to it—if I break the enchantment. I need to know more before I charge in, else I could rupture something that canna be fixed." He hesitated for a beat. "I wouldna be quite so cautious but for the link to Taltos that we already know is here."

Fionn stepped away from her. "Let me help. We can explore it further."

The Celts raised their hands and chanted. Aislinn watched intently. Magic fascinated her. It always had, even when she'd thought it the purview of fairy tales. The crypts became clearer as the mists shrouding them moved aside. Made of shiny stone that looked like beige marble, they glowed warm against the dark of the attic. She repositioned herself so she could see beyond Fionn and Gwydion. The bodies lying in the crypts were amazingly well preserved. They didn't look dead. The faces were pink, the flesh full. What had Marta done? Were her parents sorcerers? Had they cooperated, or been duped?

Gwydion's staff blazed with blue light that made her eyes ache.

Fionn moved to the far side of the crypts, hands extended, chanting in the odd language Gwydion had used before.

The woman sat up and tossed a leg over the side of her crypt. Gray hair cascaded over her shoulders. She shook her head, as if she'd been asleep. Brown eyes fluttered open. She gazed from Fionn to Gwydion. "I am guardian of the gate," she pronounced. "How dare you disturb me?" A second leg followed the first.

From the expression on Fionn's face, it looked like he'd commanded her to stay put, but his magic wasn't doing the trick. The woman was pushing right through it.

Fionn shouted for Arawn and Bran. Footsteps pounded on the attic stairs. They raced to Fionn's side, apparently strengthening his binding.

The woman tried to get the rest of the way out of her crypt, but this time, she couldn't move and drew her lips back into a snarl. "I tell you, I hold the gates. Destroy me at your peril." A crafty look crossed her face. "I can do just as good a job with the gates if I'm awake."

Her gaze drifted about the room. "Where is that daughter of mine? Last I remember, she got Dad and me good and drunk on something." She reached for Fionn's leg, almost grabbing a handful of fabric before he sidestepped out of her way. "So long as I'm up, *boys*, how about a little fun? You're a likely looking bunch, and I've been asleep for ages." She tried for a come-hither expression, but all she managed was to look like a whore well past her prime.

Fionn and Bran grimaced.

The man in the other crypt stirred and made a low moaning sound. "Who dares disturb me?" emerged from his half-open mouth as a breathy sigh, words slurry. His voice sounded rusty. It must have surprised him, because his eyes popped open. They were the same muddy brown as the woman's.

Gwydion sketched something in the air with his staff, and Aislinn saw the protections around the two resurrecting themselves.

"Aye, good idea," Arawn muttered, adding layers to the enchantment as he shoved the woman back into her crypt.

"You're putting them back to sleep," Aislinn gasped. "Why? I thought the whole point was to see what they know."

"Hush," Fionn said. "We'll explain later."

Because she didn't see the point in watching four magicians work on a binding she'd done her damnedest to unravel, Aislinn went back down the stairs.

"Did they free them?" Rune asked.

"Yes and no." Aislinn poured more mead and settled in to wait.

It didn't take long before the men returned, but when she got to her feet, she was decidedly tipsy. It felt good. "Well?" she said, hands on her hips. Then she looked at Rune. "Maybe you might not want to listen to this."

"She was my bondmate. I have a right."

"Aye, that he does." Gwydion pulled out a chair and sat heavily. "They truly are guardians. They hold the pathways open between this world and many others. If we destroy them, there willna be a way to return the dark gods to their realms."

"Or to oust the Lemurians," Bran added. "Thank Christ ye dinna destroy the binding, lass." He tugged out a chair for himself and gestured for everyone to sit.

A sudden chill marched down her spine. Had her naïveté almost doomed Earth? *I have no business dabbling in arcane magics. None. I don't know enough.* She shivered, remembering her impressions from the photographs she'd found in the study. "You said they weren't human. Did you figure out what those things upstairs are?"

"We think so," Fionn answered. He threw his leg over a chair, picked up the mead bottle, and drank. "Hmph. Nearly empty."

"There would be more where that came from," Arawn said.

"You didn't answer me." Aislinn felt like a nag, but she had to know.

"The ones in the crypts were not exactly spilling secrets," Bran said dryly, "but we believe they are the product of humans who mated with Lemurians."

"If that's true," Fionn added, looking grim, "it means the Lemurians plotted for years to create gateways to allow the dark to infiltrate Earth so they could ally with their power. The last Surge was only one piece of a much-larger puzzle. Though they don't look it, the Old Ones are a dying race, which is why they attempted to blend their bloodlines with humans. How they managed to have such a pairing take is beyond me."

"How does Marta fit into all of this?" Aislinn was mystified.

"That's easy," Arawn said. "The Lemurians struck a deal with some greedy humans—likely scientists. Who knows how they twisted DNA to come up with viable offspring. The two in the crypts are brother and sister. Marta was their child."

"Were they the only ones?" Aislinn asked. A macabre fascination filled her, along with an understanding of why Marta was so tall.

"We have no idea," Gwydion replied. "But if the Lemurians have been successful bringing human DNA into their bloodlines, their alliance with the dark may well prove unstoppable."

"I told you we needed to act," Fionn muttered.

"Aye, that ye did," Bran agreed. "And here we thought ye were simply besotted with the MacLochlainn." He shrugged. "At least we know the feel of the hybrid race now. 'Twill make it easier to hunt them."

"No wonder Marta went mad." Aislinn felt disgusted and impressed at the same time. The woman must've been amazingly powerful to trap her parents into holding the gates between the worlds so she could travel back and forth to Taltos and probably other places as well.

Then she remembered the wolf. "Rune. I'm sorry."

"I wondered why she did not smell entirely human." The wolf was on his feet, clearly agitated. "She raised me. I thought all humans smelled that way until I met others." A growl emanated from the back of his throat. "I should have asked more questions."

"It wouldna have mattered," Gwydion said. "She wouldna have answered."

Aislinn went to Rune and knelt next to him. She searched for a way to tell him Marta hadn't been in her right mind. That maybe human intelligence couldn't coexist in the same body with anything Lemurian, but he shook her off and left the kitchen. With a worried-sounding squawk, the raven followed him.

"There is much we doona know," Arawn said. "Marta may have embraced her Lemurian side or despised it. Mayhap she only hated her parents. I'm not as certain as Gwydion that the two above hold all the gateways. Yet, they hold enough of them that 'twould be fool-hardy to disturb the binding."

Aislinn stumbled to her feet. "From what I overheard in Taltos, Marta hated the Lemurians and did everything in her power to subvert them. How soon can we go back there and obliterate those bastards?"

"'Tis the dark gods who have to go," Bran said thoughtfully. "Without them, the Lemurians wouldna have enough power to bother anyone."

"And the human-Lemurian spawn—if there are more of them," Fionn added.

"Tricky of them," Gwydion muttered, "to make something that looks so like a human we never would've thought to look twice."

"So Taltos isn't the answer?"

Aislinn looked around at the men. No one answered her. For some reason, she felt thwarted. She'd found something she could handle, but it wasn't the salvation she'd hoped it would be—not for Earth, and not for her. Even if she'd been able to destroy the harmonic, it wouldn't have affected the dark gods at all. A complex strategy she could only begin to guess at linked the Convergence and its Surges to the Old Ones, the dark gods, and their minions. She hoped they could figure it out before it was too late. Maybe her nerves were playing off the urgency in Marta's journals, but she didn't think any of them had much time left.

"We need to talk with Dewi," Fionn said thoughtfully.

"Aye. If nothing else, mayhap she can tell us why she's still in Taltos and not with us," Arawn muttered, sounding annoyed by the dragon's defection.

"Don't we need more of a plan than that?" Aislinn demanded. The beginnings of a headache pounded behind one eye. She knew she needed sleep.

Gwydion nailed her with his sharp, blue gaze. "Humans are hasty, lass. Better to take the time to make sure of your strategy than to bludgeon your way through something and make a fatal mistake."

She thought about the crypts and winced. "Touché. Think I'll catch a couple hours' sleep before I fall on my face."

Fionn got to his feet and placed an arm around her shoulders.

They hadn't made it five feet down the hallway when Arawn called him back. "We need you here, Fionn, not rutting in yon bed. Bid the lass a good night, then return to us."

CHAPTER 20

*A*islinn didn't even remember the rest of the walk to her bed. She woke once to find Rune stretched out beside her, snoring softly. Part of her thought she should go look for Fionn, but before she could force her body out of the warm nest she'd made under the covers, she fell back asleep.

Something tugged at her shoulder. She ignored it. She wanted to stay asleep. She'd been dreaming that she was riding Dewi, soaring above a medieval-looking castle while wearing tight-fitting leather breeches, lace-up boots, and a form-fitting leather jacket. The deer hide garments cut the wind so she was toasty atop her mount, gloved hands curved around spines growing out of Dewi's shoulders. She hadn't realized it in the dim light of the cavern, but the dragon's scales were blood red. *We make quite the pair,* Aislinn laughed to herself. *My hair almost matches her coloring.*

"Yes, daughter," Dewi spoke into her mind. *"We were made for one another. Never forget that."*

"Aislinn. Wake up. 'Tis important." Fionn's voice was insistent. He tugged harder on her shoulder. Then he bent and kissed her neck, nuzzling it.

"Go away." She tried to sink back into her dream, but it was impossible. She rolled over and put her arms around Fionn's neck. "I was having the best dream." She pulled him toward her. "Lie down as long as you're here."

"Nay, lass. There's not the time for that, though I dearly wish it were otherwise. Ye must be up." He straightened and gazed fondly down at her. "Ye've nearly slept the clock round as 'tis."

"You sound like my mother—in more ways than one."

He inhaled audibly and blew out a breath. "Ye must hurry, Aislinn. We've been talking with Dewi. She wants you to come to her. Now."

"Why didn't you say so?" Aislinn sprang out of bed, realized she was mostly naked, and shrugged. It wasn't anything Fionn hadn't seen before. "I was dreaming about her."

"Why am I not surprised?" He handed her clothes from off the floor. Warmth spilled from his eyes as he helped her dress.

Aislinn pulled the flannel shirt over her head and slithered into Marta's pants. She hunted in the semi gloom for her boots and a pair of socks. "What did the dragon have to say?"

Fionn fired his mage light so she could find her other boot. "I think I'll let her tell you. Ready?"

She followed him down the hallway, took a turn through the kitchen, and they went out through the back door. "Where's Rune?"

"Right here." The wolf ran to her. The new day yielded just enough light for her to see his eyes gleaming gold. He looked happy.

"This way." Fionn led her around to the back of the house. Dewi lay on her belly, but Gwydion, Arawn, and Bran still had to look up to meet her whirling gaze.

"My MacLochlainn," Dewi purred and stretched out a taloned foreleg. "I have waited long for this." Her voice was musical and multi-toned. It reminded Aislinn of the Old Ones when they spoke English.

The dragon's words sank in, and Aislinn stopped in her tracks. "What do you mean?" Even though the men seemed to be looking right into Dewi's eyes, Aislinn avoided them. What if they sucked her in and she couldn't get away?

"You are the last of the Cenél nEgoghain, child. Eoghan was son to Niall Niogiallach. I brought him into his own as sacral king of Tara over a thousand years ago. The clan lived in Lochlann, a place of myth and magic far to the north—"

"Stop." Aislinn shook her head. "Too many names. I'll never remember, let alone be able to pronounce any of them." She glanced at Fionn. "There's that Irish history you wanted to force feed me."

"A wee bit," he conceded.

"Come closer, child. I will not eat you. I promise." Dewi lowered her snout and puffed a tiny flame Aislinn's way.

I rode her in my dream...

"It was not a dream." The dragon chuckled. Smoke curled from her nostrils. "Come." She crooked a claw at Aislinn and then glanced over one shoulder to her broad back in clear invitation.

"I-I can't," Aislinn whispered.

"Och aye, ye can and ye will." Fionn came up behind her, placed a hand on either side of her waist, and gave her a none-too-gentle shove. "Ye wouldna want to risk offending her. She is sacred to us."

Aislinn's heart pounded. She tried to swallow, but her mouth was dry as a riverbed after a year-long drought. The men parted to let her through. Heat engulfed her as she got closer to Dewi.

Aislinn laid a hand on the glittering scales. They were beautiful. Looking up at the huge body, she spied the two horns she'd grasped in her dream, but how on earth would she ever get to them? "Could one of you bring me that ladder over by the garage?" She barely recognized her voice as her own. It sounded thin and shaky.

One of the men stifled a laugh. "Come to the front, lass. She'll pick you up."

"Oh." Aislinn let herself be herded to the proper position. When the dragon's curved talons closed around her waist, she shut her eyes, afraid to look. *What if she drops me?*

"I could, but I won't. Not unless you give me reason. Open those eyes. Put your hand on my shoulder and swing yourself up. Catch one of the horns on my back or my head if you need help."

Aislinn felt awkward, but somehow, she ended up astride Dewi. She looked down at Rune, Bella, and the men. It was a long way to fall, and they hadn't even left the ground yet. Fear thrummed a tattoo against her neck and chest. She tried to get herself under better control. *This will be just like in my dream.*

"Only better." Dewi laughed and spread her enormous crimson wings. They were covered with leathery skin, not scales. A couple of pumps, and they were airborne. Aislinn held the horns at the base of Dewi's neck in a death grip. She focused on a small pattern of scales right in front of her, terrified to look down. Even that felt like too much, so she squeezed her eyes shut tight.

"Your eyes are closed," the dragon chided. "How will you ever learn to fight from my back if you cannot even open your eyes?"

"Is that why we're doing this?"

"Do you know nothing of your ancestry?" Despite the wind rushing past them, Aislinn heard a note of incredulity in Dewi's question.

"Not the ancestry you mean." Aislinn forced her eyes open. At first, she looked outward, marveling at the vista of east central Nevada spread below her. *Okay, this isn't so bad.* She realized she was breathing again. Her heartbeat, though far from normal, had slowed enough she wasn't worried about passing out and falling to her death. Dewi flew in large, lazy circles, with Marta's house as an epicenter.

"Hang on."

"Whoa, I was just getting comfortable."

The dragon laughed again. "I know. But child, we do not have the luxury of you spending a hundred years learning to ride me. You will sit upon my back and lead the charge against the dark."

"Me?" Aislinn's voice came out as a squeak.

"And who else? When I ride to war, it is with one of your blood astride me. That is how it has always been."

"Who was the last?"

"That would be Ian Gwinn MacLochlainn."

"When?"

Dewi laughed. Fire belched from her mouth. Smoke swirled and eddied past Aislinn. "I do not keep track like you humans, but sometime during the seventeenth century. Or maybe it was the sixteenth." The dragon banked, turning sharply first one way, then the other. After the initial swoop that left her stomach behind, Aislinn found it was rather like a carnival ride. She grinned, face plastered into the wind. "I think I'm going to like this."

"Of course you will. You were made for this, as was your mother. Too bad she fled the Old Country before her magic ripened." Something—maybe sadness, maybe disappointment—hung beneath Dewi's words.

The circles tightened as they got closer to the ground. At what seemed like the last minute, Dewi spread her wings like huge sails, and they landed far more lightly than Aislinn would've thought possible.

She threw a leg over, prepared to slither down Dewi's side, but the dragon reached back and plucked her down, depositing her into Fionn's arms. "My scales are sharp," Dewi said. "That would not have been a good way to dismount."

Aislinn wriggled out of Fionn's grip. So full of life she wanted to embrace the entire world, she danced around the yard, weaving in and out of the men with Rune nipping at her heels and barking. An undercurrent of Gaelic followed her. The only thing she made out was something like, *let the lass have this moment. 'Twill end all too soon.*

Aislinn spun and wove her way back to men and dragon. "Amazing!" She breathed deep. "Simply amazing." She looked right into Dewi's eyes, no longer afraid. "When can we do it again?"

"Soon. You need practice marshaling your magic in flight—and hitting targets from the air." Something warm brushed Aislinn's face and traveled down her body. Dewi was breathing on her, marking her. The warmth felt maternal somehow, with a tenderness that brought tears dangerously close to the surface.

With her scales glimmering in light from the newly risen sun, Dewi became progressively more insubstantial. In moments, she was gone. Aislinn wrapped her arms around herself. Without the dragon's warmth, the chill of dawn ate into her. "Where'd she go?"

"To gather as many of us as she can find in the Old Country—and other places." Gwydion's voice was deadly serious. "We go to war, lass. The sooner we mobilize worldwide, the better our chances will be."

"Yes, either we oust the dark, or surrender to them. There is no middle ground," Arawn snapped.

"You're only just now realizing that?" Aislinn stared at them, arms akimbo. She sounded rude, but didn't care. "Christ, I've known that ever since I watched my father die at their hands three years ago."

Fionn motioned for her to be quiet, but she ignored him. "Whoever Dewi went to find, I'll bet it's not the humans I've fought side by side with. Who's going to tell them what's happening?" She scanned the group, but the men seemed to be looking elsewhere. "We need to warn them. Remember, the Old Ones gave us our orders. That's how we knew where to go and who to fight. We had no idea they were in league with the dark."

The more she thought about it, the madder Aislinn got. Finally, she picked up a good-sized rock and chucked it at a nearby fence. It plonked off, and she chucked another. "Pretty fucking convenient, if you ask me. No wonder we never made any headway."

She ran to Fionn and grabbed his arm. "We have to let what's left of my race know. Otherwise, the Old Ones will lure them right to their doom. Plus, they'll fight for us. I know they will. They want to rid Earth of the dark more than anyone. We're the ones who've suffered most, watching everyone we ever loved die."

The tears that had threatened earlier overflowed and streamed down her face, but she didn't care if they made her look weak.

"Just how are ye proposing to do that?" Fionn's voice was gentle.

She brushed at her wet cheeks impatiently. "I know where some people are. I could tell them. They could tell others. It would be like a chain."

"How long would that take?" Gwydion, who'd walked over to them, asked.

"I don't know. Does it even matter?"

"Ye canna save them all—" Gwydion began.

"I know that," she broke in. "The important thing is that we at least try to warn as many as we can. We could start right here. There must be people between here and the Utah line." Spinning on her heels, she ran for the house.

Fionn and Rune dashed after her. "What are ye doing?" Fionn called.

"I'm going to get a few things together. Then I'm leaving. There's nothing for me to do here right now." Pounding up the steps, she slid through the wards and into the house.

"If ye insist on going, I'm coming with you," Fionn said. "But hold up, there are things ye need to know that might make this easier."

"I am coming, too." Rune panted. "We are bondmates. That means we stay together."

"What things?" Aislinn was in the bedroom, tossing things into her rucksack.

"Ye have all the human gifts—"

"Ridiculous," she spat, not bothering to look at him. "I had Mage and Seeker—"

"And ye added Healer and Hunter in the blink of an eye," he interrupted. "That leaves Seer. We discussed it while ye were getting to know Dewi and agreed ye must have that talent as well. MacLochlainns carry all the gifts. I told ye that ye had magic long afore the Surge. 'Tis not my fault ye dinna believe me."

"So?" She tossed her pack over one shoulder. "I'm ready to go. I plan to use my Seeker skills to find others like me."

Fionn closed on her, his blue eyes glittering. "Use your Seer skill first. It will show you a number of…probabilities. The best part is if ye doona like the future ye see, sometimes ye can change it."

"I suppose you have all five gifts, too?" She looked hard at him.

"Och aye, Lass. And a few more to boot." He took her hands, his gaze never leaving her face. "This willna take long. Let me help."

He hummed a low, hypnotic melody. Without understanding how she knew what to do, she picked up a harmonizing thread. Not unlike the day she'd slipped inside his head, a scene blossomed before her. She was back near her cave. Bodies lay strewn in the streets. Coming close, she recognized many of them, and her heart ached. Somehow, Travis wasn't there. Did that mean he was still alive? Was any of this real? Or was it a future that hadn't yet happened?

She asked a Seer's question, trying to sort what was real from what her eyes showed her. The bodies vanished, and she heaved a sigh of relief. Shelving her Seer magic in favor of Seeker skills, she went looking for others like herself and found them in caves and grottos, hiding from things that were trying to kill them. She tried to communicate, but no one recognized her presence, no matter what she did. She wondered what sort of magic rendered her totally invisible. Whatever it was, she needed to learn more about it. Though it was a problem now, she could think of lots of situations where it would be a boon. Finally, she grabbed a stick and wrote her message in the dirt. She put it lots of places so people would have to see it.

Danger. Do not trust the Old Ones. They are allied with the dark. Fight with us. Come to Ely as soon as you read this. Look for magic there, and you will find us. Once you've read this, destroy it.

For all their erudition, she was fairly certain the Lemurians couldn't read English. *I sure hope not. If they can, we're in for a bunch of unwelcome guests.* She thought she heard Fionn chuckle in the back of her mind. God, but she loved him.

"Good ye figured that out, mo leannán," echoed in her head.

So now I'm his sweetheart...

She wrenched herself back to Seer mode. The scene shifted to Salt Lake City. Her childhood neighborhood didn't look any worse than when she and Rune had left it. *Good.* It meant there'd be people to save. She wondered if she could do something from her trance state besides scratch messages in the dirt. It would sure save a lot of time. Ducking into a tunnel that she knew led to a Hunters' den, she ran through it. Sure enough, three Hunters and their animals were home. They looked gaunt and worried. Aislinn touched one, but he didn't so much as flinch. The bond animals—a cougar, a wolf, and a German shepherd—sniffed the air. They sensed her, but couldn't quite put what they perceived into a cohesive whole without a visual.

Aislinn pulled Mage magic. Fionn poured power into her, helping. She'd never tried to combine two gifts at once—she'd always used them sequentially—but she was desperate. She was here. The Hunters and their animals were here. If she tried to return later with her body, they might be gone. *She held her breath. Please, please, let them sense me.*

The mixture of magics did the trick. One of the Hunters, a solidly built woman with greasy black hair, hissed. "Something's here."

"Yes, my name is Aislinn—"

The woman's head whipped round. She raised her hands to pull magic. "Show yourself."

"I cannot. I am far away. But trust that I am human. I come to warn you—"

AISLINN WOULD HAVE FALLEN to the floor if Fionn hadn't caught her. They'd visited at least a hundred humans, spreading the word and exhorting them to tell everyone they knew. He backed her toward her bed. "Ssssh. Lie down, *mo croi.* Let me get you some mead."

Rune jumped onto the bed, licking her face and chiding her about leaving—even astrally—without him by her side.

"She'll be fine, laddie," Fionn assured the wolf. "Stay with her. I'll be right back."

When he returned carrying a flask and a bowl of food, she'd kicked off her boots and stuffed a pillow under her head. She tried to smile, but it felt beyond her. "Why do I feel like an entire team of mules kicked me in the guts?"

He grinned. "Because ye just used more magic than ye're used to —a whole lot more."

"Look at all we did." Pride filled her. "Once I've had something to eat, we can hunt down more people to warn."

He sat next to her on the bed, offering first the flask, then the bowl of yesterday's stew. "I have to admit it was a good idea. We'll need all the manpower we can gin up. A hundred humans would help a lot."

"What if we can find two hundred? Or five?" Aislinn spooned food into her mouth. Even though she was almost too done in to chew, she needed fuel before she could leave again. "How much of that was your magic?"

He shrugged. "Maybe a third. Maybe half. 'Tis hard to quantify such things."

"Thank you." A thought occurred to her. "Will I get stronger? So I won't need as much help from you?"

"Och aye, lass. 'Twill be interesting to see just how strong ye become."

Handing him the empty bowl, she opened her arms. Fionn shucked his clothing, snuggled next to her, and smoothed hair back from her face. He kissed her, his mouth gentle against hers. Before when they'd come together, they'd clawed at one another, desperate with need. This time, their lovemaking was slow and sweet. His hands glided under her clothes, caressing rather than grabbing. She covered his face with kisses and strung them down his chest until he moaned low in his throat. Murmuring endearments in Gaelic, he moved enough of her clothes aside to slip a hand between her legs. She wriggled against it, savoring the climax that rippled through her.

When she reached for him, he was hard. Christ, he was *always* hard. Aislinn smiled and wrapped her hand around him. She licked his chest and belly, positioned herself between his legs, and took him into her mouth. She'd never done that to him before. They'd always been in too much of a hurry to slam their bodies together. Licking, sucking, and stroking, she worked her way up and down his shaft, gratified by his gasps and moans. His cock swelled and got even harder, though that scarcely seemed possible. She cupped his balls and knew he was close by the tension in them.

He put a hand on either side of her head and pulled her off him. "I want to be inside you." His voice was rough with emotion. "To feel your body around me."

"Are you sure, because—"

"Aye, quite sure." He pulled her on top.

She spread herself to accommodate him. He felt so incredible that it was hard to breathe when he buried his full length inside her. Sex had never, never felt this mesmerizing. He pulled nearly all the way out, hands on her hips to keep her still. The tip of him danced just at the entrance to her vault, teasing her. She tried to slither out of his grip so she could get him back inside, but he wouldn't let her. When she thought she couldn't stand anymore, with every nerve ending on fire, trembling on the edge of another climax, he pushed into her ever so slowly. She came before he hit bottom, crying and shaking against him. He made that incredible sound like a big cat on the prowl and juddered hard inside her. The jolts of his release rocked her as his hands on her hips moved her just the way he liked.

Tears streaked her cheeks. Where had they come from? Overcome with emotion, she kissed him, murmuring his name over and over in between kisses.

"We shouldn't have." Guilt roiled through her as she pulled away. "There's so much to do..."

He offered her a crooked smile. "That may have taken all of ten minutes, fifteen tops. I say it was time well spent. Get dressed. Go toss some water on your face, and we'll have another go at warning more of your kinfolk."

"How long do we have?"

"At least until Dewi returns. Then she will require all your attention."

"You never told me why she was hanging out with the Old Ones, masquerading as their dragon, Orione. While you're at it, does anyone know what happened to him?"

He grinned. "That sounds like the woman I love. A piss pot of questions, to be sure."

"Are you going to answer any of them?" She couldn't help it. She grinned right back. "By the way, I like the sound of what you just said. The part about loving me."

His eyes softened from the midnight of a deep ocean to a mellower blue. "As do I, lass. Ye asked about Dewi. Originally, we, um, assigned her spy duty under Taltos. She'd run into a patch of difficulties and needed to get away from Ireland and us Celts. Once she was ensconced in her tunnel, though, somehow she knew ye would turn up sooner or later. Orione was weak. She killed him and used illusion to take his place."

"Do you know how long she waited for me?"

"Not exactly. From the sound of the tale she told us, at least a couple hundred years."

Aislinn sucked in a surprised breath and blew it out in a whoosh. "That's a hell of a long time before the last Surge—"

"I keep trying to tell you. The Convergence and Surges are a really small part of what's happening right now. Think bigger, Aislinn." He put his hands on her shoulders. "The key to survival is focusing on the right things. Never forget that. Now come on. We have work to do."

CHAPTER 21

"**G**ot it!" Aislinn exclaimed. "Damn. I finally hit something."

Dewi chortled, banked, and suggested, "Try another. We want to make sure it wasn't just a stroke of luck."

The dragon had returned hours ago. They'd been in the air for most of that time. So long that light was fading from the day. Aislinn pressed her legs into the dragon's sides. She'd gotten better at balancing without having to hang onto Dewi's horns, but it wasn't easy lobbing magic at a target when you were on the move. If it weren't for the marksmanship inherent in the Hunter gift, she didn't think she'd be able to hit the broad side of a barn.

As the dragon circled, getting ready for another pass, Aislinn's thoughts drifted. After she and Fionn made love, he'd joined his magic to hers. Sex seemed to fuel the linkage, because they'd accomplished even more than with their first round of warning visits. Aislinn was coming to appreciate the Seer gift. It was by far the most powerful of the five, because if the wielder was strong enough, they could truly turn back time.

She lost count of how many humans they reached before Fionn called her back. Body and soul reunited in the bedroom, she'd been so weary she stumbled and had to grab onto a chair so she wouldn't

244

fall. She'd looked longingly at her bed, but Gwydion stood in the bedroom doorway, beckoning her.

"What? Is the dragon back already?"

"Spent a wee spot of time in that bed, did ye?" the warrior magician had inquired archly. "Ye needn't answer that, lass. I smell sex in the air."

She colored. "That happened hours ago. I was looking at the bed because I'm tired."

"Doesna matter. I have a sharp nose. And eyes, too. Come. Dewi is many things, but patient isna one of them."

"Gwydion said that, did he?" Dewi's voice was sharp.

Jerked back to the present, Aislinn muttered, "If you don't like what you find in my head, stay out of it."

The dragon snorted. "I see what is in your mind. All of it. Fionn is a comely thing. Maybe I will invite him to my bed."

Aislinn was shocked at the pang of jealousy that shot through her. Fionn was hers. No other woman—

"We could share," Dewi suggested roguishly.

"Over my dead body. There, I hit the target again. Look."

"I have always shared what the MacLochlainn values," the dragon went on smoothly.

"Not this time." Aislinn ground her teeth together. She lobbed another jolt of magic. It hit home, dead center on one of the targets the men had set for her.

"Do it one more time," Dewi challenged, "and I might reconsider."

"There." Aislinn loosed magic. "Twice. See, I hit that one and the one right next to it."

"Very good, Daughter. Now listen to me. Anger is the key. Not too much. But the right amount fires your magic, makes it potent. I don't really want your man." Dewi huffed laughter into the air, blowing smoke so thick Aislinn could barely see. "But I made you angry, and your aim improved."

Aislinn gripped the dragon's horns and tried shaking them. Her aim had gotten better *before* the dragon baited her. If Dewi wanted anger, she'd… "Oh my God, look." Argument forgotten, she pointed. Humans poured into the yard, popping out from jumps from God only knew where. "Put me down, Dewi. I need to greet them. And reassure them, too."

"Do you truly believe arriving on a dragon's back will reassure anyone?"

Aislinn chuckled. Her giggles morphed into a deep belly laugh. "Now that you mention it, probably not. But it's one more reason to get me on the ground."

"You have half an hour. Then we will have another practice round." Dewi began the tight circles that would return them to Earth. "Remember, this will be much harder when the enemy is spread beneath us, trying to shoot me out of the air and you off my back."

She'd been spotted. Humans queued in knots, pointing at the sky, hands raised to call magic. Though it was nearly full dark, Dewi glowed, shedding enough light for Aislinn to see clearly. Fionn, Bran, Gwydion, and Arawn moved among the people, probably trying to calm them. Somehow, Aislinn didn't think the Celts would engender much more in the way of comfort than Dewi.

The dragon touched down. Reaching back, she helped Aislinn dismount and then folded her wings behind her and shut her whirling eyes. "I shall rest. See that I'm not disturbed."

"Did you really mobilize others to join the fight against the dark?"

Dewi opened one eye. "Of course. Now leave me be."

Aislinn wanted to ask where the other Celts were. It would be good information to share with the humans flooding Marta's yard. She considered telling Dewi she could find better places for a nap than a yard teeming with new arrivals, but she bit her tongue. After a final, pleased glance at targets she'd hit dead center every time, she moved toward one corner of what was rapidly becoming a crowd.

Probably should've sat with the men and come up with a strategy…

Aislinn realized they hadn't done so because none of them truly believed her frantic call to arms would yield more than a few stragglers. Enough humans crowded into the yard to really make a difference, and more were arriving every minute. Hundreds milled about, spilling onto the country road bordering Marta's house.

"Aislinn."

She spun, hearing her name. Travis loped to her, civet at his heels. She hugged him and said, "I'm so glad you're still alive."

"I thought it was you when I heard the message to assemble here. The Hunter who told me said your sending was pretty insubstantial, but he got the red hair and golden eyes right. You're the only one I know who looks like that." He gestured toward Dewi's bulk. "What's with the dragon? Are you a Hunter now, too?"

If you only knew the half of it...

"She is, and I am her bondmate." Rune emerged from the shadows under the back porch steps and trotted over. "Not that reptile over there."

The civet hissed. Rune growled back.

Travis rolled his eyes and clucked to the civet. "She doesn't like me to talk to other bond animals." He shifted his gaze to Aislinn, his brown eyes glowing with pleasure. "I'd been hoping I'd run into you again..."

Fionn materialized at her other side, with Bella perched on his shoulder. "Aislinn, ye need to be coming with me, lass. Gwydion is trying to organize them so ye can talk to small groups."

"Who's this joker?" Travis stepped between them.

"And I might be asking you the same thing." Fionn's blue eyes snapped dangerously.

Oh, crap. I do not need this.

Fionn's penetrating gaze shifted to her. "Friend of yours?"

"Yes," she said. "Travis was, ah is, a friend."

"Should I be leaving the two of you alone, then?" Fionn inquired much too smoothly.

Aislinn grimaced at the loaded question. Fionn was trolling for information.

"Great idea." Travis smiled, showing lots of teeth.

The civet hissed again. Bella shrieked and batted the air with her wings.

"No," Aislinn cried and stepped back from all of them. She was so tired her eyes ached in their sockets. Inhaling sharply, she watched both men. They circled one another, practically dripping testosterone.

"I've found out lots of things about myself." She aimed her words at Travis. "One of those things is I have a centuries-old bond with Fionn Mac—" She bit her tongue. "Uh, never mind."

"You don't even know his damn name," Travis sneered, "and you haven't been around for centuries. Give it a break, Aislinn. If you decided fucking me was a mistake, just tell me and be done with it." Hurt ran beneath his words.

She felt terrible. She'd never wanted to hurt him or anyone else. "I..." she started, but words wouldn't come. What could she say? Yeah, I liked you fine, but now there's someone I like a whole lot more?

Travis stalked off, civet in tow.

Fionn tipped her chin up with a forefinger and forced her to look at him. "If ye are wanting to follow him, best get on it afore he's lost in the crowd."

Anger brimmed and spilled over. "God damn it! He was just a man I fucked once. I liked him. Okay. But it's nothing compared with what I feel for you. Pull in your horns. You just carved *mine* all over me."

Shock bloomed on his face, and then Fionn threw back his head and roared. "So I did, lass," he managed to choke out when he could talk again. "Glad ye recognized it. Follow me."

Staggering from weariness, she struggled to keep up. "What would you have done if I'd said Travis was really special?"

"Killed him."

Good to know. She shook her head, sorry she'd asked. Fionn was talking to her, and she'd missed most of it. "Could you repeat that, please? I'm about done in. Wasn't listening, sorry."

He turned to her and scanned her face. With a curt nod, he put a hand on either side of her head. Energy flowed into her. She suckled him like a starving child.

"Better?" He took his hands away.

"Much. Thanks. Now, what were you trying to tell me?"

"What I should have before I got into such a snit seeing you with that Hunter. All of us, Dewi included, drafted a plan while you were riding her—"

Annoyance surfaced. "Why wasn't I included?"

"Because you had enough to think about between flying and target practice."

"Hmph." She crossed her arms over her chest. "What'd you decide without me?"

He eyed her, but didn't rise to the bait. "We believe it best to begin with the lesser dark gods, leaving Perrikus and his mother for last. They will be most difficult. Actually, we're hoping they'll leave if we can vanquish the other four."

"What about the Bal'ta, the wargs—"

"Not sure." He cut her off. "'Tis possible they may alter in some way so they're no longer a threat, once the dark magic fueling them leaves."

"How about human hybrids like Marta?"

He tossed his hands in the air, palms upward. "It's frustrating because there are many unknowns. Same answer, lass. They're even more nebulous, since none of us know if there are any more of them."

She nodded. It truly was amazing how much better she felt. "What did you do to me back there when you put your hands on my head?"

A corner of his mouth turned upward. "Fed you. And I will do it again. All ye need. I fear 'twill be a verra long time afore either of us can rest again. Or find comfort in one another's bodies."

Arawn took her arm. "This way. Think carefully afore ye speak. We need their help. None of us had any idea so many would heed the call."

Aislinn drew into herself, thinking. She was the one who'd started this particular train down the tracks. It was up to her to keep it from derailing.

"Do ye want me by your side?" Fionn asked.

"Always." The smile she gave him came from her heart.

Fionn clasped her hand and squeezed.

Aislinn stood tall. She knew how young she was. She'd have to do something to make them respect her, to gain and hold their attention. Suddenly, she knew what to say. Gwydion had them arranged in groups of about a hundred. Doing a quick nose count, she realized close to a thousand people had come. Her heart soared. They were going to win this war. Earth would be theirs again. She just knew it.

"Thank you for trusting me enough to come," she began. "My name is Aislinn Lenear. My father was killed the night of the last globally synchronized Surge. My mother went mad and was herded into the vortex. Over the last three years, nearly everyone I've cared about has been killed. When the Old Ones convinced me I was special, that I had magic, I was told I had Mage and Seeker gifts, with Seeker being the weaker of the two.

"About a month ago, I was ordered to Taltos under the guise that my gifts had come to the attention of the dark and I needed special training. Along the way, I found I had Hunter and Healer gifts as well." She whistled. Rune walked to her side and stared at the crowd. "This wolf taught me I was a Hunter. He was gravely wounded within the first twenty-four hours after I met him. Desperation helped me discover my Healer gift.

"Then I met the man standing beside me." She took a breath. She hadn't asked Fionn about this part and hoped it would be all right with him. "Against hope and reason, he is Fionn MacCumhaill, the Celtic god of wisdom, creation, protection, and knowledge. Somewhere in the crowd tonight are Gwydion, Bran, and Arawn, more Celtic gods here to offer help. According to the dragon, still more Celts are on their way. Because they live so long, they measure time differently than we do. They were waiting to see what would happen after the dark gods showed up. Well, they're not waiting any longer."

A muted roar rose from the crowd. Aislinn waited for it to die down.

"According to the Celts, the Lemurians are a dying race. Long before the last Surge, they plotted to overrun Earth, but knew they couldn't do it alone. They allied themselves with the dark gods and figured out a way to mate with humans. Results from that mating are in the house standing over there. Thank God they're protected by an enchantment. There may be more Lemurian-human hybrids. Now that we know they exist, we can watch out for them."

"How?" someone called.

"They're very tall. Like the Old Ones. According to my bond wolf, they smell different."

"So our best bet is to team with a Hunter and trust their animals?" a different voice asked.

"That's a good start," Aislinn agreed. "Besides, they'll stick out like sore thumbs. Not many of us are six-and-a-half feet tall."

"Go on," someone shouted.

"Yes, tell us more."

Aislinn threw her hair back over her shoulders. She blew out a breath. This was working, truly working. She had their interest. They believed her. She'd been so worried they'd turn away.

"The Celts think we should target D'Chel, Tokhots, Slototh, or Adva." Her stomach roiled. The names of evil rolling off her tongue sickened her. Fionn grabbed her hand. His touch calmed her, and the nausea subsided. "Sorry," she said. "Their names make me feel like I've eaten poison."

A sympathetic murmur rose from the crowd.

"What about their minions?" a voice called.

"The truth is, we don't know," Aislinn answered, aiming for absolute accuracy. "Without their dark masters, they may lose enough power that they're no longer a threat. Or they may leave."

"What about Perrikus and that mother of his?" It sounded like the same voice.

Aislinn peered into the crowd, but couldn't see who'd spoken.

"We save them for last."

"But if we killed them first," the voice argued, "the others might pack up and go. There are only two of them and four of the others."

A low murmur swept through the group, rising in intensity. The crowd seemed of two minds.

Fionn raised his hands. "Quiet." His American voice was back. "In the first place, killing the dark gods will be very difficult. They have a nasty habit of not staying dead, even when you've driven a stake through their heart."

"How do you know?" someone asked.

"Did you do that?" another chimed in.

"The short answer is yes. When I was certain the bastard was dead, I made the mistake of retracting my wards." Fionn shrugged. "I have a hell of a scar. Would anyone like to see?"

Aislinn visualized the thick white line traveling from the midpoint of Fionn's chest down to his pubis. She'd wondered how he'd gotten it. Good God, it was a miracle he hadn't faded away to the *Dreaming* or wherever the Celtic gods went once they'd been gravely wounded.

Once the laughter and ribald commentary—mostly from the women—that followed Fionn's question died down, Aislinn started talking again. "What I haven't told you yet is that my mother was descended from Irish kings. Apparently, she was supposed to remain in Ireland and produce an heir for the MacLochlainn line. Instead, she fell in love with my father and skipped across the Atlantic." She spread her hands in front of her. "My fate found me anyway. And that fate includes the dragon napping over there. She will battle the dark for us with me on her back."

A cheer obliterated her next words. Aislinn's heart thudded against her chest. She'd always been an intensely private person. To share so much was harder than she'd ever imagined it would be.

"Ye're doing fine," Fionn whispered against her ear. "In fact, ye may be done."

Aislinn recognized wisdom in his words. She'd sat through lots of speeches that had gone on far too long. When the crowd settled, she said, "That's really about all. We will decide where to strike first, travel there in small groups to maintain the advantage of surprise for as long as possible, and do our damnedest to get our planet back."

The applause was thunderous. Aislinn wondered who hadn't heard her and how many times she'd have to go over the same ground. Gwydion led her to another group, and she began anew. It wasn't as bad as she feared. Anxious to hear, people crowded together. In all, she only had to deliver her message five times. Rune stuck to her through the hours she stood on her feet talking. She could tell he was tired, but he never sat down. During a lull, she asked how he was. He licked her face and told her he was proud of her.

She was just following Fionn into the house, intent on something to drink and eat, when she heard Dewi deep in her mind. *"You did well. Now is time for more practice. You have had far more than the half hour I allotted you to be away from me."*

Fionn looked at her. "What does she want?"

"You can't hear her?"

He shook his head. "I know 'tis her, but I canna hear the words. Would I be asking you what she said if I already knew?"

"Time for more aerial games."

Fionn looked thoughtful. "Ask—and very carefully—if she minds you taking a handful of minutes to eat."

Aislinn's eyes widened. It would never have occurred to her to ask anything of the dragon. She was still in awe of her. But it wouldn't do to pass out and fall off her back, either.

"Do you mind if I take just a short time to eat and drink?"

"If you must. Hurry, Daughter. I miss you."

"She said yes." Aislinn quirked a brow at Fionn. "Gee, she's nearly as possessive as you are."

"Mayhap we'll be duking it out one day."

"Ha! She already said she'd like to fuck you."

"That," Fionn said, an odd light in his blue eyes, "would be verra interesting. I could spin you a tale of one of my ancestors who lay with a dragon—"

"Later." She made a chopping motion with one hand. "I need to eat. It's a long way past dinnertime." Aislinn stood over the stove and stuffed leftovers into her mouth, not bothering to heat them. Nearly everything they'd cooked was gone, so she ate dried meat and fruit to fill in once the pot was empty.

Footsteps sounded outside the door. She figured it was Arawn or one of them, so she didn't even look up until she heard a muted snarl from Rune, who stood guard nearby. Fionn flowed between her and the doorway. She couldn't see through him, so she took a couple steps to the side.

"Arguments are breaking out," a red-haired man with green eyes said. He was about five feet ten and looked like a tired, worn thirty-something.

"About what?" Aislinn asked, chewing.

"Whether we should throw in our lot with anyone who's not completely human."

"How do you feel?" Fionn asked softly.

"I'm here, aren't I?" the man asked defensively. "Figured if you knew, maybe you could do something before a bunch of us leave."

*a*islinn looked at Fionn. Asking for advice went against the grain, but he had far more experience in battle tactics. "What should we do?"

He raked a hand through his hair. "I think you should get on Dewi's back and give them a pyrotechnics display," he said with a flawless American intonation. She wondered how he kept how to talk to whom straight.

Explosives, my ass. "What am I, fucking Joan of Arc?" she demanded and wiped the remains of her meal off her mouth with the back of one hand.

Fionn smirked. "If you could channel that one, our problems would be over. Get moving."

"Who's Dewi?" The man sounded confused.

"The dragon." Aislinn sprinted for the door. She'd no sooner yanked it open when the buzz of angry voices reached her. The man's laughter followed her down the steps. *What the hell is so funny?*

Sending her Mage gift spinning outward, she heard snippets of conversation. People thought she wasn't what she'd told them. She'd disappeared, for God's sake. Maybe it was because she needed to replenish her magic so she'd look human again.

She eyed the crowd. Fionn was right. By the time she wove through the mass of humans and tried to settle them down, many would've already left. She needed something dramatic to stop them in their tracks. Aislinn raced to Dewi's side. "Okay," she said, panting. "I'm ready. We have to do something to keep all of them"—she gestured behind her—"from leaving."

"What did you have in mind?" Understated humor ran beneath Dewi's words as she lifted Aislinn to shoulder height.

"Mostly fire from you."

The dragon laughed, puffing smoke. "That can be arranged. Shall we?" Her powerful wings caught air under them, and she flew in slow, lazy circles. Her aim was incredible as she shot gouts of flame into the middle of small groups. It didn't take long before everyone was looking up, pointing. Unbelievably, someone—probably a Hunter—attacked.

Aislinn flattened herself against Dewi's neck, shock registering as a killing blow zinged toward them. The dragon evaded it easily. Once the danger was past, she didn't hesitate. Fire spewed from her. Someone on the ground turned into a pillar of flame. "That should take care of anyone else who seeks to harm us." An exultant note ran beneath the dragon's words.

Grief for the unknown human filled Aislinn and left a bitter taste. Dewi was just so...casual about taking life. Then she thought of Fionn. He'd meant what he said about killing Travis.

Shouts rose from the crowd. Raised fists shook their way, and she knew she had to do something. Focusing her Mage gift to make herself heard, Aislinn cried, "There's an enemy out there. It's not me, or any here. You waste time in paranoia. It would be more productive for you to gather others to help in our effort."

"You killed Richard," someone shouted.

"He tried to kill me," she countered. "What was I supposed to do? Deliver myself up to him?"

The crowd quieted. They were still talking amongst one another, but the edginess seemed to have dissipated. Aislinn projected her voice again. "Do what you must to ready yourselves. If you can bring more people here—or at least warn them not to heed the Old Ones—it would help."

"What are you going to do?" a woman asked.

"Practice focusing my magic from up here," Aislinn called back. "This is only my third time on Dewi's back." She waited, but her answer seemed to satisfy those on the ground. Aislinn drew in a shaky breath. At least for the moment, the crisis had been averted. Fionn and Rune stood on the back porch, looking right at her. Fionn gave her a thumbs-up gesture.

Aislinn shut her eyes for a moment, weary beyond reckoning. When she opened them, she thought she could actually see the warding around the house. She asked Dewi if that were possible.

"Of course it is. I've known it was there from the moment I arrived. The more you and I practice, the better you will get at seeing things through my eyes."

Aislinn thought about that. It made sense. Rune could merge his senses with hers, so why not Dewi? "Do you agree with the men about how to go about this?"

"What men?"

"Fionn, Arawn—"

"Oh, them," Dewi interrupted. "They seem like boys to me, since I've known them their entire lives."

"You didn't answer my question."

"Try for that target, and then I will."

"But that one's really far away," Aislinn protested. "And it's dark."

"Stretch your wings. It's the only way to expand your horizons."

Aislinn extended all her senses, feeling for the target with magic, since she could barely see it. "Hey!" Pride ripped through her. "Got it."

"Your facility with the Hunter magic is improving. Do it once more."

Caught up in honing her skills, Aislinn forgot about her question until Dewi touched down. "You owe me an answer," she said as Dewi helped her to the ground.

"So I do." The dragon chuckled, pluming smoke. "I am of two minds. If we could eradicate Perrikus and that mother of his, and Adva who controls portals and knowledge shared by all of them, the others would leave."

Aislinn waited, but Dewi didn't say anything else. "Why is that two minds?" she asked at last.

"Because agreement amongst leaders is key to success. The men, as you call them, felt differently. I was but one voice out of five."

"How hard will it be to kill the dark gods?"Dewi's hypnotic eyes drew her in. "My, what a predatory question, my dear." She hesitated. "I'm not certain they can be killed. The best we may achieve is to, shall we say, declaw them for a time."

"Would it be better to focus on the Lemurians?" Now that Aislinn had Dewi talking, she wanted to get as much information as she could. The Celts hadn't been nearly this forthcoming.

The dragon narrowed her eyes. Scales clanked against each other. Apparently, Dewi was considering how best to answer her. "I don't think so. The one large unknown is how many human hybrids they managed to make. If the only ones are here, the Old Ones' power is nearly at the end of a long cycle."

"And if they made a lot of hybrids?"

Dewi snorted. Flames sprayed from her mouth. "Then there is a whole new race that needs to be exterminated." Scaled lids dropped over Dewi's eyes, effectively severing the link between them. "Go now. I will let you know when I have need of you again."

Feeling cast adrift, Aislinn scanned the yard, looking for Rune. A newly risen moon was half full. It lent just enough light to help. Not seeing the wolf, she hunted for Fionn or the others. Finally, she caught sight of Gwydion and walked toward him. She tried for a brisk pace, realized she didn't have the energy, and settled for just putting one foot ahead of the other.

He spotted her long before she reached him and closed the distance between them. "Ye look as if ye lost your last friend."

Aislinn shook herself. "Sorry. Just tired. What's happening?"

"Things settled once Dewi killed that boy. Some went to warn, some to bring reinforcements."

"When do we leave?" She eyed him, taking in the hard planes of his face, blond braids, and chilly, blue eyes.

"With the dawn." She must have looked nonplussed, because he laid his hands on her shoulders and turned her toward the house. Letting go, he gave her a swat on the rump. "Get some rest. Can't have you falling off Dewi, now can we?" The laugh that followed her held a stony edge.

Hmph. Sounds as if he'd like to chuck me right off Dewi's back... Rune fell into step with her. She thought about asking where he'd been, but it didn't really matter. "Where's Fionn?"

"Inside with the other three."

"But I was just talking with Gwydion."

"And I just left all three of them sitting in the kitchen," Rune insisted.

Gwydion's a sorcerer, she reminded herself, *with power I can only imagine.* As she dragged herself up the steps, she wondered about Fionn. Was she making a mistake not to be wary of the magic that blazed from him? When it came down to it, who was anyone loyal to? *Yeah, probably not some young chickie they just met, prophecy be damned.*

She let Rune and herself into the kitchen and tried to corral her sour mood. Gwydion looked up from where he sat and gave her a broad wink.

Aislinn couldn't help herself. "How'd you do that?" she demanded.

"Do what?" Fionn moved his gaze from a piece of paper, where he'd been sketching something with a stick of blackened wood, to her.

"I just talked to him outside. But he's not there, he's here."

Fionn rolled his eyes. "Och aye, and that's an old trick of his. Pay it no heed."

From her perch atop the stove, Bella cawed. It sounded like the bird was laughing.

"While we're at it…" Aislinn slid her body down a wall, ending up in a heap on the floor. "Why was that guy who warned us about the crowd laughing when I left?"

"I think 'twas because the idea of a real-life, fire-breathing dragon enchanted him, lass." Fionn's gaze sharpened. "There's little enough laughter. Doona begrudge someone a wee bit of mirth."

She dropped her head into her hands. A headache pounded behind her left temple. Her eyes ached. When she took a general inventory, scarcely a body part had escaped damage. Everything was complaining. Her eyes fluttered closed, and the rise and fall of conversation turned into a muted hum. She felt Fionn's energy beside her. He lifted her, cradling her against his body as if she weighed nothing.

"Rest," he murmured into her hair as he laid her on their bed. "I'll wake you once we've put a meal together."

He commanded Rune to watch over her. The wolf's growl was the last thing she heard before darkness fell like a heavy curtain, obliterating everything.

∽

SHE WOKE LONG ENOUGH to eat from the bowl Fionn brought and wriggle out of sweat-soaked clothes that had dried on her body. The next thing that awakened her was his mouth trailing kisses up her leg.

"Is it time to go?"

"Soon."

Bella flapped around the room, looking for a place to light.

Aislinn reached for consciousness, feeling fuzzyheaded. "I talked to Dewi. She thinks we should target Perrikus first."

"Aye, I know she thinks that."

"She's old and wise. Maybe we should listen to her." Aislinn scooted to a sitting position. The chilly bedroom air turned her upper body to gooseflesh.

Fionn interrupted his kisses long enough to shoot her a patronizing look with his brows furled.

Damn, he's playing the god card again...

"I am not." He repositioned himself so he was sitting on the bed and looking at her with a solemn expression. "Even with all the human help, ye need to understand the odds of us prevailing aren't high."

"Why not? Until they showed up here, the dark gods were just characters in Marvel Comics."

He barked a harsh laugh. "Never believe that, lass. Whoever penned those illustrated books had run-ins with the dark gods. 'Tis why they ended up memorialized in what ye call comics. The dark gods are real. And they are old. Far older than any of the rest of us."

"Dewi said the best we could hope for was to slow them down."

"Did she now?" A corner of his mouth twitched. So did the muscle under one eye. "I'm not surprised. She's battled them afore."

"So have you." She traced the scar that ran up his midline with a finger, realizing as she did so that he was naked. Aislinn set her teeth in a determined line. "Both of you are still alive, so maybe it's not as hopeless as you think."

"Why do ye suppose the lot of us were waiting to see what would happen? No one wants to throw their life away—"

"Can you die?"

He snorted. "Och aye. Mayhap not dead exactly, but I can be driven to a place where I might wish I were."

"I can Heal whatever happens to you."

"If ye find me in time."

"What happens if I don't?"

"I wander forever, soul separated from body, longing for you."

He traced a fingertip around one of her nipples, then bent and kissed it. His tongue felt warm, swirling around mounded flesh that had already hardened into a point from the cold air in the bedroom.

A jolt of desire rocked her, and she closed her arms around him, pulling him close. "Do we have time?"

He raised his mouth from her breast. "Not much. But Aislinn, this may be the last time we have together. Battles are never certain. One of us may not come out the other end of it intact."

Her throat closed. Caught between lust and dread, breathing became a struggle. His mouth covered hers. His kissed her as if they had all the time in the world. The spicy, musky scent that was his and his alone enveloped her. She pushed thoughts of the battle to come aside. It wasn't as if she hadn't seen combat. But the stakes had never been so high. Before, she'd trusted that the Old Ones were orchestrating everything. They'd provided a buffer between her and the dark. She was just thinking how stupid she'd been, and how naïve, when he shoved the covers down more and spread her legs.

"I am all that will be in your mind, *mo leannán*," he murmured just before his mouth settled between her legs, breathing heat into her.

He licked at her, tasted her. She lifted her hips and twined her fingers into his hair, trying to get closer. What he was doing felt incredible, but he amped the intensity tenfold when he sucked on her clitoris and sank fingers inside to press something that made her crazy. She wasn't even sure what he was doing, but it made her come over and over, the orgasms so close that she wasn't sure when one stopped and the next began.

He slid his body up hers and buried himself inside her. She raised her legs, locking them around his hips. He told her he loved her in Gaelic over and over before he closed his mouth atop hers. She tasted herself on him; it made her wild with lust. They rocked together for an eternity that ended all too soon. He made that sound she loved—a purring low in the back of his throat—when he came, juddering hard. She'd come so much that another climax seemed impossible, but he carried her with him, hands gripping her ass and pulling her even tighter against him.

"'Tis time to be off," Bran said from the doorway. "What is it with the two of you? Shy of pulling one off the other, or dumping a bucket of cold water over you, I couldna get your attention."

"Ye're just jealous." Fionn gasped. He balanced himself on his arms and pulled his cock out. Still hard, it glistened with their fluids.

"Doona believe him, lass." Bran laughed. "Just say the word, and I'll show you mine. 'Tis bigger than his."

Aislinn giggled. "Yeah, and I'll just bet it's hard all the time, too." She wiped at herself with a sheet and started tossing clothes on, aware of Bran's gaze.

"I can see why ye picked this one." Bran stepped close enough to jab Fionn in the arm. "She's a beauty."

"She's mine," Fionn growled. "Never forget that. Leave us. We'll be out soon enough."

Aislinn layered on clothes and stuffed extra things she thought she'd need into her rucksack. "Are we taking any food?"

"Nay, we can hunt for what we need."

"May I talk with you?" Rune left the shadows in a corner of the room and padded to her side. "Alone." He looked pointedly at Fionn, who furled his brows.

"And here I was thinking we were friends, lad."

"That has nothing to do with it."

Maybe it was something in the wolf's tone, but Fionn finished dressing quickly, held out an arm for Bella, and left the room.

"What is it?" Aislinn hunkered down so she and Rune were at eye level.

"I do not like it that the dragon will take you where we cannot fight together."

Aislinn thought about that and realized she didn't like it either. She said as much, adding, "It can't be helped for now. You'll be on the ground when I land—"

"Not the same," he snapped. "Bondmates were never meant to be separated. I fear it will bring us bad luck."

"I can ask Dewi. Maybe she'll know some other way."

To Aislinn's surprise, Rune snarled. "She won't help. In her mind, you are her bondmate, not mine."

Aislinn placed a hand on either side of Rune's head. "You're a part of me. Have faith. I'll figure something out."

<h1 style="text-align:center">CHAPTER 23</h1>

*A*islinn emerged from the house into the gray of a new day. Clouds were thick in the sky, and the air smelled like snow. Winter had been mild since the snowstorm when she'd waited for Travis, but it looked like the trend was about to change. Fionn, Arawn, Gwydion, and Bran circulated among the humans. She assumed they were issuing final instructions. Slototh was their first target. For some reason, the men thought he'd be the easiest to provoke into making a stupid mistake.

The basic plan hadn't changed, despite Dewi's concerns. The humans would jump to an area in the southwestern Arizona desert, landing just outside Yuma. At least it wouldn't be snowing there. Aislinn would jump with Fionn. The other Celts would leave before them. Dewi would get there in her own way. She'd tried to talk Aislinn into flying on her back a few minutes ago, but Aislinn had demurred.

"It's too far. I'd be tired by the time we got there. And I need to link to Rune to make sure he comes out at the right place."

Dewi had bristled, especially after Aislinn mentioned Rune. She did it on purpose to test his theory that the dragon saw him as a rival. As usual, the wolf's instincts about others were spot on. Dewi argued, cajoled, even tried to force Aislinn with compulsion, until Gwydion called her off, saying, "We havena the time for this." It was actually a relief when Dewi made a leap for the skies and was gone. Aislinn raked her hands through her hair and hoped the dragon would've moved past her pique by the time they regrouped in Arizona.

Looking every inch a warrior, Fionn walked briskly to her and Rune, with Bella riding on his shoulder. He'd changed into tight-fitting leather breeches, a leather shirt, and a mailed hauberk. Vambraces hugged his arms. The only parts of his attire that hadn't changed were lace up leather boots that came halfway to his knees. "Ready?"

She felt like quite the rube in Marta's rolled-up black work pants, sadly worn leather boots, green wool shirt from the McCloud Fishing Lodge, and black Gore-Tex jacket with a black watch cap pulled nearly to her eyes. *Oh well. Not exactly a fashion contest here.* She met his gaze, tried to smile, but couldn't. "No. I don't think I could ever be ready for something that might mean we lose our planet to the dark."

"Good you're on edge. It means ye'll be careful. We leave in about ten minutes."

She buried a hand in Rune's ruff, taking comfort from his simple, animal warmth. Since she had time, she pulled off her hat, separated her long, thick hair into two sections, and braided it to keep it out of her eyes. "Are you scared?"

Fionn shook his head.

"Why not?"

"Lass, 'tis only the first of what will likely be a long string of battles. It could take years to rid ourselves of four dark gods—if 'tis even possible. We'll find out soon enough if we need a different plan. Doona forget, the dark gods are only part of the problem. There will be others to fight along the way."

"Like Dewi. I think she's jealous of Rune." Aislinn's hand flew to her mouth. She hadn't meant to blurt it out like that. Braids done, she jammed her hat over them to mask her discomfort.

Fionn laughed. "Dragons are jealous of everyone. 'Tis the way of things."

Rune's jaws snapped together. "Not funny, human." Bella cawed her support.

Fionn stroked the wolf's head. "Not to worry. Aislinn belongs to you and me."

And Dewi. What about just belonging to myself, goddammit?

Aislinn shielded her thoughts. She stole a quick glance at Fionn, but it didn't seem he'd noticed. He had to be inside her mind to read it. Problem was he could sneak in there without her knowing. As much to cover her inner turmoil as anything, she asked, "What happened to the other Celts Dewi supposedly went to the Old Country to raise?"

Fionn skewered her with a grim look, his brows drawn together. "Aye, lass. Now that ye mention it, we'd all like to know that."

She felt him pull the magic that would take them where they were going. While it would've taken her several jumps to get from Ely to their destination, Fionn assured her he could do it in two. They'd probably arrive before most of the humans, but it would allow time to finalize their plans.

For a moment or two, she felt sad about leaving Marta's house. It was where she'd realized she was in love with Fionn. Then she thought about the ensorcelled hybrids in the attic and decided she and Fionn could do better elsewhere. They'd have to come back sometime and destroy the bodies, but that was way down the line. Years, from what Fionn suggested. Or maybe never if they needed the gates between worlds to remain open.

A weightless sensation began in her feet. She felt for the outlines of Fionn's spell, made sure it encompassed Rune, and they were gone.

∾

A surprising number of humans were already there when Aislinn and Fionn arrived. Arawn, Bran, and Gwydion had set up something like a field headquarters, complete with chairs for themselves, in a huge indentation where massive, black rock walls butted against one another. They checked the humans in by having them write their names on some sort of tablet. It lit, absorbed a name, and cleared itself for the next person. Aislinn stared at it, fascinated. What mix of electronics and magic could do something like that?

Arawn and Bran were outfitted similarly to Fionn. Gwydion wore his trademark robe, red this time. His staff leaned off to one side. Aislinn wondered if he was still barefoot. Fionn trotted toward the other Celts. She followed, looked around for Dewi, and was relieved to not find her.

"About half the humans are here," Gwydion informed them.

"So soon?" Aislinn felt stunned. Had their magic been that much weaker than everyone else's?

"Surprised us, too." Arawn told her. "'Tis all the magic directed at one place. Apparently, it eases the journey, though we've lost the element of surprise—if we ever had it in the first place."

I need to remember that Fionn's not the only one who can read my mind. Aislinn nodded, while trying to maintain a neutral expression. She wanted to tell him to stay out of her head, but figured they'd be wasted words.

"Listen up, lass," Gwydion said. Something in his tone made her glance sharply at him. "Slototh is holed up in the remains of a prison in Yuma, surrounded by human shades and Bal'ta. Because he absorbs everything that has been discarded, the shades cling to him, drawn like lodestones, hoping to recover something of themselves. 'Tis possible there will be some you recognize. Doona let yourself be distracted from your task."

"To me, Daughter."

Aislinn's head whipped around. Dewi. But where was she?

"Right here. I have been here all along. We must refine your eyesight."

Sure enough, when Aislinn focused her Mage senses, she saw the dragon squatting in the dirt off to one side. Seemingly satisfied, Dewi withdrew whatever spell had kept her hidden.

Aislinn turned to Fionn. "Take care of Rune."

"Aye, that I will." He bent to kiss her.

"I will watch over your bond animal as well." Arawn nodded curtly.

Moving away from Fionn, Aislinn crouched next to Rune. "I will only ride until we get to the battlefield. Then I will fight by your side." The wolf leaned into her, and she hugged him.

Aislinn waved to Dewi. "Be right there," she called brightly. The antagonism between dragon and wolf felt wrong. She didn't like being in the middle, and she felt protective of Rune.

"How many are here?" she asked Gwydion.

"Better than twelve hundred, but it's finally slowing down." He spread his arms wide. "Thank you. This was your idea."

Her mouth split into a crooked smile. "I had no idea it would work out so well. How soon before we leave? And how far is it from here to that prison?"

"Less than a mile. We are splitting into four companies, one led by each of us." Gwydion's gaze swept over the mass of humanity gathered into four camps and at the few still signing in. Getting up, he tapped Arawn and Bran on the shoulder. "Marshal your companies and leave. Fionn and I will do the same as soon as we are done here."

"Why did you get everyone's names?" Aislinn asked. "Most people's families are dead, so what difference do names make anymore?"

He gave her a sad, slow smile. "Ye have never truly been in wartime afore, lass. We do it to keep track of the living—and the dead."

"MacLochlainn!"

"Whoops, Dewi is *not* happy." Blowing a kiss to Fionn and Rune,

Aislinn took off at a dead run for the dragon, a plethora of excuses running through her head.

Smoke plumed from the dragon's nostrils. "I told you it was time for us to go. Why did you not heed me? Next time, I will make you sorry you disobeyed."

Aislinn stood in front of Dewi, the palliatory words she'd planned evaporated in a rush of anger. Seething, she crossed her arms over her chest. "Now you look here," she snapped. "We're supposed to be partners. You think you call the shots and I jump to your whistle—and maybe that's how things were in the Middle Ages —but I can't operate like that. I'm nobody's lackey. Not even yours. So either we come up with some way we can make this work, or I'm going to the battle with Fionn. Your choice."

Something like a growl came from the dragon. It was so loud, the packed dirt beneath Aislinn's feet vibrated, but she stood her ground. If she backed down now, she'd be no better than a slave.

"You dare to speak thus to me?" Dewi spoke very clearly, enunciating each word.

"I guess so. I just did." Aislinn spread her hands in front of her. "I'd like to make this work. You're old and powerful, and I could learn a lot from you, but you can't treat me like a child, even if that's what I seem like to you."

Dewi huffed. Smoke blanketed Aislinn so thickly she began to cough. "Stop that," she gasped, spitting black-flecked phlegm. "I need to leave. Am I flying with you or not?"

"Get on. We can talk about this later."

Aislinn smiled inwardly. She'd won. Or had she? What if Dewi tried to dump her off as soon as they were in the air? She was practically certain she could pull enough magic to soften her landing, but not positive. *I'll take my chances.* She swung into place where the dragon's neck and body connected. *She needs me, waited hundreds of years for me. She's not going to kill me. At least, not right now.*

"Perceptive of you," sounded in her mind. The words held a snarky

you may have won this round, but I have more cards up my sleeve intonation.

"Damn it!" she muttered. "Between you and Fionn and Rune, I don't have any privacy at all."

"What were you talking with Gwydion about?" Dewi ignored Aislinn's comment.

"Strategy. I needed to hear what he had to say. All my fighting until now has been done either alone or with one or two others."

The whirr of the dragon's wings—soothing and hypnotic—was loud in Aislinn's ears. She rather liked her perch atop Dewi, at least when the dragon wasn't being possessive and demanding. The massive bulk of what had to be their objective was just coming into view. Like most buildings in the southwest, it was stucco, with rounded archways and a flat roof. Much of the structure had fallen in. She was astonished something that sturdy had succumbed to decay in only a few years. *Maybe the prisoners trashed it when they escaped after the Surge.*

"Well." The dragon sounded annoyed. "Are you going to share *our* strategy with me?"

Dewi's question startled her. "Sorry. I figured you already knew. That you'd talked to one of the other Celts. Anyway, Gwydion and the rest of them have split the humans into four groups; one will approach from each direction. You and I will touch down in the middle. I will join Fionn's group, and we'll storm the gates."

"What will I be doing?"

"Uh, I'm not sure. Can you make yourself small enough to get inside the prison?"

Dewi snorted. "Maybe, but I do not like this. I want the battle outside, so I can kill the enemy. I suffered the Old Ones, pretending to be something I was not, for long years while I waited for you. Now I would indulge my baser passions."

"I'll do what I can," Aislinn murmured, not at all certain she'd have any control over much of anything once the fighting heated up. She thought about apologizing for Dewi's long wait, but didn't.

After all, it wasn't her fault she was linked to a clan dragon. She hadn't even known about her until she'd gone into Taltos.

"Look sharp," Dewi crowed.

Aislinn's thoughts scattered like so much dust. She scanned the ground. Bal'ta poured out of the prison ruins. "Looks like you'll get your wish." She grinned. Now that it came down to it, she welcomed a chance to kill those bastards. "Wait a minute."

"What?"

"They used to be light avoidant. That's why we were sure we'd be fighting them inside. What happened?"

"Simple enough." The dragon made an *hmphing* sound. "Slototh wove a spell to protect them. In fact, I can see it. Look, Daughter. It's that blackish shroud hanging in pieces over everything."

Aislinn sharpened her vision with magic. Sure enough, translucent sheathing drifted in the air. It was worrisome she'd needed the dragon to point it out. She vowed to be more observant. Sloppiness could get her killed quicker than anything else.

"Did the Celts tell each human to ward himself?" Dewi broke into her thoughts.

Aislinn rolled her eyes. "They'd have done that without directions. Do you think we're so stupid we want to die?"

"Just checking. In battle, as in everything else, details make all the difference." She paused a beat. "You need to work on your attitude."

Like hell I do.

Flames belched from Dewi's mouth. She banked low over a mass of Bal'ta. Dragon fire blasted through the sheathing and engulfed them in flames that didn't go out, even when the abominations rolled on the ground. Slototh's mantle reknit itself around the hole. Fear settled in Aislinn's belly. Slototh was powerful. Maybe the Celts had underestimated him. If he was the weakest of the lot...

Don't think about that. I need to fight what's in front of me.

Aislinn took careful aim, thrilled when a Bal'ta exploded. She did it again. And again. Her worries dissolved in blood lust. All four companies were in the thick of things now. The stink of magic hung over everything. Every time dark magic collided with their magic, an explosion buffeted them. Aislinn clung to the dragon with her legs and called destruction down on so many Bal'ta, she lost count. The hairy ape-like creatures blanketed the ground. Dead humans did, too. Not as many, but their side was suffering losses.

"No more." Disappointment ran beneath Dewi's words.

Craning her neck, Aislinn realized Bal'ta had stopped racing out to the slaughter. Either they were all dead, or Slototh, recognizing a frontal attack wasn't working, had called them back. Dewi circled lazily. They watched the four companies regroup and start toward an archway leading inside.

"Looks like we're back to Plan A," Aislinn said. "Put me down so I can go with them."

"From a military perspective, it would be better for us to stand guard out here. That way we could pick off—"

"You're more than capable of doing that without me," Aislinn broke in, her voice cold. "I asked nicely for you to land so I can get off. If you don't, I'll pull magic and jump to the ground."

The dragon's body heated beneath her legs. Aislinn figured she was royally pissed, but at least they were losing altitude. They connected with the ground so hard Aislinn's teeth clanked together. She waited for Dewi to reach back for her, decided the dragon wasn't going to make it easy, and worked her way down, catching both skin and clothing on scales. Dewi hadn't been kidding when she'd warned that wasn't a good way to dismount. The closer Aislinn got to the ground, the sharper the scales got.

She surveyed the cuts on her hands. They weren't deep, but they stung. To minimize further damage, she jumped the last four feet, landed in a tuck, rolled to her feet, and sprinted after the tail end of one of the companies just disappearing into the prison. Fionn and Rune were nowhere in sight. Maybe she'd find them inside. She knew better than to use her mind voice to call. If one of them was sore pressed in battle, that single moment where their thoughts diverted to her might mean their death.

The terror she'd packed away in a corner of her mind wanted out. She stuffed it untidily back away. *Not now.* Her mouth was dry, but she didn't have time to get water from her rucksack. She passed under the archway and scanned a large interior room, blinking in the dim light. It seemed she was alone. Which way had everyone gone? How the hell had they cleared out so fast?

Feeling an off-key vibration low in her spine, she warded herself and spun hard to one side. Something was targeting her, but what? *Christ! After all my big talk to Dewi, how could I not have warded myself?* Breath rattled in her chest. She pivoted her head from side to side, Mage senses wide open. If she was the only one here, who was trying to kill her? Aislinn looked harder, using tricks Fionn and Dewi had taught her.

There. In that corner. Like the Bal'ta, but more so, sat a blackness that swallowed everything. Impossibly high, not far from what had to be a ten-foot ceiling, a pair of red eyes glowed. Whatever it was, its head must be huge, since the eyes were a foot-and-a-half apart. Aislinn bit back panic. She swallowed hard and wondered if it was Slototh. Then she knew it had to be. For some unknown reason, he'd let everyone else race past him. She eyed one of three openings at the far end of the room and then looked back at the door she'd come through, but the dark god moved and blocked her egress that way.

Pulling invisibility, she sidled away from him.

"I can still see you." Laughter, deep and raucous, filled the air.

Fear sank sharp teeth into her belly. She ran for the far end of the room, her lungs on fire with effort. *Almost there. Not much more.* The doorway she'd been heading toward slammed shut in her face, and she skidded to a halt, panting.

Okay. Escape isn't an option. Turning, she faced the spot that drew darkness. "What do you want with me?"

"I could ask you the same thing, human. Why am I suddenly host to four Celtic gods, a dragon, and humans, all hell-bent on destroying me?"

She drew herself up tall. "Because we want you to go back to the world you came from before the Surge."

More laughter. The temperature in the room plummeted. Ice chips rattled down on her. She wrapped her arms around herself trying to keep warm, trying to think. Because Slototh was the god of filth, she'd expected rancid odors, slime, and debris. Maybe Gwydion had made a mistake, and this was one of the others.

"You got it right the first time," Slototh said once he stopped laughing. "I am the god of all that is discarded. Filth and slime are common misperceptions. Why, I even have some things of yours," he added slyly.

"Like what? How could you possibly have anything of mine?"

"Try your hopes and dreams. The ones that shattered three years ago. I have the future you had hoped for. Your husband and the children that will never be." He made a snuffling sound that might have been a chuckle. "I have everyone's, of course, but I have enjoyed yours far more than most. What a treat that you delivered yourself to me. You saved me a great deal of trouble finding you."

The blackness shifted. If felt as if someone sucked all the air out of the room. Her lungs ached. She clutched at her throat. Just when she was certain she was going to pass out, a man stepped out of the darkness, and air returned to the room.

"I suppose I should've warned you. I'm so used to it, I don't even think about it." He paused. "I thought you might like me better this way." The man standing before her was every bit as gorgeous as Perrikus or D'Chel. He had gleaming black hair, dark blue eyes, prominent cheekbones, and a strong jaw. A cream-colored linen shirt clung to the muscled lines of his chest and shoulders. A pair of crisply pressed black slacks snugged around slender hips. He wore expensive-looking leather loafers. A pale blue sweater was slung over one shoulder. He could've passed for a male model or a movie star.

Dewi was right. I should've stayed with her. Aislinn waited for a jolt of sexual energy, for the lust that would bring her to her knees, but it didn't come.

"Well," she stared defiantly at the man before her, "aren't you going to try to seduce me where I stand, like Perrikus and D'Chel?"

He smiled. It was a beautiful smile that made the corners of his eyes crinkle with delight. "Oh no, my dear. What would be the sport in that? I prefer my women to beg for me. It ruins things if I've cheated. They spread their legs, but I know they didn't really want to." Something feral gleamed in the back of his eyes, but it extinguished itself so fast that she wasn't certain she'd seen it.

He held out a hand. "Coming?"

"That depends. Where are you taking me?"

"It will be a surprise."

Aislinn shook her head. "I'm not into surprises."

Something rippled across those perfect features, but Slototh got control of himself. "I could take you anywhere I wanted, with or without your permission."

"Okay." She stared right at him. "I'm waiting." Aislinn fanned magic around herself. She reached for Dewi and felt the dragon link to her, seeing through her eyes. Shock and outrage surged from the dragon, and then power poured into her so fast Aislinn wasn't sure what to do with it all. She raised her hands, surprised to see flames shoot from the tips of her fingers. Then she realized the link to Dewi was a two-way street. Secrets roiled through the dragon's mind. Aislinn wanted to dig deep, to know what Devi knew. Instead, she borrowed the dragon's power to reinforce her warding.

She danced from side to side on the balls of her feet, taking in her adversary. "Come and get me," she snarled.

"Never forget you asked." The voice was silky smooth, radiating danger. "Before we are through, you will discard a few more things for my collection."

The air shifted again. Slototh, back in his light-sucking form, closed the distance between them. Fire didn't faze him. She threw all the magic she had at him. It bounced off and sizzled when it hit the stone floor. She tried to dart behind him, to run outside to Dewi and freedom.

He grabbed her as she ran past, plucked her off the ground, and raised her so his red eyes could bore into her. "Your wards are a joke. So is that thing out there. You're coming with me. Enough games."

Fire roared through the arched doorway where Dewi tried to cram her bulk inside. The flames danced around Slototh, as if they were afraid to touch him. Filled with helpless rage that twisted her stomach into knots, Aislinn ground her teeth together.

There's got to be a way out of this. But what?

A pressure differential made her ears hurt. Her skin burned with icy heat where Slototh held her. They came out in a large room. She saw an enormous bed next to one wall and an array of things that looked like medieval torture devices along another. In places, the floor was splattered red. Before she could take in any more, he dropped her. She tried to tuck her body together, but landed wrong. Pain shot up one arm. Aislinn curled onto her side, wondering if she'd broken anything. Her gaze lit on a rack, complete with pawls and bars. She shuddered.

"Get up."

"What if I refuse?"

Pain ratcheted through her. It felt as if her skull was about to explode. She staggered to her feet. When she hunted for the link to Dewi, it was gone.

"That's better. Your dragon pest cannot penetrate the wards around this room. By the time I'm through with you, the little war you foisted off on me should be over."

"How? You're not there to run it, and the Bal'ta aren't smart enough." *Maybe if I keep him talking, I'll think of something I can do.*

"Remember the labyrinth?"

She nodded.

"I built one here. The Celts and their stupid human sheep

followers should be good and lost by now. They'll be lucky to find their way out in a hundred years. By then, everyone will have starved to death."

"They can use magic."

"It will boomerang right back at them. Funny acoustics in the labyrinth. That Minotaur was crazy, but smart as a whip. I took his ideas and did them one better." Slototh inclined his head. For one bizarre moment, he looked like an emcee at an awards ceremony. "The Minotaur is here. He liked the idea of fresh food. It's been a long while since anyone thought to send him human sacrifices." The dark god sighed. "I miss the old days. Things were so much…easier."

He morphed back into man form. The transformation sucked the air out of the room again. She gagged, but maybe because she was expecting it, she didn't have the same sense of being half suffocated this time.

His eyes gleamed as he looked at her. "Take your clothes off. They'll just be in the way."

What do I have to lose?

Pulling every ounce of magic she could summon, Aislinn heaved it at him. When it didn't do much other than bring a surprised look to his face, rather like he welcomed a challenge, she glanced about. Desperation burned through her. If magic wouldn't do it, maybe something else would. An iron rod leaned against the wall next to the rack. She lunged for it and swung at him, connecting with his neck.

CHAPTER 24

The crack sounded loud against the silence of the room. Not waiting to see if she'd hurt him, Aislinn swung again. This time, the bar thunked against warding. *Shit!* She used her Mage gift to blast a hole and drove the rod through right behind her magic. Iridescent blood spewed out, steaming and hissing where it contacted the stone floor.

Slototh bared his teeth. The sound of his breathing, ragged and breathy, eddied between them. His human form shimmered.

Nooooo! She was sure he was more vulnerable as a human. She did *not* want him back in beast mode. Her heart stuttered in her chest. She pulled her top up, exposing herself. "Don't change back."

"What? You like it rough?" A knowing smile spread across his face. "Never would have guessed that from your discards."

She managed to nod. The wound she'd opened in his neck was closing rapidly. She wondered if she could hurt him enough to buy herself time to jump out of there. He walked toward her, flexing his hands. She forced herself to keep her breasts out. Anything to bring him within reach again.

"Drop that piece of iron."

Dredging up what she hoped would pass for a genuine smile, she let go of it. The rod clanked loudly as it clattered to the floor.

He closed a hand over one breast, twisted the nipple, and then lowered his head to bite down on it. She felt his warding fall when he touched her. Excitement thrummed through her, but she batted it aside—and waited. She'd have to pick her moment carefully. If she blew it, she wouldn't get a second chance. His mouth moved to the other breast, then to her mouth. Blood, hot and salty, flowed where he bit into her lips. She ignored the pain and focused her mind.

The cadence of his breathing increased. Something huge and hard as stone pressed into her stomach. His cock. Christ! It felt as if it was two feet long. She tried to twist away, but he just bit harder. Shoving both hands between them, she closed her fingers around his shaft. She dug into it as hard as she could. He bucked against her, obviously enjoying the hell out of what would have reduced any other man to shrieks of agony.

Her lungs smarted from the effort of fighting him. She tried to knee his balls. Anticipating her, he kicked her leg aside, doubled up a fist, and punched her full in the face. It sounded like a cannon went off inside her head, and she felt the bones crack in one cheek. More blood filled her mouth. She spit it out, gasping for air.

Slototh was done toying with her. She didn't think she had much time left before he finished her off. Reaching deep, she channeled her pain and despair into anger. Magic hurtled out, aimed for his carotid artery. She gave it everything she had, willing the walled vessel to burst. Her exhilaration when she felt it rupture was heady. *I haven't won yet. The bastard might be able to heal himself.*

He leapt back from her, a horrified expression on his face, and clapped a hand to the side of his neck. "You bitch," he snarled. "You fucking bitch."

She felt him grope for his beast form. *Can't let that happen.* Weaving fire and air, she built walls around him, praying they'd hold, that he wouldn't just shatter them with a thought. His throat was swelling visibly because there was nowhere for all that blood to go. How long did it take a human body to bleed out? Eight minutes? Ten? How long would it take him? Aislinn added reinforcements to the barrier keeping him in his human body. Her breath rasped, harsh in the still air, and then plumed white, as the temperature in the room dropped. She heard him struggling to breathe, too. A gurgly, grating quality raised her hopes that he might actually be dying.

Ha! Wishful thinking.

Could he die? If Fionn couldn't, why would she delude herself this thing could? *He doesn't have to die. I just need five minutes to get out of here.*

His neck was twice its normal size, the skin stretched so taut she was amazed it didn't fracture and burst burst. Maybe the key was to create an injury that got worse faster than they could heal themselves. Speaking of which, she took half a second to glance at her wrist. It was grotesquely swollen, probably sprained. Maybe broken. She patted her smashed face gingerly and winced. No matter. She'd take care of herself later—if there was a later.

Slototh sank to the floor. His eyes fluttered shut. Iridescent blood trickled out his mouth, nose, and ears, picking up speed as internal channels opened. Was he far enough gone? Could she risk a jump, or would he grab her when she was most vulnerable? She checked the wards around him. They were solid. If he could've broken through, he would have.

Aislinn reminded herself to breathe. She'd never been so terrified in her life. *Can't think about that now.* Her top was still north of her breasts. She yanked it savagely back down. *Okay.* She took one last look at Slototh. He was turning gray. There would never be a better chance.

Frantic to escape, she summoned power, expecting him to spring to his feet and sabotage her in the middle of her jump preparations. It didn't happen. She visualized the yard where she'd left Dewi, wrapped herself in magic, and was gone. When she tumbled out into a brightly lit day, she was so relieved sobs ripped through her, making her broken face ache.

Dewi. Where was Dewi? Aislinn looked about, frantic. From out of nowhere, familiar talons grabbed her and slung her into place as the dragon's wings beat the air. Aislinn wrapped her arms around Dewi's neck. They wouldn't go very far, not nearly all the way around, but she hugged Dewi as hard as she could. Jagged pain lanced up her arm. She remembered her wrist and drew back. One side of her face throbbed.

"Tell me," Dewi hissed. "Everything."

Aislinn did, shamelessly sucking every ounce of compassion the dragon laved on her, drinking it down like mother's milk. "Anyway, I couldn't have been very far away, because it only took a few minutes to jump back to where you found me." She paused to draw breath.

"He probably had you somewhere in that labyrinth he told you about. Wonder how extensive the tunneling is and if I could fit in it." The dragon banked, swinging them into another large arc.

When she thought she could stand to hear the answer, Aislinn asked, "Do you think he's dead?"

Such a long silence pulsed between them that Aislinn thought Dewi wasn't going to answer. At last, the dragon said, "Probably not, but it will take a long time for him to resurrect himself into something menacing."

Well, that's a piece of good news. "You need to put me down."

"Not a good idea. Look what happened last time I did that."

"I have to Heal my wrist and face."

"That's not the real reason."

Aislinn winced. It made her face hurt worse. The dragon was canny. The time they'd spent in one another's heads had given Dewi sharp intuition about how Aislinn's mind worked. "No, it's not. Once I'm done with my injuries, I'm going after Fionn and the others. I can't let them die."

"Did Slototh really tell you the Minotaur is somewhere down there?" Dewi sounded fascinated.

"Yes. Why? Is he a long lost relative or something? Ah, sorry. I didn't mean that." In spite of the backlash from the wind, Aislinn felt heat rise to her face.

"Now that you mention it, we're sort of like cousins, in a very distant way, of course." Dewi started the tight circles that meant they were landing. This time, she helped Aislinn down and sat guard over her while she Healed her injuries. Shucking her pack, Aislinn found a water bottle and drank until it was gone. Her belly clutched with hunger, but she couldn't take the time to hunt or prepare anything. She kept hoping someone would come out the archway leading into the prison, but no one did. Other than her and Dewi, it was silent as a crypt.

"Shall we use magic to try to see something?" Dewi's voice was uncharacteristically soft. "If you insist on going in there, you need all the information you can get."

"Wherever Slototh took me was deep. Made my ears hurt."

"Do you want to link to my mind?"

"Yes." The word was no sooner out than her perspective shifted. It was like sharing Rune's senses, but amped up a hundredfold. The dragon's vision was multi-dimensional. She sent it auguring into the earth beneath them. Time passed. A part of them—their astral selves?—oozed through walls and floors, seeking what had become of the Celts and humans.

"Enough of this." Dewi's voice sounded as if it were coming from the bottom of a very deep well.

Aislinn blinked. The familiar ground in front of the prison shimmered into being around her. "That bastard! He lied to me. There's no one down there. I didn't get any sense of their passage."

"They went somewhere," Dewi observed.

Aislinn stumbled to her feet. "I'm going back inside. I can track them with Seeker magic." She met the dragon's whirling eyes, daring a contradiction. "We tried it astrally. It didn't work."

Dewi puffed smoke, started to say something, and then clanged her jaws shut. Her double rows of sharp teeth made a grinding sound. "We will establish and maintain a mind link so I can see what you do."

Aislinn smiled. "Thanks. Even though I know you can't rescue me, it'll be nice to not be totally alone." Shouldering her pack, she trotted toward the arched entrance. Every bone and muscle in her body ached. Part of her was afraid Slototh might've gotten a second wind, patched himself up somehow, and would be lying in wait to pounce the second she crossed the threshold.

That's ridiculous. If he could've killed me, I'd be dead.

She slipped inside the relative coolness of the stucco building and summoned her mage light. Sweeping the area with her Hunter senses, she looked for the enemy. Hunter magic wouldn't pick up shades, but she wasn't worried about them. She felt the dragon inside her head, urging her to use Seeker magic.

"I'm getting to that," she told Dewi. *"Wanted to make sure it was safe first."*

The Seeker gift sent streamers of glimmering light through the large room and beyond. It took more magic to make a visible trail, but Aislinn didn't want to have to keep checking her bearings. "Please," she sent up a prayer to whoever might be listening, "don't let me be too late."

She walked for a long time. The large room led to another. From there, she took several flights of stairs down into the earth, passing multiple levels holding empty cells. Rats scurried along walkways littered with scraps of clothing, human waste, and the odd dish. She left markings each place she reached a choice point, hoping they'd help her find her way back if something happened and she couldn't use her magic. Corridors gave way to tunnels weaving ever lower. She found water running down a wall and took a few minutes to fill her belly and her water bottle. Occasionally, she tried her link with Rune, but came up dry. She was just starting to question if her Seeker gift had somehow gone awry, when she heard distant footsteps pounding the ground. Aislinn pulled her magic and her mage light back quickly and flattened herself against a wall.

She heard grunting before she saw the thing. Impossibly huge and glowing, its horns spanned the width of the tunnel. It slowed as it got close to her, its bull's head turning this way and that on a thick stalk of a neck.

"Fascinating," Dewi breathed. *"See if you can get him to talk to you."*

"I'd rather stay out of its way."

"Come on, girl. Grow a set."

Aislinn snorted. She'd expect a comment like that in a seedy bar, not from a thousand-year-old dragon. She turned her attention back to the Minotaur. It had stopped about ten feet from her. She heard it breathing, a wet, sloppy sound.

"What are you doing in my realm?" Its voice was low and rumbly and made the walls vibrate. It took another step toward her.

"Looking for my friends. Have you seen anyone? Just tell me, and I'll be on my way."

Aislinn held her breath. The thing towered over her. Christ, it was almost as tall as Slototh's beast form had been. In a moment of unpleasant revelation, she wondered if it was really Slototh and not the Minotaur at all. *Can't be. He feels different.*

"Are you the one who hurt Master?"

Shit, oh shit, he knows. "What do I do?" she asked Dewi.

The dragon laughed. *"Incredible. He's really there with you. Tell him none of us have masters. He probably would've killed Slototh himself if he could've figured out how to get away with it."*

Aislinn wondered what Dewi meant by *us,* but she didn't have time to sort it out. She risked a flicker of magic for her mage light. It streamed pale against the darkness. In its light, the Minotaur looked even more daunting, like the creature out of myth that he was. Brown fur merged with skin midway down his chest. He was naked and had the biggest cock she'd ever seen. Fully erect, it curved against a flat stomach. Enormous balls hung between legs heavy with muscle that bowed out slightly. Aislinn swallowed. She might not be able to outrun the thing in front of her, but if it came down to it, she figured she was far more agile.

"Yes, it was me."

She met wide-set bovine eyes. The Minotaur bared squared off teeth and snarled.

"I should kill you." It snaked out a shockingly fast hand and closed it around her upper arm.

Aislinn pulled fire. Her skin heated, but it didn't make any difference. The Minotaur held fast. He didn't even seem to notice the smoke rising from his hand or the smell of burnt flesh.

"Young," he hissed wetly and licked his thick lips with a white-flecked tongue. Twin fires danced in the backs of his eyes. "Young like the ones they sent me in Knossos."

"Oh no, I'm not," she countered still trying to pull away from him. It felt like she was chained to a mountainside. "They were children. I'm not."

He trailed his other hand down her body and backed her against a wall. His enormous cock pressed into her breasts. A trail of saliva hung from his lips, glittering in her mage light. "No matter. You'll do." He jammed a hand between her legs. She writhed, trying to get away.

Aislinn reached for magic to fight him, but ran up against a barrier. *Damn! It has to be the Minotaur—or the dragon.* She tried to sever her connection with Dewi to see if the dragon had turned on her for some unknown reason, but it was too late. Aislinn felt her body stretching, changing. Her neck grew, wings sprouted. She looked out through whirling eyes, hot with lust. Dewi had taken her over, using their link as a conduit to inveigle herself into the tunnel.

Goddammit! She wants to fuck the Minotaur.

Horrified and violated, Aislinn was also swept away by passion so deep and primal it obliterated everything else in the world.

"Why couldn't you do this when Slototh nearly killed me?" she demanded, clinging to a thread of sanity in a river of sexual sensation.

"I tried." Dewi sounded defensive. *"He blocked me."*

Desperate to escape the dragon's body, Aislinn took a different tack. *"Let me go. Distant cousins, my ass. You and the Minotaur know one other."*

"You might say that. Hush. I am done talking—until after."

Helpless, trapped inside Dewi, wave after wave of erotic fascination rolled through Aislinn as the dragon positioned herself for that immense cock. Aislinn wanted to run, but couldn't figure out how to separate herself from the dragon. She wanted to stay and have the Minotaur fuck them forever.

Dewi wriggled back against the Minotaur and twisted her tail aside, seating him inside her. Fire belched from her mouth, and she roared her delight. The Minotaur settled his hands on Dewi's haunches. He lifted them as he slammed himself home over and over again. Just when Aislinn thought she couldn't stand another second of sharing her body with the dragon, Dewi's body spasmed, giving Aislinn the most intense orgasm she'd ever had in her life. It shattered her, felt incredible—and wrong. As wrong as sex with one of the dark gods would have been, no matter how her body reacted.

I've got to get out of this. "Dewi! Let me go right now. Damn you. If you ever want me to do anything with you ever again, release me from your body."

"But you enjoyed him as much as I did," Dewi panted deep in her mind. *"I did it for us. We can share your Celt the same way."*

"Not a fucking chance. And I say bullshit. You did it for you. I don't care how many hundreds of years it's been since you got laid. I want out of your body. Now."

Aislinn felt herself shrinking. Arms took form, then legs. Shakily, she stepped away from the dragon and her consort, noticing they were still coupled. From the looks of things, they'd be going at it for hours. The Minotaur's breath caught as he jammed himself into Dewi. Gripping her scaled sides, he threw back his head, laughed, and told her he'd forgotten what a little vixen she was.

Little vixen? Not exactly her view of Dewi. If she hadn't been so intent on escape, Aislinn would've laughed until her sides hurt.

She slipped deeper into the tunnel. She had to find Fionn. What she didn't understand was why she hadn't found him yet. She'd been following the Seeker magic. She clapped a hand to her head. Perhaps some of what Slototh said was true. He'd told her the labyrinth perverted magic, made it bounce back in unusual ways.

"Maybe I marched right by them and didn't take the right side tunnel," she mumbled.

"Where are you going?" Dewi demanded.

"To find Fionn and the others."

"I could help—once I'm done here."

"I'll keep it in mind." Aislinn snorted.

Right. It will be a cold day in hell before I ever trust her again. Or let her into my head for anything.

She considered retracing her steps, but changed her mind and pulled magic to jump back to the chamber next to the front door. If Seeker magic wouldn't do it, she'd use her Seer gift and ask it to take her back in time to when Fionn and Rune had entered the prison.

More than anything, the length of time it took her to return to the chamber told her how far underground she'd been. Much farther than where Slototh had dragged her. Something nagged at her. The dark god's name. She could think it now and say it without struggling not to puke. Did that mean he was neutralized? At least for now? She dared to let herself hope.

Settling near the open, arched doorway, she reveled in feeling sunshine on her back. Was it still the same day, or had she been underground so long it was tomorrow? She shook her head hard. It didn't matter. The only thing that did was finding Fionn, Rune, and the others.

Unbuckling her pack, she shoved it under her butt. She still felt sore and stretched from the Minotaur's bulky member. How the hell had Dewi done that?

The same way Rune merges with me. The difference is he respects me. She doesn't.

Recalling exactly what Fionn had done when he'd led her into her Seer magic, she closed her eyes and summoned a trance state. When she thought she had it, she asked the magic to show her Fionn leading his company through this very room. Spectral bodies marched past her. Ones that got close dissolved when they ran up against her, only to reanimate on the other side. She sent her astral self trailing after the last of the company.

Shades blocked her way, but she shoved though them. Her astral projection wasn't warm, so she didn't have anything they wanted. The ghostly company went into the prison itself, not down where she'd been. As Aislinn followed them down long, stone walkways, she was amazed how large the place was.

Must have housed thousands...

Finally, she saw dazed humans, wandering from cell to cell, and her heart leapt. They were here after all. It was the damned labyrinth that had confounded things. Her joy faded as she watched them. It was like they'd been hypnotized, eyes glazed, staring straight ahead. Fionn! Where was he? Or Rune? He should be easy enough to find. She tried calling, then realized no one would hear her. She needed her body for that.

Because she didn't need the spectral soldiers to show her the way, Aislinn sped back to her body, shoving shades out of the way as she went. The disorienting thump as astral and physical bodies collided practically flattened her. She wondered how long it had been since she'd eaten.

Pushing the thought away—there'd be time to eat later—she took off at a lope for where she'd found the humans. The shades were more than an annoyance this time. She was warm and breathing. They wanted what she had, so they swarmed her, clawing at her with skeletal fingers. One sliced her with a knife, but the cut wasn't deep. She kicked the blade out of his hand and pocketed it so he couldn't jump her from behind. Enemies who were already dead were such a pain in the ass.

Shoved hard from the rear, she sprawled face down on the floor, spitting out dirt. God only knew how many piled on her and pushed her down. Aislinn reached for her magic, but it was useless against shades, since they were beyond feeling pain.

"Let me go," she begged. "You have to let me go. Friends are trapped in this building." She wondered if telling them that was a mistake. Shades fed on life. If they didn't already know a bunch of live bodies could be found nearby, she'd just torn the lid off that can.

"And you'll be a'lettin' her go," a low, melodic female voice with a strong Irish lilt said. "Now. I won't be a'tellin' you agin."

Aislinn gasped as the weight holding her down evaporated like dew on a hot morning. She'd know that voice anywhere. Getting to her feet, she ignored the cut places on her hands. She searched the gloom, didn't find what she sought, so she cranked more lumens into her mage light.

"Mother? I know you're here. Show yourself."

$\mathcal{T}$ara Lenear stepped out of the mass of shades. Her red hair was still long and luminous. Her golden eyes glowed with delight. She held out her hands. The nails were cracked, the skin split and desiccated. "Ach, *mo leannán*," she crooned. "I never thought to see you agin in this life."

Aislinn's throat thickened with unshed tears. "Thanks, Mom," she managed brokenly. "If you could keep the rest of them off me, I have people to rescue."

Cold, dead fingers closed on Aislinn's hand. She squeezed back. Stepping close, she hugged her mother. Underneath the stench of dead meat, she could still pick out the smells she'd always associated with Tara: lavender, cinnamon, and vanilla.

"Could I be helpin'?" her mother asked.

Aislinn didn't have to think long. Having her mother by her side again was impossible to refuse. "Sure. Let's go." She sprinted down the corridor.

When she got close to where she'd seen the humans Aislinn opened her mind, questing for Rune, and found him. *"Where are you?"*

"Locked behind a magic barrier." He growled. *"Fionn is here, but something is wrong. I cannot rouse him."*

Aislinn didn't think she'd ever heard anything quite so welcome as the wolf's voice in her mind.

"Who are you talking to?" Tara demanded. Her eyes narrowed. "Fionn who?"

I can't tell her everything. It will take too long.

"Mother, I know you have magic. It's where mine came from. Can you help me find a barricade held in place by a spell?"

Her mother's head snapped up. It seemed she was scenting the air. "The dragon," she muttered. "That *uafásach* dragon is down here somewhere."

"No shit." Aislinn snorted. "She's not the problem, Mother. Focus! I have to find Fionn."

"Really, why? Watch your language, child."

Aislinn blew out a frustrated breath. *I do not have time for this.* "It's Fionn MacCumhaill, Mother."

"Och aye, why didn't ye say so? He was my betrothed, afore your Da. I ran like hell to get away." Tara Lenear faded from sight.

"Glad we've got that straight," Aislinn muttered, staring after her mother.

A wandering human bumped into her. Aislinn grabbed him by the shoulders and gave him a good jolt of magic. His eyes cleared. "Shit," he muttered. "What happened? Last thing I remember, I was marching behind Ted…"

Aislinn released him. "Wake up everyone you come across. Once you wake another, tell them the same thing. Out is that way." She pointed back over one shoulder. "Just keep taking right turns. It should start to look familiar once you come to the parts before you ran into this ensorcellment."

Knee deep in lifting what fortunately had been a weak spell for every human she saw, Aislinn didn't pay any attention when her mother's bony hand closed over her shoulder.

"Ye never did listen well. I tell you, I've found 'em. Come wi' me."

Heart in her throat, Aislinn raced after her mother. Tara floated rather than walked—and she moved fast.

"Ach, 'tis here." Tara threw her hands upward in a helpless gesture. They crashed down soundlessly on something invisible. "I canna break it. What's left o' my body isna strong enough."

Aislinn's magic was already spinning outward. She felt the shape of the working immediately. It was intricate. Because it might be booby trapped in some way that would blow all of them to kingdom come, she felt her way carefully, wishing she wasn't so hungry and tired. She was more likely to make mistakes when she couldn't think straight.

Fionn's there, she told herself. *Just on the other side of this.*

"Can ye no' see the working, Daughter?" Tara asked.

Aislinn looked at her mother. She'd been so intent on unraveling the convoluted magic that she'd nearly forgotten about her. The first layer had fallen. Many more crowded beneath it, each seemingly more interwoven than the last. "Tell me what you see." She met Tara's gaze, so like her own, golden in the glow from her mage light.

"'Twould be easier to start from the bottom corner, just over there. Ye needn't dismantle the entire thing. Just a wee hole big enough to crawl through would do the trick."

Mom was always smart.

Aislinn shuffled over to inspect the place her mother had indicated. Excitement coursed through her. The weave was grainier there, not so tight. She started snipping strands with her Mage gift, letting it show her the next one in line.

"It's big enough," she told Tara. "I'm going through."

"Careful, lass. Ye—"

A whine and the scrabble of claws on stone broke into her mother's words. Rune launched himself at her and drove her to the ground. Aislinn closed her arms around him. He licked her face over and over again, and she realized she was crying.

"Quick," she said, "I need to see what's happened to Fionn."

"This way." Rune belly-crawled back through the opening, with Aislinn right behind him.

The air felt thick inside the working. Tendrils dragged against her, cooing soothing nothings. *"No worries. None at all. Lie down. Rest. You are so tired. Rest is what you need. Rest and dreams..."*

She fought the casting. It was like something out of fairy tales, where the princess slept for a hundred years. Anyone not paying attention would fall asleep. *Let's hope a kiss is all it takes to wake Fionn...* She crawled to where he lay crumpled against a rock wall, one arm thrown across his face.

"Fionn!" She shook him. Tears streamed down her face. She reached for him with her heart, laid her face next to his, and showered him with kisses while she ran her hands over his familiar body.

"Won't work." Rune stood next to her. "I've licked him, bit him, talked to him. I don't understand what happened. One minute, we were leading a company. The next, we stumbled through something like sticky spider's webs. Fionn recognized what it was. He cursed and tried to backtrack, but he couldn't focus his magic on the wall that closed behind us."

"Whatever this is doesn't affect you?" Aislinn considered how she could leverage that if it were true.

"No." Rune verified her suspicions. "Not me, but Bella's just as far under as Fionn."

"Bella!" Aislinn felt ashamed. She'd totally forgotten the bird. "Where is she?"

Rune trotted to a dark corner. Aislinn followed and scooped up the raven, who'd frozen into position, her head under one wing.

"Do you have any idea what happened to Gwydion and the others?"

"No."

Cradling Bella against her, Aislinn tried to link with Fionn's mind, but it was closed to her. She tried again, pushing hard with her Mage gift. Then with her Seer gift. It was like running up against a castle wall. She took his hand. Thank God it was warm.

Something he'd said slammed into her. She'd blithely told him she could Heal him, and he'd replied only if she found him in time. Then there'd been that part about his body being severed from his soul.

She rocked back on her heels. She needed Gwydion or Arawn or Bran. Someone who knew more than she did. Even Dewi. No, scratch that. She didn't trust the dragon as far as she could see her.

Tara materialized by her side. "Och aye and 'tis thick in here. We need to drag him outside this enchantment."

"Are you sure we won't hurt him?" Aislinn locked gazes with her mother.

Tara cocked her head to one side in a gesture Aislinn remembered so well it tore at her heart. "Nay. But we canna leave him in here. That will kill him for certain. Mayhap not kill," she amended, "but he will sink so deep, 'twill no longer matter. Where did ye get the bird?"

"It's Fionn's bonded one."

"Aye, then, and it must be the same one. A nasty piece, she was. I am certain time hasna improved her temperament." Tara Lenear chuckled coldly. "Mayhap we could be leavin' that one asleep."

Between her and her mother, they managed to drag Fionn outside the enchantment. Rune tried to help, but all they did was fall over one another. Aislinn had to make the hole bigger, but not all that much. She made a second trip for Bella and tucked the bird into a protected corner. Her head spinning from weariness, Aislinn sank to the stone floor next to Fionn and caught her breath. He looked about the same. She watched the rise and fall of his chest and tried linking to his mind again.

Why can't I get in?

She rocked back on her heels and dredged through every magical possibility she knew, but nothing fit her needs. "Do you know what's wrong?" Aislinn eyed her mother, floating a few inches above the floor.

"Aye."

Aislinn waited, but Tara didn't say anything else. "Are you going to tell me?"

The shade that had been her mother shrugged. "It willna matter. I doona think ye can fix it."

"Tell me anyway." Aislinn drew one of Fionn's hands into her lap.

Rune whined. "I am sorry. The air did not feel that tainted to me, or I would have warned him."

"Not your fault." Aislinn turned toward Tara. "Come on, Mom. Talk."

"Hmph! Ye used to be more respectful."

"Sure, when I still had a normal life and two parents."

Her mother looked so sad Aislinn wished she'd kept her mouth shut.

"The avenging one knew all of you were coming," Tara said at last. "He had a scrying pool—"

"How do you know that?"

"And how else, Daughter? I spied on him. He were no friend to the likes o' us. We had little enough left, and he would have been stealin' even that if we would ha' let him."

All that is discarded... "Go on," Aislinn said softly. Compassion for her mother thrummed through her. "I won't interrupt again."

"He knew the four Celts. I heard him cursin' them roundly from that obscenity of a bedroom of his. Particularly Fionn. For some reason, Slototh hated him with a fury. He set traps for the Celts— breathed their names into them, he did. T'others, he just let wander, confused. I'm thinkin' he dinna believe humans would be canny enough to find their own way out."

Well, that settles what happened to Gwydion, Arawn, and Bran. "Mom, hold up a minute. I know I said I wouldn't interrupt, but since you know the feel of Slototh's traps, would you mind seeing if you can find the others?"

"I will." The wolf took off at a lope before she was done talking.

Tara shook a finger at her. "Ye shouldna say the wicked one's name aloud. 'Tis bad luck."

Aislinn laughed bitterly. "Yes, I've had more than my share of that. You said you know where Fionn is. Why can't I reach him now that he's lying right in front of me?"

"Fionn barricaded himself deep to keep the evil one out. He could be in the *Dreaming*. He might be elsewhere. All I know is that he isna here. I canna feel him, though I sense his warmth." Tara hesitated. "Ye need Gwydion, master enchanter that he is. Or the dragon."

Aislinn clenched her jaw. The last thing she wanted was to ask Dewi for help, not after the trick she'd pulled with the Minotaur, but she wasn't about to let Fionn waste away wherever he was, either. "There's got to be another way," she muttered.

"Where did ye learn about magic, Daughter?" Tara's question had an edge to it.

"It was either embrace it or follow you into the vortex."

"Oh." A pause, then, "I am sorry. I dinna prepare you verra well. But I couldna find my way back to a world without your Da in it."

Aislinn reached out a hand. "It's okay, Mom. You didn't know what was going to happen."

"Och aye, but I did." Tara jabbed her bony index finger skyward. "The Seer gift, it runs strong in me. I told Jacob we should stop goin' to anything linked to the Convergence, but he insisted." One corner of what was left of her mouth turned downward. "I never could refuse that man anything."

Crouched in a dark stone corridor, clutching Fionn's hand, with her mage light suspended off to one side, Aislinn wanted to scream at her mother. To remind her she'd had a duty to her daughter as well. She bit back bitter words. This wasn't the time. Besides, it wouldn't change anything. Anger was an indulgence, and she barely had enough strength left to keep herself conscious and moving forward.

"Where did you get yourself off to?"

Gritting her teeth, Aislinn answered Dewi. *"I am in the prison itself, many hundreds of feet above where I left you. Did that...thing leave?"*

"He's really quite sensitive—"

"Can it. Is he gone?"

Dewi chuckled. *"He's asleep. I must have worn him out. Men are so fragile that way. Open your mind so I can find you."*

"In a pig's eye. You'll have to find me the old fashioned way or not at all."

The dragon didn't answer.

"Well, either she's on her way here, or we got lucky and she's mad at me and not coming," Aislinn mumbled.

"Who?"

"Your old nemesis, the dragon."

Tara's expression softened. Aislinn took a good look at her mother. Most of her face from her cheeks upward was still intact. It was only lower down, where gashes interrupted what had once been living tissue, that she didn't look like herself. Wounding was permanent for shades. Since their blood no longer circulated, they couldn't heal themselves. Flesh rotted where skin no longer covered it.

"I loved her when I was little." Tara's eyes filled with a faraway look. "She took me flyin'."

"What happened?"

Tara tossed her hands in a Gaelic *je ne sais* gesture. "I dinna care for my future bein' mapped out from afore the day of my birth. Dewi never gave me a minute to myself. I couldna keep secrets from that one. Once I was old enough, I left. Then I met your Da and rewrote my future."

Aislinn's Seeker gift pinged a sour note. Her mother had left some things out. She opened her mouth to ask what pieces Tara had omitted, when she heard Rune's claws scrape against stone as he rounded a corner.

"I bit my way through," he crowed. "Got Gwydion. He was trapped, but not asleep. Not deep, anyway. He came around as soon as I nipped him in a few key places."

Footsteps sounded, bare skin slapping against stone, punctuated by the tap of a staff. "There ye are," the mage growled at the wolf. "I told you to wait for me. I'm still foggy from Slototh—" Gwydion's mouth fell open. "Tara MacLochlainn, as I live and breathe. Lass, ye've been killed. Why are ye not on the far side of the veil?" He hastened to her side and gathered her close. Strong emotion rippled through the muscles in his face and jaw. Dead or no, Gwydion liked having her mother in his arms. He looked like a dying man who'd been given a second chance.

Rune nudged her hand. "I'm going to find the other two."

Aislinn bent and kissed the top of his furred head. "Thank you."

"Thank me when all are safe."

Aislinn turned back to Gwydion and her mother. "You loved her," she blurted, seared by sudden understanding. Tara hadn't told her that part. It was what she'd been hiding. Her mother had been promised to Fionn, but she loved Gwydion. Tara had solved the problem by running away.

"Aye, lass." Gwydion still clung to her mother's shade. "And I love her still. Fionn never did. He only wanted her because of the ancient prophecy." Resentment churned beneath his words.

"She was neither of yours," Dewi boomed. "The MacLochlainn belongs to me. Now and always." She slapped Aislinn none too gently as she lumbered past her. "You would do well to remember that, girl."

Aislinn lurched to her feet. "How the hell did you get so close without me hearing you?"

"I can be silent when it behooves me," Dewi informed her haughtily and grabbed Gwydion's shoulder with a taloned foreleg. "Give me the MacLochlainn."

Tara spewed a string of curses in Gaelic, grew progressively less substantial, and walked through the wall behind Fionn.

Good for you, Mother! Tara had told the dragon she'd see her in Hell before she'd be owned by anyone or anything.

"Ye great stupid snake," Gwydion shouted. "Now see what ye've done. Ye frightened her just as ye did when she was but a wee bit of a thing."

"She hasn't learned a damned thing." Dewi spat back. "Doesn't have any more sense than she did when you started pawing at her when she was only fourteen. I tried to protect her—"

"Stop. Both of you," Aislinn shrieked. "Mother's dead. She doesn't need your attention. Doesn't even want it, from the looks of things. Fionn's the one who needs you." She sank to her knees next to his body and laid full length atop him, covering his lips with hers. She tried to push into his mind, but the same shielding repelled her.

"Appears it'll take more than a kiss from a princess to bring him back," Dewi noted dryly.

Aislinn curled her body into a sitting position right next to Fionn. "What will it take, dragon? The way things stand, I figure you owe me one."

Gwydion, still looking shell-shocked, dropped to the floor next to her and Fionn, robes puddling around him. He took one of Fionn's hands, grabbed his staff with the other, and began to chant. The staff glowed blue-white; Aislinn felt the spell he wove. It dripped power so ancient she could only guess at its origins.

The scent of lavender and jasmine filled the air. Gwydion's voice increased in volume and cadence. Aislinn wanted to watch, to understand the magic, but it made her dizzy. When she tried to look, the air was thick with multi-colored runes morphing into one another, forming new runes like an aerial ballet. The staff blazed so bright, she even saw it through her closed lids.

"Now would be the time for ye to kiss him and call to him." Gwydion nudged her with the staff. It burned where it touched her. "I find I am needing help."

Aislinn glued her lips to Fionn's and added her magic to the mix. After a heart-stopping few moments when she was afraid he was lost to her forever, his body stirred beneath her touch. She lifted her mouth from his and cried, "Fionn. Beloved." Arranging her body half on top of him, she kissed him again. When his lips moved beneath hers, she kissed him harder, slid her hands into his hair and her tongue into his mouth. As if from a great distance, she heard the raven caw.

"*M*o *croi, mo croi*," Fionn whispered against her lips. He threaded his arms around her and tightened them. "How did ye find me?"

"She didn't," Gwydion spat. "'Twas I who brought you back, though I had many second thoughts. Aislinn helped a bit, but she couldna have reached you without me." The master enchanter hesitated. "Tara was here. She reminded me of…many things."

"Where were you?" Aislinn asked Fionn. "Why couldn't I reach you?"

"Slototh was after me. I secured myself in the one place he couldna follow: the *Dreaming*."

"And a good thing I know your mind," Gwydion muttered. "Saved a great deal of trouble tracking you down." Using his staff for a lever, he pushed heavily to his feet.

Bella flapped over and settled next to Fionn. She pecked gently at him as he moved Aislinn to one side and worked his way to a sit. He rubbed his face with his hands and gazed blearily at everyone. "What are we doing here? We shouldna be unwarded with Slototh about. Hell, we shouldna be here at all. The wicked one caught me at the height of my strength. Now I'm weak as a newborn colt. We must leave."

Aislinn felt him summon magic. Bella attempted to fly to his shoulder. It took her two tries. "Ssssh." Aislinn laid a hand on his arm. "I don't think he's a threat for the moment."

"Why not? What happened? I have to get up. Find my men. Get ye to safety." His head thrashed from side to side, eyes rolling wildly. He gripped her hand so hard, it hurt.

"Hopefully, the humans are on their way out of here. They were wandering about like zombies, but it didn't take much to snap them out of their trance state." Aislinn hesitated. "Nothing like you. No matter what I did, it wouldn't penetrate the wall you'd slapped up— or hidden behind."

She couldn't stop touching him, even though warning gongs echoed inside her head. All the things she didn't know mocked her. Had she just been a prophecy substitute when her mother became unavailable? Gwydion intimated as much. Was it like it was with Dewi? He only wanted her because she was a MacLochlainn? Her head hurt. She was so tired she could sleep for a hundred years.

Maybe it would be okay if I never woke up.

An inner warning voice blared. *Got to get myself outside. Now.*

She shook her head to force order into her thoughts. *I can't leave until we find everyone.*

"Aislinn." Fionn tapped her arm. "Ye dinna answer me."

She met his gaze, locking her golden eyes onto his blue ones. "Sorry. I need food and sleep. And we still need to find Arawn and Bran and their companies."

"I could take care of that," Dewi snorted, "but if you aren't going to make use of my talents, I may as well go back and entertain myself."

Aislinn lurched to her feet and walked to the dragon. "That's the best idea you've had in a while," she snarked. "Why don't you do that?"

"Aye, strong thinking, lass." Gwydion glared at the dragon. "Be gone." He shook his staff.

Dewi blew smoke out her nostrils, made a very annoyed-sounding grunt, and vanished.

"Thank fucking God," Aislinn muttered. "I want to tell Mother goodbye before we hunt down everyone else."

"Is she gone?" Tara oozed back through the wall. Her gaze shifted from side to side. "Och, I was certain that one was goin' to follow me. She spent years chasin' me once I moved to Salt Lake. Had to build wards to keep her out."

Gwydion closed his arms around her again. He murmured to her in Gaelic, and she murmured endearments back. Bella cawed stridently. Apparently having recovered somewhat, she flew to them and pecked Tara's hair.

Fionn took two strides, snatched the bird in both hands, and chided her. Aislinn didn't catch all the Gaelic, but the bird was complaining that Tara should've been Fionn's.

With an arm twined around Tara's waist, Gwydion turned to face them. "I am going to send her to her rest in the halls of the dead," he said solemnly. "There is aught here for her. She would bid you farewell." He gave Tara a gentle shove toward Aislinn.

"Mom, oh Mom." Aislinn was crying, unable to control the emotions flooding her. "I love you. It's like losing you all over again."

Tara pulled her close and held her against her half-decayed body. She crooned in Gaelic like she'd done when Aislinn was small. "Never forget ye are my baby girl. And 'tis proud I am of how ye've turned out." She took Aislinn aside then, whispering low. "Fionn loves you. I see in his eyes what was never there for me. I know ye've heard things here today that might make ye doubt him, but doona make that mistake. He is a good man." She kept an arm around Aislinn as they walked back to Gwydion.

"I am ready," she said simply, "after one last piece of motherly advice. Watch out for the dragon. She's on no one's side but her own."

Fionn, who'd kept a tight rein on Bella, tipped his chin at Aislinn. "Let's give them some privacy."

Aislinn's throat was so tight she couldn't force words past the lump in it. Tears burned just behind her eyes.

She looked at her mother, who smiled at her. "There's nothing more to say, *mo leannán*. We will meet again in the Summerlands, the kingdom of the dead."

Fionn transferred Bella to a shoulder and hooked his arm into hers. "Come," he said gently. "Where's Rune?"

"Hunting for Arawn and Bran." She snuffled, feeling perfectly wretched.

"Why don't you call him? Maybe we can help."

Fionn led her away from Gwydion and her mother, keeping hold of her, much as he was doing with the raven. It was as if he knew she'd run back to Tara, given half a chance.

Aislinn's heart screamed in protest. All the pain she'd buried when Tara walked into the vortex hadn't really gone anywhere. It was still inside her, waiting to chew her up and spit her out in little, jagged pieces. Being so exhausted she was worn to a nubbin didn't help.

At least this time, I got to tell her goodbye...

So what? I'm still an orphan.

Only children are orphans. I haven't been one of them for a long time.

"Call Rune." Compulsion ran beneath Fionn's words.

Once, she would've been angry, but she understood the wisdom behind his action. She was dangerously close to falling apart, and he knew it.

"Rune. Rune. Did you find them?"

"Yes, both. All are on their way outside. The humans who were awake found them about the same time I did. I was just on my way back to you." The wolf hesitated a beat. *"I tried to tell you that, but you didn't answer."*

"I'm sorry. No excuses. Where are you?"

Rune shot an image into her mind. She didn't recognize it. *"Tell me how you got there—"*

"I will find you."

Fionn had obviously been listening. He jumped into their conversation. *"Good. We'll wait here."*

Aislinn pushed her mother's face out of the center of her mind's eye. There'd be time to grieve when it didn't hurt so much. She dribbled power into her mage light to crank it up a notch and then turned to face Fionn. "It appears Slototh targeted you. Is he the one you tangled with? The one who ripped you up the middle like a slab of meat."

"Aye, lass. He hated me."

"Why? What did you do to him?"

"What else?" A crooked smile lit his eyes. "I stole a maid he valued and made her love me, not him."

"What happened to her?"

"She was a Selkie. She returned to the sea." Fionn spread his hands wide. "Doona be looking at me like that. Slototh had stolen her skin. He forced her to remain in human form. I freed her, returned the skin, and gave her a choice."

"How long was she with you?"

"And why does that matter?" He tipped her chin so her gaze met his. "'Tis you I love."

His words warmed her soul. Tired as she was, Aislinn vibrated with longing for him. She wanted to believe him, had never wanted anything quite so badly, but they needed to talk. She had a lot of questions that needed answers before she could fall into his arms. He reached for her, but she shook her head and retreated a few steps.

Rune slipped out of a shadowed hallway, looking very pleased.

"We're all present, then." Fionn smiled, but it held a sad edge. "Let us leave this place." He eyed Aislinn. "Ye've been quite the question girl. I've a few of my own once ye've had a bit of a rest."

"I don't know if I have enough magic left to get us out of here."

"I do." He settled the wolf between them and put an arm around her.

Power zinged through the air when he called it. She wondered why he couldn't have rescued himself.

"'Twas a tradeoff," he said, eying her as he held onto his spell easily. "I couldna leave even the slightest chink, or Slototh would have followed me through. Once one like me winds himself into our special place in the *Dreaming*, only another can unravel the magic. I was working on finding a way around that, though."

"If that's the only place you're truly safe," she said with a frown, "it seems like a flawed system. You put yourself there, but can't get yourself out."

He favored her with half a grin. "I was verra near to blowing a hole in my shelter, especially after I heard you calling me."

"Do you mean to tell me I could've gotten you out of there?" She looked askance at him. "It sure didn't feel like it. That magic Gwydion used..." She blew out a weary breath. "No matter how many years I practiced, I could never, never—"

"Ye doona know what ye'll be able to do. Your magic is still growing, lass. If I'd trained you, ye might have been able to free me."

"Yes, too bad you couldn't have foreseen every single thing I might've needed to know." Her sarcasm left a bitter taste. "Don't mind me," she muttered. "I just felt so fucking helpless. Didn't like it much."

"No one does." He had such a tender look on his face that a part inside her melted. "Are ye wanting to use the magic I called up for us? Or would ye rather stand here trying to sort things out?"

"I want out of here."

"Then let's go."

Aislinn staggered into a waning day. Fionn had jumped them to where they'd started, a mile or so from the prison. Humans milled about, leaving in groups of twos, threes, and fives, presumably going home. Arawn and Bran gestured from where they sat, sheltered by the same rock walls they'd chosen earlier. When Aislinn got there, she noted they were checking each human soldier out, much as they'd checked them in.

"How many did we lose?" she asked.

Arawn looked up. "So far, one hundred fifty-three have not passed through here." He glanced at the line queuing behind her. "We will see. My estimate is not more than fifty or sixty."

"Excellent." Bran smiled. "I'd thought we'd suffer far more losses."

Aislinn lowered her gaze. She wanted to share their enthusiasm, but to her, the loss of even one more human life, on top of all those forced through the vortex, was too many.

Movement caught her attention out of the corner of one eye. Aislinn groaned as Dewi settled to earth, folding blood red wings behind her.

"Daughter."

Aislinn ignored her.

Fionn grabbed one of her hands. "Dewi is calling you. Ye canna ignore her."

"Oh yes, I can."

His forehead creased. For a minute, she thought he was going to censure her and girded herself to ignore him, too. "What happened, lass? Did she injure you?"

The gentleness in his voice was almost more than she could bear. She didn't trust herself to talk, so she just nodded. Fionn's face darkened, and he drew his brows together into a thick, furious line. With Bella on his shoulder, he strode toward Dewi, planted himself in front of her, and crossed his arms over his chest. "What did ye do to her?" he demanded.

"Included her in an adventure," Dewi trumpeted defiantly.

"What kind of adventure?" Suspicion thrummed beneath his words, but apparently Dewi didn't hear it.

"Well..." The dragon lowered her head conspiratorially. "After we'd done an astral search and not found anything, we linked minds when she went inside looking for you. It was terribly exciting. She came across an old friend of mine—"

Fionn held up a hand. "Ye can stop right there. This tale has a familiar ring to it. 'Twas the Minotaur, was it not? I havena seen that particular gleam in those ancient eyes for any other creature, except perhaps my kinsman, Uther Pendragon. Or your mate, Nidhogg, when he still walked the Earth."

"Yes," Dewi gushed. "Smart of you to guess. Of course it was the Minotaur. And he was just as powerful as ever. Why, do you know…?" The dragon must've seen a warning flash from Fionn's eyes, because her voice ran down.

"Ye dinna force her, did ye?" he ground out.

"I thought she'd like it." Dewi's jaws parted in a lascivious grin. "What woman wouldn't? A cock of steel that can go almost forever."

Fionn dropped his arms to his sides and balled his hands into fists. Aislinn saw his jaw clench. "She is my woman." He spat the words through gritted teeth. "Ye will never force her into another sexual encounter without her express permission—and mine. Do ye understand me?"

Dewi bared her teeth in a snarl. Apparently, being chastised wasn't an experience she'd had often. Fire belched from her mouth. It came close to Fionn, missing by scant inches. The dragon turned away.

Relief swept through Aislinn. Fionn had defended her. Against a creature he'd told her was sacred. *He does love me. He really does.*

"Of course I do," he muttered and made his way back to her side. "And don't get all pissy because I was inside your head." He still looked angry enough to spit nails. "Why didn't ye tell me what she'd done to you? I'm going down there to get rid of that damned atrocity once and for all. He's been nothing but a nuisance ever since Pasiphaë fell in love with her husband's Cretan bull, fucked it, and created him." Fionn rolled his eyes. "All those children he ate. I doona understand why someone else dinna kill him long since."

The air crackled as Fionn summoned magic.

Aislinn made a grab for him. "I didn't tell you because I've hardly had a chance to tell you anything. Leave him be. I don't think he can find his own way out of the labyrinth. Besides, killing him won't undo what happened. The dragon's just as guilty as he is."

Fionn met her gaze, his blue eyes dark as midnight. "He would have raped you, lass, dragon or no, and killed you if Dewi hadn't shown up."

She nodded. "I know that." A knife-like smile split her face. "I'm pretty good at getting to men while they're lost in lust. Somehow, I would've been fine. The real problem was Dewi. She blocked me from my magic."

Rune, hackles raised the length of his back, growled and said, "I told you she was trouble." What he'd heard pass between Aislinn, Fionn, and Dewi must've upset him terribly. He ran in circles, unable to contain himself. Making a dash for the dragon, he barked and snarled, fell back, and then did it again. Aislinn called him, worried Dewi would turn him into cinders if she got angry enough, but the wolf didn't listen.

Fionn reeled in his magic. "If ye are certain ye doona wish me to avenge your honor—"

Aislinn shook her head. "Save your magic for when I really need it." *Besides, you'd have to kill both of them to truly avenge anything.*

"I think we're about ready to go," Arawn said, once he'd thanked what looked like the last human to check out. "We did better than I expected. Losses on our side totaled forty-six."

Gwydion, who'd shown up during Fionn's discussion with Dewi, let out a low whistle and rubbed his hands together. "Aye, good news indeed. I canna think of another battle where we had so few casualties."

"We need to hear about what happened betwixt you and Slototh." Bran shot a meaningful look at Aislinn. "But not here."

"Wait." Dewi stalked close. Her unsettling gaze zeroed in on Aislinn. "This is an apology to the MacLochlainn. I'm sorry. I didn't mean to hurt you. It's not as if you were a maid, after all. I honestly didn't know you'd be so upset."

Aislinn moved from under the protective arm Fionn had draped across her back. Squaring her aching shoulders, she faced the dragon. "If you mean that, apology accepted. We can talk more later when I'm not so tired. For now, can you promise you'll never do anything like that to me ever again?"

Dewi nodded.

Sensing a trick, Aislinn snapped, "I need to hear you say it."

"I will never pull you into something we have not agreed upon again."

Aislinn closed her eyes. They felt gritty. She opened them and held Dewi's whirling gaze. "I'll hold you to that," she said solemnly.

"Somehow, I do not doubt it." Dewi threw back her head and laughed, spewing fire. She was still laughing when she spread her wings and took flight.

"Nice work." Gwydion dusted the palms of his hands against one another. "That one has needed a good come-uppance for better than a thousand years." He gazed around the group. "Where are we going?"

"How about back to Marta's?" Aislinn suggested. "There's more food there than any place else I know. Unless one of you has a better suggestion."

The men looked at one another. Something silent passed between them that Aislinn was too tired to decipher. Left to their own devices, she supposed they'd go back to the Old Country.

"Agreed." Arawn tried to smile, but he looked as done in as the rest of them.

Fionn held out his arms. "Come here, *mo croi*. I'll have you home in no time. Once we're there, I'll see ye get rest and food."

He whistled for Rune. The wolf came at a lope. He'd chased the dragon's flight path from the ground, apparently intent on making certain she was really gone, not simply hiding behind something.

With Bella on his shoulder and the wolf between him and Aislinn, Fionn called power to transport them back to Ely.

islinn didn't remember much about the journey back to Marta's. True to his word, Fionn carried her down the hallway and tucked her into bed. She thought she should clean up first, but couldn't even get the words out before she fell asleep. She remembered waking to eat. Fionn handed her a bowl, but her efforts to manipulate the spoon were pathetic. After watching her fumbling efforts to feed herself, he filled the spoon and guided it to her mouth until the bowl was empty.

Finally, her eyes opened, and she felt more-or-less like herself. She wondered how long she'd been dead to the world and if it was day or night. Fionn had drawn the curtains, so it was hard to tell. She swung her legs over the side of the bed and walked to the window. Pushing the heavy drapery material aside, she peeked out. A stellar sunset, the sky a panoply of perfect pastels, brought a smile to her face. "Nice to wake up to," she murmured.

Rune padded into the room, came to her, and licked her hand. "You're awake."

"How long did I sleep?"

"Dawn came, and then came again."

She blinked. It had been nearly night when they'd arrived back at

Marta's, so she'd slept for the better part of two full days. When she turned away from the window, Fionn stood framed in the doorway, the raven perched on his shoulder. "Sleeping beauty. I was wondering if you'd ever waken. Another twenty-four hours, and I'd have gone hunting for a counter spell."

"American English," she blurted. "You must really want to be on my good side."

He shrugged. "Och aye, lass. There, 'tis that a wee bit better, now?"

She laughed. "I think I've gotten to where I actually don't care anymore. Before it hurt because of Mother, but I got to see her again." Sadness welled. "At least this time I had a chance to tell her I loved her—and goodbye."

Bella loosed an outraged squawk and flew into the hallway. It bothered Aislinn that the bird hated her mother so, but she couldn't do much about it.

"I'll talk to her," Fionn said, "but later. This is far more important." He crossed the room and pulled her into his arms. His heartbeat thudded beneath her ear. They stood like that for long moments. Finally, he murmured, "I can draw you a bath. Would ye like that?"

She twisted in his arms, wrinkling her nose. "Yes. I'll bet you would, too. You'd think I would've gotten used to how badly I stink, but I haven't."

"I doona care how ye smell—" he grinned down at her "—so long as ye're alive."

As he readied her bath, she walked to the bathroom door, sucked in a breath, and said, "Tell me about Mother."

He turned to face her. "She was part of the prophecy. I was to wed a MacLochlainn, and Tara was the first possibility in many hundreds of years. I think I told you that before." The lines next to his eyes deepened. His American diction was crisp, as if it were less painful to tell the tale that way. "I didn't love her. Gwydion did. I knew she loved him, but I pushed forward anyway. Duty drove me. Gwydion understood. He didn't like it, but he understood."

"There's something you're not telling me."

Fionn nodded. A corner of his mouth turned down wryly. "Remind me to dull that Seeker gift of yours. Gwydion and I—we had words. Tara overheard. She was afraid we'd hurt one another over her. That, combined with pressure from Dewi, was enough to drive your mother out of Ireland."

"You didn't go after her."

The tub was full. Fionn turned off the taps, but Aislinn wasn't ready to take off her clothes. Not yet. Not until she'd heard everything.

Fionn offered her a sad smile. "I already lived in the United States. But no, I didn't try to find her."

"Why not?"

"Because something Gwydion shouted at me that night sank into my thick skull. He told me I'd make her miserable and myself, too. That Tara MacLochlainn was a fey creature, with only one foot in this world and the other in the *Dreaming*."

Aislinn nodded. She knew that about her mother. "So you walked away."

"Aye." He quirked a brow. "Are ye wanting to get in afore the water turns stone cold?"

"You can make it warm for me again."

His mouth twitched. "Get in, wench. I'll go bring you some dinner."

"No." Her mouth went suddenly dry. "I want you to stay."

"Why?"

His gaze settled on her. She saw hope in his eyes, and something else, too, flickering in their depths. Was he afraid she'd spurn him now that he'd told her the truth?

"Because I had to expose myself to Slototh and feel his disgusting hands and mouth on me. I was held hostage by Dewi and raped by the Minotaur. This is something I want to have happen on my own terms." She tried to smile, but couldn't. Turning away, she stripped out of her filthy, stinking clothing, stepped into the tub, and lowered herself into the steaming water.

He didn't try to talk to her, just sat looking at her as she soaped herself. The water took on a grayish hue. At last, she met his gaze. "You've been getting quite the eyeful. Like what you see?"

His breath caught in his throat and made a clicking sound. "Ye are quite possibly the most beautiful creature I've ever laid eyes on, lass. With all that red hair floating about you, ye look like a latter day angel. Do ye know how hard it's been not to scoop you out of that bath, lay you on the floor, and have my way with you?"

"Thanks for not." A smile began in her heart before it spread over her face. "I needed time for myself." The smile morphed into a grin. "But the water's pretty disgusting, and I'm ready to get out."

"I could heat more," he began and then frowned. "Those bite marks on your breasts and mouth. Did Slototh do that?"

She nodded and tipped her chin up. "I had to lure him closer."

He shook his head, his eyes blazing with compassion. "Nay, doona be defensive. I'm just so sorry. It hurts my heart that I wasna there to protect you. Now, are ye certain ye doona wish more hot water?"

"Yes. We can take another bath later. Together."

Gripping the sides of the tub, she came to her feet with water streaming down her body. He handed her a towel. She wrapped it around herself and then grabbed another to soak up water from her hair before stepping out of the tub.

He stood before her, still just watching, giving her all the space she needed. She traced the familiar lines of his body with her gaze, taking long moments to appreciate his wonderfully broad shoulders, slender hips, and powerful legs. He wore a cream-colored cotton shirt and snug-fitting jeans. The outline of his cock, hard and waiting for her, was obvious through the fabric. Though it was a challenge to look away, she moved her focus upward to his face. To his incredible, long-lashed eyes shading to deepest blue and the strong, graceful bones in his cheeks and jaw. His lips were slightly parted, waiting. She knew he was waiting for her. Just for her. Only for her.

Aislinn opened her arms. The towels fell to the floor.

Kicking them aside, he came to her and drew her close. "*Mo croi,* I love you. More than is good for me. I love you."

He crushed his mouth down on hers. His hands roamed down her back and settled on her ass. He pulled her against him and moaned. She heard need and desperation and fear that he'd lost her in the sound, overshadowed by relief that he hadn't.

She drew away from him long enough to say, "I love you, too. When I thought you were lost to me, I went a little crazy, because I didn't want to live in a world without you in it."

He scooped her up as if she weighed nothing and laid her tenderly on the bed. His hands worked the buttons of his fly. He freed himself and then knelt over her, stringing kisses down her body. He nuzzled her breasts, sucking the nipples gently until she reached for his hips, desperate to feel him inside her. He wriggled out of her grasp, slid farther down her body, and settled his mouth over the engorged spot between her legs. She came almost as soon as his tongue twirled around her clitoris, hips bucking against his mouth. He dug his hands into her hips, urging her higher as his tongue worked her. No one was more surprised than she when the spasms of a second climax jolted through her.

"One of these days," he said as he positioned himself over her, "I'm going to make you come ten times doing that." His voice was rough with passion. "But just now, I canna wait to feel your body around mine. Ye doona know how close I came to taking you while ye slept. I wanted you that badly, lass."

She watched his face as he pushed into her, watched his eyes half-close in ecstasy as he withdrew and then, very slowly, slid back inside. She wrapped her legs around his hips, pulled hard to get him to bury himself deep and stay there. Her fingers dug into his back, and she rocked her body against him.

He kissed her, tongue pushing inside her mouth as his cock slammed into her. Gentleness gone, they grappled with one another, gasping and panting, grinding their bodies together seeking release. He groaned, made the wonderful sound like a lion purring that meant he was close. She shoved herself against him, met him stroke for stroke. Feeling him shudder inside her brought her over the edge again. Aislinn clung to him as if he were the only solid thing in a world spinning out of control.

"If the two of you could keep your hands off one another for a few minutes," Gwydion said, "the lot of us need to talk."

Rune, who'd been standing guard over them, growled.

Aislinn opened her eyes. The warrior magician stood in the doorway. A deep purple robe was belted at his waist. Unbraided, his blond hair spilled down his shoulders. Blue eyes twinkled merrily.

"What is it with you?" she managed, struggling to catch her breath. "First Bran—or was it Arawn?—and now you. Are all of you voyeurs?"

He grinned at her. "Lass, ye doona know the half of it."

"Food," she said. "I need to eat while we talk."

Fionn hoisted himself up on his forearms. He eyed Gwydion. "Leave us, and we'll get up. Ye'll want to give the lass a spot of privacy."

"Now why would I want to do that? She's a lush sight for these old eyes." The slap of his bare feet mingled with laughter as he disappeared down the hall.

THEY SAT around the kitchen table. Arawn and Bran were still in battle leathers, Fionn back in his jeans and a shirt. She'd dredged more clothes out of Marta's closet, finding a black skirt that came to her ankles and a fluffy teal sweater. The woolen garments felt soft against her skin. Rune must have liked them, too, since he'd curled right next to her, his back against her skirt where it fell to the hard-wood floor.

Aislinn had eaten until she felt full enough to burst. In between bites, washed down with plenty of mead, she told them about Slototh. "I asked Dewi this." She glanced around at the men. "Now I'm asking you. Do you think he's dead?"

All four shook their heads.

"Well, if he's not dead, where is he?"

"If we got verra lucky, he's back in the world that spawned him," Arawn answered, a murderous look in his dark eyes. "Fionn's not the only one of us who've tangled with that one."

"Is there any way to know for sure?" Aislinn asked. She'd feel a whole lot better if she knew Slototh wouldn't be lurking in some dark corridor, lying in wait for her.

"Nay," Bran said. "I'm thinking we'd be better off trying to solve the human hybrid problem."

Bella squawked from where she'd taken up residence atop the refrigerator.

"What about the other dark gods?" Aislinn asked.

"Aye, there is that problem as well." Gwydion shot a lascivious look her way.

Fionn must have noticed, because he glared at Gwydion.

"Stop it, you two." Aislinn rolled her eyes. "I thought we were supposed to be figuring out what to do next." She looked first at Fionn, then at Gwydion. "I'm not Tara. Mother was only a girl when the two of you started haggling over her—"

Aislinn's jaw clanged shut. Quick as a nod, she was on her feet, hands raised to meet the magic she felt coming toward them. Rune stood next to her, growling. Though she hadn't seen him move, Fionn was somehow by her side, with Bella on his shoulder. Gwydion, Arawn, and Bran closed ranks, making a wall in front of them. She glanced at Gwydion's staff, but it wasn't glowing. Did that mean something magical wasn't coming? Or was it that the magic wasn't a threat? She couldn't tell from the warrior magician's demeanor. He looked grimly ready for anything.

The air shimmered on the far side of the room. Travis and his civet took shape.

Aislinn blew out a breath. "What the hell, Travis? You scared the crap out of me."

"Hmph." Fionn's face darkened. It was obvious he remembered the Hunter all too well.

Travis looked from one to the other. "Thank God I came out in the right place. I left in a hurry, and I wasn't sure I had it just right."

"What happened, lad?" Bran asked, concern etched in his face. "Ye sought us out. There must be a reason."

Bella flew around the room, cawing. The civet hissed at the bird.

Fionn grabbed his raven out of the air. "If ye doona behave better, I'll be shipping you back to the Old Country."

"You'd never do that," the bird informed him haughtily. She pulled out of his grasp and landed on the top of the kitchen door.

"Watch me," Fionn said tightly and settled his gaze on Travis. "I suggest you talk, lad. Something is amiss. I see it in your eyes."

Travis nodded. "We're under attack. From the Old Ones."

Aislinn gasped. "Holy crap! That's terrible. We figured they'd turn on us, but not this soon. What happened?"

"I'm not sure." He shrugged. "We'd just gotten back from Arizona and were settling in—you know, hunting and trying to get some rest —when a whole herd of them closed on us. We didn't think anything of it. I mean, we'd never seen quite that many in one place before, but we figured they were just going to give us more orders." He took an uneven breath. "We wanted to act normal, so they wouldn't know we were onto them."

Travis looked down. His jaw worked. Aislinn figured he was struggling for control. "They just started killing us. Stopped our hearts where we stood." His voice broke. He cleared his throat and went on. "Some of us have stronger magic than others. We threw up wards and jumped out of there. Later, once we'd had a chance to think, we decided the best thing was to see if you'd help us. I volunteered to come here because my jumps are the most accurate."

"What were your losses?" Gwydion asked.

"Twenty-something when I left. Probably more than that now."

Travis dragged his gaze—brown eyes flecked with his green power color—up off the floor and looked at each of them in turn. He settled on Aislinn last. Pleading shone from the depths of his eyes. "Please," he said. "We need help."

"You'll get it," Aislinn snapped, outraged by what had happened. After shoving a goodly portion of Earth's population into that damned vortex, now the Lemurians were killing the rest of them outright. What had the vortex been? Something for show?

"Hmph." Gwydion grabbed his staff. "We were trying to figure out what to do next. Seems that decision has been made for us."

Aislinn glanced at her skirt and sweater. "I need to change." Spinning, she dashed for the bedroom with Rune right behind her. As she rifled through drawers, she was grateful Marta had been a bit of a clotheshorse. Snugging into dark green work pants with lots of pockets, she rolled the bottoms. Clean socks came right before she shoved her feet back into her boots. She eyed them for a moment. They really were in bad shape. She needed to find another pair —and soon.

She pulled a black long john top over her head and followed it with a thick green jacket made of something fuzzy and synthetic. It was cold here, and it would be cold where they were going. She rummaged through her rucksack, checking to make sure it still had everything she might need for contingencies. Her hand closed on her water bottle. It was empty, so she filled it at the bathroom sink.

By the time she returned to the kitchen, Fionn was back in battle leathers, hauberk, and vambraces. She wondered where he kept them when they weren't on his back. *Sometime, I'll have to ask him.* Pulling cupboards and drawers open, she grabbed handfuls of nuts, dried fruit, and dried meat and stuffed them into a large pocket of her rucksack. Being half-starved hadn't worked well for her in Arizona. She was damned if she'd make the same mistake twice.

"Are we going back near where I used to live?" she asked Travis.

"Yes. I sent the men an image of where we need to come out while we were waiting for you. Guess I'm going with him." He pointed at Gwydion. "They didn't think I'd be fast enough on my own."

"How many jumps?" she asked Fionn.

"Maybe only one." He smiled reassuringly at her, but worry flashed behind his eyes.

None of them had foreseen the Old Ones engaging in a direct frontal attack. It hadn't been part of any equation they'd drawn. They'd viewed the Lemurians as relatively passive, without teeth, reliant on the dark gods to mastermind their destructiveness. Aislinn sucked in a breath. If they'd misjudged the Lemurians so badly, what other mistakes had they made?

An unpleasant truth intruded. She bit her lower lip and looked at Fionn. "Do you think the dark gods are behind this?"

"Who else?" Arawn growled. "News travels fast. They would've heard what happened to Slototh by now."

"Aye, lass," Bran muttered. "They're out for revenge. The Lemurians owe them, and they're calling in their chips."

"Okay." She clucked to Rune, slipped her pack straps over her shoulders, and buckled the waist belt. "I'm all set."

Bella back on his shoulder, Fionn stepped to her side, sandwiching the wolf between them. Magic filled the air until it was hard to breathe. Linked to Travis and his civet, Gwydion was the first to leave. Arawn and Bran shimmered and disappeared.

"Ready?" Fionn asked.

She felt the thrum of the spell he held in check, waiting until everyone else was safely away.

"More than ready." Aislinn tensed her jaws. "I hate the Lemurians. They killed my parents. If we have to blow through an entire army of them to get to the dark gods, it's fine by me."

The jump seemed to take longer than she expected. After a while, she couldn't feel Fionn or Rune. It worried her. When darkness finally fell away, Aislinn saw the rubble of what was left of a city, except nothing looked familiar. She turned in a full circle before realization slammed her like a kick in the guts. Fionn and Rune weren't with her.

"What the hell?" she sputtered and called their names.

A triumphant whoop turned her blood to ice. Travis stepped out of a gateway in the air, civet in his arms. "Damn! Didn't think I'd be able to slip away from that Celt. Still not quite certain how I managed it." He loped over and grabbed her arm.

Aislinn tried to pull away, but his fingers gripped like pincers.

"What did you do?" she cried, still trying to wrap her mind around Travis's plea for help being nothing but a sham. "Where are Fionn and Rune?" She reached for her magic, intent on escape, but couldn't latch onto it. The threads wouldn't respond to her call. Fear clutched at her belly.

Travis curled his lips into a snarl. "You're human. You belong with us."

"Yes." Regnol, Travis's Lemurian magelord, slithered out of the gateway Travis hadn't closed off. "There's the little matter of Metae's death—and my other comrades your wolf slaughtered. You are coming with me."

The Old One's gaze shifted to Travis. "You have done well. You may go now."

Horror filled her—and fury at Travis's betrayal. She watched dumbstruck as he and the civet stepped through the gateway and were gone in a flash of blue-white light.

Her face an impassive mask, Aislinn turned to face Regnol and stared into his whirling, alien eyes. He already had her. There was no reason not to make eye contact. "Where are you taking me?" She forced a bravado she was far from feeling.

"Where else?" What passed for Lemurian laughter rasped like a saw blade attacking metal. "To Taltos."

~

You've reached the end of *Earth's Requiem*. The story continues in
Earth's Blood
And is completed in *Earth's Hope*
All three books are available in print and e-format
Read on for a sample of *Earth's Blood*

ABOUT THE AUTHOR

Ann Gimpel is a USA Today bestselling author. She's also a clinical psychologist, with a Jungian bent. Avocations include mountaineering, skiing, wilderness photography and, of course, writing. A lifelong aficionado of the unusual, she began writing speculative fiction a few years ago. Since then her short fiction has appeared in a number of webzines and anthologies. Her longer books run the gamut from urban fantasy to paranormal romance. She's published over 50 books to date, with several more planned for 2018 and beyond. A husband, grown children, grandchildren and three wolf hybrids round out her family.

Keep up with her at www.anngimpel.com or http://anngimpel.blogspot.com

If you enjoyed what you read, get in line for special offers and pre-release special reads. Sign up for Ann's newsletter on her website or her blog.

EARTH'S BLOOD, CHAPTER ONE

BOOK TWO IN THE EARTH RECLAIMED SERIES

Fionn tumbled through a gateway and leapt to his feet. Something was decidedly wrong. The wolf and raven were right behind him, but he'd lost all sense of Aislinn's presence in the traveling portal. It made him half-crazy with fear, but there was nothing he could do until the spell spit him out. Mouth dry, heartbeat thudding in his ears, he waited to see who would follow him out of the ragged hole he'd left in the ether.

For the love of the goddess, please let me be mistaken about this.

Rune emerged. A howl split the still air. *"Where is she?"* the black and gray timber wolf demanded. He reared up and plunked his paws on Fionn's chest. *"What happened to my bondmate? I cannot feel her anywhere."* He howled again. It was a mournful sound, full of grief.

Fionn wrapped his arms around the wolf, but Rune dropped to the ground, apparently not interested in comfort.

"Yes, where did Aislinn go?" Bella demanded, bouncing forward with her awkward avian gait. Ever cantankerous, the raven was bonded to him, so Fionn was used to her moods. She spread her large wings, took to the air, and cawed her displeasure.

He stared after her and struggled to manage a mounting sense of panic while balling his hands into fists. Both bond animals knew the truth: Aislinn had disappeared somewhere between Ely, Nevada and wherever they were now. He barked a word to close off his magic. The place they'd rolled out of shimmered and disappeared.

He loosed a string of Gaelic curses. "What the fuck went wrong?" he muttered. Fionn drew magic to augment his night vision and gazed wildly about for clues. They were in the midst of rubble that could well be Salt Lake City, so at least that part of his casting had been true. *No,* an inner voice corrected him, *I doona know that. This could be anywhere.* He shoved straggling strands of blond hair out of his eyes and sent his magic spinning outward to gather data. His heart beat a worried tattoo against his ribcage.

The air to his right took on a pearlescent hue. Bran and Arawn leapt through a portal in a flash of battle leathers, the snug-fitting garments indistinguishable from Fionn's attire. Arawn barked a command, and their gateway winked shut. His midnight gaze scanned the small group. "Why is Gwydion not here?" he demanded. "He left afore any of us."

Rune threw his head back. Another desolate howl split the night.

Bran's coppery eyes narrowed. "Aye, and where is the lass?"

"And that Hunter scum, Travis," Fionn growled. He spread his hands in front of him. "I havena felt Aislinn since a few moments after we entered the portal. Join your magic to mine so we might figure out what has happened."

Bran nodded curtly. "Aye, Travis must have lied to us, but to what purpose?"

"To save his own sorry hide, what else?" Fionn snapped. "Or mayhap because he wanted Aislinn for himself."

The air took on an iridescent waviness. Gwydion stumbled out of the odd-looking place. Tangled in a welter of blue robes, he clutched an intricately carved staff; blond hair swirled around him. "Be gone, I say—Wait, what happened to—?" He took in the tableau as he lurched unsteadily to his feet. Fionn almost heard wheels turning as Gwydion tallied who was missing. The warrior magician pounded the end of his wooden staff into broken asphalt. Lightning crackled from the end of the staff, betraying his annoyance.

Something snapped in Fionn. Bright, brittle anger lanced through him, and he launched himself at Gwydion, driving the other Celtic god to the ground. "Bastard," he screamed. "Ye were in charge of Travis. What? Ye couldna control a simple human? Look what your slipshod seeds have sown!" He raised a fist and drove it into the side of Gwydion's face. It was more satisfying than using magic. Closer and more personal.

Rune jumped into the fray and sank his teeth into Gwydion's leg. Bella cawed her disapproval. She tangled her talons in the mage's long hair and pulled as she pecked at him. Gwydion bellowed in pain. The air thickened and developed an electric quality as he reached for his magic.

Fionn had just cocked his arm back to hit Gwydion again—before his fellow Celtic god shielded himself—when strong arms closed about him and dragged him back. Magic surrounded him, forming a barrier.

"That willna help," Arawn, god of the dead, revenge, and terror, said, his voice stern with command.

"Aye, it willna get your lass back," Bran agreed. God of prophecy, the arts, and war, he often had a gentler approach than the other Celtic deities.

Gwydion rolled to a sit, looking dazed. He placed his hands on the wolf and raven, muttering in Gaelic. After a time, both animals retreated. He touched the bloodied places on his thigh; the flesh mended quickly. The master enchanter and god of illusion didn't make any move to get to his feet. He settled his blue gaze on Fionn, bowed his head slightly, and said, "I am most sorry. Ye are right to be angry with me. The lad came at me flanked by Lemurians. I never even knew how many. When I sent my magic spiraling out to find Travis, he was gone beyond my reach."

"Why didn't ye tell me?" Fionn growled.

"How?" Gwydion countered, sounding weary. "Communication isna possible in the portals."

Fionn groaned inwardly. He knew that. Where were his brains? *Taking a wee holiday,* a sarcastic inner voice suggested. Fionn jerked against the magic holding him. "You can let me go now," he told Arawn and Bran. "I've returned to my senses."

He stepped forward and extended a hand to Gwydion, who grasped it. "I'm sorry I lost my temper."

Something sparked from the mage's blue eyes—compassion laced with pity. Gwydion stood and then brushed off his robes; dust flew in all directions. He bent to retrieve his richly carved staff. It glowed blue-white when he touched it, and he arched a brow at Fionn. "See, the staff knows battle lies ahead. The important thing is what we do now. A good start would be not tearing one another to bits."

Though Fionn agreed, he secretly wondered if Gwydion might have tried harder were it not for the bad blood between them over Tara, Aislinn's dead mother. As a MacLochlainn, Aislinn was bound to him, just like her mother had been. But Tara had loved Gwydion. To avoid marrying Fionn, she'd given herself to a stranger and run away to America, effectively severing an age-old bonding. Tara MacLochlainn had been an Irish queen. Under laws of blood and dynasty, she should have belonged to him, Fionn MacCumhaill, Celtic god of wisdom, knowledge, and divination...

Guess she had other ideas about that. What a fankle. Mayhap one we're still paying for. Fionn forced his mind to stay in the present. No point in dragging old bones out and chewing them half to death. Rune's large black and gray head rammed his side. The wolf bared his fangs and growled.

"I understand." Fionn settled his blue gaze on Rune. "We have to find her. And we will."

"Let us go over what we know." Bran stepped closer. Blond braids were tucked into tight-fitting battle leathers. He had a dreamy look about him, but Fionn wasn't fooled. The god of prophecy's mind was sharp as a whip.

"Good idea," Arawn echoed. Dark hair cascaded down his leather-clad shoulders. Looking as grim as the dead he commanded, his face etched into harsh lines. Eyes, so dark that iris and pupil were indistinguishable, flashed fire.

"Let us ask the goddess's blessing," Fionn intoned. A weight like a cold stone settled into his guts. They couldn't afford to make any mistakes. Aislinn's life depended on them getting this right the first time. *And my life right along with it.* Fionn thought about the next thousand years without the only woman he'd ever truly loved, and his soul shriveled. He cursed his immortality. Life without Aislinn wouldn't be worth very damned much.

Gwydion began a Celtic chant. The other three joined in at proscribed intervals, punctuated by Bella's shrieks and Rune's barks, whines, and howls. Night yielded to a sickly orange sunrise as they sang.

"I believe we are ready," Gwydion murmured.

"Aye, I feel a goddess presence," Arawn spoke reverently. "'Twill provide a balance point against all our male energies."

"Let us return to cataloging what we know." Fionn gestured impatiently. Though he understood the wisdom of securing divine assistance, he wanted to get moving before something lethal happened to Aislinn. A vision of her being tortured—long limbs splayed over a rack—rose to taunt him. He muffled a cry, but his mind wouldn't clear. Blood ran down Aislinn's face and blended with the red of her hair. Her golden eyes were glazed with pain. He bit down hard on his lower lip, feeling powerless. Adrenaline surged, leaving a sour taste in the back of his throat.

Bran nodded. "We are, indeed, ready."

Fionn latched onto the sound of Bran's voice and let it pull him out of the black pit his mind had become. He crooked two fingers. "Talk, goddammit."

Bran inhaled sharply. "The Hunter, Travis, sought us out. I dinna try verra hard to test his words, but there was enough truth in his tale to satisfy me."

"And I, as well," Gwydion agreed. "So mayhap his small group of humans truly was set upon by Lemurians—"

Fionn snapped his fingers. "I have it. That putrid poor-excuse-for-a-human cut a deal to save himself. Mayhap part of it was designed to wrest Aislinn away from me since he was in love with her, too. She told me—" The words curdled in his throat. He couldn't bear the thought of Aislinn fucking anyone else. She'd been with Travis once.

If she was telling me the truth... Mayhap she was with him many times and softened the telling to spare me.

Arawn cocked his head to one side. "Even though ye stopped midstream, what ye did say made sense. Travis agreed to serve as bait in exchange for his life—and mayhap the life of his bond animal, as well. If he had his eye on the lass afore all this, well, the pot would have been all the sweeter."

Fionn waved him to silence. "Ye say ye felt Lemurians?" He looked at Gwydion, who nodded. "Well, then, she must be in Taltos. Where else would they take her?" Relieved to have a destination and something to do, Fionn pulled magic, intent on leaving immediately.

"Hold." Gwydion put up a hand.

"What?" Annoyed, muscles strung tighter than a bow, Fionn locked gazes with him and sparred with a pair of blue eyes nearly identical to his own.

"Ye canna go off half-cocked. There are not enough of us." Gwydion hesitated. "As the god of wisdom, knowledge, and divination, Fionn MacCumhaill, I would think ye would know that without me having to tell you."

Frustration fueled rage. Fionn opened his mouth to tell Gwydion what he really thought of him. "Why you sanctimonious—"

"Never mind that," Bran spoke up. "We need a strategy."

"And mayhap more of us," Arawn added.

"Aye, and what about Dewi?" Ignoring Fionn's bitten off words and the challenge beneath them, Gwydion furled his brows.

Fionn blew out an impatient breath; his anger receded. The others were right. Dewi, the blood-red Celtic dragon god, was linked to the MacLochlainn women. She'd also spent centuries in the tunnels beneath Taltos, spying on the Lemurians. Yes, they definitely needed the dragon.

"All right," he ground out through gritted teeth. "I get it. I agree we need Dewi and probably more of us as well."

"We must return to Marta's house. As soon as we can."

The wolf's voice startled Fionn. He turned to look at Rune. The wolf padded closer. *"I have been to Taltos both ways,"* the wolf reminded him, growling low. *"It is much easier and more direct if we enter through the portal in Marta's basement. That way we maintain the element of surprise. The Mount Shasta gateway is akin to going to their front door and ringing a bell."*

Fionn kicked himself. *Even the wolf is thinking more clearly than me.*

Rune had been bonded to Marta and knew her secrets. She'd been onto the Lemurians, delving deep into the extent of their lies. Before they killed her, she'd managed to figure out that the war against the dark gods was a sham. The Lemurians were actually in league with the dark. They were the ones who'd masterminded cracking the veils between the worlds to allow the dark ones access to Earth. An ancient race, the Lemurians understood they were dying. They'd needed an infusion of magic, so they cut a deal. Access to Earth in exchange for—

Fionn filled his lungs with air, blew out a breath, and did it again. He had to get hold of himself, or he'd be less than useless hunting for Aislinn. *That will not happen. Focus, goddamn it. Pull it together.* Fionn pushed the ache in his heart aside and buried it deep. He couldn't afford emotion. Or mental forays into Lemurian treachery. Not now. When he'd met Aislinn, she'd been a foot soldier in the Lemurian army, branded so she couldn't use her magic against them.

Voices flowed over him. When words fell into coherent patterns again, he heard Gwydion ticking off a plan on his fingers. Apparently one the others had formed without any input from him. *How dare they?* Anger flared hot and bright. Fionn welcomed it like a drowning man might grab a spar. He needed the energy to find the woman he loved.

"...agreed, Bran will hunt for Dewi. Arawn will return to the Old Country to muster as many of us as he can find. Fionn, the bond animals, and I will return to Marta's house. We will sneak into the tunnel a time or two to see what we can discover, but we will not move to rescue the lass until you arrive with reinforcements."

Gwydion nailed Fionn with his blue gaze. "Aye, and ye have returned to us. Did ye hear—?"

"Aye." Fionn cut off Gwydion's next words. "Let's get moving."

The master enchanter inclined his head. "As ye will."

Fionn looked at him and wondered if it were mere coincidence that Gwydion would end up babysitting him. He decided to test those waters. "I really would be fine with just the bond animals. Feel free to join either Arawn or—"

"Pah!" Gwydion interrupted. "Not on your life. I know you, Fionn MacCumhaill. If ye returned alone, ye would turn Taltos upside down to find your lady love. Then the rest of us would have two to search for."

Arawn moved forward and laid a hand on Fionn's arm. "Remember," he said, "the Lemurians came from Mu. They may still have a way to retreat there. If they do so, we willna be able to follow. Or they might strike a deal with the five remaining dark gods and go to one of their worlds if they feel threatened. We can travel to the border worlds, but it isna pleasant. Nay, if they have truly taken Aislinn to Taltos—and we doona know this as a fact—it is imperative they remain there. So doona do anything foolish."

"I understand." Fionn clamped his jaws shut. Thoroughly chastised, he felt like a child again. He hadn't considered either of the alternatives Arawn just outlined. Apparently they'd come up in the part of the conversation he'd missed while wrestling with himself.

"I know ye do." Arawn favored him with a rare smile. "Bran and I are leaving." The words had scarcely left his mouth when the air around both mages took on a numinous quality.

Fionn locked gazes with Gwydion. "Are ye ready?"

"I am." Rune took up his traveling position next to Fionn's side.

"As am I." Bella settled on his shoulder in a flutter of wings.

Fionn stared at the bond animals. They'd returned to audible speech; that must mean they'd gotten their anger under control. *If they can do it, so can I.*

Gwydion nodded slowly. "I doona believe there is aught else to be done right now, so the answer to your question would be aye."

The air thickened as Gwydion drew magic to open a portal. Blessedly numb inside, Fionn added his own to the mix, buried a hand in Rune's neck ruff, and stepped through.

AFTER THEY RETURNED to Marta's house in the ruins of Ely, Nevada, Fionn spent the next hour rattling through it, looking for clues that might help them. He started in the bedroom, but Aislinn's scent, a mix of honey and musk, clung to everything and nearly undid him. When he caught himself pulling her pillow to his nose, he threw it against the wall and stormed out of the room they'd shared.

The rest of the house hadn't yielded anything. Fionn didn't bother going up to the attic. Marta's parents were there, trapped in a state of suspended animation by a strong spell. Best leave them to their rest, since they held the gates between the worlds open.

Because there wasn't anything else to do, he settled at the kitchen table with a bottle of mead and nearly emptied it. The anesthetic effect he hoped for hadn't happened, though. At least not yet.

"Would ye like to talk about it?" Gwydion's melodic voice interrupted Fionn's bleak thoughts.

He swiveled his head to look at the mage standing in the doorway, flanked by Rune and Bella. Dirt clung to his robes; Fionn wondered where he'd been. Gwydion had told him where he was going, but Fionn hadn't paid much attention.

Hmph. Even the animals deserted me.

I'd have deserted me, too, a different inner voice inserted dryly. *The way I banged around in here wanting to kill something—anything—if only it would bring Aislinn back to me.* Fionn understood at a level beyond reckoning that if he ever laid eyes on Travis again, the Hunter would be dead before he saw what hit him.

He tipped the bottle in Gwydion's direction. "Not sure what there is to say," Fionn mumbled.

"Och, and there is much to be said between us." Gwydion clomped to the table, hooked a chair out with one of his perpetually bare feet, and sat heavily. "For example, we havena ever truly talked about Tara—"

"With good reason," Fionn snapped.

Gwydion shook his head. "Ye doona trust me. I sense your hesitation. We must clear the air."

Fionn opened his mouth, but Gwydion shook his head. "Hear me out. That empty place inside you? The one ye're trying your damnedest to ignore—or drown with spirits? 'Tis akin to how I felt when Tara fled Ireland to escape having to choose you or me. She wanted me, but the ancient bond demanded she wed you."

"I know all that. I still doona see—"

"For the love of the goddess, would ye stop interrupting?" Gwydion's blue eyes flashed dangerously.

Fionn subsided against the back of his seat.

"'Twas no skin off your ass when the lass left Ireland, yet I mourned her loss every day. It's been years, but I miss her still. 'Twas a gift to see her once again in the tunnels under Slototh's lair —even if she was already dead."

Something in Gwydion's words penetrated the desolation surrounding Fionn. He'd known Gwydion cared for Tara, but he'd never appreciated the extent of his loss. Truth hit home, and shame washed over him. When Gwydion waved it in front of his nose—no, make that shoved his nose right in it—Fionn recognized kindred pain. He drew his brows together. "Why were ye not angrier at me? We had words, but it seemed we made things up soon enough."

"Nay, I simply buried my resentment. What would've been the point in holding a grudge? I tracked Tara to America. By then, she'd wed another and made it painfully clear she wanted nothing to do with you or me—or the dragon—ever again."

"At least part of that was my fault. I could've—"

A bitter laugh bubbled past the close-cropped red-blond beard on Gwydion's face. "Aye, ye see it now. Ye dinna see it then. All ye could see then was that she was the MacLochlainn. *Your* MacLochlainn."

Fionn looked at his hands. What Gwydion said was true. He hadn't loved Tara, and he'd known she didn't even like him, yet he'd insisted on pressing forward with marriage. Of course, there was the niggling problem that he already had a wife, so he'd been finagling a divorce. Tara, finally eighteen, took matters into her own hands and left Ireland.

"I really am sorry. I should've been more considerate—of both of you."

"Och, aye." A thread of magic forced his gaze to meet the master enchanter's. "I forgive you."

A corner of Fionn's mouth turned downward. "The question is whether I can forgive myself."

Gwydion held out a hand for the mead. Fionn passed it to him. Eyeing what was left of the bottle's contents, Gwydion said, "There never was a drink that offered enough oblivion to purge Tara from my thoughts."

"Wasna working for me, either." Fionn snorted. "I should know this. Ye told me, but I wasna paying attention. Where did you and the animals go?"

"We did the same outside as ye were supposed to be doing within. That would be hunting for clues Travis may have dropped while he was here."

Fionn waited. Instead of talking, Gwydion tipped the bottle and drank until it was empty. "Did ye find aught?" he asked after it appeared the other mage wasn't going to say anything else.

Gwydion's forehead creased. He shoved blond hair over his shoulders, pulled a leather thong out of his robes, and bound it out of the way. "It was odd," he murmured. "At first we all"—he gestured toward Rune and Bella—"thought we sensed Old Ones—ah, I meant to say Lemurians. When I looked more closely, though, whatever had been there was gone." He shrugged.

Something tugged at Fionn's internal alarm system. Attuned to danger, it rarely failed him. "Do ye suppose they were after Marta's parents?"

For a moment, Gwydion looked confused, but then his features smoothed. "Och, ye mean the Lemurian-human hybrids ensorcelled in yon chamber." He waved a hand over one shoulder. "Mayhap. There is little else here to draw the Old Ones."

Fionn thought about the genetic manipulation that must have gone into hybridizing the couple in the attic and shuddered. Did the Old Ones want Marta's parents' blood so they could do the same thing to Aislinn?

"At least Aislinn is likely still on this side of the veil," Gwydion muttered.

Fionn looked sharply at him, realizing the other mage must have read his thoughts. He dragged a hand down his face. "Aye, we all hope that."

Something sharp closed over his calf. Rune had bitten him. "It is time. We should go into Taltos. I must see for myself whether my bondmate still lives."

"Can ye feel her?" Fionn asked.

The wolf's amber eyes gleamed in the dim kitchen. "No, but if she is in Taltos, I will know once we open the gateway and I cross over."

"They might've her shielded in some way—" Fionn cautioned.

"Enough words." Rune nipped Fionn again. As if to support her fellow bond animal, Bella landed on Fionn's shoulder and dug her talons deep.

A wry smile split Gwydion's face. "It would appear the animals have spoken."

"We did tell the others we'd do a reconnaissance." Fionn stood.

Gwydion followed suit. Both men went to the corner of the kitchen with the hidden trap door. Fionn kicked the rug aside and tugged the door upward. When he looked back, he saw Gwydion's staff glowing with a blue-white light.

Fionn worked his way down the ladder, helping the wolf. It was awkward. When Aislinn had gone into Taltos without him, she'd used magic to transport the wolf to the gateway. The thought of her seared his soul. His throat felt thick. A pulse pounded behind one eye, promising a mother of a headache if he didn't focus magic to soothe the inflamed blood vessels.

At the bottom of the ladder, he strode to the section of wall holding the gateway and began the incantation from Marta's journals. Gwydion's energy vibrated next to him. Stones scraped against one another as the gateway swung open. Fionn bent to give Rune instructions, but the wolf bounded through the opening and disappeared into the dark.

"Damn it." Fionn swore softly. "Ye stay with me," he said to Bella.

"I am not going past this doorway," the bird informed him. She fluttered from his shoulder to a chair and perched on it. "Fewer of us, less chance of discovery. Safer for Aislinn."

Fionn couldn't help but agree with her. His bird had warmed to Aislinn, much to his relief, since she'd taken a perverse delight in making all the other women in his life—including Tara—miserable.

"Mind speech," Gwydion said sharply. *"And precious little of that."*

"I suppose we follow the wolf. He gave us little choice."

"After you."

Fionn stepped through into a dark tunnel. Careful to mute his magic in case the Lemurians had posted guards nearby, he turned left and trailed after Rune. Guts tight, barely breathing, he moved beneath Taltos, the city built by Lemurians deep inside Mount Shasta. Desperation thrummed through him.

I have to find her. Failure is not an option.

www.ingramcontent.com/pod-product-compliance
Lightning Source LLC
Chambersburg PA
CBHW070825190726
48292CB00006B/2116